THE BETA FILE

MIKE UPTON

authorHOUSE

AuthorHouse™ UK
1663 Liberty Drive
Bloomington, IN 47403 USA
www.authorhouse.co.uk
Phone: 0800.197.4150

This book is a work of fiction. People, places, events and situations are the product of the author's imagination. Any resemblance to actual persons, living or dead, or to historical events is purely coincidental.

© 2016 Mike Upton. All rights reserved.

No part of this book may be reproduced, stored in a retrieval system, or transmitted by any means without the written permission of the author.

Published by AuthorHouse   07/12/2016

ISBN: 978-1-5246-3724-8 (sc)
ISBN: 978-1-5246-3725-5 (e)

Print information available on the last page.

Any people depicted in stock imagery provided by Thinkstock are models, and such images are being used for illustrative purposes only.
Certain stock imagery © Thinkstock.

This book is printed on acid-free paper.

Because of the dynamic nature of the Internet, any web addresses or links contained in this book may have changed since publication and may no longer be valid. The views expressed in this work are solely those of the author and do not necessarily reflect the views of the publisher, and the publisher hereby disclaims any responsibility for them.

The Beta File is as usual dedicated to several people:-

- ❖ To my wife Brenda, my two daughters Catherine and Victoria and my Granddaughter Holly

- ❖ Of course to Sarah my former pa always there with a cheerful smile and a helpful word

- ❖ To all my friends who continue to encourage my writing

- ❖ To everyone at AuthorHouse for their cheerful helpful professional help in changing the manuscript into a finished book

- ❖ To all those people around the world who put themselves at personal risk by taking part in legitimate drug trials

- ❖ Most importantly to all my readers. I hope you enjoy The Beta File.

MIKE UPTON
Summer 2016

CAST OF KEY CHARACTERS

People working for TV-12

Kim Harding	Chief investigator Highlight programme
Samita Patel	Works for Kim
Fergal O'Connor	" " "
Toby Brewer	Head of Highlight programme - Kim's boss
Peter Holmes	Managing Director
Lawrence Armstrong	Marketing Director
Ruth Baverstock	Advertising Director
Elaine Rees	Financial Controller
Jason Moran	Head of Programme Planning
Penny Proctor	Senior Producer - documentaries
Rick Stevens	On location cameraman
Jamie Wilson	Investigator for Highlight (similar job to Kim)
Julie Patterson	Junior research assistant
Levi Edelman	Head of Legal Services

People working for Furrina Pharmaceuticals

Brian Moffatt	Scientist
Marylyn Goodrich	Chief Executive
Louis Farmer	Head of Drug Development
John Andrews	In Market Drug Test Controller
Fay Roper	Head of Human Resources
Steve Jackson	Head of IT

Other players

James Dixon	Kim's fiancé
Golda Lowenthal	Barrister
Sally Foster	Golda's junior barrister
Anna Dorrington	Friend of Kim

Indian minor characters - Mumbai

Lead guide/coordinator	Sanjay
Guides	Amrit and Girish
Drug trial subjects	Ganesh, Ashan, Dipti
	Chetana, Kumar, Mala, Prakesh

INTRODUCTION

The Beta File portrays events unlikely to take place in real life - I hope, because Pharmaceutical and Drug companies throughout the world are scrupulously careful in observing strict protocols concerning trials of new drugs and medicines which are normally conducted amid great secrecy but also within very carefully controlled and monitored conditions and if any adverse reactions are encountered the trial is stopped; the reasons for the undesirable symptoms evaluated and before restarting every possible effort is made to understand why it occurred and thus learn how to avoid a repeat of the unfavourable effect.

Of course from time to time things do go wrong. Indeed that is precisely why such trials take place - to test out the characteristics, performance and any possible side effects of them once administered to human beings before their widespread introduction into general use. This is normally done on a small group of volunteers where the effects and results are most carefully evaluated by various regulatory authorities before a licence to permit the general introduction of the drug is given.

Government controls throughout the world are extremely stringent and demanding of drug companies who have to report in great detail before a licence to test on humans would be granted and this process can take many years to complete. Therefore the idea that a major Pharmaceutical Drug development company would deliberately act in the way this novel depicts is not only improbable but almost certainly implausible.

On the other hand investigative radio and television programmes certainly *do* exist and have often revealed major problems and scandals within many companies from corruption to fraud and so the scenario that TV-12 - the fictitious TV company depicted in this book would investigate alleged malpractice of the type depicted if they were made aware of it by a whistleblower, is therefore entirely realistic and thus the scenario depicted in The Beta File might occur.

PROLOGUE

Mid December was bitterly cold. Christmas revellers were on the streets of Northampton but by ten o'clock the man was curled up in an old sleeping bag that one of the church do-gooders had given him. It was threadbare and had hardly any stuffing but it was at least something to help keep out the biting cold. Beneath him were two layers of corrugated cardboard and some newspapers which again helped stop some of the cold seeping up into his body from the stone step on which he was lying in a shop doorway in one of the streets off the centre of the city. It was quiet and he'd used this place for several nights now.

It was always risky kipping down in doorways as some people liked to give sleeping homeless people a kick or a punch or spit at them as they passed but for the man that was all part of his life now and he accepted it.

Fast asleep, the first he was aware of danger was when he felt wet on his face and assumed it was raining. But opening his eyes he saw jean clad legs above black boots and looking up he saw a penis squirting urine straight at his face.

'Oh God no don't do that please' he yelled trying to put his hands over his face as he started to crawl out of the sleeping bag.

'Why not' yelled the youth giving him a savage kick in the ribs and laughing but to his relief the stream of warm liquid stopped. 'Here we've got plenty for you yet mate' added the youth as he stepped aside and his two companions took his place, one peeing onto his face and head while the other aimed at his chest and then sprayed his sleeping bag and cardboard.

'Please stop' the man begged again trying to push himself up, 'please' then he spluttered as the stream of warm liquid splashed in his open pleading mouth.

'Fucking tramp' yelled one youth as he slammed a violent kick into the supine man's face who felt his jaw break and some teeth get smashed. 'If we had some petrol we'd burn you'.

'Yeah that'd warm you up wouldn't it you piece of rat shit' added another of the youths laughing as he finished peeing and kicked the man's arm away causing him to collapse on the ground half in and half out of the doorway.

In the next few minutes the three thugs rained kick after kick and blow after blow on the defenceless man on the ground who after trying to ward off the attack gave up as he felt more teeth break, a sharp pain as ribs were broken and then lost the sight in one eye as the first thug jumped in the air and landed hard on the upper half of his face.

'Come on guys one more kick each for luck eh?' stated the first youth and taking aim at the defenceless man's head he slammed his boot into the back of the skull. The next lad kicked the groaning man in the chest breaking yet another rib while the final kick from the giggling third boy, who was only just sixteen, landed under the man's chin flicking his head backwards violently.

'Loser' yelled one of the attackers lighting a cigarette as he walked off.

'Tosser' laughed another as he joined up with his friend.

'Useless wanker' added the third giving the comatose man a huge kick in the genitals which brought forth a scream and then still laughing one more kick this time again in the mouth which finally dislodged most of the remaining teeth. After a pause and laughing loudly the three thugs wandered off down the street as the sound of the Christmas carol "Oh Come All Ye Faithful" could be heard coming from a nearby late opening shop.

It wasn't too much later that a young couple heading back to their car to drive home after a meal in a nearby restaurant found him motionless but groaning with blood all over his face and more spilled on the shop doorway step and pavement. Using his mobile the man dialled the emergency services, gave the location and agreed to wait until help arrived which it did in the form of two police officers who took one look and rang for an ambulance.

Although the emergency department doctors and nurses did what they could the man died that night never properly regaining consciousness. He had no identification on him and his face was so swollen, bruised and smashed and with most of his teeth gone the police decided that it was no use issuing a photograph so his body was taken to the mortuary.

No one came forward to claim the body. Perfunctory checks by the police on their DNA data base showed no match, nor did fingerprint checks which wasn't surprising as the man had never been in trouble with the police.

So the body of the "Unknown White Male" remained in the morgue for the next fourteen months until the pathologist needing to free up space in the chilled cabinets requested permission for its removal, following which a decision was made by the coroner's office to permit burial.

On a wet windy cold grey February morning the unknown man was quietly buried in an unmarked grave to the side of the unremarkable cemetery of a small church in an unfashionable district of Northampton.

The only people present were the four pall bearers who slowly and solemnly lowered the coffin into the newly dug burial place, bowed and stood back as the vicar softly intoned 'We commend to Almighty God the body of this poor soul, unknown to us but known to and loved by Him in the sure and certain knowledge of his resurrection into eternal life. Amen'.

Call no man happy till he is dead.
Aeschylus.

CHAPTER 1 - EIGHTEEN MONTHS EARLIER

*It is the act of a bad man
to deceive by falsehood.
Cicero*

'Highlight office' Kim Harding said glancing at the office wall clock as she picked up the ringing phone and seeing it was twenty past one understood why she was feeling hungry as she hadn't yet had anything to eat since her cereal and yoghurt breakfast.

'Umm hello .... yes err ...... is that the Highlight people?' asked an apprehensive sounding male voice.

'It certainly is. How can we help?'

'I know of an issue which the company I work for is hiding. I mean it is a really *serious* issue and I don't think that they should be allowed to get away with it'.

'Well that's what we're here for. To make sure they don't'. There was a pause where the man didn't say anything although Kim could hear him breathing and recognising that he was obviously very nervous and anxious she continued in a soft friendly tone of voice. 'So can you tell me a little of what it's about?'

'Look if I do I will be protected won't I?'

'Yes of course. We can and will ensure that your name and details don't become known to your employer. I can assure you that we have an excellent record of protecting people's identity'.

'Right'.

'Would you like to tell me your name?'

The caller paused and then said quietly 'Brian'.

'Okay Brian. So what is it that you know and about which company?'

'It's the firm I work for'.

'Which is?'

'Furrina Pharmaceuticals'.

'What about them?' she asked tapping the company name into her computer search engine and moments later the screen was filled with the usual type of corporate "wallpaper" relating to this company.

She saw that Furrina Pharmaceuticals were a very large organisation that tended to shy away from publicity but had achieved considerable success over the past few years with a number of new drugs which they'd got to market. Although big with turnover of almost £15bn and continuing to grow fast, there were many of their competitors and other operators in the market who were much bigger. Nevertheless if they were up to no good then they were big enough to make an excellent scalp for the Highlight team.

There was a long silence before he asked 'You're not recording this are you?'

'No. Would you like me to do that?'

'NO' he exclaimed loudly almost panic stricken.

'It's okay. Calm down. Now what is it about Furrina Pharmaceuticals that you know?'

'I've never done this before …… you know told tales about my employer'.

'Well perhaps there's not been a need before but if you think something's wrong then you need to tell us'.

'No there hasn't. Been a need I mean'.

Another long pause but Kim didn't get irritated as experience had shown her that when people rang in with information about their employers doing something wrong it often took such whistle blowers a little time to actually say what it was that they wanted to disclose. So she was patient and didn't hurry whoever this whistleblower man was. But after a long period of silence finally she asked 'Would you find it easier to meet and talk about whatever it is?'

'I don't know'.

'We could meet wherever you like. You choose and I or one of my colleagues will come to you wherever that is. Whereabouts are you by the way?'

'Milton Keynes. At least that's where Furrina's plant, lab and offices are. I live in a small village a few miles out of Milton Keynes'.

'Would you like me to come to Milton Keynes?'

'No I think not as we might be seen'.

'Alright' she replied thinking that even though she'd never been there Milton Keynes was a big place and it was unlikely that she and this Brian chap would be spotted in all the crowds, however if he didn't want to meet there that was fine. 'So if not there then where Brian and what is it that you want to say about Furrina?'

'They're fiddling ....' then he stopped.

'Go on' she said in as encouraging voice as she could muster. 'What are they fiddling? Money? Financial results?'

'Test results' he said so quietly it was almost a whisper.

'Test results? What sort of test results?'

'Drug test results'

'Then I think we should meet and talk about this as soon as possible'.

'Do you?'

'Yes I certainly do. So where would you like to meet? What about here at our offices?'

'NO!'

'Alright. Where do you suggest then? You choose'.

'Somewhere private and away from everywhere but look I .... I need to think about this before we go any further'.

'I understand that but Brian if you know that Furrina Pharmaceuticals are doing something wrong then it is really your *duty* to speak out about it. And there's no better group of people to tell than us. We can expose it without reference to you'.

'They'll be bound to find out that it was me'.

'Why?'

'They just will. You don't know them'.

'No I don't, but I give you my word that we will *not* disclose the source of our information' she said firmly. There was another period of silence so she said in what she hoped was an encouraging tone of voice 'So when and where shall we meet?'

'I don't know. I need to think about it a bit more'.

'Look just come and talk with me. That can't do any harm can it? An initial discussion?'

'I'll ring you back'.

'*WAIT!* Don't ring off. Let me give you my mobile number and you can ring me on that anytime night or day'.

'Okay' and he repeated the number back after she read it to him then rang off.

'What was that all about' asked Toby Brewer the head of the Highlight programme who'd dropped by Kim's work station to check on a couple of things with her but he'd kept silent while she was on the call.

Highlight was an investigative show on TV-12, a fairly new television station and one of the station's flagship programmes. Since the first programme aired nearly twelve months ago it had quickly established for itself a fierce reputation for investigative and perceptive undercover reporting of wrong doing conducted mainly, but not exclusively, by major British based companies.

However recently there had been some grumbling by the senior management of TV-12 that Highlight's exposés were insufficiently hard hitting or sensation creating and that they were becoming too tame.

Toby was aware of the criticism but unsure what to do about it as their output of hard hitting programmes entirely depended on people bringing issues to them to investigate and if they didn't get meaty tough issues then it was hard to make the subsequent programme hard hitting.

'Some guy called Brian who says that Furrina Pharmaceuticals are fiddling drug test results' said Kim.

'Blimey! Are you going to meet him?'

'He's rung off but I've given him my mobile and I've made a note of his number so I'm sure he'll call me again. If he doesn't then I'll ring him'.

'Fine. Keep me posted' he said thinking that if this was real then fiddled drug results might be just the sort of thing they could get their teeth into and make a really good programme. 'How's your current investigation coming along?'

'Alright but some way to go on the background research yet before I've got something concrete I can to come to you and others with regarding a possible programme'.

'Okay. Keep me posted on that too and especially on this drug trial lead'.

'Sure' and she turned back to her screen, studied Furrina Pharmaceuticals for a while, then switched to her e-mail in-box, groaned when she saw how many there were and began the task of sifting, weeding out, reading and answering them.

Among them was one which made her smile. It read:

Only 2 days to go. Can't wait baby. James xxx.

She fired off a reply:

Umm me too and that's 2 days too long! Be patient. Remember the old saying – 'everything comes to he who waits' – and I'll give you everything when I see you Friday. Grrrrrrrrrrrrrr. Kim xxxxxxx

Grinning broadly she turned to some other work and was soon immersed in that and so both the mysterious Brian, and her lover James, were forgotten. But later as she stood in the crowded tube carriage on her way back to her apartment in Balham, James's face and then his body came vividly to her mind and she passed the remainder of the journey quietly dreaming of the week's break the two of them were taking leaving Heathrow this Friday evening.

She lived in an apartment, which was one of twenty in an old converted warehouse and so had high ceilings, wooden plank floors and odd bits of metal machinery partly buried part in the walls as features. Stripping off she put on her jogging gear and was soon pounding the pavements. This three mile run was the second part of her daily exercise routine, the first part being the ten minute strenuous exercise schedule she conducted every morning as soon as she got out of bed.

As she ran, her mind flickered over many different things including a couple of potential investigations that she was working on at the office, the strangely interesting call from the very nervous Brian but inevitably her coming week's holiday with James and just thinking of that and him made her smile as she ran.

Back at her apartment she stripped off and showered to wash away the sweat from the run then slipping into fresh underwear, a white tee shirt and slim fit jeans she walked barefoot from the bedroom to the kitchen where she took out of the fridge the remains of a vegetable smoothie that she'd whisked up this morning.

After a run she liked to wait for about half an hour before eating so she took some dirty clothes out of the washing basket, pushed them into the washing machine to join those clothes already there, added the powder, peered at the controls then pressed the appropriate buttons and nodded when the machine began operating.

Plonking down into the dark green settee at one end of the long through sitting room/kitchen she opened the paper which she'd bought at the tube station and quickly scanned through the day's news as reported by the London evening paper. Finally checking her watch and seeing that it was a quarter past eight she went to the kitchen and rustled up her supper of smoked mackerel, salad, two crisp breads and a glass of dry white wine which she took to the trendy brightly coloured kitchen table and sat down to eat as she tried to solve the Sudoku printed in the paper.

Today it wasn't difficult and she finished the puzzle about the same time she finished eating so getting up she loaded the dishwasher, wiped down the table, made herself some decaf coffee and walked with it to the settee where she switched on the TV and was just in time to catch the start of this week's episode of a complex police drama serial on TV-12. At ten as the programmes were changing from the serial to the news she poured herself a small whisky and sat sipping that while watching the daily outpouring of disasters and misery from around the world and in the UK. When it finished she got up, put her coffee mug and whisky glass in the dishwasher, checked that the front door was locked and bolted, set the burglar alarm and was soon snuggled down in bed. Wishing James was there with her she sighed, ran her hands down her body, hugged herself pretending it was him doing that and turning onto her side to go to sleep noted that the bedside clock showed 10.52.

Moments later her mobile rang and sitting up she reached for it and stared at the screen, initially not recognising the number but then the last three digits rang a bell as she said 'Hello. Kim Harding'.

'Oh hello. It's Brian. We spoke earlier today. I hope I'm not ringing too late' said the voice she immediately recognised as the potential whistleblower from Furrina Pharmaceuticals.

'No that's okay. How can I help?'

'Look. I've thought about it and I *would* like to meet you and talk'.

'Right but not tonight. I've just gone to bed'.

'Oh sorry. Shall I ring back tomorrow?'

'No it's fine to continue now. I wasn't asleep so where do you want to meet?'

'Could we meet in Hyde Park?'

'Sure but Hyde Park is a big place you know' she chuckled. 'Is there a particular spot you have in mind?'

'Do you know the Serpentine Lido? You know where people can swim outdoors. In the lake there?'

'Yes I do. I've swum there myself'.

'Oh right. Nice I should think. I haven't as I'm not a very good swimmer'.

'So what day and time?'

'I've got to come to London for a meeting in the morning. It'll be finished about eleven thirty so could we say midday at the Lido?'

'Midday? Sure that's fine. Now what do you look like in case there's lots of people milling about?'

'What do I look like?'

'So that I can recognise you?'

'Ah yes. Well I'm medium build, five foot nine, forty five years old. I'll be wearing a dark blue jacket and grey trousers, pale blue shirt, no tie but carrying a small document case. Will that enable you to recognise me?'

'Without doubt' she chuckled. 'Now I'm a couple of inches shorter than you, and a bit younger at thirty one, slim, shoulder length blonde hair, not bad looking but I don't know what I'll be wearing yet. I tend to decide on that when I'm having my morning shower. But I'm sure we'll link up alright'.

'Fine thanks. Till tomorrow then. Sorry to have rung you so late'.

'Not a problem Brian. See you at midday'.

'Yes thank you. Goodnight'.

'Well well' she mused aloud as she put down the phone, checked that it was plugged into the charger properly and lay back down where after a bit of tossing and turning she dropped off to sleep not waking until her alarm shrilled at six thirty.

CHAPTER 2

She was there by the Serpentine Lido at eleven fifty and stood looking around then thought it might be better if she sat down on one of the many park benches so she did and waited. Checking her watch she saw midday come and go and wondered if the mysterious Brian had chickened out, but at about ten past twelve a man stopped in front of her.

'Excuse me. Are you Kim?'

'That's me' she smiled looking up at him.

'The Kim from TV-12 .... err Highlight?'

'Yes. I'm Kim Harding from Highlight. You must be Brian'.

'Yes'.

'I'm very pleased to meet you' she said standing up and holding out her hand which he shook with a rather flimsy and gentle handshake. 'Where would you like to go to talk?'

'Can we walk? You know walk and talk?'

'Sure. This way?' and she set off along the path beside the lake. 'So you've been at a meeting here in London have you?'

'Yes'.

'Was that to do with Furrina Pharmaceuticals?'

'Yes'.

'Furrina is an unusual name for a business. Does it have a special meaning?'

'Furrina was a Roman Goddess with some connection to water. Furrina started out years ago by manufacturing water purification tablets and have grown gigantic since then of course and now are a fully fledged drug manufacturer. Our Chief Executive Marylyn Goodrich is a woman although I wouldn't describe her as a goddess. No certainly not. More of a devil really, that is if you can have a female devil' he mused. 'Do you think there's a female devil? Maybe a male one and a female one?'

'I don't know but whether you can or not do I gather she's not a very nice lady?'

'She is a one hundred percent thoroughly horrid *bitch!*' he said with real feeling.

'Right' and she waited for him to contribute more to the conversation but as he didn't she spoke again. 'And have you worked for Furrina for a long time?'

'Ten years'.

'That is quite a time. And what do you do there?'

'I'm a research scientist'.

'That must be interesting. So what sort of research scientist are you?'

'I work on new drug developments'.

'Sounds impressive'.

'Not really. It's just a question of following certain procedures, practices and pathways then thinking as broadly as possible to try and find something new that will benefit people who are suffering from a particular disease or illness'.

'I see. And what are you working on?'

'Leukaemia'.

'So is it something to do with your work on leukaemia that caused you to ring us yesterday?'

'No'.

Thinking that trying to get information out of this man was like pulling teeth that didn't want to come out, nevertheless she kept her voice pleasant, quiet and smiled as she looked at him. 'So it's something else then is it? Another drug?'

'Yes'.

They'd walked about two hundred yards by now and as they were approaching another bench she said 'Look why don't we sit down and then you can tell me whatever it is you want to?'

'Alright' but as they sat down he twisted round in every direction peering carefully around them.

'Is someone watching you?'

'No. At least I hope not'.

'Look Brian. We're in the middle of a public park. We are two people sitting on a park bench chatting. We could be husband and wife, boy friend and girlfriend, office colleagues, lovers, old friends, brother and sister. Anything but I really don't think you need to be paranoid about being watched unless you have reason to think that you are under surveillance for some reason?'

'I don't know. They watch everyone all the time' he said quietly.
'Who do?'
'Furrina'.
'Oh come on Brian. They can't watch *everyone all* the time!'
'No maybe not' he admitted. 'But they do watch'.
'What do they watch for?'
'Disloyalty. Competitors. I don't know. Everything'.
'Are you sure you're not being a bit paranoid?'
'No I'm not. *You* don't know them. *I do*'.
'Okay' she soothed. 'So you're not being paranoid. But what is it you want to tell me about. This other drug?'
'They're ....' he paused and looked frightened.
'They're what?' she asked with a deliberate little edge in her voice.
He turned and looked at her and she was struck by his eyes which really did look frightened. 'They have a potential new drug on trial'.
'And so what does this drug do? What's the illness or condition that it is intended to improve or cure?'
'Stomach cancer but they're hiding the results of some of the tests that have gone wrong'.
'What went wrong?'
'Some of the people that they've been testing this new drug on have developed serious side effects but Furrina have hidden that as they race to get the drug to market'.
'What sort of side effects?'
'Mainly serious eyesight defects and in some cases partial strokes'.
'Strokes and eyesight defects! They can't hide that sort of thing!'
'They *can* because that's exactly what they *are* doing. The incidence of these side effects is a very low percentage of those taking the drug but I think that in time more people will exhibit more problems the longer they are taking the drug'.
'How low a percentage?'
'Less than nought point three percent' he said.
'That *is* a small figure'.
Yes but scale it up. If a million people took the drug and had those symptoms then you're talking three thousand people. If ten million took the drug then you could be talking thirty thousand people. One hundred

million would give you three hundred thousand affected people. Remember prescription drugs are a global supply business. Just because Furrina is British doesn't mean that it will only be supplying this drug in the UK. It's got a worldwide sales, marketing and supply operation. So people all over the world could be affected. And if Furrina don't manufacturer it themselves in all the overseas countries in which they operate, they'll licence its contract production to other pharmaceutical manufacturers for them to make it and supply the market, with Furrina picking up a big fat royalty'

'I see'.

'And so the numbers of people just with direct effects from this drug could be huge. But if I'm also right about the potential longer term effects then more people could develop adverse symptoms *later on* from taking this drug. In that case the numbers could be absolutely enormous. Horrendous'.

'Of course. But don't they test new drugs on laboratory animals before humans? You know rats and monkeys?' she wanted to know.

'Yes and they did. First they tested on mice and rats but when some adverse reactions appeared they ignored them saying that it was a species issue and went on to test on dogs which started to show adverse reactions, so once more they again said it was a species issue and thus not typically capable of translating into human results. So they moved to testing on monkeys and I have to admit that there were none of the side effects noted there, so they ignored the adverse data from the earlier animal tests and just used the monkey data to get a licence to be able to launch a test of the product on humans'.

'Christ. But look Brian. You keep saying *they*. But aren't you part of this test programme yourself?'

'No. I was taken off it eighteen months ago and transferred to the leukaemia project but I've managed to keep track of it. I shouldn't have done that. But I have'.

'Why were you transferred off it?'

'Because I kept querying the test results and highlighting the adverse effects. I said they needed to do much more work on the substance before moving to human trials'.

'I see. But isn't that what you scientists are supposed to do? Evaluate, test and re-evaluate?'

'Of course. But Furrina don't like it when their pet major projects get screwed up or delayed and as I was seen as a sticking point I got moved off it'.

'So where in the UK are these human tests being carried out?'

'No not here. They're doing it in India which is well out of the way where they can much more easily hide the adverse reactions'.

'But surely they won't eventually launch generally into the world with this known problem?'

'No obviously not but they'll use these results to refine and then re-test the drug. Effectively they are running a kind of real life human laboratory on-going experiment. The test is not to cure stomach cancer it is to test compatibility of it on people. Healthy people who don't have stomach cancer.

That's how these sorts of tests are done. The product is tested on *healthy* people who *don't* have the disease to evaluate how it is tolerated by a healthy person. As in this case it is intended to tackle stomach cancer then if someone doesn't have stomach cancer it should just pass straight through the test subject with no ill or side effects. That's what they're trying to find out.

If not they'll learn from that and amend the drug accordingly. Normally you do that as a result of animal tests not knowingly from human results.

Once they've got sufficient satisfactory tolerance results they can use that test data along with the data from animals to apply for a licence to enable them to move onto limited trials on human volunteers who *do* have stomach cancer. These are likely to be people who are very seriously ill with that manifestation of the disease and so although they would be volunteers they know they are taking a risk but then as they're near the end of their life they are generally willing to take the chance. After all what have they got to lose? Nothing really.

Now obviously from time to time drug tests *do* go wrong. Every pharmaceutical company has had its share of problems during drug development. That is a fact of life. But when that happens the test stops, everyone examines what's gone wrong and then decides how to proceed, what modifications are needed or whether to scrap the drug completely. And that is often the outcome. Scrap it and start again completely anew.

But they're *not* doing that. They are continuing to administer the drug and as a result people are being damaged'.

'That's bizarre and very worrying'.

'I think it's criminal'.

'Yes it probably is' she agreed. 'Is there anything else you can tell me?'

'Lots. What do you want to know?'

'I'm not sure at this stage. Look I'd like to talk to the rest of my team and then we'll get back in touch with you and see how we can progress this further. Is that alright?'

'Ye-es'.

'You don't sound too sure'.

'How long will it take ……. before you get back to me I mean?'

'A few days. I'm going away tomorrow for a week but I'll ensure that the team work on this while I'm away then when I'm back we can meet again and I'll let you know whether we want to take this on as a Highlight investigation'.

'Oh. Might you not then?'

'Well you see the problem is that we do get an awful lot of things fed to us to investigate. We can't do them all. We simply haven't got the resources to do that and even if we did we only have a one hour a week slot of airtime on TV-12 for the Highlight programme. So if we decide to take it on then we have to believe that it is worthwhile and stands a real chance of going on air and leading to a proper issue for Highlight'.

'It *is* real' Brian said earnestly looking straight into her eyes. 'People are being damaged by this drug. *Badly* damaged. And heaven knows what long term side effects might accrue from its use. Remember thalidomide? This could be another of those ……. only *worse!*'

'Alright Brian. What is this drug called by the way?'

'Its proper chemical name is Betanapotraproxiflevien-g3, but as that's hard to pronounce even for us scientists then it's just called Beta for short'.

'Okay. Well it certainly sounds the sort of thing that we *could* and probably *should* investigate. We'll look into it and come back to you. My boss is Toby Brewer. If he needs to contact you while I'm away for anything is it alright if he rings you?'

'Yes I guess so but he mustn't say he's from TV-12 or Highlight. That's terribly important' he stressed looking almost beseechingly into her eyes.

'Don't worry. He'll be discreet and just use his name not who he works for'.

'Alright thanks' he muttered getting up. 'Look can we part in different directions. I'll walk on this way and you go back the way we've come. Okay?'

'Fine'.

'Thanks and I'll wait to hear from you or Toby'.

'Sure. Bye Brian' and with that the two people separated and walked away in opposite directions.

Kim strolled slowly and deep in thought. If what Brian had said was correct then they could have a massively explosive expose on their hands, but it would undoubtedly be difficult to get the proof and evidence. On the other hand if human beings were being used as guinea pigs and suffering real physical and possible mental damage in the process then Highlight had to find a way to bring that out into the open, expose it and stop them.

Back at TV-12 she went straight to her boss's office and once inside, leant against the wall and asked 'Hi Toby. You got a few minutes?'

'Sure. Is this about this Brian guy you went to see? Anything in it?'

'Could be' and she proceeded to relate everything that Brian had told her.

Toby listened carefully, asked several questions, said it sounded interesting and what was she planning to do about it now?

'Well I'll do some background research about Furrina Pharmaceuticals and the drugs they've got on the market, see if I can find out anything about any drug trials they're running but that'll be about it before I go away tomorrow for a week's holiday in the sun. Maybe Samita or Fergal could do some more work on it while I'm away?'

'Good idea. I'll get Samita working on it for you. Will you update her please before you go? I want Fergal to carry on with this sex and financial probe in to that town council we're almost ready to break cover with'.

'Okay fine' and she left Toby's office and went to her own desk in the open plan office area and again tapped Furrina Pharmaceuticals into her computer.

While she had returned to her work area and began to study the company in detail, Toby back in his own office sat thinking hard as he considered the phone call he'd just had with Jason Moran the Head of Programme Planning who'd said that worries regarding Highlight was beginning to cause real concern among the senior management and that Toby had better get ready as it was expected that he'd be summoned to a very top level meeting early next week to discuss the current state of Highlight and its likelihood of being allowed to continue in its present format and frequency.

Unaware of this Kim worked hard for the rest of the day starting to assemble information and data related to Furrina Pharmaceuticals and when she went home that night her head was spinning, but her evening run and shower afterwards cleared it. Then she dressed and left her apartment to meet up with a girlfriend with whom she'd arranged to have supper.

She got a taxi to the wine bar which was only about fifteen minutes away from her apartment. It wasn't crowded tonight and Anna who was already there nursing a glass of red wine, grinned, slid off the high bar stool, cheek kissed Kim, pointed to another glass of red wine and said 'Got you one ready'.

'Thanks' and taking a small sip she smiled and added 'lovely'.

'So how are you then?'

'Great'.

'You do look well I must say. Obviously your love life is firing on all cylinders' laughed Anna.

'It certainly is and James and I are going away for a week tomorrow'.

'Away away? Like abroad away?'

'Uh huh. To Sardinia'.

'Nice. Luxury hotel or is he going to make you skivvy and wait on him hand and foot in a villa doing the washing up, cleaning, cooking, then servicing his carnal needs whenever he feels like a good........'

'No chance!' interrupted Kim with a grin. 'We're going to an hotel. Quite small and a bit bijou but looks really nice in the brochure. Pool, bar and restaurant but I expect we'll eat out in local tavernas'.

'Tavernas are Greek not Sardinian darling' Anna corrected with a laugh.

'Whatever! Taverna or restauranté they're all the same I'm sure' and adopting a French accent she grinned 'it will be très magnifique ma cheri'.

'I know your command of French is wonderful but Sardinia is an Italian island so I doubt if French will be much use to you there!'

'Ancora meraviglioso anche se cara!' Anna looked puzzled so Kim went on 'It means still wonderful though dear!'

'Oh alright cleaver clogs I forgot your degree was business studies with modern languages'.

'Any rate whatever the language I'm sure we'll have a lovely time by the pool, on the beach and poking around little streets and finding out of the way restaurants'.

'When you're not furiously rutting away in bed that is' chuckled Anna.

'Yes when we're not doing that' agreed Kim with a smile. I haven't seen him for about ten days as he's been in Dubai on business. He gets back into Heathrow tomorrow around midday and I'm meeting him there at the airport then we're hopping off late afternoon.

'Sounds lovely. And if he's been apart from you for ten days he's going to be so horny he'll probably rip your knickers off there and then and bonk you against the check-in desk at Heathrow' she giggled. 'Enjoy. Now I'm peckish so shall we order?'

They did and the two of them ate, drank their wine, chatted and laughed about their jobs, the economy and their respective love lives.

Kim had known James Dixon for about twelve months but things had quickly got serious between them and he'd moved into her apartment around five months ago. He was a couple of years younger than her and she sometimes joked with him, especially when they were in bed, that he was her toy boy. James was a high end estate agent as his firm concentrated on mega deals, buying and selling blocks of apartments, departmental stores, sites for hypermarket developments, out of town shopping centres and similar. Not for them fiddling around with individual houses or flats. It was a tough world but he was good at what he did and had already established a reputation for being a very good property deal maker.

Anna though was single and said she was currently dating two different men, both of whom she liked but she didn't think either was her potential "lifetime partner" so until *he* came along she was happy to date and sleep with each of them.

'Anna Dorrington you are very naughty you know cheating on them both' chided Kim.

'Nonsense! I'm *not* cheating on them. I'm *enjoying* them. Both of them!'

'There's a difference?'

'Yes there certainly is! Each of them knows that I'm dating someone else and while they're happy with that then so am I? Very happy in actual fact. Having two men on the go at the same time is great as they each really try hard, especially in bed, or wherever else we do it! Certainly stops the sex getting boring!' she laughed.

They parted about ten thirty and by eleven thirty Kim was tucked up in bed looking forward to the coming holiday and seeing James, but especially sleeping with him again as the sex with him was always very good.

But while Kim was consumed with happy thoughts of James and her coming week of sun, sea, swimming, relaxation and sex in the sunshine, Anna wearing only a pair of dark blue hold up stockings having just disrobed the matching bra and panties, was enthusiastically rutting with Imran, a currency trader in the City and one of her two current men friends about whom she'd talked with Kim. The other was a man called Gordon a senior insurance assessor but right now she was entirely focussed on Imran whose parents had originally come to this country from Pakistan and raised him and his sister here in this country. He was lying on his back, wrists pressed down by her hands as she not only slid her fully shaven pussy along his erection gently squashing it between their two bellies, but also teased him by constantly dangling first one and then her other nipple from her small breasts onto his lips. But as he tried to lick and suck she'd jerk it away, a process she tantalisingly continued for some time until she reached down, found his erect prick and holding it upright slowly impaled herself on it.

'Now baby let's rut' she whispered as she began to move on him gradually getting faster before slowing right down then speeding up again. Several times she did this until eventually she rather noisily reached her first orgasm but without stopping and still riding him to prolong her sexual satisfaction she soon groaned deeply as she hit her second orgasm just as he muttered that he couldn't hold back any longer and with several quiet grunts began ejaculating.

But while Kim was tucked up in bed alone, and Anna was wondering how long to wait for Imran to get his breath back and then stimulate him to love her again, Brian from Furrina Pharmaceuticals was nervously chewing his finger nails in his little house in Wilken a village a few miles outside Milton Keynes and so worried about what he'd said to Kim he just couldn't get to sleep. So after tossing and turning he got up and tried to read a book but was unable to concentrate on the pages as his mind kept going to the drug trial but crucially the fact that he'd split the beans. He'd become a whistleblower and he was really concerned about where it might all lead and the possible implications for him?

If Furrina found out what he'd done they'd not only fire him on the spot but ensure he was blacklisted throughout the industry. His contract of employment specifically prohibited him from disclosing any information or details about their drug development programmes and the penalty for breaching that was instant dismissal without notice or compensation. At forty five he knew if he got fired at his age it would be very difficult to get another job, because blacklisted throughout the industry as someone who breached the non disclosure of his contract terms he'd be completely finished.

'Oh why did I ever tell that Kim woman?' he moaned aloud then after a moment's thought he added 'because someone's got to know about it. What Furrina is doing is wrong'.

Throughout his life he'd been a mild man who followed the rules, did as he was told, developed his career carefully without making waves or problems and just consistently worked hard to achieve good outcomes for his research work. As a result he'd been slowly but steadily promoted to higher grades, generally received pay increases in line with or occasionally above the average, was liked and respected by his peers and bosses and seen as a reliable, trustworthy and honest if somewhat boring company employee. He'd never had any problems with any employer until he'd argued with Furrina about Betanapotraproxiflevien-g3. But even their irritation with his persistent challenging had died away after they'd moved him onto the Leukaemia work instead.

Unmarried he found it difficult to talk to women outside work. In work he conversed happily and without difficulty with women about pharmaceutical project matters or other business subjects, but anything else or outside the business then socially he became tongue tied, nervous, hesitant and was thus unable to form any proper relationships. So he didn't go out much, was virtually teetotal and as well as enjoying classical music about which he was surprisingly knowledgeable his main interest was his collection of model soldiers which took up a large section of his third bedroom.

In fact the room was completely empty except for a selection of wooden boards about three feet off the ground on which were built the scenery for various battle scenarios, both ancient and more modern. They included houses, castles and other buildings, walls, trees, hills, rocks, and on one which he used for first or second world war enactments there was a railway line and a tunnel. Along one wall he had glass cabinets filled with various model soldiers. It was truly a wonderful collection which he'd built up over the last many years and he could and regularly did lose himself for hours to anything else as he moved his various soldiers into different positions on his extensive layout.

He had various modes including Roman armies fighting barbarians; Greek warriors; German and English modern soldiers; Russian and American infantry; Middle Ages knights and soldiers some depicting the Houses of York or Lancaster.

It was a hobby that absorbed him and so unable to sleep tonight he went in to his model soldiers room and spent a couple of hours in there replaying the battle of Hastings which was one he'd not done for some months. Enjoying the sight and positioning of the members of the two armies and with a CD playing sounds of a medieval battle enabled him to completely forget about Furrina and what he'd done, until around two thirty he did begin to feel sleepy so leaving William The Conqueror's army at a crucial stage of fighting their way inland he went to bed and was soon asleep.

CHAPTER 3

Next morning Kim was in the office early as she had a lot to do before going away at lunch time and was engrossed in her work when Toby her boss and head of the Highlight unit arrived at eight thirty, smiled, commented on her early start, grinned good naturedly when she reminded him she was finishing at mid-day and went off to his office where he settled down to his own work.

Julie Patterson the junior research assistant and Samita, Kim's assistant arrived a little after nine. Julie looked fashionably scruffy which went quite well with her pretty appearance, whereas Samita was, as always, immaculately turned out.

Kim briefed the other two about Furrina and they worked out some ideas together before she left them to work on the project alone while she finished off the work she'd been doing before Brian had made contact and brought this Furrina Pharmaceutical matter to her.

Finally around twelve she shut down her computer, said goodbye to everyone in the office, made a point of going to see Toby and bidding him goodbye for the week, and then she was striding out of the building and down the street, a shoulder bag dangling from her left shoulder and a suitcase on wheels being pulled by her right hand.

On and off a couple of tube lines before boarding the Piccadilly Line which took her all the way to Heathrow where she made her way to Terminal 5, checked in, went through passports and security and was soon walking into the BA Business class lounge. Peering around she looked for James but there was no sign of him and with a sigh of disappointment she handed over her boarding card for checking at the reception desk, signed in and was about to go into the lounge when a quiet cultured male voice behind her said 'Excuse me Miss but I get rather nervous flying so I wonder if you'd sit next to me and hold my hand on the plane?'

With a little squeal of delight she twisted round, flung her arms around James's neck and plonked a big kiss on his lips then leaning back said quietly 'I'd be delighted to hold your hand'.

'That's nice' he grinned back.

Her tummy did a funny little lurch as it always did when he grinned like that and looking at him with his suitcase, laptop bag and briefcase she asked 'You just got here?'

'Umm. I followed you in and thought I'd surprise you'.

'You'll need to keep an eye on the indicator boards as we don't announce flights in here' said the BA lounge stewardess pleased to see two people so obviously happy with each other, then checking James's boarding pass she looked at her computer screen and said 'I imagine that they'll be calling the flight in about three quarters of an hour sir .... madam'.

'Thank you Kim smiled taking James's hand and leading him to a pair of comfortable seats overlooking the tarmac outside where lots of planes, mainly British Airways but also some other airlines could be seen, parked or slowly manoeuvring around the hard standing.

'It's really lovely to see you again' she said quietly still holding onto James's hand even though they'd sat down then raising it to her lips she trailed a kiss across it and added 'I have missed you'.

'And I you. You know when I'm away from you I know how beautiful you are, but when I get back and see you I am always simply astonished by two things. Firstly that my memory of you is never as good as actually seeing you in person. Secondly I can't believe that I'm so fortunate to have you as my girlfriend'.

'Well you have and I think I'm a bit more than your girlfriend aren't I?'

'Yes you are *much* more. But I don't know how to describe you though? Partner sounds a bit formal. Girlfriend, I agree sounds too casual. Lover? Bit newspaper reporterish! So what do I call you?'

'Don't worry about it. Girlfriend will do for now'.

'Okay girlfriend. So tell me about your week'.

They chatted happily together until getting up to check the departure board James said that their flight was showing as "boarding".

The hotel was all they'd hoped it would be. Calm, quiet, luxurious and set in delightful grounds leading to the small beach. Their room was large, romantic with a large balcony terrace and overlooked the sea. They embraced, kissed, said they loved each other, showered, changed and were soon sitting in the restaurant enjoying their first Sardinian meal. Later they went to their room, made love and drifted off to sleep folded into each other's arms.

During their week they swam in the hotel pool, swam in the sea, wandered outside the hotel's grounds and explored the local countryside, found some restaurants and little bars where they ate lunch or dinner or just had a drink.

They were due to fly back on Saturday but on Thursday morning James's mobile phone alarm woke them really early. Wriggling across to her side of the large bed he kissed the still sleeping Kim and when she stirred whispered 'Come on time to get up'.

'What time is it?' she queried still almost asleep.

'Just after four'.

'Four! What the hell are we doing awake at this time? Have you gone mad? We're on holiday!'

'I know but please get up. I want to watch the sun rise over the sea and then swim as it rises'.

'James have you gone potty? To hell with the sunrise. I'd rather stay here in bed' and she snuggled down on her side facing away from him.

Without a word he got out of bed, went to the bathroom soaked a flannel in cold water then returning to the bedroom, approached her and suddenly tugged off the duvet and squeezed the flannel over her recumbent and naked body.

She screamed and sat up, told him he was the most hateful man she knew; that she hated being soaked like that; hated this time of the morning; hated being woken early on holiday; but *most* of all she hated him.

He just laughed and said 'No you don't. You love me' and gently pulled her out of bed. 'Come on. It'll be lovely' and while he slid on a pair of swimming trunks and shrugged a swim robe around himself she allowed herself to be persuaded to dress in a bikini, put a robe around herself, slip her feet into some sandals and then holding one of James's hands as he had a grip type bag in the other they made their way through the deserted hotel, nodded in reply to the receptionist's 'Buongiorno' (*Good morning*) greeting and walked out of the hotel, across the lawns, along a path through manicured gardens which led to the beach. Once there James led them along and around a rocky promontory onto another tiny deserted sandy bay which faced east.

'Come on' he grinned as he took a towel out of the bag, spread it on the sand and they sat down and cuddled together. The sun was just beginning to appear over the sea horizon and in spite of yawning and still feeling very sleepy she had to admit it was a beautiful sight as it began to materialize and climb slowly into the sky. They sat and watched for a while until it was fully on show and then he turned to her, twisted her head towards him and kissing her very gently said softly 'A beautiful start to a new day'.

'S'pose so' she pouted prettily.

'And it could be much more than a beautiful day' and reaching into the bag he took something that she couldn't properly see out of it, then disengaging from her knelt in front of her sitting form and said quietly 'Kim I don't just love you. I adore you. Look we've not known each other for very long, only about a year but you mean so much to me. You are my life. My everything'.

'And you are mine too' she smiled.

'Kim darling. We've just seen the start of a new day. I'd like to see the start our lives together. Will you marry me?'

'Marry you?' she gasped quietly. 'Is this why you've brought me here this morning at this ungodly hour to ask me to marry you?'

'Yes. Will you? Please?'

'Oh James you darling man' and she stared happily at him for a moment her mind racing then she grinned and said 'yes I *will*. Oh yes I *certainly* will thank you'.

'Thank *you*' and taking her left hand he showed her what was concealed in his hand. A little blue box which he gave to her.

'Is this what I think it might be?' she queried softly.

'Open it and see'.

She did and as she looked at the diamond ring nestled within tears came to her eyes. 'Oh darling it is just beautiful. Put it on for me'.

He did and then he kissed her. 'You have no idea how happy you've made me' he said and kissed her again but this time deeply and passionately before gently pushing her onto her back. Lying on top of her as she wrapped her arms around his waist they kissed for a long time and she felt his erection pressing against her tummy but eventually they disengaged and sat holding hands and panting a little.

'Swim?' he queried.

'Okay'.

Standing he shrugged out of the robe, grinned, looked around then took off his trunks and stark naked but fully erect said 'Come on. Skinny dip there's no one around.

'You're mad' she giggled also standing up then after a quick look around to ensure they really were alone she too stripped off then saying 'wait' pulled him to her and folding him into her arms kissed him hard as the two of them stood pressed together for a couple of minutes until easing back she whispered 'I do love you'.

'And I you. Now come on. Swim time' and the two of them ran hand in hand down to the sea and plunged beneath the water.

As they surfaced they kissed again and reaching down to take find his prick she chuckled 'You did look funny running like that with this stiff thing wobbling about. Mind you the cold water will soon put paid to your hard on' and with a laugh she let go of him and set off swimming strongly out into the little bay. He went after her and they swam together for about five minutes until turning back they swam slowly and happily back towards the beach.

When they were closer but the water was still around four feet deep they stopped and kissed again and as her hand again felt for him and discovered he was now completely flaccid she grinned and said 'That's better. Very forward and impertinent of you flashing a stiffie at your new fiancé in the early morning'.

'Go on. Bet it gave you quite a thrill though at err' and he paused to look at his waterproof watch 'four forty in the morning'.

''God is that really the time? I'm not sure anything can give me a thrill at this time of day? I should still be asleep!'

'Aren't you glad you're not and here with me though?' and as he pulled her to him she wrapped her arms around his neck and her legs around his waist and with a cheeky expression rubbed her pussy against his flaccid prick.

'Buongiorno. Bella giornata per una nuotato' *(Good morning. Lovely day for a swim)* called a voice and looking they saw an elderly man with a fishing rod and bag making his way to the rocks at the side of this little cove.

'Oh God. Now what do we do?' giggled Kim disentangling herself from James.

'Don't know. Make a run for it to the beach and hope he doesn't notice?'

'Of course he'll notice. We're starkers! Oh bloody hell' she exclaimed as another man appeared also carry a fishing rod and began walking towards the first man but seeing them he smiled, waved and stopping to look at them called 'Buongiono'.

'Buongiono' James called back.

'Spero cheto non hai paura il pesce vis!' *(I hope you haven't scared the fish away!)* he replied.

'Sorry I don't speak Italian' yelled James then turning to Kim said 'come on. Be brave'.

'No I can't. Not run stark naked past two leering fishermen!' she grumbled.

'Well you'll have to, or stay here all day and the risk is that even more fishermen may come along or perhaps some people to sit on the beach'.

'God no'.

'Well it's now or never'.

'There's not much else we can do is there?

'No'.

'If you hadn't woken me up for this adventure we wouldn't be in this predicament would we?'

'No but aren't you glad I did?'

'Yes unfortunately I am *very* glad. We'd better go then'.

'Come on. Let's give 'em an early morning thrill' and taking hold of Kim's hand James led her as quickly as they could from the deep to shallow water near the beach and then they started running and splashing their way through the gentle waves breaking on the sand and on up to where their robes were.

Both Italian fishermen immediately stopped what they were doing in setting up their fishing tackle and stared open mouthed as Kim and James ran nakedly across the beach to the relative safety of their bath robes which were soon wrapped around themselves. They didn't bother with swimming costumes and James bundled them into his bag from which he extracted a bottle of champagne and two glasses.

'Champagne I think to celebrate you getting up this early, us getting engaged and both of us becoming flashers!'

Kim watched as he took off the foil and metal cork cage from the bottle, eased off the cork and carefully poured two glasses. They were both concentrating on that and it was only as they lifted their glasses to toast each other that they became conscious of approaching footfalls on the sand and looking up they were horrified to see the second fisherman was walking to them and had almost reached them.

'Engleesh?'

'Si. Err I mean yes. Sorry I don't speak your language' James replied.

'I speak a leetle bit Engleesh. You make holiday here? At 'otel?'

'Yes'.

'Is nice 'otel I think?'

'Very' smiled Kim.

'You must be careful for swim with no clothes'.

'Yes sorry about that. We didn't realise anyone like you would be about'.

'I not mind. I like see pretty lady with no clothes' he grinned making Kim blush. 'And you much pretty lady' and she blushed even more. 'With lovely body' and as he kissed his pinched fingers and waved them in the air her blush deepened. 'Magnifico! Bellissimo! Meraviglioso! Perfezionare. (*Magnificent. Beautiful. Wonderful. Perfect*). No ees not me. Ees police who not like. I much like but if they see you with no clothes on beach or in water they ...... err I do not know right word. They make you pay some money' and he rubbed a forefinger and thumb together in the universal gesture to indicate expected receipt of money.

'Ah you mean a fine'.

'Si si. Yes. A fine. Si'.

'Okay well thanks for telling us. We won't do it again' said Kim.

'Ees shame' he smiled. 'Police are fools' and with that he turned away then looking over his shoulder grinned as he said 'You are *much* pretty lady. Squisito'. (*Exquisite*)'.

'Thank you' simpered Kim.

'You drink for special something today eh?' asked the fisherman pointing at their glasses.

'We've just got engaged' she replied.

'Engaged? Sorry I no understanding'.

'I asked her to marry me' James said.

'Marry? You going get marry?'

'Yes we are' nodded Kim enthusiastically.

'Ees good. Very good. I am married for forty one years. Good woman my Maria'.

'Forty one years. That's a long time'.

'Si ees long time ...... but good time. I leave you now. Molta fortuna a tuttie e due' (*much luck to you both*) and with that he walked back towards the rocks and had soon set up his fishing gear and was standing casting into the sea alongside his friend who had already caught one fish.

Kim and James finished the champagne by toasting each other and their future lives together then they got up, waved to the fishermen and walking hand in hand made their way slowly back to their hotel room where they showered to get rid of the sand and the salt after which James gently led her to the bed, laid her down and began to kiss her lips, eyes, ears, nose, breast, nipples and pussy before lifting himself above her where she felt for his erection and guided it into her ready and very willing body. It was a wonderful lovemaking and afterwards they lay quietly together, relaxing and happy.

'James I love you more than I can say but darling will you promise me one thing for our future lives together?'

'What?'

'You won't make a habit of waking me up at four o'clock in the morning to watch the sun rise and skinny dip?'

'I don't need to now do I?'

'No darling you don't'.

Later that day she rang her mother who squealed with delight at the news then she rang Anna who gasped 'Gosh how lovely'. A couple of other close friends also said they were delighted for her and gave their congratulations. James rang his parents but no-one else.

For the rest of the day the two of them were in a kind of daze and couldn't stop grinning, holding hands, touching, and just being blissfully happy with each other and the thought of their future lives ahead.

On Saturday morning they flew back to England and once returned to Kim's apartment they spent the rest of the day, evening and night being happy with each other and making love. On Sunday they lazed around in bed, made love, got up late then after Kim did her exercise routine they had breakfast and started to talk about getting married, where they'd live and the many things that they had to discuss and agree.

At lunch time they walked to a nearby pub, had a drink and a sandwich then went back to the apartment and spent the rest of the afternoon being lazy and happy with each other's company. She went for a run at six and in the evening they watched TV and went to bed around eleven where she lay for some while thinking not only about her work at Highlight which inevitably made her think again about Brian and Furrina Pharmaceuticals, but also about the wedding, what sort of celebration she wanted, large or small, where to hold the reception and so many other things.

Her brain went round and round until eventually she forced herself to stop, clear her mind and think about her love for James so calming down and cuddling into him with an arm across his waist she finally drifted slowly and happily off to sleep.

CHAPTER 4

Back in the office on Monday morning people said she looked sun tanned and well after her holiday and when she started to show her ring everyone congratulated her especially the women who were thrilled for her.

Toby smiled said he was glad she was back and that when she'd got up to speed with everything that had been going on while she was away, to come and see him as he wanted to talk some things through with her. It was around ten o'clock that she knocked on his door and walked in.

'So James is going to make an honest women of you is he?' he grinned.

'Yes'.

'Lovely. Did you know he was going to ask you or did he drop down on one knee and surprise you?'

'No and yes'.

'Eh?'

'No I didn't know and yes he did go down on one knee ...... well two knees actually' and she briefly told him about the sunrise proposal and their early morning swim although she didn't mention it was in the nude.

'Well I'm really delighted for you. Now two things. Firstly we've done some work on Furrina Pharmaceuticals while you've been away. Background stuff mainly and from that we've discovered a couple of years ago there was a bit of a whiff of scandal about another drug test of theirs but after it went wrong they pulled it and as far as we can discover it's never come to market'.

'What was the scandal?'

'Some adverse reactions by some people involved in a drug trial to which the company didn't react very quickly and they were strongly criticised for not doing so'.

'Interesting. Now according to Brian they're not reacting again. Have you or anyone been in contact with him while I've been away?'

'Yes and no'.

'Pardon?'

'Just playing you at your own game' he grinned. '*Yes* they seem to be at it again but *no*, no-one has been in contact with Brian'.

'Right well I'll do so today'.

'Fine. Look there's something else. I haven't told anyone else about this so I'd ask you to keep it to yourself. Completely confidential. Okay?'

'Sure. Sounds mysterious!'

'No not mysterious but we *do* have a problem. With upstairs' he said pointing an index finger at the ceiling indicating the floors above on one of which the Directors of TV-12 had their offices.

'Oh what problem?'

'They aren't happy with what we're doing'.

'Why?'

'Sit down and I'll explain' he replied pointing to the side of his office, where there was a settee and a couple of matching armchairs all in pale cream leather. She walked across and settled down in one of the chairs as he took the settee and looking at her reflected that not only was she a very attractive young woman she was also very good at her job and what he had to say would undoubtedly cause her some concern as he began to update her with the details of what had occurred on the first Tuesday that she was away in Sardinia.

The previous Monday evening just as he'd been about to go home for the night, Peter Holmes the Managing Director had rung down and asked Toby to come to a programme discussion next morning at nine o'clock. Not thinking anything was amiss he diarised it and went home where Sue his wife had invited a couple of friends to supper.

On the Tuesday morning he'd been at Peter's office at the requested time but on entering was surprised to see Lawrence Armstrong, the Marketing Director; Ruth Baverstock, Advertising Director; Elaine Rees, Financial Controller and Jason Moran the Head of Programme Planning were also there.

'Hi everyone' he said cheerily wondering why such a gathering had been convened. 'Looks like Peter's got all the top brass out' he chuckled.

'Toby come and sit down' suggested Peter Homes with a rather serious expression on his face as he indicated the long glass table positioned on the far side of his large office. He took his place in the middle of one side as the other senior employees of TV-12 also ranged themselves beside him along that side.

Toby took position on the opposite side and although concerned at this gathering of the big-wigs thought he'd still try a little levity and raising both hands palm out to those on the opposite side of the table said 'Okay gov I give up. I'll come quietly'.

As there was a complete lack of any flicker of humour then he knew that whatever it was they were going to be talking about was obviously something serious.

'Toby. The reason we wanted to talk with you is that we are concerned about Highlight' said Peter opening the meeting.

'In what way?'

'It seems to have lost its edge. When it first aired it produced tough, hard hitting exposes. It really did *Highlight* in every sense many different things. It earned and justified its name and quickly established itself as one or the best investigative television programmes. Indeed you got short listed for awards at two different TV ceremonies and even though you didn't win it was good getting nominated. But now I don't think you'll be nominated for any awards. The programmes you are producing are dull, lightweight and tending towards being, dare I say it .... boring'

'Boring? Don't be daft'.

'He's not' interjected Lawrence Armstrong the Marketing Director. 'I mean look at the last four programmes. Last week's edition was about how the Church of England wasn't supporting its vicars properly financially. Is that cutting edge? No it bloody isn't. Half the audience won't care and the other half will be made up of Muslims, Hindus, Sikhs, Rastafarians, Catholics, Jedi Knights, atheists or some other bloody mob but *none* of them will be in the slightest bit bothered about Church of England vicars!'

'Well it's of concern to the vicars especially when the Church of England is worth billions'.

Lawrence sniffed and continued 'The previous edition you aired a wholly uninteresting programme about the failure of the Government badger cull. Fucking badgers. Who cares about them?'

'Plenty of farmers who are having cattle slaughtered because of Bovine TB. They care!'

Ignoring Toby's retort Lawrence went on 'Before that we heard about boarded up shops on the high street; before that yet *again* on the high street we had a programme all about the growth of so called "pound" shops. I say again. Who the fuck cares about that? I mean what's the problem with pound shops eh? They're only successful because people like to shop in them!'

As Toby was about to reply Lawrence went on 'It just isn't good enough Toby. It's not what Highlight is supposed to be about'.

'We can only make programmes about subjects that are brought to us. You know our slogan *"If you know something that should be exposed tell us and we'll Highlight it"*.

'Exactly but boarded up shops, pound shops, hard up vicars and fucking badgers doesn't fit that slogan at all' rejoined Ruth Baverstock the Advertising Director. 'I mean come on Toby. They're crap subjects. Utter crap ......'

'As well as thoroughly boring' interjected Elaine Rees the Financial Controller.

'Not to the people involved they're not crap or boring' rejoined Toby.

'Well they are to our viewers and our advertisers' snapped Ruth. Viewing figures for Highlight are down ten percent on what they were earlier this year. Ten percent! That's an *enormous* drop and our advertisers have seen that'.

'I've had three clients contact me to ask for their ads to be re-slotted out of the commercial breaks in Highlight and into something else' said Ruth. 'That is not good when advertisers want to start moving their advertising around. Next step is that they pull the ad away from us altogether and give it to another channel'.

'And we can't afford to lose advertising revenue' warned Elaine. 'Finance is tight as it is. If we get clients wanting to pull out of Highlight or worse still switching their ads to another station the word will get around. Others will do the same and then quick as winking we're in difficulty'.

'They won't do that' protested Toby.

'Oh yes they will' responded Lawrence. 'I've already had Commercial and Overseas Bank's advertising agency with whom we were close to tying up a long term ad campaign tell me they've changed their mind and are putting their money into another station's investigative programme. Also a couple of discussions with other potential advertisers, one a car company and one a toothpaste brand have gone cold. So yes Toby they *are* switching away from Highlight'.

There was a tense silence for a couple of minutes then the under fire executive said slowly 'Okay. Although I don't agree I won't argue with you as I don't think there's much point but I say again we can't just magic up items to investigate. We respond to what's brought to us. I don't have the staff or budget to start off our own investigations and *find* subjects to expose. I rely on subjects that come to us'.

'I understand that' soothed Peter Holmes.

'Any rate Toby we can't allow things to go on as they are so we're thinking of making a change to the time and frequency that Highlight airs' Jason said quietly. 'Currently it goes out at eight o'clock. We're considering moving it to ten o'clock'.

'Oh shit no! That's a death slot for a small TV station like us. People will be watching the main news channels on BBC, ITV, Sky, BBC World and so on. Ten o'clock will kill us'.

Ignoring Toby's impassioned plea Lawrence went on 'We're also thinking that weekly is probably too frequent for it and it might be better for the programme to go monthly. First Thursday of every month'.

'And we'd like you to consider making the programme half an hour not a full hour' suggested Ruth with a smile.

'Every month, ten o'clock and half an hour? You *will* kill us!' Toby yelled.

'Look I realise that this has come as a shock and you're upset about it ....'

'You're right it is a shock and you bet I'm upset'. Toby said interrupting Peter Homes. 'It's a big shock and I'm not just upset I'm fucking furious!'

'Look we haven't made any final decision yet and we're prepared to give it another couple of months in its current time duration, time slot and frequency as it is before implementing any changes'. Peter said calmly. 'The three changes *are* under consideration but *not* yet decided as to whether we do one, two or all three of them. Or none. However we thought you ought to know what's in our minds'.

'What's in your minds is to kill off a bloody good programme which employs some damn good people who work their arses off to bring real investigative journalism to the screen, often working long hours, not especially well paid by other station's standards and totally committed to what they do. How dare you criticise like you have. How fucking dare you!'

Mike Upton

'Calm down' and Ruth now waded into the discussion. 'Shouting, swearing and getting all histrionic about it won't help'

'Look I've said we haven't decided to implement those changes' Peter said in an attempt to placate Toby 'but unless something changes for the better and damn fast then we certainly will'.

'Well if you do, you can do it without me then!' yelled the irate Toby as he got up. 'Highlight stays as it is currently formatted, timed and aired or I *leave*' and without another word or a backward glance he got up and walked out of the room.

After he left there was a short pause before Lawrence said with a rueful grin 'That went well then didn't it?' and in silence everyone left Peter's office to return to their own offices or work stations.

'Christ! So do you think they'll do it? Ten o'clock, half an hour and monthly? asked Kim after Toby had regaled her with the outcome of last week's stormy meeting in Peter Holmes's office.

'I fear they might. They looked pretty determined to me. Probably not all three but maybe one or two of them. I've thought about it since last week and if they're determined to make changes then in least bad order for the programme would be making it a half an hour programme; then moving to monthly but worst of all would be moving it to ten o'clock'.

'So what do we do?'

'We'd better find something to get our teeth into that we can make into a programme to blow their balls off. I want to fuck them up hill and down dale and show the stupid tossers how wrong they bloody are!'

Entirely unphased by his crude language Kim said 'It might be that this pharma drug thing with Furrina that Brian's brought us could be a real belter of a programme'.

'Yes. Well you'd better make sure it is. In the meantime I need to see that Jamie's next programme about the county council corruption is top notch. It's a good subject and right on track for Highlight. Exposing corruption in local government is bound to be a good programme as long as Jamie has done his homework properly.

I mean look what a furore there was a few months back about corruption in a London borough that the BBC discovered. Well a big shire county council corruption ought to make just as much of a stink didn't it? If not more!'

'Yes. I know that Jamie's pretty fired up with what he's got'.

'Hope so. Everything has to be top notch from now on. No second best or nearly best'.

'Will do boss' and with a smile she gave a little salute and went back to her work area where she sat and thought about what Toby had said.

In a way there was a tiny flicker of feeling not surprised as she knew in her heart of hearts that their last few programmes *had* been disappointing, but this drug thing could be just what was needed. Hopefully also Jamie Wilson's council corruption programme which was the next Highlight programme scheduled would be good. As would her pharmaceutical issue but with that the problem was at the moment she simply didn't know if it was going to turn out to be a big scoop or a damp squib?

Picking up her phone she rang her pharmaceutical man Brian who answered almost straight away.

'Brian hi there. This is Kim from TV-12. How are you?'

'Err alright'.

'Can you talk?'

'Not really' he said.

'Someone nearby?'

'Yes exactly'.

'Right do you want to call me on this number when you're free to do so? I'd like to follow up on our previous discussions. We've decided that what you've told us could be something that we'd be prepared to investigate'.

'Right thanks'.

Putting his lack of an enthusiastic response down to the fact that he obviously had people close to him she shrugged and put down the phone conscious that if it was important to Brian it had suddenly become mightily important to her, Toby and Highlight!

It was after lunch that he rang her, apologising for not being able to speak earlier but said that he was now able to talk quite freely.

'Okay well I've discussed this with my colleagues and yes we'd very much like to follow up your project'.

'Good. So how do we proceed from here then?'

'We need to meet again and talk in much more detail. I'll probably bring a colleague so we can get a couple of brains onto the matter'.

'Right'.

'Now where do you want to meet?'

'I don't know. Somewhere very private. It must be discreet and where we can't be overhead or seen together'.

'What about my apartment? That's private enough and we can talk freely there'.

He paused before replying then said quietly 'Umm yes that sounds a good idea. Where do you live?'

'In London. Balham'.

'I don't know London very well but I'm sure I'll find it. Yes that will be fine. I'll come on the tube. Can you give me directions? Are you far from the nearest tube station?'

'No about a ten minute walk but if you like I'll meet you at the tube station and we can walk to my flat together'.

'Alright thank you'.

They fixed the meeting for seven tomorrow evening at the tube station and rang off.

Kim spent the rest of the day studying more about Furrina as well as beginning to make a list of questions to ask Brian when they met tomorrow evening. She also enlisted Toby's help with that and then sat down with Samita her assistant, updated her on where they were, stressed the importance of the project, although without disclosing the worries over Highlight's continuation and was pleased with the interest and enthusiasm that her subordinate showed.

Samita was twenty six years old, single, had a degree from Leeds University in Broadcast Journalism, was very dedicated, lived at home with her Indian parents and younger brother, and had already proved in the six months that she'd worked for Kim to be a cheerful, hardworking, innovative thinker with a nice sense of humour.

'If it is correct what this man Brian says then it is truly awful' she said with her very dark almost black eyes looking directly at Kim's pale grey ones. 'I mean to knowingly go on with drug trials that are causing physical harm to people must be stopped'.

'Of course. That's why we need to expose them' nodded Kim.

'And doing it in poor countries where they think they'll get away without any hoo-ha is very terrible. Whereabouts in India are they doing it?'

'I don't know. We'll add that to the question list for when I meet Brian tomorrow night. Look here is the list of questions that I've already created' and she printed off what was on her screen and handed it to Samita who studied it intently. 'If you think of others let me know'.

'I will of course. Thank you'.

Once again struck by how polite the young Indian woman was, Kim smiled and added 'Hey why don't you come to meet him as well tomorrow? Two minds on the case not just mine'.

'Thank you. I would be delighted to do so'.

'Great. Tomorrow we'll travel together from here to my apartment where I've arranged to see him. Leave about five thirty?'

She got home that night about eight, kissed James who'd already arrived, went for her run, showered when she got back, giggled but refused his request to stay naked for the rest of the evening and dressed in fresh panties but no bra, short yellow skirt, white blouse and bare feet. He said she looked lovely and almost as good as she had a few minutes ago when she'd walked out of the shower. She grinned and stuck her tongue out at him.

They had an enjoyable evening, ate together, watched some TV while cuddled on the settee, but after the news was finished Kim pointed the remote at the set to switch it off and after kissing James with increasing levels of passion whispered that she thought they ought to go to bed. He needed no second invitation and shortly they were making love. It was good and she delighted in hearing him quietly groan 'Oh Baby that was just *so-oo* good' as he reached his climax.

'Yes it sure was. A good rutting session' she grinned as she lay still savouring the sensation of his erection slowly subsiding until it slid slowly out of her.

'A good what session?' he queried getting off her and flopping down on his back alongside her.

'Rutting! My friend Anna always refers to performing the sexual act as rutting. I think it's quite fun. Not vulgar but slightly risqué!' and plonking a wet sloppy kiss on James's nose she snuggled down and resting her head on his chest slid her hand down to his prick where she just allowed it to lie on the still wet and now almost flaccid member.

They stayed like that for a while with him every now and then leaning to her and softly and almost possessively rather than passionately kiss her while her hand gently stroked and occasionally squeezed hm.

Eventually by mutual consent they decided to go to sleep and as she turned onto her side he sidled against her back, put his arm around her, kissed her neck, told her he loved her and soon the pair of them were asleep.

CHAPTER 5

On Tuesday she started the working day by having a detailed "think-in" with Samita and Fergal as they together discussed everything they knew about Furrina Pharmaceuticals.

Fergal had found some references on-line to the drug trials which were taking place in India but it was quite limited. Nevertheless it was a start to finding out more. Kim thanked him and asked him to go on digging to see what else he could find.

'I will. This could be a really interesting project you know'.

'I do know. That's why I want you to find out everything that you can about it for me'.

'I might check with the Indian Embassy here in London. I'm sure they've got a commercial section and as Furrina is a British based pharmaceutical company then I bet they know what they're up to? I thought I'd call them or maybe go and see them'.

'Okay fine. Sounds like a plan. Now Samita have you found out anything about what Furrina are actually up to in India?'

'A little. The trial seems to be taking place in Mumbai and is being run by their Indian Division which is headquartered there but the information I've got so far is quite sparse and limited. But it *is* a start. I'll go on seeing what else I can find'.

'Thanks do that, but in the meantime we really need to talk with Brian tonight. I'm sure that will give us a lot more to go on'.

Fergal and Samita worked on their separate pieces of the project while Kim put the Furrina investigation aside for the rest of the day in order to run her eyes over the investigation that Jamie Wilson the other senior investigator for TV-12 was developing. He wasn't quite as experienced as Kim but had been busy investigating allegations that younger women, in return for giving sexual favours to certain council housing officers in one Berkshire Borough were apparently being given significantly preferential treatment and jumping the waiting list to get a council property very much more quickly than the standard waiting time.

So at eleven o'clock she had a meeting with Toby and Jamie who had developed, studied and brought this particular investigation now almost to the point of being ready to go on air. Jason Moran the Programme Planning Head was also in the meeting.

After close on two hours detailed discussion they felt they were ready to put the programme out and now would take it to the legal department to get their approval to proceed.

'Thanks for your help' Jamie said to Kim as they all broke up. 'I think this could be a good story. After all corruption in local authorities is not unknown but always makes good news especially with the sex element! So how's your drug thing coming along?'

'Slowly at the moment. We're right at the start. I've got another meeting with the whistle blower tonight and we'll know much more after that'.

'Good luck' smiled Jamie as he went off to find the Head of Legal to explain what they wanted to put on air.

Kim watched him walk off down the corridor and noted his slight mincing gait and wondered as she had many times before whether Jamie was gay? Not that it mattered to her if he was. Shrugging she walked out of the building to a nearby coffee shop and bought her lunch of tuna salad and a small carton of freshly squeezed orange juice which she took back to the office to consume.

The afternoon went by quite quickly as she dealt with a number of different issues and then she and Samita left together, walked to the tube station and by six thirty they were opening Kim's front door who with a smile said 'Come on in' to her Indian subordinate.

Inside they took off their coats and Kim poured herself a glass of red wine, a glass of soda water for Samita who said she only drank very occasionally and the two of them sat down and small talked until ten to seven when Kim suggested Samita stayed in the apartment while she walked to the tube station to collect Brian.

'Help yourself to anything you fancy' she said as she left.

The street was quite crowded but she hovered outside the tube station and watched the myriad of people coming and going until a little after seven there he was. Walking quickly to him, she smiled, held out her hand, shook his again noting the lack of firmness in his grip and said briskly 'Nice to see you again Brian. Come on. This way, it's not far'.

They waked together in virtual silence until she led him into her apartment where Samita stood and smiled.

'Right introductions' announced Kim. 'Brian this is Samita who works with me and will be taking an important role in developing this project. I will also have someone else, a chap called Fergal working on it but I thought the two of us were probably enough to talk with you tonight'.

'Right' he replied nervously looking around the large open plan apartment. 'This is very nice. Kind of trendy. Modern yet old'.

'Indeed it is. I loved it when I first saw it. You live in Milton Keynes don't you?'

'Well near to Milton Keynes I have a small old Victorian house in Wilken not far from Milton Keynes. It's very ordinary and nothing special but it does me fine'.

'Are you married?' Samita asked.

'Err no. I…….. well that is…….. umm ……. the fact is that I don't seem to find it too easy to get on with girls. Well ladies I mean'.

'That's a shame. So what interests do you have then?'

'I'm a model soldier enthusiast'.

'How interesting' she said although thinking quite the reverse.

'Yes it is. It is real past military life in miniature you know. I read history books about battles and then re-enact them on a small scale at home. I've got a spare bedroom room devoted to it. My models range from ancient people right up to World War two. Display cases, boards for battle scenes, even CD's with sounds of fighting. Perhaps you'd you like to see some pictures?' and without waiting for an answer he took out his smartphone, tapped a few keys and then held it out to her. 'Here see? Scroll through'.

Samita duly did so making suitably impressed noises and as she clicked onto each new picture of model soldiers, army vehicles and many other elements of the paraphernalia of Brian's hobby, Kim watched Brian gradually relaxing.

'Would you like some coffee or tea or a glass of wine. A beer perhaps?'

'Could I have a cup of tea do you think?' he asked somewhat diffidently.

'Sure'.

'Milk and a little sugar if that's okay'.

'Coming right up' and she bustled off to the kitchen area and flicked on the kettle and while it boiled watched Samita listening to Brian talking about his hobby.

'So here we are' Kim soon announced as she walked back to Brian and put a mug of tea and a tin of biscuits down on a coffee table next to him. 'There I hope that's alright for you?'

He took a sip, nodded and said it was fine.

'Good. So now tell us more about these drug trials and what's going wrong'.

'Look first of all if this goes on TV I won't have to appear will I? On screen I mean!'

'It's up to you. We have a well known television technique of interviewing where you'd be in shadow *or* with your back to the camera. Either way it means you can speak on camera without being identified. And if you're worried about someone recognising your voice we can either distort it or run a voice over using an actor to speak what you're saying'.

'Right. I've never been on TV you know'.

'Most people haven't but if, and I say *if* you need to do so, then we'll coach you. Remember you're on our side and we're on yours. You're one of the good guys, so we'll help and guide you in how we'll interview you. In fact if you watch the Highlight edition this week which is about .... oh I'd better not say yet what it's about, but if you watch you'll find there's a chap there similar to you and you can see how he is interviewed to get the facts and information out but without disclosing who he is. You'll be just like that'.

'Okay I'll do that'.

'Good. So now tell us everything you know. If you don't mind I'll record our conversation so that we don't miss or forget anything' and she put a small recording device on the coffee table and twisted it so the built in microphone was facing towards the very nervous Furrina employee.

'Right Brian' and sitting back in her chair she ran a hand through her hair and pushing it off her face smiled in as reassuring way as she could and said quietly 'Tell me all about Furrina Pharmaceuticals and these drug trials that you're so worried about'.

Brian looked at her then at Samita, appeared to have a brief final tussle with his conscience, took a deep breath which he exhaled slowly before beginning to speak initially quite hesitantly and then more fluently.

'Where to start? At the beginning I suppose' and he gave a nervous laugh. 'I've worked for Furrina for ten years. I'm forty five years old and after I got my degree in chemical engineering at Southampton University I began to work for a small drugs company in Portsmouth.

At that time I lived in digs in Waterlooville, which is a little north of Portsmouth. I enjoyed my work there as it was a happy company, unlike Furrina' he added with an obvious touch of bitterness. 'I got on well rising up from junior trainee to technician then to senior technician but although the work was interesting and as I've said they were a nice company to work for, I couldn't see much opportunity to progress above where I'd got to at that time.

So I looked around for an alternative job in the similar field and found one with another drug company but in Slough. I took that and moved up to that area and rented a little flat. But although they'd promised lots of opportunities in reality I knew as soon as I started that I'd made a mistake as it was immediately clear that what they'd said at the interview wasn't right. They just wanted bench technicians working on drug developments. Why do companies do that?'

'Do what? Need bench technicians do you mean?' asked Samita.

'No. Promise one thing at the interview but the reality is quite different'.

'I don't know. It's not something that I've experienced myself'.

'I hope you don't. Right so where was I?'

'You'd gone to Slough and weren't happy there' prompted Kim.

'Ah yes thanks. No I wasn't happy there at all however I stuck it out for about two years and then saw an advert for a job with Furrina which I applied for and got.

It was about the same level of job as the one in Slough but the pay was considerably more. That's one good thing about Furrina. Probably the *only* good thing! They pay well but they want to own you lock stock and barrel as a result. Nevertheless the work was interesting I was given plenty of freedom to experiment and develop new lines of thinking in product development and the drug projects I was given were interesting.

Mike Upton

Initially I worked on a drug to reduce the side effects of diabetes. It was work that had been going on for some years already and so I continued that and developed it further. It wasn't earth shattering stuff but working with another colleague we did make some improvements to the efficiency of the drug that was already in fairly widespread use. The good thing was that as it was only a development of an existing drug it didn't have to go through years of testing and after a short six month's test programme on people suffering from diabetes without problems and with some improvement to their condition it got its licence for general prescription'. He paused and finished his tea then looked at Kim. 'I say I don't suppose it's possible to have another cup is it?'

'Sure' smiled Kim pleased to see that he was relaxing but slightly worried that the interruption might destroy his thought process and flow of information. After all so far all they'd got was his early career history and nothing of any importance for a Highlight programme but nevertheless she paused the recording machine and trotted into the kitchen area, switched on the kettle which was still quite warm and so it soon boiled. Making his tea she took it back to the sitting room and put it on the coffee table in front of him saying 'There you are'.

'Thank you. Right well I'll continue shall I?'

'Please' nodded Kim pressing the machine's record button again.

'Okay so as that diabetes project came to an end I was asked to be part of the team that was working on a new drug development for the cure of stomach cancer. It was a complex development that had been going on for some years and they were at the stages of detailed animal testing'.

'Go on' encouraged Kim.

'Umm yes well it wasn't to test on mice that had stomach cancer but to test the general acceptability of the drug and to see if it sparked any adverse reactions or side effects'.

'Right'.

He looked at her and at Samita then nodded and continued speaking. 'The tests on mice were disastrous. Several animals died and others developed awful deformities. But worse than that was the fact that some of the offspring that were subsequently born from parent mice involved in the trial that had seemed to exhibit no adverse signs, were also either deformed or very weak. It happened several times. And a number were born dead.

Mice breed very quickly you know. The gestation period is only around twenty days and they have on average somewhere between six and eight offspring but it can be up to thirteen or fourteen. Also one female can have anywhere between five and ten litters per year. Therefore you can get lots of generations of mice very quickly.

But the problems not only occurred in the mice being tested but also their immediate offspring but interestingly not in *their* subsequent offspring. So for example there could be problems with Mother or Father, also with sons or daughters but seemingly not in grandchildren mice, however there were then problems in some of the *next* generation …… the great grandchildren. So it seemed to somehow skip a generation. That is unusual but I guess probably not unique.

Now normally the emergence of these problems would ring serious alarm bells but Louis Farmer who is the Head of New Drug Development at Furrina expressed the view that it was a species issue and told us to move to testing on rats which are also fast breeders'.

'Sorry Brian but can you explain to us as laymen err laywomen' she smiled 'what exactly does a species issue mean?' queried Kim.

'Oh yes. It means it is something that is only going to affect that particular species and not animals in general. In other words Louis said it was an issue with mice and not with anything else. He of course didn't know that for sure it was just something he thought'.

'Right thanks. Go on' she encouraged.

Yes so we did and began testing on rats and again similar problems arose including parents, children, not grandchildren but again manifested in great grandchildren just like the mice testing. But instead of either abandoning the test programme Louis insisted that this was another species issue and instructed that we move to testing on dogs'.

He stopped and stared into the distance as he also took several sips of his tea. 'Nice tea' he said thoughtfully.

'Thanks' smiled Kim.

'Not everyone can make a good cup of tea you know'.

'Glad it's to your satisfaction'.

'Umm' and with a little nod Brian again began speaking. 'Yes dogs. They *can* be difficult to replicate human results although generally they're pretty reliable but again adverse effects emerged quite quickly in a few of the dogs receiving the test drug and there were also downstream effects'.

'Downstream?'

'With the offspring …….. their puppies. But because of the longer gestation times for dogs we couldn't evaluate the results on grandchildren or great grandchildren'.

'Ah right'.

'So Louis demanded that we stop testing on dogs and begin testing on monkeys. I thought and indeed said we should cease testing altogether and go back to the original development stage of the drug and try to ascertain what was going wrong. Well I mean we knew what was going wrong, but I said we needed to find out *why*. In other words *stop* what we were doing with the drug as it was and look to re-develop it. But Louis absolutely refused and insisted we go ahead with monkey testing.

I wrote a long paper saying that I thought it was wrong to do that and we should completely abandon the work to date and start anew. They didn't like that at all and I got hauled over the coals by Louis who utterly refused to countenance any deviation from the test programme and insisted we continued. So I wrote to Marylyn Goodrich the company Chief Executive and said that I thought the programme should be stopped in its current format and redeveloped'.

'What happened' asked Kim.

'I was summoned to her office and she read the riot act to me. I've never been bollocked …… oh sorry, err been told off like that before. She is a nasty vicious woman and she really went for me. When I came out of her office I felt like crying. I mean here was I trying to help. Using my years of professional experience and knowledge to assist the development of a new drug and they were ignoring me. Worse than that they were continuing with the testing'.

'Awful for you' Kim said quietly.

'It was' Brian agreed. 'The next day Louis summoned me to his office and gave me an ultimatum. Stop complaining about the project and get on with it, or if I wouldn't agree to that I could be transferred to another quite different project. If neither of those options were acceptable then I'd be fired right there and then'.

'Wow' said Samita with a sympathetic expression on her pretty Indian face.

'I really didn't want to get fired as jobs like mine are hard to get. You see although I'd worked hard for many years I had nothing spectacular or exciting to show for it. I'd not made any important breakthroughs and had just worked as part of a team, or on my own, on scientific research and drug developments.

Firms taking on people like me for really senior jobs want to see track records of achievement. Breakthroughs. Discoveries. Exciting new routes forward. I had none of those and so I knew I'd probably not get another job at my seniority and therefore pay level and would at best have to take a job at a much lower down level.

So I guess I panicked and said that I couldn't in all honesty continue on the cancer development that was clearly causing problems in animals and accepted the alternative role I was offered on the leukaemia development which I'm working on now and have been for the past three years'.

'And you think Furrina are continuing with this dodgy development on your previous project do you?' asked Kim.

'I *know* they are'.

'How do you know that?'

'Because I have a friend who is working on it but he doesn't seem to be as worried as I was. Am. I don't have many friends you know' he said wistfully 'but John has always been quite friendly to me.

Any rate they continued the monkey development programme, testing and trials which didn't seem to show *any* adverse side effects or problems. But just like dogs because of the timescale involved they hadn't been able to evaluate the drug's effect on children or grandchildren. So based on the results of that trial data they got a licence for human testing.

Now oddly they went to India to do that. Normally human trials are done under very strict conditions and extremely closely monitored in developed countries with all the medical safeguards in place to protect those subjects undergoing the tests. They're often university students, who get paid a surprisingly small amount of money in view of the potentially great personal risk they're running in being part of a drug test programme. But Furrina switched the live human trials to India where they've got a big business and it's there that the trials are being conducted'.

'So is no-one from the UK involved?' Kim wanted to know.

'Oh yes. Louis is always hopping on planes to various places in the world and undoubtedly he'll have been monitoring and checking on progress, problems and issues. There's another guy frequently out there too from the UK called John Andrews. He's the In-market Drug Test Controller so quite high up and always involved in major test programmes. I imagine that the live market tests are being run under his direct control. He reports to Louis who reports direct to Marylyn so she'll know too. Undoubtedly the Indian company's senior management will know all about it as well especially the MD there Mister Chandra Singh. But none of them are coming clean with information about the problems?'

'Why?' questioned Samita.

'Because the incidence is very small for immediate human side effects and they may not be permanent. Those people affected *may* recover. Obviously they don't know whether that's right yet, nor do they know about any downstream effects on any children of the human guinea pigs or of course of grandchildren or great grandchildren. *Yet!* They'll only find out about that in due course of time. Many years away'.

'That is truly awful' said Kim with feeling. 'So do you know exactly where these trials are being held? I mean we've discovered that they're in Mumbai in India so we know that much but Mumbai is a very big place. And do you know how the individuals were recruited? What criteria were used? Where the people came from? Where exactly they live? After all Furrina could hardly just wander down Mumbai high street and ask if people wanted to be part of a drug trial could they?'

'No. They'd have given their Indian operation the required criteria such as age, gender, married or single, body type ...... you know large men, small men, large women, small women, lifestyle such as smokers or non smokers, drinkers or teetotallers, past illnesses and so on. It would be a very rigorous set of parameters against which they'd recruit people. That would all be determined from here in the UK at head office in Milton Keynes, discussed and agreed with Mumbai and then that business would do the recruiting and signing people up against the agreed criteria to partake'.

'And these people taking part would be paid?' queried Samita.

'Yes but another advantage of doing the trials where they are is that they'd only pay a tiny amount of money compared to what they'd pay in developed countries like Europe, Australia or the USA. I mean drug trial payments even in developed counties are not large but where *they're* doing it in India the amounts will be tiny'.

'That it also shocking' snapped Samita. 'Just because the country they're using is generally less well developed then that is no reason to exploit their people who are the guinea pigs in this trial!'

'Oh course it isn't' soothed Kim.

'Anyhow that's about all I can tell you' said Brian looking at his watch. 'Gosh is that the time. I've been here for over an hour'.

'Does that matter? Do you have another appointment' Kim wanted to know.

'No but I didn't think it would take as long as it has'.

'It is an important story and we at TV-12 need to ensure we get all the facts. Tonight has been just the start. We'll need to see you again if you want to leave now'.

'I could stay a bit longer' he said 'but I'd like to excuse myself?'

'Excuse yourself?'

He looked embarrassed as he said quietly 'I need the toilet'.

'Oh sure. All that tea I expect' Kim chuckled. 'This way' and getting up she led him from the room through the door and pointed out another door further along the passageway that led to the bedrooms. 'That red door there on the right'.

'Thank you' he replied as he gingerly opened the door she'd indicated.

Back in the sitting room Kim spoke to Samita. 'Well what do you think? Something genuinely bad here or just an employee with a grudge?'

'I think there is definitely something bad there that needs investigating. Something *wicked*".

'Yes I do too' and the two women sat in silence until Brian came back.

'Thank you that's better' he smiled.

'More tea?'

'No thanks'.

'Drink? Beer, wine, scotch?'

'Erm ....'

'Go on. Do have something'.

''Might I have a small lager then?'

'Sure you can. Do you want anything?' she asked looking at the Indian girl.

'Just some more water?'

'Fine. Now Brian you talk to Samita while I go and get the drinks'.

As she left the room to go to the kitchen area she heard Brian say to Samita 'Umm what shall we talk about?'

'Whatever you like'.

'I don't really know. You see I'm not very good at small talk, especially with ladies'.

'Okay. So why don't you tell me where you went for your last holiday?'

'Oh right. Yes well last year I went to Hamburg. There was a very big model soldier exhibition and gathering of enthusiasts from all over the world. As that's my hobby I spent three days there. You needed all that time because the exhibition was in several large halls. Really enormous it was so it took time to do it justice. It was very interesting to talk with people from lots of other countries about the hobby'.

'I'm sure it was' she replied trying to inject some enthusiasm into her voice.

'Yes very much so' he confirmed as he remembered that holiday where he had indeed spent the three days looking at and discussing model soldiers, miniature battle layouts and scenes, which were of all sizes, types and kinds, with many people from lots of different countries either exhibiting, or just visiting the event like him.

What he didn't tell her though was that each day after the exhibition closed at five o'clock, he'd then spent the evenings and late into the night prowling around the many and varied offerings available in the Reeperbahn, Hamburg's famous red light district. The whole area was a veritable hive of erotic stimulation and sexual opportunity with immensely varied offerings of activities and where prospects existed to satisfy every conceivable normal, unusual and perverted requirement.

He'd visited many of the sex shops and marvelled at the range of stimulating and arousing items on sale; bought some very explicit pornographic magazines which he'd brought back to England; gone to clubs to ogle exceptionally uninhibited, frank and raunchy sex shows on stage; ambled along the Davidstraße where countless prostitutes stood in the street openly offering themselves to whoever was interested; and sauntered up and down the Herbertsraße looking at the many hookers sitting in the lighted windows displaying themselves for all to see.

In many ways he was like a child let loose in a sweet shop and his nocturnal activities were not just confined to looking, as on the first night he'd had sex with Helga a tall, fairly slim blonde German prostitute, while on the second night he'd gone with a dark haired, chunky, big breasted Polish girl called Felicyta.

But on the third night and knowing it was his last there, he decided to take full advantage of the almost limitless sexual opportunities on offer and around seven o'clock he'd had sex with Noora a petite, quite pretty, small breasted Arabic girl originally from Iraq but who having fled the chaos and turmoil in her home country following the overthrow of Saddam Hussein, now lived happily in Germany and made a good living working in the sex trade there.

After he'd left her flat he went to a bar and drank a small stein of local beer before finding a restaurant where he ate a typically Germanic meal washed down with some more beer. Next he visited another couple of clubs where in each he watched some extraordinarily extreme sex shows.

Finally as this was his last opportunity to indulge with such ease in the sexual enjoyments so freely, openly and easily available, around ten thirty he'd gone with a Russian girl called Inga with whom he struggled a bit to reach his second climax of the night but eventually puffing heavily had successfully erupted into the condom.

When he'd finished she waited a short while then patted his bottom with one hand while gently pushing his chest upwards with the other indicating that he should get off her. He nodded and rolled onto his back and watched as she leaned over to him and expertly peeled off the filled condom. She smiled and said several words in Russian.

'Sorry I don't understand'.

'I ask .... err, how you say in English? Yes. I ask. Was good for you?'

'Yes thanks' he replied as she knotted the rubber and looked at the contents. 'Not much there' she pouted. 'You not enjoy your sex with me?'

'Oh yes I did but it's the second time tonight'.

'Second? Sorry I no understand? You want have sex with me again? Second time? Ees possible but you must pay again'.

'No I don't mean that I want to have sex with *you* again. I meant I had sex with *another* lady before I came to you tonight'.

'You already have sex with another lady tonight?'

'Yes earlier this evening. Little arab girl so this time with you was second shag'.

'Ah. You sexy man having sex with two ladies in one night. No wonder not much spunk in here' she grinned tapping his balls while waving the condom in front of his face. Getting off the bed she dropped the used rubber in a small cardboard box which already contained several others. He too got off and started to get dressed as she picked up her tiny black thong, pulled it up her legs into position after which not bothering with a bra she shrugged herself into a short somewhat grubby white dress where the neck line was so low that her large breasts almost fell out when she leaned forward to put her high heeled red shoes back on.

'Here we are' Kim said cheerfully, instantly jerking Brian's thoughts back to the present and away from his sordid sexual adventures in Germany as she handed him a glass of lager, Samita a glass of water tinkling with ice and carefully carrying another glass of red wine for herself sat back down in her chair. 'Cheers'.

'Oh yes cheers' he replied taking a sip of his beer. 'That's nice. Thank you'.

'So is there more you want or can tell us?'

Brian was torn as to what to do. On one hand he wanted to get away and stop being a whistle blower as it felt wrong to be betraying his employer like this. On the other hand he strongly felt that he really had to ensure that the wicked things Furrina were doing came out into the open and the Highlight programme would undoubtedly do that. And furthermore he enjoyed looking at Kim and Samita.

Both were attractive but Kim was especially so and he couldn't help staring at her face and chest while he'd been talking and when she'd got up he'd revelled in seeing her bum move so cutely in the tight confines of her pale grey trouser suit.

'Perhaps I could stay a little longer just while I drink this' he suggested slightly raising his lager glass. 'I know the addresses of the Mumbai offices, labs and manufacturing plants but not the addresses or names of the subjects used in the trials'.

'That'd be a good start. And do you know how they recruited the people they're trialling this drug on?'

'No' and he looked crestfallen.

'Could you find out?'

'Probably'.

'It would be *really* helpful if you could do that for me' smiled Kim seeing Brian blush as his eyes which had been staring at her chest moved up to look at her face.

'I'll try' he said softly.

'Thank you' she smiled reaching forward and patting his hand which made him blush all the more.

He filled in a little more information, answered several more questions the two young women asked him and then having finished his lager said that he ought to leave.

'Do you want me to walk you back to the tube station?' asked Kim.

'Oh no I'll remember the way thanks' he replied getting up.

Kim led him to the door, shook hands with him and when he'd gone returned to speak with Samita who said 'He's obviously still very nervous about being identified'.

'I know and although we'll do all we can to protect his identity there *is* always a risk that somehow someone or other will eventually put two and two together and come up with four and work out that it was him blowing the whistle'.

'I guess so'.

'Now are you hungry? I am and I'll get us something to eat if you like'.

'Well now you mention it then yes I am peckish'.

'Come and talk to me in the kitchen while I rustle something up'.

The two chatted while Kim bustled about producing omelettes and salad for them both and as they ate Samita asked about James.

'He'll be home later. I asked him to stay away while Brian was here as I didn't want to frighten our whistleblower by having three of us, one of whom is nothing to do with TV-12'.

It was just on ten o'clock when Samita was making "time I was going noises" that the sound of a key was heard in the door and James entered the apartment, peered into the sitting room and said 'Hi. Is it okay for me to come in? Has your chap gone?'

'Yes come in and let me introduce you to Samita who as you know works with me'.

James and Samita shook hands, introduced themselves to each other after which he plonked down in the settee. 'So did it go well? Did he spill the beans for you?' he asked.

'Yes he's started to. I think there's much more to find out but undoubtedly there is the making of an excellent programme which is right up Highlight's street' agreed Kim. 'Now before you make yourself comfortable. I want you to run Samita to the tube station for me to save her walking alone at this time of night'.

If he minded he didn't show it and with a little bow grinned and said to the Indian girl 'Be a pleasure. Come this way madam, your carriage awaits you'.

'Thank you. See you tomorrow Kim' and with a smile she left with James leaving Kim alone to think about what Brian had said.

He returned after about a quarter of an hour, said he'd seen Samita safely into the tube station and had come back and parked his car in one of the two spaces allocated for each apartment next to Kim's Mini Cooper.

'Hope you didn't scratch my lovely little car parking that great gas guzzler of yours?' she asked.

'No I didn't'.

Brian meanwhile had made his way via the tube and train back to Milton Keynes where he extracted his three year old Ford Fiesta from the station car park and drove home to his village of Wilken. Once indoors he made himself a cup of tea and sat thinking about the evening in general, including the very pretty Indian girl Samita, but most especially about Kim who he thought was simply stunning.

Even when he went to bed later that evening she was still at the forefront of his thoughts and he wished he had a girlfriend like her. Well to be honest he told himself he wished he had a proper girlfriend, *any* girlfriend, for company, fun, companionship and of course sex rather than paying women to let him have sex with them.

Yes someone like Kim would be wonderful as she was really attractive, had a delightful figure, lovely long legs and was obviously fun and interesting. As he thought about her he fantasised and wondered what she'd look like without any clothes on? And the more he thought about her in that way the more sexually excited he became.

So imagining that she was there with him in his bed, he slid his hands down into his pubic hair then on to his penis and pretending that it was her hand touching him closed his eyes and gently stroked himself. When he'd fully erected he began to masturbate, slowly at first and then more quickly. It didn't take long before he muttered 'Oh Kim yes yes yesssssss' and with a happy sigh ejaculated copious quantities of semen into his dark green pyjama trousers. When he'd stopped squirting he let go of himself and whispered 'Thank you so much my darling'.

Finished and happy with the satisfaction he'd given himself, he turned onto his side enjoying the sensation of the warm wetness in the trousers pressing against his upper leg but knowing it would dry there overnight.

Then with Kim's pretty face in his mind's eye he smiled and went to sleep.

CHAPTER 6

Unaware of how she'd fuelled Brian's sexual fantasies, when James had returned from taking Samita to the tube Kim flung her arms around his neck and stretching up on tip toes, pulled his head down so she could kiss him. At six foot two he was several inches taller than her but she didn't mind and found it reassuring to have a tall man with her.

After they'd kissed she poured them both a glass of wine and when he'd plonked down into an armchair she clambered onto his lap and twisting to part face him they talked generally about their respective days then she explained what Brian had told her.

'But that is horrendous' he exclaimed.

'Isn't it!'

'So are you going to make a programme about it?'

'You bet. We're really going to expose them'.

'Could be tricky though couldn't it? To get the proof I mean? It's all very well having this Brian chap snitch on his employer but you'll need to get real proof of what he says won't you?'

'Of course'.

'So how are you going to get that? Break into their offices at Milton Keynes and search for the evidence?'

'No of course not you idiot' she chided. 'To be frank at the moment I don't know where or how we're going to get the proof'.

'Maybe you need to go to India and meet the guinea pigs and see for yourself. Film them then present the evidence to Furrina?'

'Possibly' she mused quietly. 'I'll talk to Toby tomorrow'.

'Sounds a good idea. But now I'd like you to talk to me' he grinned.

'Would you? What about? Something special?'

'Yes. I'd like you to tell me if we're going to make love here in this chair, or go to bed to do it?'

'Who said anything about making love' she said quietly raising an eyebrow.

'You definitely did this morning. You said that I should stay away while you had your secret man here and then when I came in later you'd ravish me in a most exquisitely passionate lovemaking experience'.

'I don't remember saying anything of the sort' she chuckled knowing very well she'd not said it.

'Oh I'm certain you did' he laughed pulling her towards him 'so I think you should drag me into the bedroom, take off all your clothes and ravish me'.

Later in bed when she asked he replied that yes he felt entirely satisfied from her ravishing of him and the two of them were soon asleep.

Next morning she was out of bed and doing her ten minute exercise work-out routine for which she just wore a pair of panties while James lazed in bed watching, as he did most mornings. He didn't undertake the morning exercise routine himself but he liked watching Kim at her daily schedule and he liked it even more when they showered together afterwards even though this morning she refused sex with him under the cascading hot water and told him to wait till tonight.

At the office Toby was expectantly waiting to be updated on Brian's revelations and once he'd heard from Kim and Samita and listened to some of the recording of what had been said last night he was convinced that there was definitely a programme to be made about Furrina's drug trials.

'The question is how do we go about getting the proof?' he mused. 'I mean we can't just go on air with vague statements. If we're gonna nail these guys we've got do it thoroughly, with evidence, proper proof and be legally fireproof'.

'Of course' replied Kim wondering why he had just stated the obvious.

'It won't be easy to get especially in those places' added Samita.

'No it won't. Do you think we can get your Brian to copy some documents from Furrina's offices?'

'Phew. He's quite a nervous chap. Always worried that he's being watched by Furrina. I don't know if he'd have the courage to do something like that?'

'We'll undoubtedly also need to go and see the situation on the ground' muttered Toby. 'I think we'd better go and talk to them upstairs as this could get quite costly what with flights to India, hotels etc. I'll make an

Mike Upton

appointment with Peter and whoever else he thinks ought to be in on the discussion'.

'You'll want me for that too I presume?' asked Kim.

'You bet. This is your project. Oh yes definitely. You too probably Samita'.

'Alright fine'.

'We'll wait to hear from you on then. Meantime I'll go and put the finishing touches to my thoughts on how we should proceed' said Kim.

Later that morning she was involved in a discussion with Fergal when Toby rang and said 'Twelve o'clock upstairs. Bring both Samita and Fergal' and rang off.

'I don't know who is going to be in this meeting apart from us and Toby so keep your wits about you!' Kim advised as she, Samita and Fergal stood in the lift to go to the top floor for the meeting with Peter Holmes TV-12's Managing Director. When the lift doors opened she led the way along the corridor and stopped outside the door marked with Peter's name.

'I've never been up here before' whispered Samita.

'Me neither' agreed Fergal.

'First time for everything' grinned Kim as she knocked on the door and hearing the command to come in opened it and led her small team inside.

'Ah Kim come in' beamed Peter 'and Samita and Fergal as well. Good. Now you know Jason Moran Head of Programme Planning don't you' and they confirmed that they did 'but we're just waiting for .... ah here she is' and the door opened to admit Penny Proctor who was one of the TV station's most senior programme producers with a sharp eye for detail and making the most of a cutting edge issue coupled with a fiercely sharp tongue if she didn't get her own way.

'Right' said Peter nodding at Penny as she sat down. 'I've been given an outline of this Furrina thing by Toby but why don't you tell all of us everything you know about it Kim. Leave nothing out. I want to know *everything*'.

'Okay' and over the next half an hour she explained how matters had developed from Brian's first tentative phone call to her, the meetings she'd had with him, the long detailed discussion in her apartment at which

Samita was also present and finally how she'd brought the whole thing to Toby who'd suggested the meeting here this morning.

'Okay everyone. What do we think?' asked Peter to the room in general.

'I think it's something that we simply have to run with' stated Toby. 'You said the other day Peter that you wanted tougher harder hitting subjects from the Highlight team. Well this is surely that'.

'I agree' announced Jason.

''Providing you get the proof then I am sure we can make it a real cutting edge programme' nodded Penny 'but if I'm going to stick my balls out on this one I need plenty of facts that I can weld into a believable and shocking story. How are you going to get them? I mean this Brian guy's statements aren't enough. We need proof Kim'.

'I know and I'll get it'.

'How?' demanded Peter.

'I'll go to India, find the people that are running the tests, find the people who've been guinea pigs, find the facts and thus get you the proof'.

'Won't be easy' commented Penny.

'Maybe but I'll do it. Trust me'.

'We do. Okay Kim go away and put a proposal together including costs and let me have it as soon as you can. I'll talk it through with Lawrence, Ruth and Elaine and we'll come back to you with a yes or no. Alright?'

'Yep sure. Will do. Great'.

'Fine. Thanks everyone. Meeting over. Oh and by the way have you considered what are we might call this programme?'

Without hesitation Kim said 'I think we should call it the Beta file'.

'The Beta file?' frowned Penny.

'Yes. The drug is technically known by its full name as, err hang on a sec'. Checking a folder she had she then slowly said 'Betanapotraproxiflevien-g3. Trips neatly off the tongue don't you think?' and grinned as she looked around the room. 'But as it is such a mouthful, the scientists themselves have shortened its nomenclature just to Beta so I think we should do the same'.

'The Beta file. Yes I like it' agreed Penny nodding slowly. 'Has overtones of menace, threat and mystery. Yep a good title and with some well chosen chilling menacing type music I think it could make great television. Well done Kim. Now all you've got to do is get the facts about this drug company and what exactly they're up to, statements from people involved in the trials explaining what's happened to them, information out of the company on what they're doing and together we'll make a terrific programme'.

'Is that all?'

'Yep! That's all' agreed Peter with a grin.

But to a large extent although what Kim and her small team had done so far was sufficient to get the senior management of TV-12 interested, she was also conscious that if she made a good programme out of this it could be one of those occasional TV events that really make waves which stretch out widely into all sorts of other media such as newspapers, magazines, social media as well as getting picked up and run with by several other TV stations, news broadcasts and so on and all that would undoubtedly help her career.

She'd seen past examples where in the fickle world of TV a sudden flash of journalist brilliance carried through onto screen and well executed, could have far reaching and very positive consequences for the instigator, in this case her. Conversely a major project like this executed badly or with wrong facts, would bring disaster down on the instigator's head with catastrophic consequences for their career.

Yes she nodded if she made a really good programme then the implications for Furrina could be enormous and devastatingly far reaching but for her personally then if the phrase "the world becomes her oyster" was too strong, it would most certainly do her career no harm at all and could benefit it enormously.

So it was a tightrope she was going to walk. Get it right and she'd be a hero and her career should blossom. Get it wrong and her career would suffer a cataclysmic failure.

All these thoughts went through her mind as she sat quietly thinking about how next to proceed. After a while she picked up the phone and rang Brian.

'Oh look' he said as soon as he answered 'no I'm not interested in claiming for PPI compensation thanks. Please don't ring me again about it' and he cut off the call.

Guessing that he had people with him and so was unable to talk she felt a flash of irritation pass through her but then it went as she realised it wasn't her risking her job and career and with someone as obviously nervous as Brian then he was clearly going to take the utmost care over his dealings with her and TV-12.

Turning to deal with Toby's request for a costed proposal she settled down to do just that; asking Fergal to check on flights and costs to Mumbai; Samita to make some assumptions over hotel costs and spending money that they'd need while she addressed herself to the knotty issue of how once there they'd actually get the evidence that they'd need.

She was locked into that issue when her mobile rang and looking at the screen she saw Brian's name appear.

'Hi there' she answered cheerfully. 'Can I sell you some PPI insurance?'

'Eh? No. I don't ....'

'Joke Brian. You used the PPI ruse to tell me rather cleverly I thought that you weren't able to talk to me at that moment'.

'Oh yes I see' he muttered. 'No I couldn't as there *were* people around me'.

'Is there a good time to talk to you?'

'Well it's always tricky at work. It's better in the evening when I'm at home. I live alone so there's no-one to overhear'.

'Okay I'll call you in the evenings in future unless it's urgent. Now look we've passed the next stage of the process to turn what you've told me into a proper project and hopefully eventually into a Highlight programme. We had a meeting with my boss, the Managing Director, the Head of Programme Planning and one of our most senior programme producers. The result is that I've been asked to put together a full proposition with costs, timescales and so on'.

'Does that mean you're going to run it then?'

'No-oo not yet. The process is that I'll put this proposal together, agree it with Toby, my boss, then we'll take it back to the MD and some of the other senior people and if they give it their approval *then* we're good to go'.

'Good to go? You mean you'll make the programme?'

'Yes but whether it then gets on air is another issue. Various people will have to see what we've made and decide whether they think it merits going on air. So we're not there yet but we *are* on our way. Now is there any chance of you coming to India with us? We'll pay all your travel and accommodation costs'.

'Oh no I don't think so' he replied immediately in a almost panic stricken voice. 'I mean I *could* but I would be so worried about being seen out there and thus identified as the person who has leaked the information about the company and what they're doing'.

'Right. I thought you might say that. So have you thought any more about what I asked when you were at my apartment about getting information on how Furrina recruited their guinea pigs out in the markets and how we can find them?'

'Umm well yes I've thought about it but it's not going to be easy to do'.

'Nothing good or important is ever easy Brian. I'm sure if you put your mind to it though you could find a way. I'd be ever so grateful' she said in a soft wheedling tone of voice.

'Right' he gulped. 'I'll try'.

'Thank you'.

'I'll ring you if I can find that out'.

'Not *if* you can find it out Brian. *When* you've found it out'.

'Yes okay ...... when' he muttered.

'Thanks. Remember we are relying on you'.

'Yes I know' he replied in a worried tone of voice. 'Is there anything else?'

'Not at the moment. As we find out more information especially from the actual market place we'll need lots of your time and help but for now I just want you to get that information for me. That's why I rang you earlier'.

'Right'.

'And of course if you find out anything more do let me know. Remember you are the expert here in this matter. We're only TV people, so we're relying on you to steer us in the right direction'.

'Right' he repeated again quietly.

'I'm depending on you Brian. Don't let me down will you?'

'No I won't. I'll try and find some more information out of Furrina after everyone's gone home this evening. It'll be quiet then and easier to do it'.

'Sounds ideal. I'll wait to hear from you'.

'Yes okay. I can't promise of course'.

'I have every confidence in you Brian. Speak later eh?'
'Yes. Goodbye'.

On Wednesday evening Kim had finished her run, showered, changed and was sitting at the table eating the evening meal which James had prepared. They tended to take it in turns over making their suppers and tonight he'd volunteered to do it and produced a spicy spaghetti Bolognese with a side salad. She was about half way through hers when her mobile rang. Looking at the screen she was it was Brian.

'Sorry darling. I must take this. It's Brian from Furrina' she smiled at James then said brightly 'Brian hello there. Nice to hear from you again'.

''Oh yes thank you. I've got some more information for you'.

'Good. What?'

'Well firstly I've found lists of names of the people taking part in the drug trials in Mumbai'.

'Oh well done you. How clever of you. That is brilliant' she gushed.

'And I've discovered some preliminary results from the latest recruits in India which I've printed off and taken a photocopy. None of the people involved are ill or have got stomach cancer. The trials are to test general compatibility with people not curative effect. I've got one copy here at my home and the other is for you. They make worrying reading'.

'Wonderful'.

'Wonderful? Oh no I didn't say they make wonderful reading. I said they make worrying reading'.

'Yes I know you did. I don't mean wonderful that they make worrying reading. I mean wonderful that you've got the information'.

'Oh right. Yes I see what you mean'.

'Now all you've got to do is get that list to me'.

'Yes okay. I've also discovered that there is a schedule of people who started as guinea pigs but who have now been taken off the trials'.

'Taken off?'

'Yes. I think that is probably because they've developed adverse symptoms. I couldn't think of any other reason why people would be removed from the trial. You normally need longevity and especially *continuity* for this sort of trial. Taking someone off early on goes right against that. So I thought that the only reason must be that they're developing or have developed problems. If that is so then the sooner you make this programme the better. People's health and possibly their lives are being put at risk by Furrina'.

'Of course. Can you get hold of that list of those people who've been taken off the trials?'

'I don't know. Let me think about that'.

'Alright but I need from you what you've already found as soon as possible. Have you printed it all off?'

'No. What I have done is to print off a few summary sheets. It's difficult to easily get the rest'.

'But without *lots* of real data we can't make the programme. A few summary bit of information won't do'.

'I know. But there's so much. Let me think about how to either reduce it or get more extracts from it'.

'Good. Now I need to get hold of what you've discovered so far. Those summary sheets. You're not in London tomorrow are you?'

'No I've got to go to Scotland for a review meeting with two doctors at Edinburgh Royal Infirmary over some leukaemia research things'.

'When do you leave?'

'Tomorrow morning on the eight forty Easy Jet flight out of Luton'.

'Okay I'll meet you there and you can hand the papers over to me before you go. I'll be there in good time and hover by the Easy Jet check in desks'

'NO! I'll have a colleague with me. We can't do that. I daren't risk being seen with you' he exclaimed clearly highly agitated by the suggestion.

'Okay calm down. How about if I come to your house before you leave tomorrow?'

'No. Look you have to understand that I have to be really very careful with this. I told you Furrina see everything that their employees do on computer. I'll post the information to you'.

'Could you scan it and e-mail it to me?'

'No they might be able to trace that I've done that'.

'How? Surely you have your own computer or tablet? They can't see what you send from there'.

'I've got a laptop but it's a Furrina machine so I dare not scan this stuff into or from that. It's too risky as they'd be bound to find out'.

'Surely not?'

'Look you don't know them. They'll find out somehow. No I've printed it off at the office and I'll post it to you. I pass a small village shop that's also a post office on my way to Luton. I'll go in there and arrange to send it recorded delivery'.

'Will they be open at that time of the morning? After all you'll be off early won't you if your flight is at eight forty?'

'It opens at six'.

'Gosh that's early and a time when good folks like me are still tucked up in their nice warm comfy bed fast asleep'.

Smiling as he imagined Kim in bed he said 'You should have it the day after tomorrow'.

'Alright. Have a good trip to Edinburgh and we'll talk when you're back'.

'Yes' but as he rang off he wondered what Kim wore in bed or perhaps she was a nude sleeper? And that thought sustained him for the rest of the evening.

Looking at her spaghetti the subject of his speculation resumed eating pleased that her meal was still warm although no longer hot'.

'Your whistleblower?' queried James.

'Umm. He really is nervous, verging on being paranoid about Furrina being able to see and keep track of everything that he does'.

'Maybe they do?'

'They can't possibly not to the extent that he implies. This is delicious by the way darling'.

'Thanks'.

The rest of their evening passed cheerfully although every now and then Kim wondered exactly what the information that Brian was going to send would reveal.

Next morning she told Toby that Brian was sending through some information and after she'd received that, hopefully tomorrow she'd prepare the official proposal for the project.

'Fine. Make sure it points up what a potentially disastrous drug this could be. We've not only got to make good television about this, but we've got to make a really hot proposition for them upstairs in order that they'll sanction the expenditure for you and your team to pursue it'.

'I know' Kim replied meaningfully.

CHAPTER 7

Everything seemed to be in limbo with her until the post arrived mid morning Thursday where among the myriad of letters, documents, junk mail and other items was a foolscap envelope marked for her attention only and with STRICTLY PRIVATE AND CONFIDENTIAL marked prominently on both sides of the brown envelope.

Kim felt her heart start to bump as she carefully opened the envelope and then a small smile spread across her pretty face as she read what Brian had sent.

It was exactly as he'd said on the phone. A summary of some of the trial results and lists of the names and addresses for the Indian trials guinea pigs, with some notations against each name which she didn't understand but no doubt Brian would explain their meaning;

There was also a hand written note from Brian saying that her was sure he could get hold of statements about the people taken off the trials, much more general documentation on the overall effectiveness of Beta, the progress of the Indian trials and finally some information about the past test programme on the monkey results with an extrapolation into human results expected from the successful application of the drug to people.

'Wow Brian my man. This looks as though it's going to be dynamite. And if this is only part of what you can get hold of we're onto a goldmine' she muttered softly. 'Well done'.

Knowing how fearful he was about being contacted nevertheless she wanted to let him know that she'd received the information so after thinking how to carefully phrase it she sent a text.

> Thank you for my birthday present which arrived safely this morning. Just what I've always wanted. Kim.

That should be okay she thought and no doubt Brian would delete it as soon as he'd read it and in that assumption she was correct because at that moment he, a colleague from Furrina and the two doctors at Edinburgh Royal Infirmary were having a short break over coffee and biscuits from their detailed discussions on Furrina's leukaemia research. Brian's mobile pinged with an incoming text, which he quickly read and immediately deleted. It was almost two hours later when locked into a cubicle in a male toilet that he replied.

> Glad u got it. I'll call you sometime this evening if that's ok.
> Brian.

'Oh Brian you are a strange man' she sighed although pleased to learn that he was going to call her so that they could discuss what he'd sent.

The more she got into this project the more excited she became about it and although knowing that it was starting to take over everything that she did workwise nevertheless she didn't mind as she knew that as a person she always threw herself heart and soul into assignments and that not only enabled her to give of her best but usually resulted in outstanding results. Where she only tackled things in a part interested or half hearted manner then the results weren't inspiring and if she was honest with herself that was what had happened on the two high street investigation programmes as well as the one about the church not supporting its vicars properly financially. Those three programmes were less than cutting edge however she took the criticism of the programme about badgers hard as she thought that had been interesting and topical as well as hard hitting.

Well she shrugged she couldn't change what had already aired but she could and damn well would make this investigation about Furrina and its dodgy drug trials a real belter of a programme.

Looking at the likely costs they were not insubstantial. Flights to India and hotels for herself, Samita, Fergal, producer, cameraman, researcher and gopher; probably payments to locals for advice and help; taxis and other out of pocket expenses. The list and hence total soon mounted up. Finally she added an unspecified amount as "contingency" as her experience was that however well you planned these things there were always unexpected costs popping up.

She added her estimate of the costs to the project document and saved it on her computer. She didn't scan and add Brian's information that she'd received this morning but summarised it and added it as an appendix. If Toby or anyone else wanted to see the complete document Brian had sent then they could.

Finally she finished and sitting with Samita ran through the proposal, listened to, agreed and added some of her suggested improvements, accepted Fergal's suggestions to shorten part of the introduction and eventually thanking her two staff felt that the document was ready to go to Toby. However she was going to wait until she'd spoken to Brian tonight to see if there was anything else that he might add which ought to be included in the submission.

The rest of her day passed slowly as she kept clock watching willing tonight to come when she could not only talk with her whistleblower again but watch Jamie's programme on council corruption go out on air live.

After her evening run, shower and glass of wine she got a couple of ready meals out of the fridge all set to pop in the microwave because she couldn't be bothered to cook anything and as James was going to be late home that evening she felt that something hot and quick would suit them both.

James still wasn't home when Brian rang and she small talked with him for a little while until she asked 'Are you free to talk about what you sent me?'

'Yes I'm in my bedroom at the hotel here. I've got the bath taps running and the radio on so I can't be overheard'.

'Brian we're in England. Well you're in Scotland, but neither of us is in Russia or North Korea where everything you say or do is monitored, measured and possibly will come down on your head like a ton of bricks. You must stop being so paranoid!'

'Sorry' he replied quietly.

'I've read through what you sent and it is very interesting. I don't understand some of it, you know the technical stuff so I'll need you to explain it in layman's language. I've also started to plan our trips. We obviously need to go to India to see the people and the trials at first hand and then depending on that will determine how we proceed further'.

'I see'.

The Beta File

'I'll take Samita and the rest of the team with me to Mumbai and then depending on how that goes I'll come back to the UK to report back to Toby, regroup then we'll tackle Furrina directly here in the UK'.

'So do you mean you'll make two programmes? One about India and one about Furrina here in England?'

'Lord no. It'll all be one programme. You must understand Brian that to get an hour's television we need *several* hours of film, interviews, discussion and so on'.

'Oh. Why?'

'Well so that we can select the best and most hard hitting sections to use in the programme. People when interviewed often ramble so we need to edit what they say to reduce its length and select the bits that support our main contention that the trials are dangerous and causing problems with people involved with them'.

'I see' but he sounded sceptical.

'Don't forget if you want to come too we will happily take you at our expense'.

'I don't think so but thanks'.

'Alright so can we now talk about what you sent through?'

'Yes'.

The discussion evolved during which Kim made copious notes, asked lots of questions and gradually found Brian more forthcoming and less obsessed with secrecy and personal concealment. She constantly told him how helpful he was being and flattered him on his skill in getting the information that he had.

'Is there any way you can get more information on the trials?' she asked.

'Ah now I had an idea about that. As you know I couldn't find it when I looked the other night but I thought that maybe if I went in over the weekend, perhaps Sunday morning and had a really thorough rummage through the computer files I might be able to uncover it. I know the pass codes for the project you see and so given time to really hunt in the computer I'm sure I ought to be able to locate it. It'll be in there somewhere. And I've bought a memory stick so I can upload it all onto that'.

'Wonderful but are you okay with going in on Sunday?'

'Oh yes. I've done it before when I've got behind on work and as there's usually no-one around then it's possible to work in peace and quiet and get lots done. Not many people go in on Sunday and the guy who is now handling the data trial information assembly and collation, is a devout Christian so as he certainly won't be there. Therefore I'm most unlikely to get disturbed' he commented.

'Well if you're happy to do that I'm sure it will be very helpful'.

'Yes. I've been thinking about it. We …… err well you, need everything I can get you so you can make a good programme don't you?'

'The more stuff we've got to choose from then yes of course the better the final programme. But as we're actually going to India if there's anything more you can get about what exactly they're doing and whereabouts over there in Mumbai then please prioritise that'.

'I will. Can we meet on Sunday after I've found out what I can?'

'Yes if you like but aren't you a bit worried about being seen meeting me?'

'No I've thought about it and you're right. I probably am being too suspicious and if we meet I can give you everything I've found and explain anything you might not understand'.

'Okay great. Where would you like to get together? Somewhere in Milton Keynes?'

'No that *is* too close. I did wonder about asking you to come to my home but I'd prefer not to do that for the same reason' he said. 'Can we meet at a motorway service area?'

'Sure which one? Newport Pagnall? That's not far from Milton Keynes?'

'Exactly. It's *too* close! Can we meet at Toddington Services? It's about twenty five miles south of Milton Keynes and therefore not so far for you to travel up from London to meet me?'

'Sure that's fine. South or Northbound services?'

'Oh it's all on one side. When going south you come off and swoop over the top of the motorway into the one service area as it's built on the side going north'.

'Right. So where do you want to meet in the service area?'

'I'll be in the newsagents browsing the magazines. We could meet by chance as it were like old friends that haven't seen each other for a while just in case anyone is there who might know or see me'.

'Fine. What time?' she wanted to know.

'Twelve?'

'Alright. A secret midday assignation it is' she laughed.

'Can I ask you something?'

'Sure. What?'

'Would you ....'

'Would I what?'

'You'll probably say no'.

'Go on try me' she said softly.

'Would you have lunch with me afterwards? Not in the service area we could go to a pub or something. No you probably won't want to do that will you? Sorry for asking. Let's just meet at twelve and chat about whatever I've found'.

'Brian'.

'Yes?'

'I'd love to have lunch with you. Thank you for asking'.

'*Really?* Do you mean it?'

'Yes of course'.

'Are you sure?'

'Yes quite sure. Now shall I book somewhere?'

'Oh no I'll do it. Is a pub alright? Or would you want to go to a proper restaurant?'

'A pub will be lovely. Thank you. I shall really look forward to it'.

'Oh so will I' he said and his feeling of gratitude and excitement came through over the phone. 'Thank you ever so much'.

'My pleasure. So until Sunday then'.

'Yes till Sunday. Thank you again'.

'Bye Brian'.

After the call disconnected she was mildly amused at his shyness but also his obvious delight that she'd accepted his invitation to lunch. He though was overjoyed at the thought of spending more time with her.

Quickly switching on the TV she left the sound down low until at eight o'clock she saw the introductory credits for this week's Highlight programme.

She watched carefully, as although she knew the content from what Jamie had told her and the work she'd done on helping him get the programme finalised nevertheless she wanted to see how the final finished programme ran on screen.

It was good and she was sure that the effect over the following days would be devastating for those people that the programme had exposed as being crooked and corrupt. The statements from the women who'd agreed to sex in return for getting pushed up the housing ladder came over clearly and in a sympathetic manner. The viewer would undoubtedly not feel disgust or that it was their own fault for agreeing to sleep with these three particular council officials, but rather sorry that they'd been so desperate that they'd agreed to do that for the benefit that was offered in housing. Also the statements from women who'd been propositioned but not succumbed were equally telling.

Several people had their faces hidden and she hoped that Brian was watching to see that the same technique would be used to prevent him from being identified.

Shortly before it finished James arrived home, walked over to her, leaned down and tried to kiss her but she twisted away' said she really wanted to watch the rest of this edition of Highlight, smiled when saying 'Okay' he dropped a gentle kiss on her head before going to the fridge and getting himself a bottle of lager which he brought with him to sit and watch the remainder of the programme which soon ended.

She texted Jamie to say that she thought his programme had come over well and had just done that when her mobile rang with an incoming call from Brian.

'Hello there'.

'I watched the Highlight programme'.

'Enjoy it?'

'Yes. That's awful what those council people were doing'.

'Indeed which is why we decided to make a programme about it after it was brought to us by a whistleblower, like you. Did you see the shadow interview technique?'

'Yes. Is that what you'll do for me?'

'Yes'.

'Right fine. Thank you. Goodnight'.

'Goodnight Brian. Sleep well'.

'I will. See you on Sunday. Bye'.

With that Kim and James watched the ten o'clock news, then poured themselves another glass of wine each, chatted about their respective day's at work and finally went to bed a little after eleven o'clock.

CHAPTER 8

Kim drove into Toddington services a little after twelve o'clock on Sunday and although the car parking area was surprisingly crowded she soon found a space to park her red, with white side stripes Mini Cooper Convertible. Blip locking it she walked into the substantial building where she found the large newsagents and wandered slowly around during which she spotted Brian on the far side studying the magazine section.

As she approached him he looked up smiled, glanced around and then spoke to her in a slightly over loud voice. 'Hello there. This is a surprise meeting you here. It must be months since we last met'.

'Yes six at least' she replied frowning slightly but he smiled and continued speaking.

'Yes it must be all of that. Maybe more. So how are you?'

'Fine'.

'Great. Do you fancy a coffee and a chat?'

'Lovely' she smiled allowing Brian to set the plan and pace of what they were going to do. They walked to the cash desk where he paid for the two magazines he'd selected and then led the way to the coffee shop on the other side of the concourse where they found a table. Putting his magazines on one of the chairs he suggested she sat down while he went and ordered her requested decaff latte and a black coffee for him.

While he was away she paged through one of his magazines and although wholly uninterested in the content couldn't help but be impressed with the quality, detail and sheer authenticity of the model soldiers and battle scenes shown in the many photographs.

'Strong black coffee for a strong man eh?' she said closing his magazine when he returned.

'Oh I don't know about that but yes I do like coffee but not too strong. It makes me twitchy and then I can't sleep at night' he responded trying but failing to look into her eyes, partly because he was nervous of doing so and partly because he was still very shy with her.

'So are your model soldiers similar to these in here?' she asked pointing at the magazines.

'Yes. Are you interested in my hobby?'

'No 'fraid not. I just looked at some of the pictures while you were getting the drinks. Needed to ensure you'd bought magazines related to your hobby and not Playboy or some dirty girly magazines' she chuckled.

'Ooh no. These are just about ......'

'I'm just teasing' she said softly.

'Oh right' he said quietly beginning to blush.

'I can see these are about your hobby but it wouldn't worry me if you had bought naughty magazines. Lots of men do'.

'So I believe' he replied blushing even more as this afternoon he had indeed intended to stop at a sex shop on his way home which had an extensive selection of porno magazines so he could stock up on some new titles.

'That's why there are lots of different ones on the shelf I guess. Naughty magazines I mean .... not men!' she laughed.

'Probably' he muttered.

'So how did it go this morning?'

He nodded and leant slightly forward. 'Yeah okay actually. In fact good. It was quiet just as I expected so I was able to do what I wanted quite undisturbed. The security man signed me in and out but as I have worked on a Sunday before if I needed to catch up on some work it didn't strike him as odd. I printed off some documents relating to my own research work on Leukaemia which I'll ensure my boss sees tomorrow when I tell him I went in to work today. Then there won't be any query as to why I was there'.

'That's very clever of you. Good thinking'.

'Thanks' and leaning further forward he spoke more quietly. 'Any rate I've got masses of stuff for you. Absolutely tons of it. More than you'll need probably but I didn't want to have to keep going in and raiding the files so I thought that one big go at it should suffice.

I know an override code to bypass the security blocks on the files so once I'd entered that then I was free to rummage around in the computer data base about this project wherever I liked. That's what enabled me to get so much. In fact I think I've got virtually everything that exists on the Beta project. I've put it all on a memory stick. I bought a sixty four gigabyte one so that I could be sure that there was plenty of room for everything I was going to download'.

'Good idea. And did all the downloads work alright?'

'Ye-es. Some took only a second or two. Others somewhat longer. In fact downloading one file took almost six minutes to complete and that's a long time in the world of computer downloads. I almost panicked as it seemed to get stuck part way through and I sat there watching for at least three minutes as the progress indicator bar when it was about seventy percent of the way across just seemed to freeze and remained stationary for absolutely ages. I was really sweating over that I can tell you, but fortunately it suddenly came back to life and started moving again, slowly at first until all of a sudden it flashed across to the hundred percent completed download indicator. That was a *mighty* relief I can tell you'.

'I'm sure it was' she replied also leaning forward to pat his hand and in so doing inadvertently giving him a brief view down her cleavage from the loose fitting cotton shirt she was wearing where the top couple of buttons were undone.

'Yes' he gulped tearing his eyes away from the sight across the table and blushing again. Seeing where his eyes had been staring she leaned back and sat up at which he coughed and looked around the coffee shop. 'I'll give you the memory stick outside' he said speaking quietly.

'Okay'.

'Will you still come to lunch?'

'Yes I'd love to'.

'There's a pub just off the motorway. Next junction north exit. I haven't been there but it sounds alright from the on-line reviews.

'I'm sure it'll be lovely' she smiled.

'Shall we go then?'

'Yes' she nodded getting up as he swigged down the last of his coffee and collected his magazines.

'Where are you parked?' he wanted to know when they'd emerged from the building.

'Here in the car park?' she grinned.

'Err yes of course. I meant ....'

'I know what you meant. Sorry you'll have to get used to my odd sense of humour. Irritates James no end sometimes' was her laughing reply.

'Is James your boyfriend then?'

'He's my fiancé' and she was conscious of the little frisson of excitement that flicked through her still whenever she used that word to describe her relationship with James.

'Oh right'.

'I parked over there on the left hand side' she continued waving a hand vaguely at the rows of parked cars.

'I'm this way' he said pointing in another direction. 'If I walk over to your car with you I'll give you the memory stick as you get in then I'll go and get my car and we can drive in convoy to the pub. Is that alright?'

'Sure' and the two walked across to her car where after she blip unlocked it he held the door for her as she got in and enjoyed the delightful sight of a long expanse of leg which became exposed as her short skirt rucked up when she slithered into the driving seat. Tugging it down she held out her hand and he slipped the memory stick with all the data into it.

'Thank you and well done' she smiled.

'I've really found lots of stuff including names of those people removed from the trials because of side effects; data on the type and duration of those side effects; the efficacy of the drug; different methods of application which they are developing. I didn't know they'd started to do that although at present it is just the capsule format they're using'.

'Different methods?'

'Yes they've almost got a version to inject as well as the capsule version. Fortunately they don't seem to have actually started to trial on humans the injectable variant ...... yet. But it appears that they are close to beginning testing that version and part of the trial purpose will be to test how one method of application compares with another. So they're really far advanced with this project if they're ready to test a second application method. Further advanced than I realised they were with Betanapotraproxiflevien-g3'.

'How the hell do you do that?'

'What?'

'Remember that complex name of Beta whatsit?'

'Oh I guess when you've spent your life working in drugs you develop a memory of and aptitude to remember them'.

'Umm. Right now shall I give you a lift to your car?'

'I can walk'.

'Get in' she chided.

He did and directed her to where his car was parked. 'There' he pointed suddenly feeling a bit ashamed of his dirty Fiesta when compared with Kim's obviously very new sparkling clean smart Mini convertible. 'Okay I've got the route from here to the pub off the internet so will you follow me?'

'Of course'.

It took about ten minutes for them to drive to the Fox and Hounds. Once inside they went to the bar where he confirmed his booking, then ordered a soda water and lime for her and a half of lager for him.

He obviously enjoyed having lunch with her but although she neither showed it nor said anything, frankly very quickly she was completely bored by him. He had little or no small talk and to break long periods of silence she had to constantly struggle to find things about which to start a new subject of conversation. On the drive there she'd done up the top two buttons of her shirt to prevent him staring down her cleavage but she saw that he was also obviously completely smitten with her legs which much as she tried to minimise their exposure, because she'd chosen to wear such a short skirt made it difficult not to continually display large expanses of them to him.

All in all it was one of the most boring hours that she'd spent in many years but as she constantly reminded herself as she smiled at him and wracked her brain for something else to talk about apart from model soldiers, which seemed to be the only thing that excited him or about which he could talk fluently and animatedly, he had already given her some important information and if what was on the memory stick was as valuable and revealing as he'd indicated then she had the components for a thunderingly good programme. And in that case she was more than prepared to put up with boringly dull Brian every now and then.

But by two o'clock she felt that she couldn't stick it out with him no longer, nor could she summon any enthusiasm to continue comparing battle tactics of different medieval army commanders so looking at her watch she said 'Brian I *have* enjoyed this lunch but I've really got to go now or James will wonder if I've been kidnapped by aliens! Or by the soldiers from one of your armies' she chuckled.

'Oh yes right. Look thank you for coming to lunch with me. I know I'm not very good company but you have brightened up my weekend'.

'Don't be silly. It's been most enjoyable learning about your hobby' she said wholly untruthfully.

'Maybe one day you'd like to come and see them?'

'Yes indeed' she lied.

'Terrific shall we ....'

'Any rate look I really *must* go now' Kim interrupted afraid he was going to try and fix a date for her to go and look at his model soldiers. So sliding out from the table she wriggled her skirt down and said 'thanks again for lunch'.

'Pleasure' he replied dragging his eyes away from her legs as he too stood.

'I'll be in touch when we've analyzed the information on this' and she patted her skirt pocket where the memory stick resided. As they walked out of the pub to their respective cars she said quietly 'Brian one thing. Are you looking for any payment for what you're doing?'

'No I just think it's so wrong and want it stopped. I don't want money'.

'Fine. See you again soon then' and on impulse she leaned forward and popped a little peck kiss on his right cheek.

He blushed bright red, muttered something that she didn't quite catch, got in his car, wound down the window, called 'Bye then' and drove slowly out of the car park utterly smitten with her and delighted that she'd kissed him.

She watched him go, shrugged and got in her own car to drive home.

On her journey she patted her pocket with the memory stick from time to time to reassure herself that it was still there. Back in her apartment where she called 'Hi I'm back' to James she took out the device, went to her computer and without sitting down switched the machine on, waited for it to fire up then plugged the little black stick into one of the USB ports just as James sidled up behind her, put his arms around her waist and pressed himself against her. Leaning forward he kissed the side of her neck then whispering in her ear 'Welcome back' gently pushed his crotch against her adding 'I've missed you terribly especially knowing you were dating another man'.

'Yes well that'll keep you on your toes won't it' she replied pushing her bottom back against him. 'Now leave me alone love as I need to see what's on here' she chuckled moving her bottom away from him and pointing to the memory stick.

'What is it? A porno film? Hey if it's a *really* dirty one can I watch too?'

'No of course it's not porn you idiot! It's apparently masses of data about the Beta drug trial problems that Furrina are hiding which Brian downloaded this morning from their computers'.

'Couldn't it wait until a little later?' he wanted to know as his hands began sliding up from her waist towards her chest.

'No it can't. Get off!' she demanded gently knocking his hands which had almost reached her breasts away from her body.

'Yes Mam' he chuckled disengaging himself and as she sat down and began staring at the screen he moved towards the kitchen and asked 'Glass of wine? Coffee?'

'Coffee please' and sitting down she began to study what was now flickering onto her screen.

Half an hour later she sat back, blew her cheeks out in a deep sigh and turning to James who was sprawled on the settee reading a colour supplement from the Sunday paper and said 'This is simply fucking dynamite!'

'It's good then I take it?'

'Good? It will blow Furrina right out of the water. Brian may be a funny little chap but he's certainly come up trumps with this stuff. It's simply amazing what he's got here'.

'What's he got then?'

'Simply all the data relating to the Beta trials. I mean *all* of it. The problems that have and are still emerging; the names and addresses of the guinea pigs although some addresses seem a bit odd but I guess that's normal for the back streets of Mumbai which is where most of the trials seem to be taking place; other trial locations; test control procedures; monitoring; full analysis back to some of the early lab research on animals; adverse reactions; people taken off the trials; oh it goes on and on. Much of it is scientific mumbo jumbo which I don't understand so we're certainly gonna need someone to explain to us what this all means and how to interpret it? Maybe Brian could do that? But it's brilliant and definitely means we can produce a project proposal for Peter and the other Directors such that they're bound to give us the go ahead. Simply bound to'.

'Great. So can you now switch off that computer and come over here? I've got a project for you to which I think you should devote a little care and attention'.

'Umm maybe' and twisting round she smiled at him and he was struck again by what a pretty young woman she was and how much in love with her he was.

'Only maybe?' he asked quietly.

'Wait a sec' and carefully invoking the "save" mode she saved all the data off the memory stick to her computer, named it Beta then double checking that all was okay, added a password to the file she'd created before shutting down the machine. Once it had clicked off she twisted round in her chair, looked at James, got up and walked slowly, almost sashaying, towards him. Reaching the settee she stood still and smiling down at him said quietly 'I think I can guess what sort of project you've got in mind!'

'To start with it involves you taking off all your clothes'.

'Really? But only me? Not you?'

'Ah well I thought that once you'd taken all yours off them you might take all mine off too'.

'Did you now? This sounds a rather naughty project doesn't it?'

'Oh yes very naughty'.

'And once I've got no clothes on then what?'

'I'm sure you'll think of something' he grinned changing from his previous semi prone sprawl to sitting upright with his bare feet on the floor and leaning back against the backrest of the settee.

'Oh did you?' she grinned beginning to undo the buttons of her blouse which she dropped gently onto the settee beside James. Next she unclipped her bra and took pleasure in sliding it down her arms and off then slowly drew it across his face, over his head and put it on top of the blouse. Standing in front of her man she began massaging her own breasts slowly and sensuously before gently flicking her nipples with her forefinger.

Then with the tip of her tongue showing at the corner of her mouth she unzipped and stepped out of her little skirt and as she laid that on top of the bra and blouse softly asked 'How am I doing on this project?'

'Quite good so far but I think you're overdressed'.

'Ooh I'd hate you to think that' she grinned and quickly slid her panties down where they soon joined the rest of her clothes. 'Better?' she asked sensuously moving her hips from side to side and back and forth.

''Much better' he grinned staring at her neatly trimmed strip of pubic hair.

'Now what would you like me to do?'

'I'll leave that entirely to your imagination!'

'Imagination eh? What about something like this perhaps?' she wheedled straddling his lap. Lifting his tee shirt clear of the waist band of his jeans she tugged it off and dropped it on top of her discarded clothes. Leaning forward she took first one and then the other of his nipples in her front teeth and nipped gently.

As he tried to pull her head to him she giggled and wriggled off his lap, knelt down on the floor in front of him and while slowly unzipping him asked with a cheeky expression 'Or something like this maybe?' as she unhurriedly tugged his jeans down to his ankles a process which he helped by lifting himself a little off the seat. Next she eased the elastic of his yellow boxers away from his body to lift them clear of his now fully erect prick and while leaning forward to drop a kiss on that throbbing appendage she slid the boxers down to join his jeans around his ankles.

'Or this?' and again lowering her face to his fully erect prick she planted a soft kiss on it. 'Or this? and getting off her knees she clambered onto his lap again, reached for his prick and after briefly rubbing and squeezing it she lifted herself, positioned him at the lips of her pussy and slowly lowered herself onto him.

Carefully she began to move on him rapidly building to a rhythm which she continued for some time as his breath came faster and faster until with a long sigh and feeling him beginning to pulse within herself she began to slow her movements until she came to a complete stop and flopped forward against his now sweaty body.

Peck kissing him she told him he was wonderful and getting off him clambered onto the settee beside him reaching for, finding and holding his hand.

'I do love you' she whispered.

'Umm and I you' he replied with a smile.

Much later they decided to shower together and afterwards they dried each other then dressed just in bath robes opened a bottle of wine and drank some in the kitchen while jointly getting their supper ready which they ate in the sitting room from trays on their laps sitting together on the settee occasionally feeding each other with a forkful of food.

When they'd eaten and James had made them some coffee and poured them both a brandy Kim insisted on again logging onto her computer to re-look at Brian's data.

She spent over an hour studying and making notes of what was on the screen and finally finished by e-mailing the file to her office computer so she could share the information with Toby, Samita, Fergal and anyone else at TV-12 who would need to see it, to enable agreement to a full investigation project to get the go-ahead.

'Come on darling' pleaded James. 'You're totally neglecting me for that computer of yours. I'll get a rejection complex!'

'Ooh poor old you' she chuckled over her shoulder. 'Just two minutes and then I'm done'.

By mutual consent in bed they didn't make love, just snuggled in together, kissed tenderly and went to sleep.

CHAPTER 9

Next day Toby became thoroughly excited immediately he saw what Kim had on her computer from the information Brian had extracted. 'This is horrendous' he exclaimed as he read page after page of the information especially the details of the problems emerging. 'I mean why aren't they stopping the trials straight away? Surely that's the right thing to do isn't it?' he asked.

'Of course it is. But that's what this is all about and why Brian came to us in the first place. He too thinks the trial should be stopped but as they're not he determined that it should come into the public domain'.

Picking up the phone Toby dialled a number, waited then spoke. 'Peter can you come down to our office area. Kim has some stuff here for the Beta project which is just dynamite. I need you to see it straight away'. He paused, nodded, put down the phone and said 'He'll be here with some others in five minutes. Get Samita, Fergal and anyone else you want and we'll go to a meeting room'.

'Look' said Kim a few minutes later looking straight at Peter Holmes 'I'll be the first to confirm that I don't understand a lot of this stuff and we are going to need someone to explain it to us. Brian could probably do that but he's so nervous I think it may be difficult to persuade him to come here to do that. However he'd be perfect as not only does he understand it all he's worked on the project and is, or rather was, an integral part of it'.

'So he knows all the ins and out of it?' asked Peter.

'Exactly'.

'You know if you can get the corroboration from your field visit to India then we really have got a potentially amazing programme here' gushed Penny.

'If' cautioned Lawrence Armstrong the station's Marketing Director. '*If*'.

'I'm sure we'll get it'.

'Have you worked out a cost schedule?' Elaine Rees the Financial Controller for TV-12 wanted to know.

'Yes. Here' and Kim handed copies to everyone.

'Not cheap and I see you've costed for business class flights. Isn't that a bit over the top? Wouldn't Premium Economy do?' demanded Elaine.

'It *would*, but they are long flights' protested Kim.

'Yes I agree' nodded Peter. 'Long flights are hell at the best of times and so I think business class is fine'.

'Thank you' smiled Kim looking at the head of the station.

'Right so tell me in simple terms exactly what you think you can discover and turn into a good programme by going to India that you can't do at present with what you've already got' demanded Jason the Head of Programme Planning.

'What we've currently got is *information*. Data, statistics, indeed piles of statistics, narrative, documents but what we haven't got is the real *life* side of the project' explained Kim. 'We need to see and talk to people undergoing the drug trials including, if we can get to them, those people who have suffered problems, adverse reactions or other difficulties from involvement with, taking, or use of Beta …… err whatever it's called' and finished speaking she looked quite aggressively at Jason.

She'd crossed swords with him before over getting a project started. His usual technique was to challenge and make the instigator in this case her, fight for approval. But once it was approved then he'd give his wholehearted backing and be a great supporter.

He asked several more questions then turning to Peter said 'Looks like a perfect fit for us. I say let's do it'.

Kim silently blew out a sigh of gratitude which got even stronger when Peter said 'I agree. Anyone not?'

Without exception everyone in the room supported the intent to run a full investigation and then make a programme exposing the duplicity, deception and downright dishonesty of Furrina Pharmaceuticals.

'Okay Kim. Looks like you've got yourself approval to proceed'.

'Thanks. I'm sure we can make something really great out of this'.

'You'd better because, as I explained to Toby recently the cutting edge of Highlight seems to have been missing on several recent programmes although James council corruption edition last week was good. In fact *really* good. So don't let's allow *this* one on Beta to fail to hit the mark with a resounding bang'.

'I won't' she promised.

'Good. Now have you got everything you need?'

'Yes as you've now approved my project proposal then I'll get cracking and soon will have everything organised'.

Back in their own work area, she and Toby settled down and ran through the detail, sorted out a time scale for getting it all done, agreed Jamie would pick up her existing work on other subjects while she was away from the office on the Beta project and generally finalised all the necessary details.

'Right now all we need are visas. I'll get Fergal to deal with that. The Indian High Commission here in London have contracted that process out to an organisation at Hounslow. We'll get the forms completed and then he can take them there. Until we get them we can't go to India. I guess we'll also need some Indian Rupees'.

'Okay fine. You get on with it all just let me know if you need any help. Have you got a date in mind to go there yet?'

'No let's get the visas organised. I've no idea how long that might take. When we know that then we can book flights and finalise the trip'.

Fergal came to Kim a little later that day to say he'd checked and the visas should be ready in five working days so if she'd bring in her passport tomorrow he'd complete all the on-line documentation and then take the forms to Hounslow.

'Right now tonight I'm going to have one more go at getting Brian to come with us' stated Kim with a determined expression on her face. 'If he was with us I just think it will make everything so much simpler and clearer and he'll be able to steer us to the right conclusions'.

So that evening after her run and before she and James had supper she had a long conversation with the whistleblower. He asked if it was essential that he went. She wheedled. He prevaricated. She got a bit cross. He got stubborn. But it was all to no avail. He absolutely refused to go with the TV-12 team to India.

'Damn' she cursed to James when she'd come off the phone. 'He is a strange man you know. Petrified of being seen there. I mean how many people live in India? Over a Billion. Good God I think there's over thirty million in Mumbai alone! I mean how the hell is he going to be spotted amongst all that lot?'

'I don't know but I suppose looking at it from his point of view if he thinks it's too big a risk then he's not going to go is he? You've said that he's very worried about Furrina finding out and therefore him losing his job. That is a pretty big incentive for him to be cautious you know'.

'Yes but how the hell are they going to find out?'

'I don't know but he obviously thinks it's too big a risk'.

'Stupid bugger!' Kim snapped almost angrily.

'Whoa. Calm down. It's not your job that's potentially in jeopardy'.

'No-oo I guess maybe you're right. But no company can be as paranoid about keeping tabs on its employees as he says Furrina is. I mean what he's described is worse than MI5 tracking spies or the old East German Stasi' she laughed'.

'Well maybe not but if he's that concerned about it then surely you should respect that?'

'I do'.

'Hmm' he mused as she walked over to her desk and picked up a file marked BETA and plonking down on the settee spent the next twenty minutes or so reading through all her notes. She only put it aside when James said that supper was ready.

'What we eating darling?' she wanted to know as she walked over to the table..

'Japanese fish curry' he replied. 'I liked the look of the recipe in that Easy Oriental Cooking cook book you bought me last Christmas and thought I'd try it. If it tastes alright then it'll have lived up to the book titles as it actually was easy to prepare. So come on give me your verdict'.

Kim took a mouthful, paused then smiled took another forkful. 'Umm nice'.

'Really?'

'Yes. It's lovely' she confirmed as she continued eating.

They had yoghurt for dessert and after they'd cleared away she went back to the settee and waited until he joined her with two mugs of coffee.

They spent the rest of the evening watching TV as there were several programmes that interested them but eventually James said he was really tired so suggested they went to bed.

They undressed, peed, washed, did teeth and were in bed around eleven thirty where she said a quiet 'Good night', dropped a kiss on his forehead and turned onto her side facing away from James.

But hardly had put her head on the pillow when she felt his hand on her hip, then she firstly felt herself being gently rolled onto her tummy and secondly she felt his prick against her upper thigh.

'Hey I thought you were tired?' she whispered.

'I seem to have woken up' he chuckled as his prick moved slowly towards her pussy.

'So I gather' she responded enjoying the sensation of his fingers playing so very gently with her vaginal lips. However when she felt his fingers from one hand begin to massage her clit while the other slid in and around those now extremely wet and very slippery lips she muttered 'Come on darling' and began to turn onto her back.

'No stay on your tummy' he whispered pushing her flat and face down then sliding his hands beneath her waist he lifted her into a kneeling position. Seconds later she twisted her head round to smile at him and waited as she felt him gently press his prick against her pussy then with a soft grunt he slid into her. As he did so her mobile rang.

'Leave it' he grunted as he began thrusting in and out but she reached for the phone and studying the screen saw it was Brian.

'I need to take this' she said wriggling away from James.

'Like hell you do' he exclaimed and slipping his arms around her waist pulled her back towards him and tried to re-enter her.

'No' she snapped moving right away from him and sitting up pressed the talk key.

'Hello' she said trying to sound bright and alert while peering at the bedside clock and seeing it showed 11.45. 'Problem?'

'Anyway who the hell is ringing you at this time of night' he demanded glaring at her in the semi darkness.

'It's Brian' then addressing herself to the phone repeated 'What is it Brian? Have you got a problem?'

'No. We're you asleep?'

'Yes I was almost. It's late. Can't whatever it is wait until the morning?'

'I've been thinking about your request for me to come to India'.

'Right'.

'Do you really think you'll be able to keep me hidden? Perhaps I could stay in the hotel all the time, in my room so no-one will see me?'

'Well you could but I'm sure it won't be necessary to go to that extent of secrecy'.

'Oh come on darling tell the stupid sod to fuck off till the morning' hissed James wriggling close to her and pressing his erection against her thigh.

'So what have you decided?' Kim wanted to know from her whistleblower while taking one of James's hands and quietly kissing it.

'Alright. I'll come'.

'You'll come? That's great!'

'So will you in a minute' James chucked quietly putting his lips to her ear and slowly inserting a finger into her pussy.

Trying to move his hand away she said into the phone 'That's great'.

'Thought you'd like it. Now put that phone down' James whispered inserting a second finger into her and taking her hand placed it on his erection.

'But you'll absolutely *have* to help me stay out of sight' pleaded Brian.

'Of course but are you really sure?'

There was a pause during which James moved his fingers to her clit and began to gently tease her there as he whispered into her ear 'Oh yes I'm sure alright'.

Removing her hand from his erect prick she gave it a gentle smack as she asked Brian again 'Are you absolutely sure?'

'Yes' he said quietly. 'I'll come with you'.

'That is simply terrific' she replied as James replaced her hand on his still fully erect prick. 'Now you'll need to get a visa' she continued giving a quite hard slap to the prick and when he quietly yelped 'Ouch' she pouted and whispered 'Oh poor boy!' then speaking again to Brian said 'If you want us to do that for you then we'll need some information about you. Quite a lot of it actually. Your mother's maiden name, full home address and phone number, date and place of birth, national insurance number, inside leg measurement ....'

'Inside leg measurement?'

'Like to measure the inside of my legs?' queried James as he tried to squirm into a position where he could re-insert his prick into her pussy.

'No' she muttered very quietly moving away and sticking her tongue out at him before continuing to speak to Brian 'No I'm joking about that but we *will* need lots of stuff about you. However the easiest way to complete it will be for you to go on-line and apply for an Indian Visa, fill in and print off the forms and then let us have them. Fergal who works for me is the person who is co-ordinating everything in that regard and he'll take the application forms to Hounslow ....'

'Hounslow?'

'Yes that's where the organisation to whom the Indian Embassy has contracted out the whole visa process is located. Fergal will take everything there, ensure that it's all okay and with luck that should speed up the process. As I told Toby my boss without visas were stuffed. No visas. No trip to India'.

'Right. I'll go on line right now and do it'.

'Well it's not that immediate. It's the middle of the night so it can at least wait till morning'.

She gave an involuntary grunt as James pushed her back into a kneeling position and slowly entered her.

'You alright?' queried Brian.

'Yes why?'

'You made a funny noise'.

'Oh I just banged my elbow on the bedside table'.

'Ah right. Any rate I'll do the visa applications stuff now. I'm wide awake'.

'Okay fine'.

'How will I get them to you?' he asked as she moved slightly to better facilitate James's penetration of her.

'A quick meeting for you to hand them over. Tell me when and where and I'll get Fergal to meet you and collect them'.

'How about that service station on the M1 where we met? In the coffee shop like before?'

'Fine'.

'How will he recognise me'.

'I'll describe you to him. You're a distinguished looking man, but to be on the safe side carry a Tesco plastic bag with you'.

'Right I will. Thank you. Good night and sorry for waking you but I've been sitting here thinking about it and I came to the conclusion that it *would* benefit you and the others if I was out there with you to help with understanding any technical stuff'.

'You're absolutely right …… aaah' she gasped as James began to really make love to her 'err sorry but my elbow does hurt. We'll also find time out there for you to interpret and explain the meaning of some of the stuff you've already given to us, especially much of what you downloaded on that Sunday sneaky trip to the office'.

'Okay fine. Good night'.

'Goodnight Brian'.

'At bloody last' grumbled James good naturedly as he now devoted himself to properly making love to her. Pressing her head down and keeping her hips and thus her bum in the air he really started pounding in and out of her as she started moving in tune with him. It wasn't long before he held her tightly and started ejaculating while licking along her back.

'God have you come?' she queried as he slowed to a stop.

'Yes haven't you?'

'No I haven't. I'm a long way off. Can you keep going?' she gasped but was then disappointed at his reply.

'No sorry love' and pulling out of her he flopped onto his back and added 'All done and it's going down'.

'Bastard' she grumbled as she wriggled away and turning onto her side said 'Well you can't leave me half way there. If your dick can't bring me off now get your tongue down there'.

He did as she requested and soon she was gasping and clamping his face hard against her as her orgasm arrived.

When she'd come off the peak and he'd moved back up to put his head on the pillow she lay down with her head on his belly. 'Thanks but you were naughty starting me off when I was trying to talk to Brian. I'm sure he realised something was going on'.

'Bully for him'. The he laughed 'Bully for Brian'.

They lay quietly together like that until surprisingly quickly James appeared to have gone to sleep. So giving a soft kiss to his belly she rolled away, turned over and also was soon fast asleep.

Brian though as soon as he finished talking with Kim straightaway dialled a number he knew by heart, listened to the introductory message, waited until he was connected and was then immersed in a dirty conversation with the woman on the sex chat line who told him her name was Heidi, that she was single, twenty seven years old, blonde, slim, tall with good legs, had cute thirty six d breasts and was wearing a red push up bra, matching panties and suspenders attached to lacy black stockings, lying on her bed and as she was feeling horny she had the hand not holding the phone inside those panties playing with her wet shaven pussy.

With that vision in mind Brian happily spent the next ten minutes indulging in an increasingly filthy conversation with her during which he began masturbating slowly at first then more rapidly until he climaxed when he thanked her for the chat.

Heidi said he was welcome and to be sure to ring again and he said he certainly would.

When the call disconnected, before taking another one Gloria who was in fact a twice married and twice divorced fifty nine year old grandmother with three children and five grandchildren, substantially overweight, wearing grubby grey jogging slacks, a dark green tee shirt with sweat stains under the armpits adding to her general pronounced body odour, had lank brunette hair which could have done with a good wash, sagging forty inch wrinkly breasts, a pronounced belly that wobbled as she moved, large hips and bottom, heaved herself out of the armchair and waddled across the room to a small side table.

She poured herself a gin, added some bitter lemon, tasted it, grimaced, slopped in another slug of gin, tasted it again and nodding with satisfaction went and sat back down again in her rather threadbare grimy armchair where she rolled herself a handmade cigarette, lit it and inhaled deeply, holding the smoke in her lungs for a few seconds before slowly exhaling through her nose. She repeated that several times then taking a final extra deep drag she pinched out the roll up and switching the phone back on waited for the next punter to come through the sex chat line to speak to her telephone persona of sweet young sexy Heidi.

It was only a couple of minutes before it rang. Picking it up she cooed 'Hi you're through to Heidi. So what's your name then lover and what would you like to talk about?'

CHAPTER 10

The flight was long but in British Airways Business Class at least the team from TV-12 were pleasantly comfortable. Samita and Fergal had never flown business class before and so enjoyed the additional luxury compared with Economy and especially compared with the cramped conditions on Easy Jet or Ryan Air flights which they usually took when going on holiday.

Penny though was used to travelling to foreign countries on business as well as for leisure and so for her it wasn't anything special as she always travelled Business class on business and usually upgraded herself to that for holidays if she was flying long distance. She was a very competent and confident woman in her late thirties and Kim was always slightly in awe of her. Not exactly frightened but wary of her seemingly boundless ability to treat the senior people at TV-12 like Peter the MD as equals and not be in any way disconcerted by him. Similarly with Lawrence, Ruth and Elaine. All in all Penny was a tough competent very self assured woman fully on top of her game and skill set. One of the best TV producers in the industry.

'Oh well maybe I'll get to be like that sometime' thought Kim as she reclined her seat into a six foot bed and looked at the engagement ring that James had given her on the beach in the early morning on their recent holiday. Smiling she re-lived this morning's cuddle in bed before they got up whereupon she'd showered and driven to the airport. She grinned as she recalled his gentle admonition 'Now don't go getting seduced by some Indian Maharaja and whisked away to an enormous palace in the hills for the rest of your days will you?'

'I'll try not to, but if I do perhaps I'll persuade him to find you a job as a gardener or handyman and then I'll be able to slip away from his clutches to enjoy a bit of illicit hanky panky with one of his servants' she'd giggled.

'Seriously take care. I've never been to India but if you're going into the slum areas be very careful as I imagine they can be dangerous'.

'We're going to check that out. We've got a proper guide organised to take us where we want to go so we won't just be blundering around in

Mike Upton

the shanty towns by ourselves. And if he thinks it necessary we'll hire a bodyguard as well'.

'Well okay but you know that India has a very high incidence of women being attacked and ....' his voice tailed off as she interrupted.

'Attacked and raped. Yes I know, but we *will* be careful I promise'.

'Okay but remember you are very precious to me and I couldn't bear to lose you or for you to be hurt in any way'.

'I'll remember' she'd promised.

As she'd left for the airport she was relaxed, warm, happy and looking forward to starting this project in earnest and that cheerful feeling lasted all the way to the check in desk where she saw an anxious looking Brian was waiting.

'Hi' she'd said as she walked up to him.

'Hello' but he didn't look at her but down at his feet.

'You okay?'

'Yes. No .... look I'm sorry but I can't do it'.

'Can't do what?'

'Come with you'.

'WHAT!'

'I just can't. Sorry. I mean what if someone from Furrina sees me or finds out somehow from their operation over there that I'm in India'.

'Even if they do and I think that's *highly* unlikely, then there's no reason why you shouldn't be taking a holiday in India. Thousands of English people do you know' she snapped.

'Yes but I'm not taking a holiday am I? We're going to be talking to people Furrina have recruited onto their drug trial'.

'And you think Furrina will find out about that?'

'You don't know them. They know everything'.

'Oh Brian for Christ's sake! What are you a man or a mouse? Now for God's sake stop being so paranoiac, get yourself checked in and let's get going!'

'Kim I'm sorry but really I can't'.

'Why not?'

'Because ....'

'Because of what?' she snapped louder than she really meant to.

'Because I am frightened of being found out. It will be the end of me'.

'Brian sweetie. You came to us with an horrendous story of awful things happening on these drug trials. We did some work and decided it was worth us investigating. We've invested time, effort and *money* into this project already. We need you on board with us. Obviously we *can* do it without you helping us in India, but it will be so much better if you *are* there with us.

You're the scientist. You know what to look for. You can help us evaluate what we find. You'll understand any results, or discussions with the guinea pig volunteers. I won't say that all will be lost without you being there but it will make one hell of a difference'.

'I know' he said quietly looking around the terminal.

'Come on. Travel with us. You told me you were going to book some holiday to cover your absence. Did you do that?'

'Yes'.

'Well there you are then. Furrina won't expect you in at work so no reason for you not to come with us'.

'No I suppose not'.

'Have you brought your passport?'

'Yes I've brought and packed everything, it's just ....'

'Just nothing. Now stop being so utterly pathetic and let's go and check in'.

He looked at her miserably for some little while then his shoulders slumped. 'All-right' he said quietly and to her great relief he stopped prevaricating and allowed himself to be steered by her to the business class check in desk.

She, Samita, Brian, Penny, Rick and Fergal completed their check in, walked though passport and immigration controls and were making their way towards to the British Airways Business lounge when Kim said for the others to go on to the lounge and she'd join them shortly as she wanted to get something to read on the flight. When she joined them they were sitting in a group and Samita was drinking water, Fergal and Rick had lagers, Brian was drinking tea and Penny had a whisky and soda. Kim went to the self service bar and got herself a gin and tonic before going to join the little group.

'Have you got anything to read on the flight?' she'd asked Brian.

'Yes I've got a novel I want to finish but I expect they'll be a film to watch as well won't there'.

'Bound to be but in case you get bored maybe these will help?' and she handed him two magazines. One was about model soldiers and the other about real life army battles.

'Ooh thank you' he smiled with genuine pleasure as he looked at the covers. 'This is the latest edition' he said tapping the model magazine.

'Enjoy' she'd grinned.

Shortly after they'd taken off she'd twisted her head, saw Brian a couple of rows behind her, smiled and was relieved to see him smile back. He still looked nervous but at least she'd got him to come with them and maybe his novel, the magazines and an in-flight film would help him forget about his worries.

It was gone midnight Indian time when they landed, made their way through a still surprisingly busy terminal, found the pre-ordered car to take them on the short journey to the Imperial Royal Hotel which was cool, quiet and an oasis of calm from the heat and bustle outside.

After they'd checked in they made their way to the bar and ordered drinks although Kim noticed Brian constantly looking around.

'Relax' she said reassuringly putting her hand on his arm and patting gently. 'There's no-one else here in the bar except us. I should think everyone else in the hotel is tucked up in bed and fast asleep which is where we will be soon'.

'Yes' he muttered immediately imagining her in bed.

'I see there's a pool here' said Samita. I'm going to have a swim in the morning. Do you swim Brian?'

'Yes but not very well. I'm a bit splashy but I might join you. Will you be swimming Kim?'

'Why not. Always a nice way to start the day'.

'I'll come too' announced Fergal then turning to Penny asked 'you too?'

'Maybe. I'll see how I feel in the morning but for now I need my bed'.

'Umm me too' agreed Kim. 'Meet at eight by the pool then?'

With a chorus of nods and "yeses" the team finished their drinks, broke apart and went to their separate rooms where they were soon all in their beds and off to sleep including Brian who was determined to go swimming even though he wasn't a very good swimmer but it would be an opportunity to see Samita, maybe Penny but especially Kim in swimming costumes.

He was in the warm although rather chlorine smelling water at quarter to eight watching carefully for any of the three women to arrive and was delighted to see Samita soon appear. She was wearing a multi-coloured one piece costume and after giving him a little wave, walked to the steps and carefully lowered herself into the water where setting off on a gentle breaststroke she swam a couple of lengths then stopped and spoke to him as he'd moved to intercept her.

'Morning Brian'.

'Morning. Lovely in here isn't it?'

'Yes. Did you sleep well?'

'Like a log'.

'Me too. Oh look here's Penny'.

The senior programme producer was also wearing a one piece costume in emerald green which although it fitted her well did rather accentuate her somewhat chunky figure but she waved at them both then took the same set of steps as Samita and was soon swimming up and down the pool. Brian also began to swim again but all the time keeping his eyes peeled for Kim's arrival and shortly his wish was granted as she too appeared poolside. He immediately stopped swimming and trod water to watch. She was wearing a blue and white bikini which showed plenty of cleavage and was tight fitting around her crotch. Walking to the pool side she waved at Brian then stretched her left foot down to test the water temperature, checked that her long blonde hair was tied back and with a smile at Samita dived neatly into the water.

It was a good dive and after a long glide she surfaced and began swimming a competent front crawl up and down the pool but after a few lengths stopped, swam over to Brian in the shallow end and standing up smiled and asked how he was this morning.

'F-f-f-fine' he stuttered almost transfixed by the proximity of her wet bikini top covered breasts, her face covered in water droplets and hair clinging tightly to her head.

'Good. Well a few more lengths will do me then it's upstairs to change, come down for breakfast and then we'll all meet in my room for a council of war to finalise our plan of action for today. I've drawn up a proposed programme of who does what, which we can discuss'.

'R-right. S-s-sounds good' he agreed looking around and noticing that Penny had got out and was wrapping a bath robe around herself was slightly disappointed that he'd missed seeing her again before she covered up.

'Hi' called Fergal as he dived in and began to swim strongly up and down the pool. Kim moved away and after doing her additional lengths swam to the steps and to Brian's utter delight afforded him a perfect view of her pert bottom as she climbed slowly up to the poolside, where she turned, called 'See you shortly' and bending forward slipped her feet into her shoes giving him an obvious view of most of her breasts as they moved forward in her bikini top.

Then he too swam to the steps and climbed up almost immediately followed by Samita who said she'd enjoyed a swim to start the day.

'Yes indeed' he smiled looking at her in her costume then he made his way back to his room where he changed then went down to have breakfast with the others before they all de-camped to Kim's room where she intended to announce the day's plan of action.

He was the last to arrive and looking round saw that Kim was perched on the end of the double bed; Samita and Penny were in the two small armchairs; Fergal was sitting on the floor as was Rick the cameraman, so he propped himself against the wall where he kept stealing glances at the bed, imagining Kim in there last night and wondering what she might have worn. A nightie, pyjamas, tee shirt or maybe she was a nude sleeper?

'This is the plan of action' she continued jerking his thoughts away from her possible night attire and to the day's activity. 'First we'll meet the guides who will take us to find the address of where the guinea pigs live.

Brian and I will brief the guides on exactly what we want to do while the rest of you wait till we've done that. Then we'll split into two groups, one guide per group and off we go to find the unfortunate people involved in this mess.

We need to track down some or ideally *all* of the people taking part in these trials here in India. The guides will take us to the various parts of this city as I'm sure we'd never find where they were by ourselves and even if we did it would take a massive amount of time. So I think that making use of them should save that for us ....'.

'Providing they know where the addresses are' interrupted Penny.

'Well if they don't we won't pay them' Kim retorted then added 'but they're from a reputable tourist guide agency which is recommended by several travel companies so they should be alright'.

'Fine'.

'The guides will be here at eleven o'clock and there should be three of them. One for each of our two groups and one is the sort of chief guide who I gather will ensure that everything is properly organised.

Finally here is a list of things we need to ask and learn from the guinea pigs. Oh look Brian is there another name we can use for these people rather than guinea pigs which sounds rather demeaning?'

'Test subjects is how Furrina will refer to them'.

'Ah yes that's better. Thanks' she smiled at him then looking back at the rest of the TV-12 team went on 'So test subjects they are then in future. Can you check through this list of questions and ensure that you're happy with them and also of course think of any other questions or points that you believe we should ask'.

There was silence for a few minutes as everybody read them through and pronounced themselves happy with Kim's suggestions, except Brian who said 'We ought to ask how long it was after first starting to take the drug when they began to experience any adverse symptoms?'

'Good point' smiled Kim.

'And also what was Furrina's reaction to that? Did they immediately take the subject off the drug or insist that they continue for a while?'

'Right'.

'And we should ask them to specify exactly what adverse reaction they had. It may be that different people experienced different reactions or conceivably different levels of intensity of reaction'.

'Fine' Kim nodded making a note.

'That should be it, in addition to this list that you've produced'.

'Thanks. See how important it is that you're here with us' she said tapping the changes onto her laptop computer.

'Yes' he replied quietly blushing slightly.

The group talked some more about the questions, agreed who would be in which team, wondered how long it would take to get round to seeing everyone and finally confirmed that they'd try and persuade the test subjects to keep secret the fact that they'd been questioned by the team from TV-12.

'Okay let's go' announced Kim brightly.

At ten forty the team were in the foyer to wait for the guides except for Kim who went to reception and explained for whom they were waiting and was assured that as soon as the guides arrived they would be directed to where Kim and the team were waiting.

She then asked to be directed to the business centre in the hotel and a sari wearing receptionist insisted on taking her there where a young woman smartly dressed in western style stood, smiled and immediately agreed to allow Kim to download a document into a printer to print off the questionnaire sheets.

'May I do that for you Madam' she asked.

'That's very kind but do you mind if I do it myself as it is a rather confidential matter?'

'Of course Madam. Here is the printer code' and she handed over a slip of paper with a pre-printed code.

'Thanks' and soon the printer was churning out several copies of the questionnaire which Kim gathered up and slipping them into her briefcase walked back to the rest of the group where she distributed them amongst the two teams.

At just before eleven o'clock three smartly dressed Indian men walked across to the TV-12 group and introduced themselves to Kim who stood and shook hands with all three of them.

They listened, asked some questions, took the typed list of names and addresses and then the lead guide called Sanjay spoke to Kim.

'This list is not in any order that we could efficiently conduct you and your colleagues to in any sort of sensible routing. We will be running about all over the city and Mumbai is a *very* large city. Doing it in this order' and he tapped the paper he was holding' will take many days. So first I think we will sit down and reorganise the list into districts, then we will put them into a sensible order and finally we will have a workable solution. Is that alright Mrs Kim?'

Smiling at the Indian way of using a Christian name after Mr or Mrs she agreed that would be fine and asked how long it would take to do what had been suggested?

'Oh not long' was Sanjay's reply and he then turned to the other two and spoke rapidly in Hindi to them. They replied in similar language and the three walked to a far corner of the foyer and sat down to reorganise the list of names and addresses.

It was about half an hour later that Sanjay came over to the TV-12 team and smiling broadly explained that they'd sorted out the lists into a sensible order and were ready to start. 'Amrit will lead one group and Girish will lead the other. I however will remain here to co-ordinate and deal with any problems' he announced somewhat self importantly.

'That's fine. If you want to order anything to eat or drink while we're all away please do so and charge to my account' smiled Kim.

'Thank you. Most kind of you Mrs Kim'.

'Right guys time to go and find these test subjects' she announced to the English group who stood, collected their things including Rick who was guarding his precious TV camera very carefully refusing to store it with the concierge. Like all such pieces of equipment nowadays it was small light and quite portable and easily fitted his shoulder. However the plan was that most if not all of the test subjects would be interviewed by the two groups today and tomorrow. Rick was going to stay behind and spend the rest of the day filming general scenes of Mumbai so that they could be cut into the final programme when it was made. The intention was to give the finished product atmosphere, life and substance as Penny described Rick's role today.

Amrit took Kim, Brian and Samita, while Girish took Penny and Fergal out of the hotel and into the heat, noise and general chaos of Indian Mumbai. They had two cars with drivers waiting and the two teams lost sight of each other as they set off in different directions for their respective list of test subjects.

Brian was delighted that he was with Kim and Samita who was the only one of the English party who felt at home in the chaotic, noisy, hot environment of Mumbai as she had visited several times with her parents to see relatives who still lived in this large Indian city.

Kim and Brian though looked around in amazement at the scenes unfolding outside their air conditioned car. They were astounded to see the juxtaposition of people, cars, motorbikes, pedal cycles, lorries and buses with assorted dogs and cows wandering along busy roads, horses pulling carts as were donkeys. It was a scene of total disarray, turmoil, unruliness and bedlam yet somehow it all seemed to work and harmonise together.

'God above. I'd never drive here' stated Kim looking at Brian.

'No nor me' he agreed.

'You get used to it' stated Samita with a smile.

'Oh yes today the traffic is quite calm' commented Amrit. 'indeed often it can be much worse'.

'Seems impossible that it can be worse than this' muttered Kim who then flinched as a lorry almost collided with the side of the car, but neither their driver nor Amrit seemed to bother and accepted it as a normal way of traffic operating.

They'd been going for about twenty minutes, at times quite quickly, at others crawling along in dense traffic jams before they turned off into what looked to be a slum area of the city.

'Here we expect to find our first contact' announced Amrit looking at his list of test subjects and then having a rapid conversation with the driver who nodded and continued driving through narrow streets, surrounded on both sides by tall buildings which were distinctly tatty and the whole area was crowded with people and very run down.

The car stopped and Kim, Samita and Brian got out and stood looking at Amrit who said 'This way Mrs Kim' and led off down a narrow pathway.

'Christ I hope this is safe going down here' exclaimed Kim quietly.

'I'll protect you' Brian said rather more gallantly then he actually felt as he too was worried at the dingy, dark and frankly oppressive area in which they now were. He knew they weren't far from where they'd left the car but map reading, navigation and knowing where he was in strange places had never been his strong point.

Kim, Brian and Samita followed closely behind Amrit until he stopped outside a small dwelling. It couldn't be called a house as it was more of a shack with two solid walls made of breezeblocks, one wall of timber and the other of corrugated iron. There was also a corrugated iron roof. The door was open and a curtain hung in the doorway.

'Here is the first' announced Amrit proudly gesturing to the shack and he banged on a side doorpost obviously glad to have successfully found their destination. 'Hello' he called then launched into a string of Hindi. Looking back at Kim he said 'I have said that there are some important people from England to see them'.

'Thanks' she replied as an Indian lady pulled back the curtain and spoke in Hindi to Amrit.

There was a rapid conversation in their own dialect for some minutes then the woman smiled and looking at Kim said 'Lady. Please to come in. My home is humble but clean' and holding back the curtain she waited for the "important people" from England to enter her home.

Inside it was dim but as she quickly glanced around Kim could see that the place was spotless and also that the Indian lady's clothes were clean as was the part of her skin not covered by her sari.

'Hello. Thank you for inviting us into your home'.

The Indian woman nodded but said nothing.

May I speak to you in English .... about the drug trial you took part in with the pharmaceutical company Furrina?' Kim asked quietly.

'My husband Ganesh also took part' was the reply. 'He is still very ill. I became ill but am now better but my poor Ganesh remains much ill. He is in bed most of the time'.

'So you both took part in the trial?'

'Yes lady'.

'When was this?'

The woman looked at Amrit and spoke rapidly to him in her own language. He replied in like speech, but finished by saying 'April' to her.

'In April lady' she said looking at Kim.

'What happened to you when you took the drug?'

'I made ill'.

'Yes but how. What went wrong with you?' asked Brian.

She looked at him for a moment then said 'I tell him' and she nodded at Amrit. 'He tell you'.

'Okay'.

There followed a long discussion between the two Indian people at the end of which Amrit said 'Her name is Ashan and she says she had pain in her head. Her eyesight became blurred and there was something else but she won't tell me as I am a man'.

'Can I help?' asked Samita looking at the Indian test subject and spoke quietly in Hindi to her who smiled and replied quickly. Looking at Amrit and then Brian Samita said 'Can you two men go and wait outside? It's a woman thing and she is embarrassed to discuss it in front of men'.

'Oh right' nodded Brian so he and Amrit went and waited outside the shack in the heat until after a few minutes Kim peered out and said they could come back in but to Brian's querying look she whispered 'Tell you later' then looking back at Ashan asked 'now is it possible to see and talk to your husband?'

'I will ask if he will talk to you' and Ashan disappeared through a floor to ceiling curtain which divided off part the room. It was several minutes during which Kim could hear Ashan and her husband talking quietly together in their own language although occasionally she heard him raise his voice as he seemed to be interrupting her from time to time. But eventually his voice quieted down and shortly after that she reappeared.

'No ladies. He will see only him and him' Ashan said pointing at Brian and Amrit. 'My husband does not speak the English'.

'Fine' agreed Kim and then the two designated men followed Ashan through the curtain behind which on the floor was a double mattress in the corner where lay a tall thin unshaven Indian man.

'So tell me what you want me to ask?' Amrit said to Brian.

'Please begin by asking him what exactly happened when he started to take the drugs. Also how soon did problems start, exactly what are they, does he still suffer and if so how? Then continue by asking him the list of questions here' and he handed Amrit the piece of paper Kim had prepared earlier.

'Okay' and Amrit spoke quickly in their own language to the man on the bed who replied in like tongue. Their conversation went on for some minutes and Brian although not understanding a word of what was being said could sense that gradually the man in the bed was relaxing and becoming more responsive to the questions and clarifications that were being put to him.

When the conversation stopped Amrit looked at Brian. 'His name is Ganesh. He says that he started to take the drugs in March and for the first few days there were no effects, but suddenly he found it difficult to focus when reading. At first he thought that as the light in here in their house is not good then his eyes were reacting to that but he discovered that outside in the light he also had some difficulty seeing properly.

He also felt breathless some of the time and often lightheaded. He fainted a couple of times which was something he'd never done before. But the worst thing was that he had a seizure of some sort and as a result is unable to use his right leg or his right arm. He cannot afford to see a doctor but a local medical man of some sort has told him that he's had a stroke. Because he has lost much of the use of his right arm he cannot use crutches to get about and so he has lost his job as a labourer and spends most of his time here in bed.

He tries to walk and do exercises to get his arm and leg working again and he thinks that there is some improvement but he is still disabled'.

'Thank you. Now can he say whether Furrina have helped him, or offered any compensation, or medical treatment?'

Another rapid exchange of Hindi took place at the end of which Amrit spoke to Brian again. 'When he first had the problem with his eyes they said it was nothing to do with the drug test and his breathlessness and fainting was also unconnected with the trial. But when he lost the use of his arm and leg they said he must have taken too many capsules and so it was *his* fault.

He says he didn't and took them only as they had advised. But they then said that the trial was over for him and they gave him five thousand rupees as a completion bonus'.

'But that's only about fifty pounds' exclaimed Brian.

'Exactly. Not much but to a poor family like this it is a lot of money'.

'But it's wrong. They've damaged his health and now they're insulting him with derisory compensation!'.

'Yes. Also they made him sign some papers and that is the last that he has heard from them. His wife has tried to contact them but they won't see her, won't let her into their building and refuse to discuss the matter'.

'Did she get any compensation when she finished the trial?'

Amrit asked the question of Ashan and then replied to Brian. 'No. They just told her that she wasn't suitable for the trial but gave her no compensation but they did make her sign some papers. She doesn't know what she signed'.

'That is truly dreadful. Alright. Now ask the man if he would be prepared to say all that into a camera so we can tackle Furrina about this for him?'

More discussion in local language took place at the end of which Amrit said 'He doesn't want to get into trouble'.

'He won't'.

More rapid exchange of Hindi then Amrit said 'He is frightened to say anything to a camera'.

'But with his help we can get justice for him, his wife and others affected like this'.

After further conversation between Ganesh, Ashan and Amrit the guide turned to Brian and said 'He'll think about it. Can you come back the day after tomorrow and he'll give you an answer?'

'Yes of course we can. But do please ask him to really think about it as we are here to help. If he can help us we can help him'.

Amrit translated and the man on the bed nodded, gave a weak smile and spoke quietly to Amrit who translated 'He says thank you. Now he wants to rest'.

Brian nodded and followed Amrit and Ashan through the curtain from the bedroom and back into the main room where he spoke to Kim.

'The man is ill. I mean really ill and if Furrina have done that to him then they need to be brought to account. And soon'.

'That's why we're all here' responded Kim.

'We should go now' said Amrit as he looked at Ashan who seemed increasingly uncomfortable with the visitors.

'Okay' agreed Kim but before leaving she went to the Indian lady and smiling took her hand and said gently 'thank you for time you and your husband have given us. We *will* help you. We will go to Furrina and demand proper compensation for you and your husband, as well as exposing them to the world', then she shook the Indian lady's hand which felt surprisingly hot.

'We'll be back the day after tomorrow' she promised as she led the way to the door where she paused to thank Ashan for allowing them into her home and repeated that they'd be back in two days.

Then led by their guide they made their way through the maze of little streets and back to the car. Once inside the team revelled in the cool of the air-conditioning as they chatted about their first interview.

'What was the other problem that lady had then?' Brian asked Samita.

She gave a quick glance at Kim then replied 'She started to have monthly problems which continue to this day'.

'Have you heard about this side effect?' Kim asked Brian.

'No. But drugs affect people in different ways. It can depend on their metabolism, if they're taking any other medicines, their general state of health and so on, but I haven't heard about this particular effect'.

'Right. We'll check that out with the other subjects' then turning to Amrit she continued 'so off to the next one then please'.

CHAPTER 11

It took about ten minutes for their driver to battle the car through the chaotic traffic but eventually he pulled onto the side of a busy road, parked and invited all the English team to get out.

'Follow me' Amrit said importantly as he led the way into another slum area. 'There are four subjects within close walking distance from here' he continued as he confidently led the way into the ever increasingly gloomy area where the dwellings were, like the first that they'd visited, made from a variety of materials. Wood, plastic sheets, bricks, breezeblocks and corrugated iron. In fact it seemed that anything that could be pressed into service to construct a dwelling had been.

Soon Amrit stopped outside one of them and rapped loudly on a door post. The curtain covering the doorway was pulled aside and a woman's face appeared. Immediately Amrit launched into a stream of Hindi but the woman shook her head, muttered something and retreated behind the curtain. Amrit eased the curtain a little aside and poking his head through spoke rapidly and surprisingly loudly for some time, occasionally pausing to be answered by the unseen woman until he stopped speaking and there was silence for a little while.

The English team looked at each other as they hovered outside in the hot, dusty and rather smelly passageway. 'What's going on?' Kim wanted to know.

'Wait please' replied Amrit.

Nothing happened for a few minutes although the sound of quiet talking from several voices could be heard from inside.

Kim looked at Amrit and raised her eyebrows but he repeated 'Wait please. They are deciding whether to talk to you'.

After a further few minutes the curtain was drawn back by a young woman wearing a bright blue sari.

'I most sorry. Please to come in' and she pulled back the curtain and held it aside as the English team plus Amrit ducked under the low doorway and walked inside. It was larger than the first hovel they'd been in earlier as here there was one large room and a couple of doors obviously leading to other rooms.

'My name is Dipti. I am speaking a little of your language. My parents do not speak the English'.

'Not a problem' smiled Kim. 'Has Amrit here explained what we want to talk to you about?'

'Yes. The drug trials'.

'Exactly. Our records show that both your mother and father took part. Is that right?'

'Yes and they wish they hadn't'.

'Can you tell us why?'

'Because they become much ill'.

'In what way' asked Brian.

'My father ....' she paused then continued 'I am not sure I can explain in English'.

'You can tell me' suggested Samita who then added some other words in an Indian dialect.

The young woman smiled, nodded and began to speak slowly at first and then more quickly. Samita interrupted her from time to time, obviously to either ask a question or to clarify a point. At times Dipti became agitated and almost angry as she spoke but finally her voice tailed away and she stood quietly looking sadly from Samita to Kim, Brian and Amrit.

'Thank you' said Samita in English then turning to Kim and Brian she said 'the situation and effects of the drugs seems to have been quite similar to the first people we saw, except the lady did not have any monthly problems but her eyesight is still badly affected and she regularly gets giddy. Her husband is confined to bed and virtually unable to walk. It seems he has also had some kind of stroke'.

'Can we talk to them?' asked Kim.

'I don't know. Although poor they are proud and don't like to admit their problems'.

'I understand but if we are to help them we need to speak, and film them'.

Dipti looked at them with a puzzled expression obviously not fully understanding what Kim had said, so Samita translated for her and a short exchange of Hindi ensued at the end of which Samita said 'Maybe her mother but she thinks her father won't talk to you'.

'Okay. If we start with the mother maybe we'll persuade her or Dipti to also let us talk to the father'.

Samita spoke to Dipti who nodded and disappeared through the right hand of the two doors returning shortly holding the hand of a short slightly bent elderly woman.

'This is my mother' said Dipti. 'Her name is Chetana. She does not speak the English'.

'Not a problem. Samita and Amrit here can translate for us and your mother'. Dipti smiled and nodded as Kim continued 'So may we start asking her some questions?'

Dipti spoke to her mother who nodded.

Over the next ten minutes or so Samita and Amrit asked many questions and the elderly woman answered freely and at times at length. Samita translated for Kim and Brian who began making written notes in his notebook.

Eventually the conversation and questions seemed to come to a natural closing point and Kim asked Dipti if it would be possible to speak to her father. She considered the request and agreed to go and ask her father if he would see the English people and disappeared through the other door from the one out of which Chetana had emerged.

She was gone for about five minutes then she returned and said 'Sorry he will not see you. He is ashamed of being unable to stand. He was a fit man who worked on the railways but now he cannot work or walk properly'.

'I understand but if he will help us we *may* be able to get him some financial compensation. I can't promise but we will try'.

Chetana and Dipti had a short and rapid conversation before Chetana went through the left hand door and she could be heard holding conversation with a man, presumably the father. After a few minutes she emerged and shook her head.

'His name is Kumar. He will not see you but if you ask me the questions I will in turn ask him but it will have to be quick as he gets tired very quickly'.

'Samita you ask in their own language' suggested Kim. 'Try and get him to tell you when the symptoms started and what they were. If he's going to keel over with tiredness rather quickly then we need the answers as fast as possible'.

'Can I go in to him?' asked Samita.

'No. I will go to him and you must ask me through the door and I will ask him and give you his answers' said Dipti.

So the slightly bizarre ritual took place with Samita checking what to ask in English with Kim, then asking Dipti who'd gone through the door the question in Hindi. She in turn could be heard speaking quietly to her father and then she'd speak more loudly to Samita who translate back into English for Kim and Brian who again made notes in his notebook.

But after a few minutes Dipti came out and looked at Amrit and the English team. 'I am sorry but he is too tired to continue. That has to be all'.

'I understand' said Kim 'and it has been very kind of him to help us as he has. Will you tell him that please?'

'Yes' and she disappeared through the door again returning shortly. 'I have told him and he says thank you'.

'Dipti we would like to film you, your mother and if he would allow us to then your father as well. To do that we will return tomorrow. May we do that?'

'I will speak to you and your camera and I can probably persuade my mother to do so as well but I doubt my father will permit it'.

'Alright we'll return tomorrow or the following day. If in the meantime you can persuade him to speak and let us film him that would be great'.

'I will try'.

'By the way did your mother and father receive any payment from Furrina for them taking part in the trials?' Brian wanted to know.

'Yes. They were paid a few rupees for the two weeks that they were taking the tablets, but when they became ill then no more. After they stopped a man from Furrina came and made them sign some papers and gave them five thousand rupees. We have not seen him since'.

'Can I see the papers your parents signed?' asked Kim.

'No. The man made them sign and then took them away. They have no copies'.

'Okay. We'll be back tomorrow or the day after then. Thank you' said Kim and turning led the team out of the room onto the dusty street.

Soon they were back in the car and on route to the next subject who when they arrived refused point blank to talk to them and angrily told them to go away and nothing that they could say was able to persuade the man to change his mind.

The same thing happened at the fourth call, but at the fifth they were invited in by an Indian lady who said that she had not taken part in the trial but her husband had and willingly invited them in to her small home which was less of a hovel but more of a rundown part of an old brick built building.

Inside they learnt that her name was Mala and her husband was called Prakash and during the trial the side effects were similar to the others to whom they'd spoken but appeared to have started almost immediately. Indeed the day that he'd taken the first capsule he'd felt ill a couple of hours later and then by the evening his vision had been affected as had his balance. He had recovered considerably now but still got extremely dizzy several times a day and was therefore unable to work. However he'd not suffered a stroke.

The English team asked many questions through Amrit as the two guinea pigs spoke a different dialect from the other people they'd seen and Samita said she had some difficulty with using it. However Amrit managed quite well and after half an hour or so they got all the information they wanted, agreed to return with a camera and left.

And so the pattern of the rest of the day was established. Some people were helpful and spoke freely; some spoke guardedly and obviously nervously; some refused point blank to discuss anything related to Furrina and the drug trials.

Later on Kim said she needed the loo at which Samita and Brian said they did too so walking back to the car after another visit Samita suggested she and Kim went around a corner and squatted down to relieve themselves. 'It's common practice here' she said with a smile. Then she told Brian to go round another corner to do the same. He did but wished he could see the two ladies with their knickers down and for a moment wondered what colour they might be?

When Kim said she was hungry, so they went to a street vendor which Amrit found and ate chapattis, samosas, curried vegetables and naan bread. It tasted good and when they'd finished they returned to the car and set off on further exploration of the city to find the various people who'd been recruited for the drug trials.

Fortunately they were all within a reasonable distance of each other which made travelling to and finding where they were not too difficult a task and would of course have helped Furrina with their recruitment and subsequent monitoring of the trials process.

By five o'clock they were all exhausted. It had been incredibly tiring in the heat; travelling through the noise and chaos of Mumbai's traffic; going from one little house, hovel or shack to another; asking the same questions over and over again; trying to persuade frightened and worried poor people to disclose what had happened to them.

'I think we'll call it a day' announced Kim. 'I need a bath and a large gin and tonic' so they asked Amrit to arrange for their driver to take them back to their hotel where they found Penny and Fergal had also just returned with their guide. After a quick greeting they all arranged to meet up in an hour's time in the bar.

Sanjay the head guide appeared to have done nothing all day except sit in the hotel waiting for any call from Amrit and Girish in case he was needed. Which he hadn't been, but when Kim asked if he was really needed on this project he with great self importance explained that the guides that they'd booked came as a threesome and he was in charge and if there were any problems he'd was immediately on hand to solve them.

Realising she wouldn't win that argument, she smiled sweetly, said 'Thank you' and that she'd be delighted to meet him and the other two guides tomorrow morning.

It was just after seven when Brian walked into the bar, looked around and saw some of the TV-12 team in the corner chatting and drinking but to his disappointment Kim was not there. However he joined those that were and was soon sipping a beer that Fergal had bought for him.

When there was a lull in the conversation he asked 'Will Kim be joining us?'

'Yes of course' smiled Samita. I expect she's on the phone to James'.

'James her fiancé?'

'Right'.

'Probably blowing kisses and talking dirty down the phone to each other' suggested Fergal with a grin.

'Don't be so horrid' snapped Samita.

Fergal just grinned again and turning to Brian said 'Horrid or not I bet that's what they're doing don't you Brian?

'Err I wouldn't know' he muttered in response.

'Mind you I wouldn't mind talking dirty to her down the phone myself'.

'Fergal you have got a nasty little mind' retorted Penny but there was a slight hint of a grin there as well.

In fact Kim *was* talking to James and they'd just started to move the conversation on a little from her just telling him what they'd been doing onto more personal aspects.

'So are you missing me?' she asked dropping her voice into a husky tone.

'Dreadfully. How long are you going to be over there?'

'We've booked for five days but if we need to we could extend it'.

'Or shorten it if you get through before that?'

'Yes I guess we could. So tell me more about how much you're missing me'.

'I keep thinking about you all the time, wondering how you are, what you're doing, if you're safe, when you're going to be back and especially when I can hold you again?'

'Just hold me' she teased.

'Well no. Much more than just hold you'.

'Sounds interesting. What might you have in mind that was more interesting than just holding me?' she wheedled.

'I want to make love to you'.

'Oh do you now. And what makes you think I'd like you to do that?'

'I just kind of know you would'.

'Hmm'.

'And when you get back I'll prove it to you'.

'Isn't that a bit forward of you?'

'Very. Now tell me what are you wearing?'

'Just a robe. I've had a bath to wash the day's grime and dust away'.

'Nothing else?'

'No. Beneath that I am naked as the day I was born'.

'Wish I was there with you'.

'So do I darling but in the meantime you'll just have to imagine me won't you?' she giggled then added 'completely naked as I am under this robe'.

The conversation went on for a little while then they did blow kisses to one another before ringing off where Kim sat for a little while holding the dead phone still hearing James's voice and seeing his face and then *his* naked body in her mind's eye but after a little while she sighed, put the phone back and slipping off the robe quickly dressed and went downstairs to join her colleagues.

Brian was the first to see her walking across the bar to them. Hair shining and down, loose cream blouse, very short maroon skirt and three inch heels showing her bare legs to advantage. To him she looked stunning.

'Hello' he smiled at her as she approached.

'Hi everyone' she trilled.

'Err c-c-can I get you that gin and tonic? Brian asked diffidently.

'Thank you' she smiled and when he returned a few minutes later with her drink she touched his hand as she said 'thanks very much'.

'P-pleasure' he said quietly blushing and again with a slight stammer.

The evening was enjoyable as the team had another drink in the bar before going to the dining room where they ate a variety of Indian food recommended to them by the head waiter. Brian needed a little encouragement to be sufficiently adventurous with the strange sounding and in some cases peculiar looking dishes but at the end of the evening he had enjoyed himself especially as he'd been seated opposite Kim and could constantly admire her face and upper body.

After they'd finished and had coffee the TV-12 team said they were going back to the bar but Brian excused himself and said he was tired and was going to bed.

When he'd gone Penny leaned over to Kim and said 'Poor Brian. You know he'd besotted with you don't you?'

'What? No. Don't be silly'.

'Oh trust me I'm not. What do you think Samita?'

'I'm sure you're right. He never takes his eyes off Kim'.

'Yeah the poor schmuk positively drools over you. Right now he's probably up in his room frantically wanking himself off thinking about you' chuckled Fergal.

'Don't be so utterly disgusting' retorted Kim sharply. 'God you've got a nasty mind'.

'Indeed he has. Great isn't it? But all the same I bet he's right' laughed Rick the cameraman.

'I think we should change the subject' suggested Penny. Everyone agreed so they ordered some more drinks and got on with enjoying the rest of the evening together.

All except Brian who upstairs in his room was lying naked on the bed with his eyes shut tight and muttering 'Oh Kim' was doing exactly what Fergal had suggested that he probably was.

CHAPTER 12

Next morning the TV-12 team met for breakfast after their morning swims. Kim had also taken advantage of the well equipped gymnasium in the hotel and because she'd not wanted to run around the streets of Mumbai alone had pounded the running treadmill for half an hour until she'd covered the equivalent distance to her usual London runs before going to the pool for a quick swim arriving just as Brian was getting out believing that she wasn't coming. However although he gave her a quick up and down glance he didn't stay as he thought it would be too obvious if he got back in to swim again just because she had arrived.

When they'd finished eating the teams set off again accompanied by their guides and the day turned out to be much the same as the previous one. Some of the test subjects were reluctant to talk but did eventually, some refused point blank but others were straight away prepared to discuss the effect on them of their drug taking experience which had caused various side effects but generally there was a pattern of similarity between all the various people's symptoms.

The team also met some test subjects who had suffered no side effects and they probed those individuals carefully to try and discover why they had not been affected but to that conundrum there seemed no clear answer except that Brian suggested they might have been given a placebo and not the real drug.

By the end of the day they were tired, in some cases irritable, but had got masses of information from sufficient subjects who'd said they were prepared to talk on camera although many took up TV-12's offer to either film them from behind, or in shadow or in some cases from the front but with the camera not showing anything above their shoulders.

Around six the team gathered in the hotel foyer and reviewed where they'd got to and debated whether they felt they had sufficient material for the next day or so for filming, eventually after considerable discussion and debate they decided that they had and so would not be solely interviewing any more people but returning to those they'd met in order to film them.

They arranged to meet in the bar at eight and all departed to their rooms to shower and change except Brian and Kim as she asked him to stay for a while because she wanted some explanations from him as to the meaning of some of the information which he'd extracted on that Sunday morning visit to Furrina. She'd summarised the parts she hadn't understood and he patiently and carefully explained what the scientific jargon meant. To her surprise he was extremely understanding of her difficulties and so his clarifications helped her as he managed to unravel the complex science and turn it into language that was more easily understandable by her.

When they finished, she smiled, patted his hand which she saw made him blush, said he'd been really helpful and that she'd see him a little later in the bar.

'Y....yes fine' he muttered as they both stood up to go to the lifts.

She was again late for the meet up arriving around a quarter past eight as she'd spent time talking to James but also had had a long telephone conversation with Toby Brewer to update him on how the project was going and he'd expressed himself pleased with what she'd said and indeed sounded not just enthusiastic but really excited at what the team in Mumbai had uncovered. He finished by asking her to ensure that Rick got the filming done effectively to make the most of whatever material the team had uncovered.

'I g ... g-got you a gin and tonic' Brian said shyly to her when she joined the rest of the TV-12 team in the bar.

'Oh Brian that's kind of you' she smiled.

'N..n.. no problem' he stuttered.

Seeing he was probably embarrassed by his shyness Kim gave him another smile and a little wink then turned her attention to Penny and chatted with her for a while although she felt the older woman was much quieter than usual. Almost withdrawn and she didn't look at all happy. Eventually they all decided to go and eat and Samita having already made a reservation they were shown straight away to their table by an immaculately dressed head waiter.

Equally smartly dressed waiters promptly appeared and it wasn't too long before they were eating, drinking, relaxing and enjoying themselves all except Penny who seemed somehow somewhat withdrawn and didn't appear to be enjoying herself. If the others noticed no-one said anything but Kim made a mental note to get Penny to herself after they'd left the table and see what was wrong.

Eventually they finished their meal having again enjoyed so many different dishes of traditional Indian food, the choices of which had been largely influenced by Samita who wanted her colleagues to experience as many different tastes and foods as possible. Leaving the table as they all began to make their way to the bar Kim took the opportunity to take Penny's arm and lead her gently to one side.

'You don't seem too happy?' she asked. 'Is there something wrong as usually you're the life and soul of the party?' Penny looked at her for a moment then to Kim's amazement tears appeared in the other woman's eyes. 'Hey whatever's the matter?' Kim asked quietly.

'It's Susan. We've had an awful row on the phone tonight, before I came down to dinner'.

'Susan? Your partner?'

'Yes. She said that she's going to a party tomorrow which is being held by Christina?'

'And is there a problem with her going to that?'

'Yes' and now the tears started falling more profusely as she sniffed, opened her handbag and searched for a tissue. 'You see Christina is her previous lover. They were living together when we met and .... well when we met and got on brilliantly, Susan left Christina and moved in with me. We've been together for almost eighteen months now and we love each other. Well I love her desperately .... and I thought she loved me, but if she's going to see Christina tomorrow then I'm really worried that she'll dump me and go back to her'.

'Oh you poor thing'.

'I told her not to go however she said that I may be her lover but I didn't own her and if she wanted to go and see Christina she was going to do so and there was nothing I could do about it. So I got really angry and started shouting at her and we had a dreadful phone slanging match and she finally told me I was an ugly controlling old cow and to fuck off and slammed the phone down. I've tried to ring her back both on our home phone and her mobile but she doesn't answer. Obviously she guesses it's me ringing and is deliberately ignoring the calls' and as she stopped speaking the tears flowed down her cheeks.

Moving to the side of the large hallway she plonked down on a settee and cried quietly as Kim sat down beside her.

'Hey is everything alright?' asked Rick who'd approached the two women. Penny turned her head away as Kim looked up at him and said 'Yes thanks.

Penny's feeling a bit faint. We're fine. She'll be okay in a minute. Just leave us alone for a little while there's a good chap'.

'Sure' and he walked away.

'Thanks' sniffed Penny.

'Look would you like to come to my room and have a good old cry?'

'Yes I think I would please if you don't mind putting up with a blubbing middle aged lesbian'.

'Not at all. Come on' and taking charge Kim led the way to the lifts, along the upstairs corridor and to her room where once inside she told Penny to sit on the couch, went to the minibar, got out a miniature bottle of brandy, poured it into a glass and handed it to the other woman. 'Drink this' she said kindly as she sat beside her 'and then tell me all about it. I'm a good listener'.

'Thanks' Penny whispered looking at her for a few moments then with a nod she began speaking.

'It was at Reading University doing my degree when I had my first lesbian encounters. I also slept with men there but I became confused as to which I liked more. When I left Reading I started working in television at ITV and there I met Steve and fell for him. We became an item and after a few weeks we started to live together. All thoughts of lesbian loving were gone and I was a happy straight girl but after a year or so I found I was beginning to fantasise about women. I'd stare at pictures of pretty women in newspapers or magazines and wonder what they'd be like undressed and especially what they'd be like in bed. I'd do the same about women I saw on the tube, in shops, at work and so on.

One night Steve was away abroad on business. He'd been gone for two weeks and wouldn't be back for another two maybe longer and so I was feeling a bit down but also' she paused then after a moment continued 'well I'm not sure what else I felt' she paused again and grimaced then continued 'yes I do. I was horny I guess.

Any rate I didn't want to cheat on Steve with another man but I did need sex so I went to a gay club in London, got picked up by a woman called Sky who was about my own age and after we'd had a couple of glasses of wine we went and had sex in one of the toilet cubicles. It was hurried, rushed, sordid and quite disgusting really. But utterly gorgeous. I *loved* it. Standing there in the loo with my blouse and bra undone, my breasts exposed, knickers round my ankles, skirt pulled right up while this other girl I'd never met before knelt down to finger and tongue me to an orgasm was simply amazing.

Afterwards we went back into the main part of the club, danced together, snogged some more and then I went home with her to her flat in Shoreditch. There was another girl there and we had a lezzie threesome. I eventually got home about two in the morning.

I thought about what I'd done and although in some ways I was sorry that I'd cheated on Steve in other ways I was so glad I'd had lezzy sex again as I'd forgotten just how exciting it was. It also kind of satisfied my craving for sex.

When Steve came back of course we spent lots of time together in bed! But every time Steve climbed onto me, or I hopped onto him I couldn't help thinking about and comparing sex with him, well sex with a man really, with sex with a woman.

'And?'

Penny paused before saying quietly 'And I came to the conclusion that although Steve was pretty good at shagging the experience with Sky in the club and back at her flat with her friend had undoubtedly reawakened my interest in lesbian sex. I didn't say anything to Steve of course and we carried on as a loving couple.

But shortly after that I got seduced by a pretty black girl called Carly who worked in Continuity at ITV. Maybe I was subliminally sending out messages that I wanted girl sex. I don't know but any rate she invited me out for a drink after work one evening and we hit a couple of bars where I had more glasses of wine than was good for me really. We got a taxi back to her place. She started kissing me in the cab and then back at her flat we went straight to bed and the sex was brilliant. The following week Jean another girl from ITV and I had sex and she told me that I was a target for two or three of them there who were all gay and they all wanted to get me into bed. I said that I'd slept with Carly and now her, so who was the third one and she told me it was the Jenny the secretary of one of the very senior managers. So that afternoon I *deliberately* got into conversation with her, invited her out for a drink after work, flirted with her and we went back to her pad where we had the most amazing sex.

I was ashamed that I was again cheating on Steve but I consoled myself that it was with women not men so in that sense I didn't feel I was *really* betraying him. Of course in reality I was and eventually it got too much and so we broke up.

Free again I started to play the field. I got my own flat as I'd been living in Steve's before we separated and I started sleeping around, with girls mainly but also blokes too from time to time. In fact I'd shag anything that was good looking. Male or female!

'Crikey!'

'Sorry are you horrified by this squalid life story?'

'Not at all. Just surprised. How old were you when all this was going on?'

'Late twenties. Old enough to know better!' Penny replied with a rueful grin. 'I then met a guy called Bill and we hit it off straight away. I mean like we met at a function at his rugby club where he'd gone with another girl. I'd gone because a guy called Graham that I knew had broken up with his girlfriend however he didn't want to miss the dinner at the club but was reluctant to go on his own. So knowing I was single he asked me, said there were no strings to the arrangement. He just needed a female companion for the evening, said he'd pay for everything and would put me in a cab home afterwards. So I said yes.

But while I was at that rugby club do, I met and danced with this guy called Bill. We clicked immediately and half way through the evening we slipped outside and had a stand up kneetrembler against the club house wall. It was January and freezing cold but we managed alright' and a flicker of a smile crossed her face for the first time since she broke down in tears.

'You seem to like stand-up quickies with strangers' chuckled Kim.

'Pardon?'

'Well the girl in the loo at the gay club and then this guy Bill'.

'Oh yes I suppose I do. And stand-ups are fun. With men or women!'

'I guess so'.

'They're not the only two stand-up shags I've had either!' she smiled wistfully.

'So what happened to the guy you went to the dinner with .... err Graham?'

'Oh I went back to him and Bill went back to his girl but we'd arranged to meet the next day. Sunday. We did and before you could say sex we were back at my place shagging ourselves silly.

'Wow'.

'Any rate Bill and I became an item for about three months I guess then he found someone else and dropped me so I was alone again until some months later I met Diana.

She was slightly older than me but lovely both in appearance but also in personality. It wasn't love at first sight for either of us but we shared an interest in modern art. In fact that's where we met at a modern art exhibition. We exchanged names and phone numbers and a few days later she rang and asked if I'd like to meet her for a drink.

I did and over the next few weeks we met up several times, had dinner together, went to other art exhibitions, waked on Hampstead Heath then one evening I invited her to my flat and said I'd cook dinner for us. It was a lovely evening and as we were having coffee we talked about sex and she wanted to know if I'd ever slept with a woman. When I said yes she asked if I'd like to sleep with her? Would I? You bet I would. And it was wonderful. So we became an item and although we kept our separate flats we spent a lot of time in each other's places. We talked about selling both flats and buying a cottage in the country because we really did think that we could spend the rest of our lives together. Get married possibly?

Then one day she came home and told me that she'd got cancer; that it was an aggressive form of the disease, incurable and that she was going to die.

It happened quite quickly and within six months from coming home that night and telling me she was ill, she was dead. I gave up work for the last two months of her life so I could be with her. Nurse her, look after her. She died one Sunday morning in my arms in her own flat. It was terribly sad but it had also been a very moving experience as she deteriorated so quickly at the end and faded away in just a few final days.

I was broken hearted and resolved there and then never to get seriously involved with anyone again. I threw myself back into work and got a producer's job at Channel 5 as ITV wouldn't take me back. The work was fine. I was fine. Alone but fine. I had several friends but that's all they were. Just friends or acquaintances not lovers. And that's how I remained for ages until I met Susan at a party a couple of years ago. For me it was love at first sight. I'd never felt anything like that before for anyone that I immediately felt for her'.

'Not even your love for Diana?'

Penny paused and looked at Kim for a moment or two then said quietly 'No. I did love Diana but with Susan it hit me like an electric bolt. We talked and got on really well but she obviously didn't have the same feelings for me as I'd instantly had for her.

She was living with this Christina woman and they'd been together for a almost two years. Before I left the party I suggested to Susan that she and I meet up for a drink. We did a couple of days later in a wine bar not far from my apartment. We chatted and got on really well so we arranged to meet up again. We did and then some more times and to say I was head over heels in love with her was an understatement. But although she was, I think, developing some feelings for me they weren't nearly as pronounced as mine were for her.

But on our fifth or maybe sixth meet-up we were in a bar and I told her of my feelings for her and that I wanted to make love with her. She didn't say anything, just looked at me. I can still remember feeling my heart thumping like mad as she sat there staring at me. I thought she was going to turn me down but eventually she smiled, lifted my hand to her lips and kissed it gently and said she'd like that too. I was just ecstatic so we went back to my flat and did so.

I think for Susan it was just pure enjoyment, a bit of fun, perhaps experimentation with another woman, maybe just simple sexual need. I don't know. But for me it was the fulfilment of such feelings of longing and needing to be really intimate with her and yes of love, that on that evening my life was so utterly complete again.

We loved and talked, and loved again and talked more. In fact it was gone midnight when she left me to go back to Christina.

That night after she'd gone I wrote her a long e-mail telling her of my feelings for her and saying that I wanted her to leave Christina and come to live with me because ....' Penny paused and looked at Kim before finishing quietly 'because I was completely in love with her. I don't just mean a bit in love. I mean utterly totally completely lost in love for her'.

Kim squeezed Penny's hand and smiled. 'And did she?'

'No not straight away. She said she couldn't leave Christina but over the next few weeks we saw more and more of each other. We went to restaurants, to the theatre, to the cinema and most times at the end of the evening she came to my apartment and we'd make love, until one day she said that Christina knew about us and had given her an ultimatum. Give me up and stay with her, or give up Christina and come to me.

I was overjoyed and thought that this was everything that I could have dreamed of but to my horror Susan said that she'd thought about it and decided that Christina needed and wanted her more than I did and so she couldn't leave her and that we had to stop seeing each other.

I was absolutely devastated. I thought my whole life had completely fallen apart. I can't tell you just how bad I felt'.

'You poor thing' sympathised Kim. 'Here let me get you another of those' and taking Penny's empty glass she poured another miniature brandy into it and sitting back down next to Penny handed the drink to her. 'So how or when did you and Susan get together again then?'

She rang me after about a month and asked if we could meet up? I jumped at it and said yes of course and asked did she want to come to my apartment or meet up at a restaurant or wine bar but she suggested just meeting for a coffee.

I agreed. I'd have agreed to meet her anywhere I was so desperate to see her again as well as wondering why she'd contacted me, but I didn't dare to hope that she might want to restart a relationship with me. So we met for coffee but it was hopeless'.

'Why?'

'I wanted to hold her, hug her, kiss her but she just sat demurely the other side of the table drinking her coffee and talking about how she couldn't make up her mind what to do. She said that she *had* developed some feelings for me but that she still had strong feelings for Christina.

Knowing that she couldn't share those feelings between us both, she was in a complete quandary as to what to do.

I asked if there was anything that I could do to help her make up her mind but she said no. She just had to work it through in her own time. As we were parting I asked if she'd like to come back to my place but she refused.

And so we parted. After she'd gone I sent her another long e-mail once again expressing my feelings for her and finished it by saying that I loved her and wanted her to leave Christina and come to me. She just sent a four word reply'.

'Which was?'

'"I know you do". That's what she said'.

'That's all?'

'Umm and for the next couple of weeks I didn't hear from her even though I e-mailed or texted her every day. I know that was over the top but I couldn't help myself. I just *had* to do it'.

She paused so Kim asked gently 'So what happened?'

'It was a Friday night, close to midnight. I was in bed asleep when my phone rang. It was her and she asked if she could come to me? Could she? I said of course she could and when I asked where she was and when she'd arrive she said she was downstairs in the foyer of my apartment block!

Any rate she came up and I was shocked to see that she had a black eye and had obviously been crying .... like I have tonight' she grimaced. 'I asked what had happened and she said that she and Christina had had a huge row because she'd discovered somehow that Susan and I had been meeting again and that during the row Christina had slapped her, thrown her against a wall then onto the floor, pulled her hair, punched her in the face so she'd run out and come to me for help.

I cuddled her, soothed her, bathed her eye with cold water, helped her have a bath, took her to bed and slept with her in my arms all night. We didn't make love. It wasn't needed. That night she wanted comfort and safety not sex'.

'Of course. And did she stay with you? I don't mean just that night but .... well you know move in and live with you?'

'Next morning we talked and talked .... and talked. She told me that she *had* developed strong feelings for me, maybe was even beginning to love me not like I loved her but she *would* like to come and live with me and see if those feelings strengthened. If not and they didn't develop then maybe we'd be better apart.

Obviously I agreed and that day we made several trips to Christina's flat as she'd gone to Newcastle for the weekend. We got all Susan's things. She wrote a letter to Christina saying their relationship was over and that she'd decided to move in with me.

I was so happy. I just can't tell you how I felt. That weekend and all the next week passed in a blur of happiness and then the next Friday night we caught the Eurostar to Paris and had the weekend there. We went to lovely restaurants, we went to a show which was a bit naughty, you know risqué but fun, and we obviously spent a lot of time in bed loving each other. Oh Kim it was just bliss for me and undoubtedly she did start to develop stronger feelings for me.

Here look I hope I'm not embarrassing you with talk of girl sex and being in bed with another woman?'

'No it's fine. So what's gone wrong then?'

'Well after Paris we settled down together and were happy. Eventually Susan told me that she was falling in love with me although to be fair I don't think her feelings were ever as strong for me as mine were for her. For me though life with her was divine.

All was well until a few weeks ago when I sensed some coolness from her to me. There was nothing I could put my finger on it was just a feeling that I had. I asked her a couple of times if there was something wrong, if I'd done something to upset her or if she was cooling towards me, but she said no everything was fine.

But I knew it *wasn't* and I started to get frightened in case she was thinking of leaving me. So we started to get a bit ratty with other every now and again. Then one evening she told me that recently Christina had rung her and asked to meet. They'd met in a wine bar and had got on really well. Christina apologised for hitting Susan and said that after she'd left she'd had a brief affair with another woman but that had finished and she was alone again and wanted Susan to come back.

I asked her if she was considering Christina's request and she said no, but I wasn't convinced she was telling the truth. In fact I was sure she *wasn't*. Any rate she started to really cool down towards me. I was still madly in love with her but we began to have rows, got irritable with each other and ……..' there was a long pause before she continued quietly 'and the sex side of things tailed right off.

Then last week I discovered that one night when I was out at a business meeting with Toby she'd had dinner with Christina and although she said they didn't, I'm quite sure they slept together. And I don't think it was the first time that she'd cheated on me with Christina.

We had a minor row just before I came away to India but tonight when she said she was going to a party a Christina's flat tomorrow it just tore me apart as I guess she'll stay there, sleep with her and our relationship could be over'. At that she began sobbing and crying again before saying 'I couldn't bear that. I just couldn't'.

'Oh Penny. I don't know what to say'.

'There's nothing you can say. Nothing you can do. Nothing anyone can do. She's there in London and going to Christina tomorrow. I'm here in Mumbai. It could be all over when I get back. I could return and find she's moved out, taken her things and I'm alone. Without her. If that does happen I don't know how I'd cope.

I know I'm older than her. I'm forty nine and Susan is thirty. Christina is thirty two so they're of a similar age. Maybe she's decided that I'm too old for her. After all I *am* older. We can't all be slim young neat size eight to ten's can we? I can't help it if I'm a size fourteen and have got a few wrinkles and bulges. That's me' and turning to Kim sitting alongside her taking her hand she said quietly 'I keep as fit and smart as I can, but I know I'm no iconic beauty. Okay I'm not unattractive but I know I'm not beautiful. Susan though *is* beautiful and Christina is equally so. Perhaps Susan wants to be with someone of her own age who is more attractive than me? Do you think that's what she wants?'

'I don't know'.

'Oh Kim whatever am I going to do?'

'Do you want to fly back tomorrow? We could probably manage without you'.

'God no. Whatever would the boss say? I've flown home because of a domestic? He'd probably fire me. No I'll stay and try not to be a wet blanket' then twisting towards Kim she said quietly 'would you give me a hug?'

'Of course. Come here'.

The two women embraced for several minutes until Penny released herself from Kim's arms and said quietly 'Thanks'.

'Better?'

'Heaps. I'll go to bed now. Maybe Susan will have calmed down by the morning?'

'Yes perhaps. Hope so'.

'Hmm. Maybe .... but we both know it's unlikely don't we?'

'I'm an optimist'.

'Glad one of us is' Penny grimaced as she stood up. 'Thanks. See you in the morning. Reception eight o'clock?'

'Fine' smiled Kim as she walked to the door and let Penny out of her room. Deciding not to go down to join the others she stayed in her room, stripped off, showered and pulling on a nightie clambered into bed, then on an impulse rang James.

'Hi' he said obvious delight sounding in his voice. 'Two calls in one evening from you. I am honoured'.

'I just wanted to say I love you, but especially to hear you say it to me'.

'I love you'.

'Say it again'.

'I love you'.

'Say it again'.

'I love you'.

'And again'.

'I love you. Now what's up?'

So she told him about Penny and when she finished he said quietly but with utter sincerity 'I *love* you. I will *never* leave you. I will *never* cheat on you. I *love* you and *only* you'.

'Thank you. Me too. Good night'.

'Goodnight. Love you'.

'Love you too'.

She broke the connection then turned off the light and rolling onto her side ran through in her mind everything that Penny had said. As she relived the conversation she wondered what making love to another woman would be like as not only was it something that she'd never done, she'd never considered it.

But as she lay there in the darkness she began to think about it and wonder how it felt to kiss a woman instead of a man and what it was like to touch another woman's breasts and pussy. And allow a woman to do that to her. Were any orgasms generated by and with a woman as intense and satisfying as they were with a man? Her conclusion was that they probably were and as she turned onto her other side she couldn't help feeling the very slightest tinge of regret that this was an aspect of sexual exploration on which she'd missed out in her life

Still she'd just have to wonder and speculate about it because as it was something in which she had no intention of ever indulging she'd never know and with that concluding thought she closed her eyes and seeing a vividly clear picture of James at the forefront of her mind whispered 'I love you' and slowly drifted off to sleep.

CHAPTER 13

Next morning was another hot dry dusty Mumbai morning full of sounds smells, bustle, chaos and general Indian life.

At breakfast when Penny joined the team. Kim looked closely at her face but she could see that the older woman was still upset and hurting though when Rick asked her if she was feeling better she nodded and said quietly 'Yes thanks' although it was clear to Kim that she wasn't.

'Okay' said Kim quietly but authoritively 'when everyone's finished eating let's move to the foyer, meet our guides and get the day going. I've mapped out a plan of activity which should enable us to get all our interviewing and filming done today. If we've still got a few candidates left over at the end of the day we can spill over to tomorrow'.

There was a general chorus of agreement and not long after they were all assembled in the huge foyer with their three guides standing in front of them looking eager and attentive.

'Good morning Mrs Kim' Sanjay the lead guide said giving a small bow. 'We are ready to take you wherever you want to go this morning'.

'Thank you. I've drawn up a route based on where we went yesterday for the team this morning. It will be Rick who is going to do the actual filming' then turning to the cameraman she said 'can you ensure you show the poverty in the areas where we're going. I'm not trying to put these poor people down in any way but I want to try and demonstrate the contrast of the quiet dignity that we saw amply demonstrated by those that we met yesterday in their simple hovels which from the outside are typical shanty dwellings but as we saw inside were clean and tidy if pretty well bereft of any real belongings'.

'Sure' nodded Rick as he shouldered his camera and picked up a grip filled with things he might need.

Looking at Sanjay she continued 'Based on where the teams went yesterday I have distilled all those visits into a list of subjects and their homes for filming. As well as Rick there will be me, Penny and Brian'.

'So Mrs Kim only one group for guiding today?'

'Yes'.

'Hmm. That is most awkward. There are two guides plus me of course in charge of all matters' he added pompously.

'But we'll only need one and I'm not sure there will be much for you to do'.

'Oh yes there is very much for me to do as I am in charge of everything'.

'I know but what will you have to do? Either Amrit or Girish will be more than adequate to take us where we want to go'.

'Oh no. It is important that I remain here just like yesterday so I am immediately on hand to solve any problems that may arise'.

Realising that she wasn't going to be able to dispense with Sanjay's services she gave up arguing about him and asked 'So as we only have one team going out into Mumbai who would you suggest we use? Amrit or Girish?'

'Oh both Mrs Kim. Both will be of use'.

It was then that she also came to the realisation that not only was she not going to be able to do without Sanjay but she was also stuck with both of the other guides. Not wanting to either cause a scene or waste any more time and as in the overall cost of this venture to India the guide's charges were eminently reasonable she nodded, smiled and said 'Well that's great then isn't it. Thank you'.

'What would you like me to do as I gather that I'm not coming on the filming trip?' queried Samita.

'I want you and Fergal to spend the day finding out as much as you can about Furrina's Indian operations based here in Mumbai. Rick took some film of the outside of their office and factory yesterday didn't you?' she asked raising her eyebrows at the cameraman.

'Yes. Outside the building, trucks coming and going, potential workers queuing up outside waiting for vacancies and work, staff and workers going into the buildings and so on. Good filler material for the broadcast'.

'Great. So Samita please talk to people there. Find out what sort of employer Furrina is? How they treat their workforce? White and blue collar employees. Try and get a picture and some quotes of what it's like to be a Furrina Mumbai employee'.

'Okay'.

'It is important and I think that you will be the one out of all of us who is best suited to do that without raising too many suspicions'.

'Because I am an Indian you mean?'

'I didn't want to put it like that'.

'But that's what you meant wasn't it? A simple post Imperialist native chatting to other similar individuals?' then she laughed. 'You're right of course. I am probably the one best suited to it'. She smiled then asked a question. 'So me and Fergal to check out Furrina?'

'Yes please'.

'Although Rick with his fancy camera won't be with us to film the people we talk to, shall I film it on my mobile?' asked Fergal.

'Now that is a good idea' agreed Kim.

'Consider it done' smiled Fergal giving her a little salute.

'Right' looking at the team and the three guides Kim nodded and continued 'okay folks. Let's get the show on the road. Wagons roll'.

Overall the day went well. Most of the people that the Highlight team had interviewed in the previous days co-operated and were happy to be filmed. Indeed one or two got quite excited about it But there were several occasions where some of the people being interviewed needed to be prompted a little, but Kim wasn't worried about that as Penny said that some clever editing would remove that and ensure that the finished interviews when shown live on TV were clear, uninterrupted and apparently spontaneous.

To the team's irritation though a couple of subjects having thought about it overnight declined to be filmed and indeed one refused to even open their door to the film crew.

Kim was particularly concerned about them as they were a couple who had suffered particularly badly and indeed were still by no means fully recovered and although not the worst affected subjects that they'd met nevertheless they were probably the second worst.

But whatever Kim said which was translated first by Amrit and then when they still refused by Girish she was unable to persuade them to change their minds. Not wanting to cause bad feelings or any upset she smiled and said they'd leave them in peace, and so the team moved on to the next subject who were very co-operative.

But later that day when they returned to the hotel Kim was still disappointed that she'd not persuaded those two particular Indian guinea pigs to speak on camera.

Rick said he was going for a swim and Brian agreed that he'd like one too but Penny said she was going to have a lie down as she'd got a headache.

'See you in the bar later?' queried Kim.

'Yes sure' agreed Penny as she walked off to reception desk to collect her room key.

Thanking Amrit, Girish and Sanjay for all their help she said they were now finished and had no further need for guide help so after much elaborate hand shaking, bowing and smiles the three Indian guides left.

Samita and Fergal who were waiting in the coffee shop off reception as they'd returned earlier than Kim's group, were very cheerful and pleased with what they'd achieved in talking to employees at Furrina's plant, as to their surprise they'd managed to get people to talk freely.

The overall impression was that Furrina was a good employer, paid fractionally above the market rate, offered decent working conditions in the laboratories, offices, factory and warehouse and there was no sign of dissention among any of the employees to whom they spoke.

Fergal's recordings on his mobile phone both still photos and also some video footage had come out surprisingly well and Kim was sure that it could be made into broadcastable material.

'That's great. Well done' enthused Kim to the two of them. 'Now I want to run an idea past you both.

Ganesh and Ashan to whom we spoke about their participation in the drug trials .... err Samita you remember she was the lady who as well as some other problems had monthly womanly problems?'

'Yes I remember'.

'Well they're now refusing to let us film them. We tried hard through our two guides but the two affected people were adamant. Absolutely no. They simply wouldn't allow us to film them and we couldn't change their minds.

So I wondered if I went back with you Samita whether just the two of us could persuade them to permit us to film them, especially Ashan? What do you think?'

'What makes you think that I an English woman, albeit of Indian extraction, could persuade them to agree to allow us to film them?'

'I don't know. I just feel it's worth a try and Samita you did seem to get on well with them, especially the lady Ashan'.

'I'm more than happy to try as long as you can remember how the hell we find our way into that slum and then to where they actually live?'

'I agree that's a problem but I don't want the whole entourage of those two guides and their boss man with us'.

'Fergal can you check with hotel reception and see if there's some way we can get guided or obtain directions into the area where these two people live?'

'Have you got an address?'

'Sure …….. err here look' and she pointed to an address on a now rather grimy and soiled sheet of paper containing the complete list and schedule of all the visits they'd made to people who'd been involved in the test programme.

Kim watched as he walked off, waited while the concierge served a middle aged German couple and then could be seen to engage in conversation with the hotel employee. Shortly he returned and nodded.

'He has a friend who would take you there. There is a charge of course for the man's services and the concierge also needs his palm wiping with some rupees for arranging the introduction'.

'Of course. That's great. Go back and ask if it can be done today?'

It didn't take long before Fergal returned and with a small smile said that he'd arranged for them to be taken in about fifteen minutes, that he'd agreed a price for the guide's services having negotiated a significant reduction in both what the guide and the concierge wanted to be paid.

'Well done' nodded Kim checking her watch. 'Right time for a quick freshen up and then off we go. Okay Samita?'

'Yes fine'.

Their guide was waiting by the concierge's desk when Kim and Samita walked over. They were introduced to him who said his name was Fred.

'Fred?' queried Kim.

Mike Upton

'Indian name too difficult for English people to say so I am called Fred when working for you people' he said in a somewhat surly manner and Kim didn't particularly take to him.

With an expression which was a cross between irritation and annoyance she led the way outside where the doorman summoned a taxi. She told Fred where they wanted to go by pointing at the address on her list. He nodded and spoke rapidly in a local dialect to the taxi driver who promptly turned to Kim and said there would be a surcharge as where they were going was not a good area.

'There was no surcharge when we went there with a different driver two days ago' she retorted.

'Today there is surcharge' he replied obstinately.

'How much'.

'Two thousand rupees lady'.

'One hundred'.

'One thousand'.

'Two hundred'.

'One thousand is lowest for surcharge'.

'Four hundred is the most I'm prepared to pay. If that's not acceptable we'll get another taxi' and she opened the door and made as if to leave the car.

'Lady. I am only a poor taxi driver. I have a living to make to feed my wife and three children and myself'.

'Five hundred?'

'Okay five hundred' he smiled. 'Pay now before set off'.

'Three hundred plus half the return taxi fare when we get to the destination. You'll get the other two hundred together with the remaining half of the fare when we come back to the hotel'.

He looked at her then nodded and took the notes she proffered to him, turned back, started the ancient car and lurched off into the chaotic traffic.

'That's only a little over five pounds. The surcharge I mean said Samita quietly.

'It was the principle of the thing' replied Kim speaking equally softly as the car jolted over a pot hole in the road and swerved to avoid a motor bike. 'I know it's not much and if this all goes well I'll probably add another few more rupees when we get back …… umm if we get back' she laughed as the car almost got hit by a horn sounding bus.

'Are you going to come back again with Rick to film them?'

'No I'll use my mobile phone and film them myself. I know it's not as good quality as Rick's proper television camera but it may be less intimidating for our subjects?'

'Could be' mused Samita.

It was about twenty minutes later that the driver pulled the car into the side of the road, exchanged a rapid flurry of conversation with Fred who then turned to Kim and Samita and said rather haughtily 'We are here' as if he alone had managed to bring the small party to the required destination.

Having paid the driver what she'd said she would she slid out of the car then leaned to him and said 'Wait right here please'. He nodded but said nothing.

'Right now you take us where we want to go' she said looking at Fred. He set off seemingly confidently and she and Samita followed him as he led the way between some dingy shanty hovels, along a narrow passageway with an open sewer filled with slow running material, around a corner, stepped across another open sewer and plunged down a dark alleyway.

'I hope he knows where the hell he's going' muttered Kim. 'This looks quite different from when we were here the day before yesterday'.

'Maybe he's taking a different route' suggested Samita.

'Hey Fred are you sure this is right?' Kim demanded.

'Yes lady' he replied over his shoulder. 'Be there soon' and he continued walking on, turned another corner and after about ten yards stopped in front of a hovel which did look familiar to both the English woman.

'Yes this looks right' announced Samita.

'Thank goodness' replied Kim with some feeling in her voice.

'Shall I try and raise them?'

'Yes please' agreed Kim to her companion's question.

Samita knocked on the side of the door and when after a few seconds Ashan appeared she asked 'Hello do you remember us?'

Ashan nodded but didn't speak.

Samita then began to talk in Hindi and she spoke for some while. It was obvious that Ashan was still refusing but Samita persisted until after a little while the curtain which served as a door was pulled aside and the two English woman were invited inside.

'You wait here' instructed Kim pointing first at Fred and then at the ground. 'Right here. Don't go anywhere. Be there when we come out'.

He didn't reply just looked at her.

Inside Ashan invited her visitors to sit down and they did so on the blanket covered chairs.

'Thank you for inviting us into your home' said Samita quietly and with a disarming smile then switching to Hindi again she spoke at length, answered what were obviously questions from Ashan and Kim could see that gradually she was winning the drug trial subject's confidence.

The conversation went on for a while then Ashan stood and walked through the hanging curtains into the bedroom at the back of the hovel. Conversation could be heard which continued for a surprisingly long time before Ashan returned and with a smile and a nod spoke rapidly to Samita who replied then turned to Kim and said 'Okay she and Ganesh have agreed to talk to camera but it will have to be in the bedroom as he is too ill to get out of bed'.

The bedroom was dim and although Ganesh could be seen lying on the mattress bed on the floor it was too dark to film.

'We need some light' Kim said quietly and immediately Samita spoke to Ashan who nodded, left the room soon returning with a couple of gas lights, looked at her visitors and asked 'Is good?'

'Yes that's fine thank you' replied Kim. 'May I speak with Ganesh?' she asked indicating the man on the bed on the floor.

Ashan nodded, so Kim knelt down and taking the man's hand which felt hot and dry smiled as she said 'Thank you for talking to us' words which were translated immediately by Samita who also knelt down.

The question and answer session didn't last long as Samita translated Kim's questions while she filmed on her phone. At the end both women stood and said 'Thank you' to the bedridden man who inclined his head and smiled briefly.

Then they spoke to Ashan and used Samita's mobile phone to film her as they asked the questions until finally the two were finished.

'Please thank her and say we hope that the programme we're making will help to get her and her husband get some decent financial compensation, as well as all the other people damaged by the tests of course'.

A rapid exchange in Hindi followed then Samita turned to Kim and said 'I think we're done. She is getting twitchy. We'd be best to go now' and with that pulling the curtain aside Kim led the way out into the dusty passageway.

'Oh shit' she exclaimed.

'What?' Samita wanted to know as she joined her.

'Well can you see our illustrious guide Fred anywhere?'

'No I can't' she said looking around.

'Nor can I. So if he's scarpered how the hell do we get back to the taxi? Can you remember the way?'

'Not really no I can't but I think it was this way' and she started walking down the passageway with Kim beside her.

'Shit, double shit and treble shit! Just wait till I get back and talk to that hotel concierge. I'll ………..' muttered Kim.

'Never mind that. I think we might need some help' said Samita in a worried tone of voice. As the two of them looked around what had previously just seemed a dim, dirty and unpleasant narrow passageway in the shanty town and which stretched for what felt like miles either side of them, now it also looked foreboding, threatening, even frightening. That feeling was enhanced by the two or three men who'd appeared and stood staring at them. Soon some other men joined them until about half a dozen had gathered. The fact that they didn't speak but just stood and stared at Kim and Samita added to the increasing feeling of menace and danger.

One of the men approached Kim and reaching out a hand touched her tee shirt. She stood still as if rooted to the spot as the dirty brown hand felt the material between his thumb and forefinger. He turned round and said something to the other men then slowly traced his forefinger up the side of the garment and across towards her breasts. She slapped his hand away and took a step back but found she bumped into someone behind her and twisting round she found more men at the back of her. Those together with the original men in front of her began to crowd together and thus closed off any attempt that she could make to get away.

Kim began to feel really frightened as she felt her jean covered bottom being touched and squeezed by several hands and then the man who'd touched her tee shirt put his hand on her left breast and squeezed.

'Get off' she yelled trying to wrench herself away but with the men behind also now beginning to fondle her body she knew she was in real trouble. She heard Samita yelling in Hindi at the several more men of all ages who'd appeared and were surrounding her.

'Help' screamed Kim as loudly as she could as she felt someone undoing the zip of her jeans and as she grabbed hold of the waist band to her horror her hands were seized, yanked away and held firmly thus preventing her from protecting herself.

Her jeans were tugged down her legs and hands touched her white panties as other hands began to try and pull off her tee shirt. She knew she had to stay on her feet as if she fell she'd be doomed to some terrible sexual assault.

Glancing over at Samita she saw that her companion was struggling in the middle of a group of men but then she lost sight of her as Kim found herself being lifted off the ground by a large strong man while a teenager grinning furiously seized her jeans and ripped them right off before taking her panties in both his hands and tugged them off as well.

'No please' she begged as she felt the panties being removed but then she was pushed to the ground and in that moment of terror as she realised that she was about to be raped she was amazed to find a thought flash through her mind that she was glad she'd put on a clean pair of undies back at the hotel when she'd had her wash and brush up before coming on this what was turning out to be a very dangerous escapade.

She also remembered James's warning about being careful. Oh if only he was here with her.

Hands slid under her tee shirt and began tugging it off. Then her bra was pulled down to expose her breasts as several men leaned down to touch, grope and squeeze various parts of her body especially her breasts. More hands held her naked legs firmly apart.

A middle aged man stood in front of her and grinning pulled his cotton trousers off followed by some extremely grubby pants. When he lifted his long shirt she saw his penis was erect as he got onto his knees and shuffled forward.

One of the younger men holding one of her legs said 'Him first then me'.

Two others holding her other leg grinned and one said 'Then us. Then them' and nodded towards the crowd of watching men. 'You get much fucked today white lady'.

'No please NO' she screamed unable to move being held so firmly by the several men as the shuffling man laid down on top of her and began groping for her pussy.

Suddenly an Indian woman appeared and yelling loudly began punching the would be rapist in the head before beginning to kick him while shouting ever more loudly at him. Kim had no idea what was being said but the man yelped as the woman grabbed his hair and tried to tug him away from Kim. He twisted and shouted back at the woman who giving up trying to tug him off Kim started kicking him again. He shouted as the woman who she now saw was Ashan started raining blows to his head and growling he began to get up and as he did so Ashan kicked his erection hard. He screamed and rolled onto his back hands around his genitals but she rushed to him and stamped down on his hands again causing a further loud yell of pain.

Ashan also yelled at the men holding Kim's legs apart who promptly let go and to Ashan's continuous shrieking they began moving away. The man who'd been about to rape her stood and with a look of pure hatred on his face pulled on his trousers as he stared down at the still naked Kim.

Her female saviour bellowed something at him then removed her cloak of sorts and draped it around Kim who was trying to cover her modesty while getting up. Ashan helped her and wrapped the cloak further around her while continuing to berate the men who began melting away into the shadows and confines of the slum shanty area.

'Samita? Is she okay?' Kim asked.

Ashan nodded.

'Samita are you alright?' called Kim looking towards her companion.

'I'm not hurt' came the reply 'But I was so frightened for you .... for us' and pushing her way through the couple of remaining men who slunk away as she walked quickly to Kim. 'They said they were going to rape you first, then strip and rape me. And that *would* have happened had Ashan not intervened and shouted that we were there to help her and her husband and get them some compensation'.

'Well thank God she did' Kim sobbed with real feeling.

Seeing her boss's clothes on the ground Samita picked them up and handed them to the still crying Kim as Ashan spoke to her in their own language. Nodding and clutching Kim's clothes she said 'Ashan says you can go into her home to dress again'.

'Thank Christ for that!'

Moments later the two women were standing gratefully inside the hovel. Kim began to re-dress but said to Samita 'Did you see my panties? They're not here with my other stuff?'

'Were they white?'

'Yes'.

'I'm afraid one of those men took them'.

'Oh God. Sodding pervert!'

'Yes. I am so sorry'.

'Not your fault. I guess we were a bit foolish coming here without a man'.

'I should have realised. It is all my fault' replied Samita with a mournful expression.

'Oh don't beat yourself up. Of course it's not your fault. I was in charge. My decision to come here. My responsibility'.

As Kim dressed Ashan spoke to Samita in their own language and a conversation developed between the two of them at the end of which Samita announced that she and Kim were to stay in Ashan's house until some trusted men could come and take the two of them back to the hotel.

'I'd rather ring and get Fergal, Rick and even dear old Brian to come and get us' announced Kim as she continued dressing.

'Do they know how to get here?'

'Oh God no they probably don't'.

'So how the hell are we going to get safely back?' and she listened as Samita spoke to Ashan again in Hindi, after which their Indian saviour picked up a mobile phone, punched in some numbers, spoke rapidly and put the phone down. Samita looked at Kim and said 'She has rung for her brother and some of his friends to come and escort us to safety. They will bring their own car. We will be safe with them'.

The Beta File

'I won't feel safe till I'm back inside the hotel' Kim said with real feeling.

'Me neither' then responding to something Ashan said she replied then looked at Kim. 'She's asked if we'd like some tea until her brother arrives. It will be impolite to say no'.

'I'd rather have a bloody great gin and tonic but in the absence of that then yes I'd love some tea'.

Ashan took a kettle that was sitting on a small stove and so was already hot and quickly made two cups of tea which she handed to Kim and Samita.

The mobile phone rang and Ashan answered it, spoke briefly then spoke to Samita who listened, then smiled and turning to Kim explained. 'Her brother and two friends are on their way. About fifteen minutes I gather before they're here'.

'Can't be too soon. I just want to bet away from his horrible place'.

'Yes me too and ....'

'And what?'

'I am so ashamed that what happened did so here in my country. India is a safe and friendly place but to have insulted and assaulted us like that is unforgiveable. I am so sorry'.

'Could have happened anywhere'.

'Yes but it didn't! It happened here in Mumbai. In India. In my country. I'm sorry'.

'I said before it's not your fault. But I guess now we know why the taxi man wanted extra money. Bloody glad I didn't pay him though. And as for that little shit Fred. You wait till I see that hotel concierge I'll report him to the hotel management. We'll get the police in too. Those bastards that assaulted us need to be locked up'.

'I doubt the police will do anything. They'll make copious notes. Take ages to listen. Ask us lots of questions. Then do nothing and eventually they'll drop the case. Especially as we're not going to be here'.

'I'll think about it' snarled Kim.

Silence descended and the three woman sat in silence until Ganesh called out and Ashan immediately went into the bedroom area. When she emerged she spoke to Samita who translated. 'He asked how we were and said he was sorry that those men had attacked us. He asks for our forgiveness'.

'Tell him there is nothing for *him* to forgive. It wasn't his fault'.

Conversation was stilted and difficult and there were long periods of silence as the two TV-12 women contemplated what had happened to them but eventually there was a commotion at the door and in came one large Indian man closely followed by two others. He glanced at Kim and Samita but went straight to Ashan, kissed her on both cheeks, held her hands and spoke quietly but quickly in Hindi to her. She replied and after a couple of minutes he turned to Kim and said in perfect English 'I am Krishna and I am so sorry that you have had such problems. These areas can be dangerous for white people as you found out, but I gather apart from the real fear that you would have had, you are not actually hurt or injured? Is that right?'

'Yes'.

'You probably want to return to your hotel straight away?'

'Yes we do' Kim said with feeling. 'As soon as humanly possible.

'Come with me then. You will be quite safe with us I assure you. Come along' and he gestured towards the door.

Tuning to Ashan Kim said 'Thank you for helping us' and as she looked slightly puzzled Samita translated after which Ashan smiled, nodded and replied in Hindi.

Samita said to Kim 'She says that she was glad she could help. Go home safely'.

With that Krishna pulled the curtain aside and led the way out into the alleyway. Another man stood waiting for the two women to appear and then he formed up on one side of them while the third man formed up on the other side so they were safely escorted by the Krishna and the two other men he'd brought through the shanty area soon emerging into a less threatening vicinity after which it seemed only a couple of minutes before Krishna walked up to a large grey Mercedes by which stood another man.

'Here is my car. Get in please' said Krishna holding open a rear door.

Kim slid inside quickly followed by Samita. Krishna got in the front passenger seat and one of the other men slid in next to Kim. The man who had been waiting by the car got behind the wheel. The other man who'd arrived with Krishna spoke rapidly to him as he lowered the car window then as he pressed the button to raise the window he walked off and was instantly lost in the crowds of people thronging the street on which they presently were.

The car moved off with the driver hooting other road users as Kim and Samita sat tensely in the back desperate to get back to their hotel and it was about a quarter of an hour later they swept up to the front of the hotel, got out of the car, said "thank you" as Krishna accompanied them to the doorman who escorted them into the hotel where the two women walked quickly to reception, collected their keys and made their way to the lifts to go to their rooms.

As they waited for the lift to come Brian appeared, spotted them and walked quickly over to ask how they'd got on?

'Tell you later' said Kim.

'Okay but did you get what you wanted? You know the interview and filming?'

'Yes but ....'

'Oh that's good. Shall we meet in the bar?'

'In a bit. Look Samita and I got into a bit of trouble in the shanty area. We need some time to get over our trauma, have a bath, change and relax. We've had an horrendous ordeal. Let's meet in an hour shall we? Can you tell the others?'

'Yes sure. But are you alright? Is there anything I can do?'

'Yes .... and no' then seeing his puzzled expression she went on 'yes we're alright *now* but no thanks. It's kind of you to ask but there's nothing that you can do'.

'Kim can we go upstairs now?' asked Samita.

'Sure. Look Brian we'll see you later okay?' and with that the two women stepped into the waiting lift.

Upstairs Kim sat on the bed and began to cry as the horror of being attacked, stripped naked and almost raped in the street by a bunch of strange men hit her and she realised just how closely she and Samita had come to being very seriously assaulted. Indeed if it hadn't been for Ashan that is undoubtedly what would have happened or worse. Maybe they'd have been killed.

She'd previously read of woman, both white and Indian being attacked and raped in India and although before momentarily experiencing a feeling of regret for the victims she'd never before given it much thought. But today she knew just how those other poor women must have felt.

Picking up the phone she dialled James. She needed the reassurance of his lovely calm voice. She needed him to hold her and tell her he loved her and although he was several thousand miles away and couldn't hold her now, just hearing his voice and speaking with him would be reassurance enough.

'Hello James Dixon speaking' came his voice when the call connected.

'Hi darling' she said struggling to hold back the tears as she decided not to tell him what had happened. There was no point in having him worry about her for the rest of the time she was in India. She was shaken and upset but alright, so it was something that she'd keep to herself. Maybe one day she'd tell him but not now.

'Kim my love. How are you?'

'I'm fine. Tired, dusty, missing you like mad but fine' and she wiped away a tear from each eye as she felt a wave of calmness surge through her on hearing his voice'.

'I'm missing you too darling. So how is it going out there?'

'Yeah okay. We got what I think will be the final bit of filming done today' and at that point she couldn't hold back the tears and she started crying.

'Hey are you okay?' James asked quietly.

'Yes I'm fine. Just tired'.

'You sound as though you're crying?'

'I am. It's hearing your voice. I love you so much'.

'And I love you. Now just a moment ago you said you were on the final bit of the project? Great! So when are you coming home?'

They talked for a few more minutes, then feeling so much calmer and relaxed she said she needed a bath and would call him tomorrow. They blew kisses at each other, said again how much they loved each other and when the call finished she sat holding the phone as the tears started again. She cried for some minutes then muttering that she needed to pull herself together she went and ran a bath, lay back and soaked for a long time. Eventually she sat up and washed her hair as she wanted to be sure that every possible element of dust and dirt from the location of their ordeal was gone.

The Beta File

Getting out she dried herself, went into the bedroom and used the hotel hairdryer to style her hair, got dressed, put on a little makeup and taking a deep breath left her room to go downstairs and join the others where Samita was obviously telling them what had occurred.

As she walked up to the group Brian stood up. 'Samita's told us what happened. I am so sorry. If only you'd let me or Rick or Fergal come with you?'

'Yes but we didn't and although we were both very frightened and I had the horror of being stripped and pawed by a bunch of strange men we are alright. But if Ashan hadn't heard the commotion, come out and begun yelling at and hitting those filthy bastards I don't know what would have happened. Well I do of course and that is too horrible to contemplate. But it didn't. So let's not talk about it anymore if you don't mind. Subject closed'.

'Right. I'll g-g-g-get you a drink. G-g-g-gin and tonic?'

'In a minute. First I'm going to see that bloody concierge. Fergal will you come with me please?'

'Sure'.

'Shall I come too?' asked Samita.

'No I think Fergal and I can manage. Come on'.

When they got to the concierge's desk Fergal spoke firmly. 'That guide you organised for this lady and her colleague earlier'.

'Yes sir' then looking at Kim he said 'was everything alright madam?'

'No it certainly wasn't'.

An immediate look of concern came onto his face as Kim explained what had happened. While she spoke his face became more distressed and when she'd finished he spoke sincerely to her.

'Madam I am so sorry. I really cannot say how sorry I am by what has happened to you. Fred is not someone we've used before but as a guide was required at short notice I rang a contact who said he knew someone. I assure you I will never use that man again. *Never*. Now shall I call the police immediately?'

'Will they do anything?'

'Of course they will investigate and hopefully bring these bad fellows to justice'.

'How will they find them? I don't know their names. I'm not even sure I could identify them. No I think although it was a very frightening experience for me and my colleague it would be best not to try and take matters further'.

'As you wish madam'.

'Yes I do. Just make sure you never use that man again'.

'Oh I will and ......'

'And?'

'I will ensure that he is black listed for all the hotels so such a thing can never again reoccur'.

'Good thank you'.

'And I know some people who will see that he is taught a lesson'.

'Oh I don't know about that'.

'Madam it is not your concern'.

'Right' then turning to Fergal she added 'come on time for that drink that Brian's getting for me I think'.

Back with the others Brian handed over her drink then turning to Samita asked 'Can I get you something too?'

'Yes you can. I'll also have a gin and tonic ...... a large one. I don't usually drink but I need one now'.

And so slowly the evening began to get back to normal and by the end of dinner conversation, laughter, banter and general cheerfulness was being exuded around the table.

Kim refused a nightcap later on and said she was going straight to bed but after she'd stripped off, peed, washed, done her teeth, brushed her hair and pulled on a nightie clambered into the extra large double bed and was about to snuggle down when there was a knock at the door.

Getting out of bed she peered through the security spy hole in the door and saw Penny standing outside so she unlocked and removed the chain before opening it to the concerned looking producer who brandishing a bottle of brandy, held it out in front of her and said quietly 'Want to talk about it?'

Immediately the awfulness of their ordeal came back to her and with a nod she invited the older woman to come in bursting into tears as she did so.

'Come here' whispered Penny putting her arms around Kim and pulling her to herself. 'Cry as much as you want'.

It was gone midnight when Penny left and Kim was alone. They'd drunk quite a lot of the brandy and Kim felt really quite drunk when she laid down in bed. Her head was spinning every time she closed her eyes so she sat up and focussed on a crack in the curtains. Provided she did that she could keep her head under control but the moment she lay down everything started to spin. Suddenly she felt sick and scrambling out of bed she made it to the bathroom just in time before vomiting violently into the toilet bowl. Several times she threw up but eventually she staggered back to bed and this time when she laid down fortunately now nothing seemed to spin any more.

She woke next morning feeling awful. Her head didn't just ache. It thumped as though a man with a jack hammer was trying to drill his way out from inside. Her tongue felt furry and she was sure that her breath would smell. Peering in the mirror she didn't like the face that looked back at her.

'Oh my God' she muttered as she made her way to the shower and stood under it for about a quarter of an hour during which she turned the water from hot to cold and back to hot and back to cold. Eventually she felt somewhat better and returning to the bedroom, dried and styled her hair, got dressed and made her way downstairs where the others were already tucking into breakfast.

'Sit here' invited Penny indicating the chair next to her.

'Thanks'.

'How do you feel this morning?'

'Like shit'.

'Hmm. I won't say you look like that but you certainly don't look your usual bright on the ball self'.

'How much of the brandy did we drink last night?'

'You had lots. Did it help you sleep?'

'No it made me sick and this morning I still feel........'

'Like shit. Yes you said' interrupted Penny with a grin.

'Absolutely'.

'It'll pass. Now I suggest you have just some orange juice, coffee and perhaps a croissant'.

'Okay'.

Later that morning the team got together, reviewed everything that they'd done whilst in India, checked and double checked the interviews, ensured they'd missed nothing of importance and by twelve o'clock declared themselves satisfied and happy with what they'd completed.

By mutual consent they went off in small groups but ensured that they stayed in the main shopping areas while they bought souvenirs, trinkets and presents for those back home.

Well everyone except Brian did as he had no-one for whom he needed to buy a present but arriving back in the hotel he went to the shop in the foyer and bought an Indian cloth decorated handbag for his mother.

CHAPTER 14

The TV-12 team made their way through Heathrow's terminal 5, queued to pass immigration, waited for their bags and finally emerged into the main arrival hall which was crowded. There were dozens of people waiting at the barrier for arriving passengers and before Kim spotted James, Penny who was beside her grabbed her arm and said 'Look it's Susan!' and dropping her suitcase rushed over to the barrier where a pretty young woman stood.

Even though separated by the metal barricade they flung their arms around each other and hugged.

'Wait I'll come round' gasped Penny but running back to Kim she said 'It's Susan. She's here. It must be alright mustn't it?' and grabbing her case and without waiting for an answer she ran back through the crowd around the end of the barrier to her lover where they kissed and hugged.

As she approached the end of the barrier Kim saw James and waved. He waved back and as she quickened her pace to get to him she called 'Bye everyone, see you on Monday' and ran the last few steps until she reached him where she simply let go of her bag and suitcase and flung her arms around him. Folding her to his body he whispered 'Welcome home darling' and kissed the top of her head, followed by her lips as she looked up at him.

'Oh James I have missed you' she whispered.

'I bet not as much as I've missed you'.

They clung together oblivious of the hordes of people steaming past, or of the remainder of the TV-12 team who smiled as some of them looked for their own friends or relatives who were waiting for them.

Except Brian who had no-one to meet him and seeing Kim and James together, Samita and her father, Penny and Susan holding hands and talking animatedly to each other, Rick with his arm around a tall black girl and Fergal reunited with his wife Mary, he wandered through the crowded concourse to get the bus to the long term car park where he'd left his car. He was soon on his way to his home near Milton Keynes, looking forward to seeing his model soldiers again and perhaps that evening if he wasn't too tired after the long flight treating himself to sex by visiting one of several prostitutes that he regularly frequented.

'Come on my darling' James said quietly as he stooped to pick up Kim's carry bag and take hold of the handle of the large wheeled suitcase and with her arm thrust through his they walked to the short term car park and were soon inside the Range Rover which was James's pride and joy.

The two of them looked at each other, leaned close, kissed, this time deeply and passionately, then eased apart and she whispered 'I love you. I just can't tell you how much as there are simply no words to describe the love that I feel for you'.

'And that is exactly how I feel about you'.

They kissed again then sat with her head on his shoulder and her hand resting on his thigh. It didn't move but stayed there feeling his strong leg muscles as she inhaled his body smell, remembered his aftershave scent and leaning up kissed his slightly stubbly cheek.

'You need a shave my man' she said quietly running her hand down his cheek. 'First job for you when we get home'.

'Actually we're not going home'.

'Oh James darling I don't want to do anything special. I'm tired after that long flight and the hard work in India. I didn't sleep well on the plane so I'd just like to go home, make love with you and then go to sleep'.

'Well some of what you want is in the plan but not all'.

'James please ………'

'Schh' he cautioned as he put a finger on her lips. 'What I have in mind will more than meet your requirements. Trust me'.

'I do but I'm tired' she replied quietly.

'Put your seat back a little, close your eyes and let me take you to be pampered, powdered and loved' and leaning across he popped a soft kiss on her lips then straightening up, clipped his seat belt on, started the engine and drove slowly out of the car park, threaded his way through Heathrow's confusing traffic system and eventually emerged onto the M4 where he headed west away from London.

'Where are we going' Kim queried as she reclined her seat.

''You'll find out when we get there' he grinned. 'Now tell me all about India' but shortly after she'd started to speak her voice tailed away and he saw that she had dropped off to asleep.

The Beta File

After about an hour's driving he turned off the motorway and soon they were travelling through countryside until he shook her gently awake as slowing they came to a pretty village which he drove through almost to the end until he came to an impressive set of entrance gates and a sign pointing to The Barleycorn Hotel and Spa.

'Here we are' he announced quietly and turned onto the driveway that led in a slow curving direction for about a quarter of a mile through immaculate gardens until he reached a tall yew hedge through which there was an open gateway. As they drove slowly through the gap they came upon an old Georgian grey stone house with a gravelled courtyard. James drove to the door and stopped.

Immediately a man appeared, smiled, bid them welcome, said his name was Walter and that he'd take their bags.

'Thanks. There are four altogether. Two for each of us'.

Inside they were checked in with quiet calm efficiency and then Walter led the way to their room which was to the back of the house, and overlooked the gardens.

'I hope you'll be comfortable here sir and madam' he said then added 'everything is arranged for you sir just as you requested'.

'Thanks very much' James replied taking the room key and passing the man a ten pound note.

'Oh James this is lovely and a wonderful surprise'.

'Good. Now knowing you'd be tired after your trip and flight I've booked you a pampering session in the spa. They are going to do all sorts of wonderful things to and for you then when you come back here *I'm going to do wonderful things to and for you*' and his smile and softly spoke word made her stomach churn in a delightful way while she also felt her heart give a sudden thump of happy excited anticipation.

Looking at his watch he said 'You've got about half an hour before your appointment, so probably you'll want to have a shower first and unpack'.

'What are you going to do while I'm away?'

'You're appointment is scheduled to last for two hours after which you've an appointment with the hairdresser here. While you're being pampered and fussed over I'll have a swim in the hotel pool, catch up on a few work things and await the return of my beautiful fiancé'.

'Oh James you are wonderful. We're staying here tonight?'

'Of course. Is that alright?'

'Yes but the problem is I don't have a smart evening dress for dinner and this place looks quite posh. I just took comfortable things to India not elegant luxury hotel dining dresses'.

'Hmm. So what you need is something like a little black dress isn't it?'

'Exactly' she nodded.

He grinned then walked across the room to where the suitcases had been placed by Walter, selected the smaller of his two bags and hefted it gently onto the bed. 'Have a look in there'.

With a frown she opened the bag and peered inside where on the top she saw a dress bag which when she opened revealed that it contained a carefully folded black dress. Taking it out she held it out at arm's length then pressed it against her body and looked in the mirror.

'James it's lovely. But it isn't one of mine so whose is it?'

'Yes it's yours. I bought it for you'.

'You bought it?'

'Well to be honest your friend Anna bought it but I paid for it'.

'Anna bought it? Why? How? I don't understand?'

'Because I told her that I was taking you away to this place when you got back from India and that you'd probably want a couple of smart dresses for the evenings and would she get something suitable. So she came round to the apartment, had a look at some of your things to get a feel of the style you liked and the right size then told me that any woman is happy with a little black dress and that's what she recommended that she should buy you. You'll see in the bag that she also bought one or two other things'.

Kim carefully put the dress on the bed turned to James she popped a quick kiss on his lips and said 'The dress is lovely. Thank you. Now what else did she buy?' and looking in the case again saw there were a couple of small bags on top of another probable dress bag.

Taking the first small bag out she peered inside then grinned as she extracted a black half cup bra which had a little red rose motif on each cup and a matching pair of knickers which were really more bikini style than full panties. In the other paper bag was a pair of holdup black stockings which she could see had a fancy lacy top design.

With a grin she said 'Well well. Naughty Anna'.

'Umm. She said that seeing that we'd been apart for a week or so if it had been her that's the sort of stuff she'd treat her man to seeing her in and she was sure you'd feel the same given a choice'.

'Did she now? Well they're lovely and I'll be more than happy to wear them to fuel any sexy fantasies that you might have now I'm back!' and her grin was broad and wide. So what else is in this other bag?' and taking out the next large bag she opened it and revealed a pale green ankle length dress which as she held it out to examine it properly said quietly 'James this is lovely too'.

'Good. There's more in the case' and he watched as she removed two more small bags. The first contained a front opening white lace bra with some matching full sized panties and the second held a complimenting suspender belt and some stockings which the pack described as "warm honey" colour.

'Oh James. These are so pretty' she said looking at the undies 'and the two dresses are wonderful. Thank you so much'.

'Glad you like them. All down to Anna's skill and decisions'.

'Well they're good choices and thank you for thinking about it and getting Anna involved. Come here' and flinging her arms around his neck she whispered 'What a wonderful set of surprises. This place, the massage and spa, the dresses, the pretty undies and this romantic room. You are the most wonderful man in England. In Britain. In Europe. In the whole world. In the universe. Ever. And a little later I'll show you how just grateful I am and how much I love you' and as she spoke she pulled him close, pressed her body against him and looking up pulled his head down to her and kissed him hard and long. Eventually they eased apart and with a smile she said 'I guess I'd better go and shower and then go to the spa hadn't I?'

'Yes I think you had. I'll walk down with you then while you're being pampered I'll have a swim'.

It was nearly three hours later when Kim walked back into their bedroom to find James sitting at the desk unit wrapped in a bathrobe and simultaneously talking on his mobile phone while also tapping away on this laptop. He twisted round, smiled and waved at her then holding up his left hand with fingers and thumb upright mouthed "five minutes" at her.

She nodded, sashayed over to him, smiled and leaning down dropped a soft kiss on the top of his head, then walked to one of the armchairs and sat down to wait for him to finish his call.

When he had he swung round in the chair and walking to her asked 'So how was it?'

'Divine. I've had an all over body massage, a head massage, a special shoulder and back massage, hot stones on my spine, a mineral and seaweed bath, my toenails and finger nails done and finished with a lovely session in the hairdressers. So how do you think I look' she asked coquettishly as she stood up.

Slipping off her robe and with one hand by her side and the other resting on a hip, one leg pushed slightly forward she stood before him completely naked, delighting in his openly admiring expression as she slowly turned right round through three hundred and sixty degrees.

'I think you look utterly beautiful' he said his voice suddenly husky.

'Thank you' and with that she walked to the bed, clambered on, laid down and smiling stretched out her arms to him adding quietly 'so why don't you come and have a closer look'.

The lovemaking was tender, languid, mutually inclusive and she groaned as several orgasms rippled through her before he said he couldn't hold back any longer and ejaculating with a happy satisfied series of grunts took her over the edge to her final prolonged climax which she felt engulfed every fibre of her being.

Afterwards they remained locked together for some time until he slowly clambered off her and pulling her to his side put an arm around her shoulders as she snuggled into his armpit.

'James that was quite wonderful. Thank you. And the massage and everything that went with it was a terrific homecoming present. Whatever gave you the idea?'

'I guessed you'd be pretty shattered after the long flight, and I wanted to take you away for a weekend but to ensure you enjoyed it to the best of our mutual ability I hunted around on the ever wonderful internet until I found what I wanted. A small luxury hotel, in the countryside, with a real spa, on site hairdresser, an especially a romantic bedroom and not too far from Heathrow'.

'Well you ticked all the boxes. And did I tick your boxes with our lovemaking?'

'Erm .... I'm not sure. I think we'll need to do it again soon so I can be sure' he grinned dropping a kiss on her lips.

'Oh do you now? I might not feel like giving myself to you again this afternoon' she chuckled.

'Oh I think you will' he whispered as he leant down to kiss the nearest nipple to him. 'Don't you?' he went on looking into her eyes.

'Um well now I think about it again then yes definitely?' she smiled.

And she did give herself to him again and this time the loving was more robust, vigorous and considerably more energetic after which they laid together cuddling and Kim soon dropped off to sleep. James remained where he was, holding her, smiling and constantly staring at her face, her lips and hair as he realised just how much this woman meant to him.

At around seven she stirred and muttered 'I think I dropped off'.

'You sure did. It will have done you good and refreshed you for the evening. Now shall we dress and go down for a few drinks and dinner?'

'Umm. I'm going to have a bath first. I don't want to shower because it might mess up my hair'.

'Hey can I share the bath with you?'

'No you can't mister. I want to relax, enjoy a really hot deep relaxing soak and if you get in as well no doubt you'd start interfering with me'.

'Of course'.

'Exactly and that's just what I don't want. I want to have a little *me* time on my own, so you go and shower in that separate shower cubicle where you can think about me while you slosh hot water over your sexy body. Grrrrr!' she chuckled.

He did as she asked and made his way to the separate shower room where he was soon twisting and turning under the hot water that cascaded from the high powered shower.

When he emerged back into the bedroom Kim was still in the bath so he peered in and asked 'You sure I can't get in there with you? There's plenty of room. I don't think I've ever seen such a big bath? And I bet over the years lots of couples have had a fling in there together'.

Mike Upton

'No doubt and I'm not saying we can't or won't .... just not right now. So be a dear and clear off to leave me alone to enjoy my bath. On my own!'

He grinned then muttering 'Spoilsport' went back in the bedroom and getting his electric razor out of his bag set to dealing with the day's stubble. He finished and was almost dressed when Kim emerged from the bathroom, all warm, pink and smelling lovely as he gently kissed her lips.

'You look great' she smiled openly admiring him now fully dressed, smelling of aftershave then picking up the pair of black panties added 'now go downstairs, ensure we've got a nice table, get yourself a drink and I'll be down shortly'.

In fact it was nearly half an hour later that she walked into the bar looking absolutely stunning. The high necked dress fitted her perfectly and showed her figure off well as it was quite tight fitting around the bust and waist but being rather short also displayed her shapely legs to good advantage.

He grinned, told her she looked stunning and watched as she wriggled up onto an adjacent bar stool being careful as she did so when crossing her legs that her stocking tops were not exposed.

'Thank you but I'd prefer you to look at my face rather than trying to get a cheap thrill looking up my dress!' she smiled tugging the hem down a little more.

'Nothing cheap about the dress or your legs' he grinned. 'Champers?'

The barman who was hovering nearby heard her say yes so he straight away poured a glass for her and handed it over asking as he looked at James 'And for you sir? Another gin or will you join the lady in some champagne?'

'I'll have some champagne but can you open a bottle and we'll take it to the table and drink the rest over dinner'.

The evening was a great success and they talked nonstop. Her about India, the country, the people, the abject and obvious poverty contrasting with the spellbinding luxury that could be seen and especially about their interview of the subjects of the Furrina's drug test programme, the problems filming and her fury at the harm that had been done to so many people and the shabby way Furrina had paid off the damaged people. The only thing she didn't mention was when she and Samita had been attacked.

He told her what he'd been doing at work, how much he'd missed her and how glad he was that she was back.

The food was excellent, the service discrete and faultless, the champagne delightful and eventually they made their way to the bar where coffee and liqueurs were served. He had a large espresso and a malt whisky while she asked for a decaff coffee and a small brandy and as she took her first sip of the spirit she was for a moment reminded of the night in Mumbai where Penny had come to her room and allowed her to talk through her ordeal resulting in her drinking far too much brandy, something she definitely wasn't going to do tonight .

Finally he took her hand and said softly 'Shall we go up?'

'Oh yes please'.

In the bedroom he eased the zip of her dress down and then enjoyed looking at her in the underwear that Annie had chosen.

'You like?' she queried with a cheeky smile doing a complete three hundred and sixty degree turn.

'Oh yes I like very much' he smiled as he undid her bra strap, freed her breasts and gently cupping them lowered his lips to each in turn taking time to gently lick and suck each nipple which he enjoyed seeing harden.

'Let's go to bed' she whispered extracting herself from him and walking to the bed which had been remade while they were downstairs having dinner. Peeling off her panties she laid down on the duvet still wearing the holdup stockings.

He was soon undressed and joined her where they made love slowly, passionately yet tenderly until they both climaxed her surprisingly noisily. Afterwards she peeled off the stockings and they slithered under the duvet and cuddling together dropped off to sleep.

The next morning they slept in late, made love, showered together, had room service breakfast then while James went for a swim Kim had another back and neck massage. When she returned to the room she switched on her smartphone and when it had fired up it pinged with a text message from Penny.

> It's all fine. Susan is
> back to stay. She isn't
> leaving me 4 Christina.
> Isn't that wonderful?
> Have a lovely weekend.
> I know I will. Penny xx

Kim texted back to say how pleased she was and that she'd see Penny on Monday at the office. She and James wandered around in the grounds for the rest of the morning, watching the many different types of birds that abounded and enjoyed seeing a couple of grey squirrels flashing through the trees.

Returning to their room once inside Kim pushed James against the wall and kissed him firmly while rubbing her crotch against him which to her delight resulted in her feeling his erection beginning and soon it was pressing against her. She began deliberately grinding herself against him from side to side then reaching down slid her hands to his trouser clip and zip and moments later had pushed them and his pants down to his knees allowing his still erecting prick to sway freely forward to complete its process of erecting.

Swinging him round so she was the one now leaning back against the wall she flipped up her skirt, wrapped one leg around his body and whispering 'Come on then' pulled her panty crotch aside and helped his prick nuzzle against her pussy which quickly moistened and as he slid into her she exhaled deeply.

She stayed with one leg around him and one leg on the floor as he pumped in and out. It was fast, furious, intense and they both climaxed surprising quickly. When they'd finished she disengaged herself pulled her panties back into position, smoothed down her skirt, dropped a quick kiss on his nose, grinned and said 'Thanks Mister. Now you ready for some lunch?'

'Sure but what was that all about?'

'Didn't you enjoy your stand up kneetrembler?'

'Yes but ……….'

'Go on' she grinned 'stop being a flasher. Pull your trousers and pants up and let's go eat. I'm hungry!'

Downstairs in the bar she had a glass of wine and he had a beer while they ate some hotel special smoked salmon and cream cheese sandwiches.

'So what was that bonking against the wall about then?'

'You enjoyed it didn't you?'

'Yes when we'd finished I told you I had when I asked the same question. Yes I did enjoy it but what made you instigate lovemaking like that?'

With a grin she told him about Penny's description of her two stand up sexual encounters and said that it had awakened her appetite to do the same. 'After all it's a long time since I did it like that' she chuckled.

'I hope it met your expectations' he smiled in return wondering just for a brief moment with which man she'd previously done it like that but the thought was instantly forgotten as she replied.

'Oh yes it sure did thanks'.

After lunch they went back to their room where Kim laid down on the bed and dropped off almost straight away. James lay for a while admiring her beauty before he too dozed. He woke first around five o'clock and made some coffee using the small percolator in the room and when it was ready he poured two cups, added some milk from the little plastic units in the room fridge and walked over to the bed where he put the coffee on the bedside table before kissing her awake.

They lay quietly together for a while chatting and drinking the coffee until they both got up, she had a bath and after initially deciding to have a shower he changed his mind and clambered into the oversized bath tub with her. They giggled, kissed, splashed and when she saw that he'd erected she took hold of it and asked with a very cheeky expression 'And what do you want to do with this thing?'

'You got any ideas?'

'Nope' she chuckled.

'You could put those pretty lips around it?'

''Nope as that'll get my hair all wet and it won't look nice for tonight'.

'You could rest your back against the end and slide your legs around me?'

'Nope. Uncomfortable for my back'.

'You could just wank me off?'

'Nope. Far too uncouth'.

'I could lie down and you could straddle me?'

'Ah ha now *that* sounds like a plan doesn't it' she grinned as she began to massage him. 'Go on then darling get yourself in position for your lady to satisfy your obviously dirty thoughts'.

'Only mine?'

'Nope. Mine too!' and with a 'grrrrr' she pushed him backwards, reached down and holding him upright queried 'ready?'. Seeing him nod she lowered herself gently onto him and began to move, slowly at first and then alternating between slow and fast movements brought them both to a satisfying climax. Finished she clambered off and asking 'Aright?' sat back to watch his erection slowly subside.

'You know it was' he confirmed.

'Tell me then how wonderful I am at making love to you in the bath'.

'You're wonderful'.

'Tell me again'.

'You are wonderful at making love. You are wonderful as a person. You'll make a wonderful wife. You'll make our lives together wonderful. I feel enormously grateful that such a wonderful person as you has committed herself to me'.

'You like me then?' she laughed slithering down to the end of the bath and as they sat facing each other she leaned her back against the end of the bath and sat with her legs spread either side of his.

'Do you think we'll always be so much in love and have fun like we've just done?' she asked sliding first one foot onto his prick and then the other.

'I'm absolutely sure we will'.

'Do you like me doing this?' she asked as she carefully put her feet either side of his prick and began to gently rub him.

'I do rather' he grinned.

'Thought so' she chuckled seeing him beginning to erect again.

'Hey stop a moment' he said leaning forward and removing her feet. Then seeing her querying expression he went on and speaking with great sincerity said 'You know Kim no-one has ever made me as happy as you do. And I don't just mean the sex. I mean everything about you, about my feelings, my view of life .... well just everything'.

'Oh James that is such a nice thing to have said. Thank you' and she reached forward took his hand and squeezed.

They lay there for some time not speaking just happy in each other's intimate company until she said 'Hey we'd better get out or we'll our skin will get afflicted like Toad's did'.

'Pardon?' he replied with a puzzled expression on his face.

'Wind in the Willows? That lovely book by Kenneth Graham? When Toad pretended to be a washerwoman and had his hands in the washing water his skin went all wrinkly. Have you never read that book?'

'Well as a kid I did but I don't remember that'.

'Philistine!' she snapped good humouredly. 'It was my favourite book for many years and I still remember large parts of it. Any rate, time to get out' and with that she stood up and got out then on an impulse leaned over him and dropped a kiss onto his lips. 'Love you lots, and lots, and lots, and lots' then wrapping a large bath towel round herself she walked to the door into the bedroom, paused and added 'and lots' before going out of the steamy bathroom.

'Me too' he called after her as he also got out, pulled the plug and taking a towel off the heated rail, dried his hair and then wrapping it round his waist also walked into the bedroom.

She already dressed in the white lacy bra and knicks enjoyed seeing him watch her as she fitted the suspender belt around her waist, clip it together then sensuously and slowly attach the four suspender straps to the brown stockings and with each foot in turn raised ensured the stockings were pulled right up, were straight and properly positioned.

Next she settled down in front of the dressing table, waved him away when he tried to kiss her shoulder and concentrated on making up her face and brushing her hair. Finished she stood and asked him to help her into the close fitting long green dress. He did so and after carefully sliding the zip from her waist up to the top gently lifted her hair away and kissed her exposed neck.

'Thank you' she smiled as she stepped away then turning to face him pressed her left leg forward revealing to his quite unexpected delight that the dress was slit up one side from ankle almost to the waist. In fact he wondered as it was split so high if when she walked she'd expose her panties, but as she stepped across the room he realised from the clever cut of the fabric that it didn't, just showed the majority of her leg including if she strode out too much her stocking top and suspender clip. 'You like?' she queried with a coquettish expression on her face.

'Oh yes I definitely like' he muttered.

'So do I' she confirmed. 'Now let's go drink and eat'.

They did and eventually went to bed around eleven, undressed each other slowly and sensuously with him delighting in undoing the front opening bra, made love and slept deeply.

Next morning they decided to be decadent and have breakfast in bed again after which they made love, showered and mid morning they packed, he paid and then they drove happily back into London to their own apartment where she was delighted to see a large notice propped up in the kitchen saying WELCOME HOME. LOVE JAMES alongside a large bunch of assorted flowers in a vase.

'You old romantic you' she smiled as she squeezed him to her side. 'Thank you' and pulling his face to hers she gave him a soft but sensuous kiss then leaning back looked deeply into his eyes as she added 'I really do love you. More than I can ever say. Thank you for arranging that weekend away. It was a truly lovely welcome home present'.

'My pleasure and it's so nice to have you back home again safe and sound'.

'And it's nice to be back ……. safe and sound' she replied quietly remembering the assault but then instantly pushing it to the back of her mind.

They made coffee then unpacked; she put their dirty clothes into the washing machine; he made sandwiches for lunch. In the afternoon they both settled down to their respective computers. He for a quick catch-up and she to complete writing the report and recommended course of action relating to the Beta File that she'd been creating while in India. When finished she emailed it to Toby Brewer her boss and then texted Brian and thanked him for all his help, added that she hoped he'd enjoyed India and that she'd be in touch shortly regarding filming him for the programme.

Next she e-mailed Anna and said the dresses she'd chosen were divine, fitted perfectly and that she also loved the undies, as did James! Almost immediately she got a response.

> Oh good. Hope the undies did the trick!!!!!!!!!!

With a grin Kim sent a reply.

> What trick's that then? ☺

Anna responded

> As if you couldn't guess!!!!!!! Lol.

Kim replied

> Oh that trick?!? Yes it did thanks. Lots of times!! Jealous?!?

The reply soon pinged back

> You bet I am! Speak soon. Love Anna. xxx

James got a lasagne out of the freezer that he'd made while she was in India and they had that with some salad and a defrosted crusty loaf which as it had been frozen wasn't really crusty now but it sufficed.

At around ten they went to bed, told each other how much they adored one another and although James would have been happy to go straight to sleep, Kim adopting a coquettish expression said quietly 'I don't think you really want to go to sleep?' and as she spoke she kissed his chest and then moving lower kissed his belly before taking his prick in one hand and his balls in the other asked 'do you?'

'Not if there's something better on offer?'

'I think we might be able to manage that' she chuckled sliding her lips over his erection and beginning to move her mouth on him.

'Oh baby' he muttered.

Letting him slide out for a moment she began kissing his now fully prick before re-swallowing him and beginning to suck and generally use her lips, tongue and whole mouth to bring the greatest of pleasure to him that she could all the way through to him climaxing. When he had she withdrew, slithered up alongside and cuddled into him.

'How do you do that so well? I mean you're not just good at it you're outstanding' he wanted to know.

'Why thankee sirr. Glad to have been of service to your lordship' she replied in a soft West Country accent looking over at him and giving a mock salute.

'No come on. Where did you learn to do that so well? It's not the sort of thing you read about in women's magazines is it?'

'Ooh you'd be surprised what is in women's magazines these days, although not half as much as there is on-line' she chuckled. 'I had a boy friend once who simply went ape for a good blow job and as I quite liked him I was happy for him to teach me how he liked it done. In fact I think he preferred that to having penetrative sex, which was fine for him as he got his rocks off alright but it didn't do a lot for relieving my sexual needs. So we split up after a few weeks. However a combination of his coaching, plus some study of the internet, added to the fact that neither he nor you are the only ones to have benefitted from my oral skills, *and* as in most things where practice makes perfect, all those various elements have I think taught me everything I needed to know about orally satisfying a man. And now *you* are the sole beneficiary of all that learning!'

As they cuddled together and began drifting off to sleep he thought about what she'd said about a former boyfriend teaching her the skills of oral sex.

He didn't ask about it as they'd made a pact early in their relationship that although from time to time they might mention former boyfriends or girlfriends, they'd never pry; never ask each other for specific details about previous relationships; never allow it to become an issue between them. They'd agreed that they were both adult, grown up, experienced sexually, had slept with others before they met but that those former lovers were just that. *Former.* In the past. Done and finished with. Confidential. To be ignored. Definitely *not* for discussion.

CHAPTER 15

On Monday morning before the team gathered, Kim walked to Penny's office and hovered outside the open door. She was on the phone but waved Kim in and soon finished her conversation.

'I just popped in to see if everything was alright? You know with Susan?'

'Oh yes it's wonderful. You got my text didn't you?'

'Yes but I wanted to be sure that ..... well I suppose that although you said on Saturday morning in the text that she was back with you I wanted to be sure she'd stayed for the whole weekend and that things are as you hoped'.

'Oh they are indeed. Susan *did* go to that party at Christina's flat and she said she did so out of spite really as I'd forbidden her to go. She was also quite honest and told me that she *had* slept with Christina after the party but immediately regretted doing so as she realised that she didn't now have any feelings for her. So she walked out and went back to my place. She baked a cake and in the pink icing on the top had put in large white letters the word "Sorry". Look I took a picture' and taking her mobile she showed Kim the cake.

'How lovely'.

'It was. She is' smiled Penny 'and can I tell you something else?'

'Sure'.

'She's asked me to marry her'.

'Oh how wonderful. I assume you said yes?'

'You bet I have. We went straight out and bought each other engagement rings. Look' and she held out her hand so that Kim could make suitable noises of admiration. 'Still enough about my love life. We've got a programme to put together. See you in the conference room in' she paused to look at her watch 'ten minutes?'

'Great' but as Kim got to the door Penny called out.

'Thanks for being so kind that night in India'.

'Pleased to help'.

'No. Not everyone would have been so compassionate and sympathetic to a sad, miserable, crying old lesbian'.

'Maybe but then I'm not everyone am I?'

'No you're not. See you in a few minutes'.

At the meeting the whole team who'd gone to Mumbai reviewed where they were, looked at the filming that Rick had taken of their interviews with the drug trial subjects and the mobile phone footage they'd also taken. Then at ten Kim rang Toby and said they were ready to see him and bring him up to date on what they had.

He was waiting in his office along with Peter Holmes the MD and Jason Moran the Head of Programme Planning and they all listened intently as Kim assisted by Samita, Penny and Fergal explained exactly what they'd been doing, who and what they'd seen and discovered. Rick joined the meeting to review the filming that he'd shot in India and at the end of two hours Kim felt quite exhausted but as she finally stopped speaking she looked at Toby's face which radiated interest and clear pleasure in what she'd presented.

Peter though was looking blank faced and she couldn't judge whether she'd gained sufficient interest from him to approve the project to go to the stage of turning it into a programme or not. Jason though winked at her when she looked at him.

'So Peter what do you think? Will you now authorise going ahead and turning all that we have into a finished programme?' asked Toby.

'Not only do I think you should, I think you *must*. What Furrina are doing is utterly reprehensible and wholly wrong as well as undoubtedly being illegal. Can you check with the legal eagles here on that point Kim?'

'Sure'.

'Right go ahead. You have my full support for it and I think it'll make an excellent programme. Just what we want Highlight to do. Expose in a hard hitting way wrongs that need public airing. Now what about your whistleblower ...... err Brian isn't it?'

'Yes. What about him?' frowned Kim.

'Will he go through with it?'

'Yes I'm sure he will. Admittedly he was a bit of a waverer to start with but now he's come to India, seen for himself the damaged people and got fully involved with what his firm is doing then I'm certain he'll stay with us and complete the project'.

'Good as he is the real key to this' mused Peter.

'I know. I'm sure we can keep him in okay'.

'Does he want any payment?'

'No I've asked him that and he said no'.

'Check again. I always like it when whistleblowers accept a payment, even a small one, as it kind of ties them to us. Puts them under an obligation as it were'.

'Indeed but if they do it without payment then in a way they're more sincere as they are doing it because they believe in what they're doing and not just for the money. Evangelical rather than avaricious'.

'Hmm maybe. Right anyone else got any points?'

Penny asked about timing to go to air; Samita queried a couple of points; Toby made a few suggestions but after another ten minutes the meeting ended and everyone left Toby's office to go their separate ways.

'Want a sandwich?' Kim asked Penny.

'No thanks. I'm popping out for lunch'.

'Anywhere nice?'

Blushing Penny replied 'I'm meeting Susan. I don't know where we're going to eat. She's coming here to pick me up'.

'Ooh lovely. Enjoy'.

'I will' smiled Penny.

From then on over the next two weeks while the work on the Beta project became fast and furious as many hours of film were honed down into what would eventually become a comprehensive hard hitting one hour programme the next Thursday slot was occupied by another investigation from Jamie exposing illegal use of farm chemicals by some farmers. It wasn't one of the best programmes that TV-12 had run in the Highlight series but it sufficed as did the next Thursday programme dealing with unscrupulous car dealers fiddling mileage and ages of cars making out they were newer than they really were.

Although Kim watched both programmes at home and complimented Jamie the next mornings all her thoughts were focussed on Furrina and her investigation. There was so much that they had but it had to be cut so that the programme was an hour. She did e-mail Toby asking if there could be dispensation to run it for an hour and a half but that idea was firmly rejected. One hour maximum so she again began to examine everything that they had. This was *always* the difficult part. Deciding what to leave in and what to take out? And in this instance they had so much.

But this was exactly where Penny came into her own. An exceptionally experienced documentary producer with a great track record of success in the industry she was determined that this programme would be one of the best that she'd ever made if indeed not the best!

There were two main reasons for this. Firstly she felt she owed a debt of gratitude to Kim who'd been so kind and understanding to her on the night of her distress in India after the phone row with her Susan. Secondly she, like some of the senior management at TV-12, had also been worried that the Highlight hard hitting documentaries had been losing their sharp cutting edge and she was concerned that if this continued it could affect her reputation.

She could only make a programme based on what was unearthed by the journalists like Kim and Jamie as however hard she tried if the basic source material was poor, uninteresting or insufficiently hard hitting then there was only so much that she could do in her role as producer to mitigate that.

However she strongly felt that this Beta File programme could be a world beater and as such she was resolved to do the very best job on it that she could.

'You know the interviews with Brian are going to be crucial to the effectiveness of this' she said to Kim one morning.

'I know and he's coming in to the studio tomorrow. We'll have to handle him with great care as he is really frightened that somehow or other his identity will be disclosed in the programme'.

'Well he can choose. Either to be interviewed from behind so only the back of his head and shoulders are seen or he can sit sideways and we'll blank him out just leaving him in profile. Either way is effective. In fact to add impact I think we'll do both so that in the finished programme some of the time he's in back view and sometimes he's in hidden profile. That'll add a bit of interest'.

'He may want an actor to voice what he says. I've said we can do that if he wishes'.

'No problem. I suggest if we go that route we use George Dunfold. He's got a nice authoritative yet approachable voice. Sort of warm, trustworthy, kindly uncle style yet with a bit of steel in it where needed. He'll bring the gravitas that we want'.

'Yes good idea. We used him on that cruise ship programme we did recently didn't we?'

'Yes'.

That evening Kim arrived home, went for her run, showered and as she slipped on some slacks and a tee shirt James arrived, smiled, kissed her, said she smelt nice and that he was starving.

'I'm going to stir fry some chicken with noodles vegetables and prawn crackers. That be okay?'

'Sounds wonderful .... just like you'.

'Creep' she laughed sticking her tongue out at him.

'Hey you'.

'What'

'Did I ever tell you that you've got a lovely tongue?'

'No I don't think you have'.

'Well you have'.

'Now isn't that nice'.

'Umm and I think later I might find something for it to do rather than just being inside those lips of yours. Mind you .... they're pretty nice too'.

'My lovely tongue and pretty nice lips as well as the rest of me are all available to you but not tonight or for the next couple of days' and seeing his eyebrows raise she added 'monthly time'.

'Ah okay. Right Miss stop talking and start cooking. Your man is hungry!'

'Yes sir. Right away sir. Immediately sir. At once sir' and dropping a quick curtsey as well as giving a little salute she trotted away to the kitchen where soon they were seated eating the meal she'd prepared.

They talked while eating and afterwards when the dishwasher was loaded and they were relaxing together on the settee she told him that

Brian was coming in to the studio tomorrow to record his pieces for the documentary.

'Is he okay with that?'

'I hope so. He's so nervous about the whole thing that I keep having a private nightmare that he'll want to pull out, or change his mind and not want us to run the programme'.

'Isn't it too late for that?'

'Yes. It's not his issue any more. It's ours. It is a TV-12 investigation and to be brutally frank we could run it now without him'.

'Really? How?'

'Well we'd introduce it by saying that we'd been made aware of irregularities with Furrina's drug testing programme and had investigated and as a result made the programme. Obviously it will be better to have him interviewed and being an integral part of it but it's now gone so far along the road that it has taken on a life of its own. We can do the Beta File without Brian'.

'So with him or without him you've got a programme?'

'Yep we sure have' she chuckled. 'Nightcap?'

'Umm scotch please'.

She poured two, one large one for him and a small one for herself which she drank quite quickly then announced that she was going to have a hot bath and an early night.

James said he'd stay for a while and listen to some music but after he heard her leaving the bathroom and going to bed he changed his mind and was soon in bed alongside her.

'Cuddle me?' she whispered.

'Come here' and he gently pulled her into his arm and cradled her as she drifted off to sleep. He left the light on and carefully so as to not disturb her picked up his book from the bedside table and read for a while until after about half an hour and finding his eyelids getting heavy he put down the book, turned out the light and carefully disentangling himself from her sleeping body turned onto his side and went to sleep.

Next morning Kim was in the office early. She'd texted Brian as soon as she'd got up to check he was still coming and knowing his paranoia about being found out had phrased it quite innocently and related to his hobby.

> Hi Brian. Looking
> 4ward 2 seeing u
> 2day 2 continue
> our talk about the
> Plantagenet armies.
> Is 10 o'clock still ok
> 4 u? Kim.

The reply arrived as she was walking to the tube station.

> Yes. I've taken a
> days holiday so
> I'll see you then.
> Brian.

Nevertheless she was still apprehensive as to whether he would actually turn up and she was mighty relieved when the receptionist rang through to her work station.

'Kim I've got a gentleman here who said he'd rather not give his name but that you are expecting him. *Are* you expecting someone?'

'Yes I'll come down and get him. Thanks Kirstie'.

She took the stairs as her work area was on the first floor and soon she was click clacking across the marble floored reception area where a very nervous Brian was sitting in the corner with his face completely hidden behind a newspaper.

'Hello' said Kim brightly.

'Hello' replied Brian from behind the paper.

'Come along this way' and as he stood she took his arm and led him out of reception to the stairs and up to her work station. 'Right here we are' she said cheerfully as she invited him to sit in the visitors chair next to where she worked.

Although it wasn't an office it was quite a large area with a desk unit, computer, TV monitor, cupboards, shelves and two visitor chairs. 'Make yourself at home' she smiled.

'Thanks' he replied looking around with a nervous expression on his face.

'Relax you're quite safe here'.

'I hope so. You don't know Furrina. They've got eyes everywhere'.

'Not in here Brian. Now stop being so suspicious of everyone and everything'.

'Right' he nodded although his expression still looked almost terrified.

'Now look I'll talk you through what we're going to do and then we'll go to a studio and record you. It won't be live so if you make a fluff of it we can redo it. As many times as you like until both you and we are happy. Penny will be there as will Samita and possibly Fergal and probably Jason Moran will also look in. Nice guy who is Head of Programme Planning. He's important as he has to be satisfied that the programme content is going to meet his requirements. Oh and there'll be a cameraman of course to film you'.

'Will that be Rick who was with us in India?'

'No. He's a location cameraman. This'll be one of our studio guys, or girls'.

'Girls?'

'Yes women are quite capable of looking through a viewfinder, adjusting the range and depth then pressing the record button you know' chuckled Kim.

'Yes of course. Sorry. I just assumed ....'

'I know what you assumed but never assume Brian'.

'No'.

For the next quarter of an hour Kim went into detail of how the filming would be done and at Brian's instance carefully explained the techniques for hiding his identity. He looked somewhat puzzled so she rang Samita.

'Hi. Sam can you get a couple of interviews on VTR that we've done in shadow and from behind. I've got Brian here and he'd like to be quite sure of which technique we're going to use to ensure his identity is protected? Thanks'.

'VTR?' he queried looking around.

'Video Tape Recording although we don't use that now as it is all digital, but we still use the old nomenclature'.

'Oh right'.

The two of them chatted for a little while then Kim's phone rang and Samita said that she had what Kim wanted set up in viewing room 3.

'Okay we'll come now' announced Kim and she led Brian out of her work area, away from the work stations of herself and Jamie Wilson, along the corridor and into a small room which had a VACANT or IN USE sign on the door. Flipping it to IN USE she led the way inside where Samita was waiting. Very shortly Penny joined them rapidly followed by Fergal and Jason.

'Right now have a look at these sections of previous programmes where the interviewee is hidden from view. You did watch the Highlight programme on council corruption didn't you?'

'Yes'.

'Good' and with a nod at Samita she stood beside Brian as one of the screens flickered into life. He watched transfixed clearly attempting to see whether he could identify the subject being interviewed but at the end he knew that it wasn't possible. Similarly with the alternative technique the TV station used. Whether it was from behind or in shadow the subject could not be identified.

'Alright?'

'Yes I think so ...... err sorry I mean yes that's fine'.

'Good so let's go to the studio we'll be using shall we?' and with that Kim led the whole group out of the door along the corridor and into an empty studio.

Brian looked around nervously. 'This is it then?'

'Oh come on Brian relax for goodness sake. You look as though you're about to be taken to the electric chair or gas chamber. You're just going to be interviewed that's all. I'll be actually doing the interview and we're on the same side. You and TV-12. The others you spent time with in India will be here so you're among friends. You know everyone except Jason who might join us and he's very much on our side'.

'You said he was a very important man'.

'He is but that doesn't mean he's not supporting what we're doing. He is. Very strongly in fact. Ah here's Fergal now'.

The latest arrival shook a still nervous Brian's hand and watched as Kim led him across the small studio to where there was a comfortable armchair, a side table with a vase of flowers, some curtaining behind the chair to give a pleasant looking backdrop and in front a camera pointing straight at the chair.

'There is where you'll be when we film. Now you've seen some of the previous stuff we've done hiding the subject's identity'.

'Yes and I'd prefer it to be the method where I'm in shadow. From behind although the viewer can't identify the subject, someone looking really carefully and knowing the person might be able to identify them from the shape of their head or hair style'.

'Fine. In shadow it is' smiled Kim.

'Err there's one other thing' prompted Brian.

'What's that?'

'You said that you could use someone else to say what I say. An actor I think you said'.

'Yes that's done quite often. We'll record you then have what you say typed up and bring in an actor to voice it. Is that what you'd like us to do?'

'Yes. Please'.

'Done' she smiled then looking at Samita she asked 'Can you see if casting have got hold of George Dunfold yet? We need an authoritative firm male voice and he'll be perfect. Give them a ring and see if they have and if so whether he's available today if possible then Brian can see and hear it being dubbed'.

Samita left the room leaving just Penny, Fergal and Kim with Brian.

'Like some coffee?' Penny wanted to know.

'Err I don't really drink coffee. Could I have a cup of tea?'

'Sure. I don't know which is worse? The machine coffee or the tea but tea coming up' and with that she left the room, soon returning with the requested beverage. 'Here. I won't say enjoy but it is at least hot and wet' she smiled.

'Thank you' and the still petrified looking man took the proffered drink in a hand that visibly shook.

At that point the door opened and a scruffy looking young woman walked in, nodded to everyone in general and approached Penny.

'We all ready to go?'

'No not yet. Come and say hello to Brian. He's the guy you're going to be filming. Shadow technique and we'll probably dub his voice. It is very important that Brian is not recognised by anyone. *Very* important' she stressed.

'Essential' stated Brian.

'No problem. Okay give me a moment or two so I can get lighting to sort that out for me' and she strode over to the side picked up a phone, punched in some numbers, waited a few seconds and then said 'Jaygo my sweet this is Fran. I need some shadow lighting for an interview .... err like now .... yes sweetie that means right away so stop doing whatever you are doing and get your pretty little body down here and sort it. *Now!*'

She grinned at the others and said 'Won't take long to set up' then going to Brian she held out a hand and said 'we'll film you in shadow profile so no-one, not even your best girlfriend, will recognise you and if they're gonna dub your voice as well you'll be totally anonymous'.

'Thank you b..b.. but I don't have a g..g...girlfriend I'm afraid'.

'Boyfriend? If so you'll like meeting Jaygo as he leans that way'.

'No definitely not'.

'No problem then. Shall we say that your own mother won't recognise you' and with a smile she walked over to where a television camera on a swivel tripod was located.

'Come and sit down so I can have a look at you through the lens'.

'You're not filming yet?' he said with some alarm.

'No relax err Brian isn't it?' and seeing him nod an affirmative she smiled and said 'no all I'm doing is checking for range and depth'.

'Right' and he settled himself into the chair that Fran had indicated.

At that moment the studio door opened and Jason walked in. 'Hi everyone. Everything going okay?'

'Yes all fine thanks' responded Penny.

Walking over to a still nervous looking Brian he said 'So you must be Brian? Heard a lot about you. Thanks for bringing this issue to our attention'.

'Fine. I thought it should not be hidden'.

'Quite right. Okay I'll get out of your hair. Make a good one people. We need a hard hitting Highlight programme. Bye then and with that he breezed out of the studio.

'Now Brian just relax. Think of nice things. What do you do in your spare time? Are you a golfer?' asked Fran.

'No. I collect model soldiers'.

'Really' replied the camera lady managing to keep any element of surprise or amusement out of her voice. 'Sounds interesting' and while she was talking Brian saw the camera moving and heard it whirring.

'Hi Franny babe what do you want' called an effeminate male voice.

'Oh Jaygo my love this is Brian and we need to film him in shadow profile. Can you sort the lighting for me?'

'Sure' and approaching Brian he held out a limp hand and said 'Hi there. Shame you want to be hidden good looking chap like you. Still won't take more than a couple of strokes of a lamb's dick and we'll have you hidden away' and with a little toss of the head he busied himself with lighting arrangements until looking at Fran he said 'have a look at that. Alright?'

'Perfect sweetie. Thanks'.

'Pleasure. Bye Brian. Lovely to have met you' and with that he minced out of the small studio.

CHAPTER 16

'Right Brian' called Fran as soon as Jaygo had gone. 'Sit up and say something'.

'What shall I say?'

'Anything you like. Tell me about where you live, where you go for holidays, what you like to eat. Anything. I just want to get the sound levels right and test Jaygo's shadow lighting'.

So Brian hesitantly at first and then more fluently started to talk until Fran said he could stop.

'Okay I'll play that back so you can see how you look, or rather see how you don't look, and hear how you sound' and after fiddling with a few machines and switches a large TV screen to the side of the studio flicked into life and Brian stared at his blacked out self. He peered intently but was satisfied that no-one could identify who he was from what was on the screen.

'That's fine' he said with much relief in his voice. 'Isn't it' he asked looking at Kim and Penny who'd also come over to watch the screen.

'Yes' they both confirmed.

'Good. Jaygo might be a rather overtly over the top gay chap but he does know his lighting effects' chuckled Fran.

'The only thing is that I'm worried that my voice will be recognised' was Brian's next point.

'It's not going to be a problem' soothed Penny. 'We're voicing it over for you'.

'How will that be done?'

'Kim will interview you and you'll answer the questions. That'll all be for real but afterwards we'll type up what you've said and get an actor to speak your words. So when the programme goes out the viewer will see and hear our intrepid Kim asking the questions, and see you in shadow with an actor's voice responding but using the exact same words that you've used. So it will be your responses and comments but spoken by someone else'.

'Right'.

'Now these are the first questions I'm going to ask you' stated Kim and she asked and he answered initially hesitantly and then more fluently as he relaxed and for a moment forgot where he was. 'Good' she smiled. Now most of the rest of the questions I won't pre-brief you about so we get an instinctive reaction not a thought out answer. That will add authenticity to the whole interview even though when it goes out your words will be spoken by an actor'.

'Now remember commented Penny 'answer openly and above all honestly. That is *essential*. Okay? Don't make anything up. Stick to the facts and what you know to be true'.

'Understood' and an expression of nervousness once again came onto his face.

'So ready to go for it?'

'Yes' he said more confidently than he felt as in reality his heart was thumping and his hands felt clammy and he knew that his armpits were wet with sweat and he could feel sweat on the back of his shirt.

'Okay good' smiled Penny. 'So Kim you go and get yourself tarted up ready for the camera. I'll look after Brian and we'll go for a shoot at ………' she looked at her watch and the big clock on the studio wall and then at Fran 'ten forty five?'

'Yeah fine' replied the camerawoman. 'That'll give me time to go and have a wee and a ciggie' and with that she nodded at Brian then walked out of the studio during the process of which Brian's eyes fixed on her taut bottom in the close fitting jeans she wore.

Noticing where Brian was looking Kim went and stood in front of him, smiled and said 'Won't be long Brian. Make yourself comfortable and try and relax. I'll be back soon'.

'Right' he gulped.

'Would you like some more tea?' Penny wanted to know.

'Thank you' and when it arrived he sat looking around him at all the paraphernalia of a TV studio.

When she returned now wearing a just above the knee dark grey dress, with her hair beautifully styled on top of her head which was something that Brian had not seen before as previously she'd either worn it down and loose, or in a pony tail. He thought she looked lovely and said so.

'Thank you. Girl has got look her best on camera. Is Fran back yet?' she asked aloud of no-one in particular.

'Yeah right here behind you with Jaygo' said the woman in question who'd followed Kim into the studio.

'So Brian take your seat' instructed Penny and he did so.

There was the sound of several switches being clicked and bright lights filled the interview area, then Jaygo clicked some more and although Kim was fully illuminated, Brian was plunged into darkness.

'Want me to stay?' queried the lighting man.

'No sweetie that'll do just fine' announced Franny. 'If we get a problem we'll shout for you'.

'Right love' then turning to Brian he said 'bye. It's been *lovely* to meet you' and left the room.

Brian licked his lips nervously and took a small sip from the glass of water that had been put on the small table beside his chair by Penny who then moved to the side of the studio and sat down in front of an array of screens and monitors then said 'Sound check please'.

'Hello I'm Kim Harding and for tonight's Highlight programme we're investigating the pharmaceutical industry ....'

'Fine' said Penny looking at the screens and monitors. 'You now Brian please?'

'Err what shall I say?'

'Anything that comes to mind. Tell us how you're feeling?'

'Oh right. Well actually I feel a bit nervous. In fact to be honest I feel *really* nervous. I am definitely going to be in shadow aren't I? No-one will be able to identify me will they?'

'That's lovely thanks and to answer your question .... no. No-one will be able to identify you' then after a glance around the studio she said 'so everyone here we go. Five, four, three, two, one .... go Kim'.

A bright light flicked onto Kim's face as she smiled directly at the camera and began to read from the autocue.

'Good evening and welcome once again to another edition of Highlight, the programme that fearlessly investigates wrongs and issues that need to be brought out into the open. Issues that companies especially big corporations are trying to hide from us the public, from their shareholders and in many cases from their own employees.

Tonight's programme is typical of that and involves the pharmaceutical industry. Specifically a large British company called Furrina Pharmaceuticals.

Furrina operates in many countries of the world and is one of the major players in the cut throat drug industry developing, manufacturing, marketing and selling products that can bring relief or help cure countless illnesses, ailments and serious conditions. That is all good and Furrina like many other companies in this industry is constantly seeking to develop new drugs to tackle a wide range of illnesses.

That process is long, often tortuous, expensive and time consuming and an important, indeed vital part of the development process is to *test* new drugs that are being developed on animals.

Now tonight we are *not* attempting to challenge or question whether the use of animals in laboratory testing of drug development is right or wrong. No. We accept that it happens and in this regard Furrina is no different from many other pharmaceutical companies. They use animals to evaluate and test for any possible side effects from the use of a new drug before it is prescribed for use on humans. Mice, rats, rabbits, dogs and monkeys are generally the animals dosed with a new drug. Sometimes just one of those species and sometimes more than one. Rarely are all species used.

The effect the drug has on them is carefully noted to determine whether there is any ill effect as well as eventually trying to see whether the drug cures whatever illness it has been designed to do. But often the testing is simply to establish the *safety* of the drug. After successful animal tests then the company will be granted a licence to use it in carefully structured and very vigilantly conducted tests on human volunteers. Provided those tests are successful then the drug company will apply for a licence to sell the drug to the medical profession for its general prescription.

If any side effects are observed during the animal testing process, it will be thoroughly investigated, analysis undertaken to find out why these side effects have occurred and once that information is to hand modifications will be made to the drug to enable more tests to be conducted. At every stage of the test process there is check and counter check. Evaluation and re-evaluation. Nothing is skimped or rushed. Nothing is overlooked.

The Beta File

That is why drug development is so expensive. It is the time taken from initial concept to final mass production involving thousands and thousands of hours of detailed work, the most rigorous evaluations, the ultimate safety test programme.

The rewards for those drug companies in the pharmaceutical industry are immense and that is why so many companies in this field around the world are chasing the golden opportunities to develop and then sell drugs to cure the illnesses from which we humans suffer such as cancer in its many forms, dementia, arthritis and many more.

But sometimes something goes wrong. Sometimes in spite of all the care that is taken during the animal testing process a problem can manifest itself when it gets to the human trials stage.

Those people who agree to become test subjects for drugs do so with their eyes wide open knowing the risks that they run. So why do they do it? The answer usually is for money. But not a lot of money. In western countries such as the UK, America, Europe it is often university students who subject themselves to this risk in order to earn a little additional money to supplement their way through college or university.

They of course do so knowing that the most rigorous pre human testing on animals has been done and that the test programme to which they are submitting themselves is as safe as it can be. Of course they sign disclaimers absolving the drug companies of any subsequent liability if something goes wrong. And of course sadly sometimes it does go wrong.

When that happens then normally the drug company involved will immediately stop the test, give whatever medical assistance is needed to help the affected subject recover and regain full health and subsequently monitor the subject over a long period of time.

But we have discovered that Furrina Pharmaceutical has been running a drug test programme on a new drug they have in development called' ………. she paused and looked at a file of papers 'Betanapotraproxiflevien-g3. As that is such a mouthful we are going to shorten its name and simply call it Beta. It is designed to treat stomach cancer but it has resulted in some serious side effects in the human guinea pigs involved in the trials. *Very serious side effects.* And what is worse, far from stopping the test they have continued it, resulting in more test volunteers being affected. Furthermore side effects were discovered during the animal testing programme which

Furrina ignored and blindly careered on with more animal tests taking no notice of these side effects in their laboratory animals.

They moved from one species to another until they found one group of animals which didn't exhibit side effects and then they used that, ignoring and indeed hiding the previous adverse results and effects in their documentary submissions to the appropriate authorities in order to get a licence to move to human testing.

That is, at best wholly unethical .... at worst downright criminal.

You may wonder how we at Highlight know about this? Well the answer is that one employee from Furrina is so concerned about this blatant abuse of trust that he has approached us and given us all the data showing exactly what Furrina has been up to.

We have seen that data and had it thoroughly examined by independent experts who all agree that what Furrina are doing is not only truly dreadful but as I said a few moments ago .... almost certainly illegal.

And tonight we are now going to show *you* that data. That evidence. That truly dreadful situation.

To add to Furrina's duplicity they have conducted the trials in India. Not here in the UK but in a third world country where people are available freely and cheaply. We have been to India where the trials are being carried out. We've seen, met and interviewed many of those guinea pigs. People whose lives have been ruined by Furrina. Poor people who in return for a *tiny* amount of money have been bought off from taking Furrina to court or seeking any other form of redress.

That is what tonight's Highlight programme is about. You will be shocked, concerned, amazed and indeed horrified that one company .... a British company at that, can conduct itself in such a despicable way'.

She paused looked intently at the camera for about ten seconds and then relaxed and looked over to Penny and asked 'How was that?'

'Fine'.

'Really?'

'Yes'.

'So we're ready to record Brian then?'

'Uh huh. Fran you ready?'

'Yep. Whenever you are'.

The Beta File

'Okay so Brian here's your big opportunity then to spill the beans in your own words in response to Kim's questions' stated Penny.

'Right' he replied visibly gulping. 'That was an awfully long introduction but I suppose in an hour's programme that doesn't matter?'

'No it doesn't' responded Kim 'but remember that when the programme goes out it won't just be showing the camera pointing at me. We'll cut in shots of India, Furrina's offices and labs, assorted pictures of pills, syringes, people in white coats working in laboratories and cute shots of rats, mice, dogs, rabbits and monkeys. There's plenty in film libraries that we can use. My voice will be continuing in the background of course'.

'I see. Thank you'.

'Two secs' called Fran as she clicked a couple of switches thus using the shadow lighting set up that Jaygo had organised and Brian was instantly in shadow.

Kim swung round and looked at him and smiled as Penny said 'Okay going after three .... one, two three go Kim'.

'I am now going to talk to the man who has brought this abhorrent situation regarding Furrina's drug trials to Highlight's attention. To protect his identity we've hidden his face, changed his name and his words will be spoken by an actor'. Turning away from the camera she looked towards Brian.

'When did you first discover that something was wrong with the drug trials for this new drug?'

'Err ....' he paused and cleared his throat 'umm it was about eighteen months ago'.

'And how did you discover that?'

'I was working on its development and involved with the animal trials'.

'Can you tell us what happened with those animal trials?'

'Yes'.

Hesitantly at first and then more confidently Brian explained about the problems that emerged in mice, rats, dogs but not in monkeys. As Kim probed and questioned him in greater detail he became more fluent and answered her well thought out probing queries well and gradually forgot where he was, the camera, the lighting and focussed on Kim and her questions.

Eventually after about an hour Kim sat back, studied her clip board of notes and relaxed as she asked him 'Anything else? Have we missed anything of importance?'

'No. Is that it?'

'For now yes'.

'So what happens next?'

'Now we'll spend the next few days, editing what you and I have said, splicing in the film that Rick shot of our interviews with those poor guinea pigs in India, as well as the shots of Furrina's factories and office buildings in the UK and India . We'll also include shots of some of their key people. Specifically, err' she paused and looked down at her notes 'Marylyn Goodrich the Chief Executive, Louis Farmer who you said was Head of Drug Development and John Andrews the In Market Drug Test Controller. To my mind they are the key people but I think we also need to get a shot of Chandra Singh the head of Furrina's Indian business. I expect there's one on their website.

Then we need to edit down my questions and your answers before dubbing an actor's voice onto what you've said. Finally we'll add some standard shots of pills, potions, tablets and so on, put it all together, tear our hair out as it'll be too long, agonise over what to cut out and what to leave in so we get it down to a total running length of fifty two and a half minutes'.

'I thought it was an hour's programme?'

'It is altogether, but we need one minute for the standard Highlight introductory sequence, two commercial breaks for adverts of three minutes each and thirty seconds for the end closing Highlight sequence'.

'Crikey I didn't realise how tightly controlled it was, down to the second!'

'That's television' said Penny who'd joined the conversation. 'Well done Brian. You did well'.

'Did I?'

'Yes you did' confirmed Kim.

'Do you need me anymore?' called Fran.

'No that's it for now. Thanks'.

'I'll be off then' she said and after powering down her camera and switching off the lighting she nodded to everyone present and left the studio.

As she did so a phone to the side of the studio rang and Fergal who'd remained silent throughout the whole session answered it, listened and said 'Hold on a sec' then looking at Kim called across 'casting have got an actor who's available today. He could be here in an hour or so'.

'Who is he?'

Fergal asked the question then called out 'Walter Mitchell'.

'Is George Dunfold not available?'

'No apparently he's in Germany so they've suggested this Walter chap. They say we've used him before'.

'We have' agreed Penny. 'He did the voice over on our programme a few months ago on how some budget airlines are skimping or taking short cuts on aircraft maintenance to save money. Odd little chap but with a really interesting voice. Yes I think he'll be fine as he'll come across as authoritative and sound as though he knows what he's talking about. Tell them to book him and get him here as soon as'.

Fergal did so then asked 'He'll be here by one. Now do you need me anymore Kim?'

'No thanks' and hearing that he left the studio.

'Err what now then?' queried Brian.

'Would you like to stay until Walter arrives then you can watch as he reads through his lines ...... in other words what you said and watch him speak those words as we dub him onto your shadow'.

'Ooh yes please'.

'Well you can either sit somewhere and wait until Walter arrives or if you've other things to do you can leave the building and come back for one by which time we'll have typed up what you said ready for Walter Mitchell to speak in place of your voice'.

'Shall I do that then? Leave and come back?'

'Up to you'.

'Yes alright that's what I'll do'.

While he was away Kim went to Toby and updated him on where the team had got to and what remained to be done.

'What about confronting Furrina? When do you plan to do that?'

'Not sure. I'm still thinking about that'.

'We need them on the programme either face to face or on film. It will fall rather flat as a hard hitting programme if we haven't got their reaction and comments'.

'Ye-es I know. As long as we can protect Brian's identity'.

'For sure. What I think we should do is wait until we've got all that you're presently working on to a more finished state, edited and so on then we'll beard the lion in his den, or lab' he chuckled. 'Are you okay to do that or do you want some help?'

'No I'll be fine. I'm a big girl now Daddy' she grinned.

'Hmm. And an impertinent one too' he laughed quietly.

When Brian arrived back Walter Mitchell had already read through the typed up script that he was to voice. He'd read it carefully and had asked to watch Brian actually speaking some of the words on the film taken earlier. He stared intently at the silhouetted figure on film answering Kim's questions and when it had been run through completely he asked to re-watch some parts, then looking at Kim he'd said 'Fine. All straight forward. Ready to go when you are'.

'Right. George this is Brian whose voice you're dubbing'.

The two men shook hands as Kim made some phone calls shortly after which a sound recordist arrived and as Brian's silhouette began to run on the screen Walter spoke Brian's answers.

It didn't take long and when it was done the actor waited while the TV-12 team involved with this part of the recording did a final run through and review of what and how he'd said Brian's words, nodded when Kim approached him, told him that was fine and if they needed him again for any additional recording they'd be in touch.

When it was all over, as he made his way back home Brian felt a mixture of emotions. Pleased that it had all gone well but in a way disappointed although at the same time relieved that his part was now done, coupled with an overall sense of concern that what he had set in motion had acquired a momentum of its own and was now wholly outside of his control.

Kim was busy tidying up some loose ends of paperwork for the rest of the day then when back at her flat she was soon changed and pounding the pavements during which she mentally reviewed what had been achieved so far. The more she thought about it she was more convinced than ever that this would be a stunningly powerful programme.

CHAPTER 17

'**K**im can you and whoever you want to bring with you pop along to my office. I want to discuss how you're going to approach Furrina' said Toby next morning when she'd picked up the phone.

'Sure. Now?'

'Say in five?'

'Okay'.

She spent the time assembling the notes she'd already made about this matter. It would be a tricky interview. She knew that. The key point was to give Furrina sufficient time prior to going on air in order to be seen as fair, yet not allowing them too much so they could not only complete the investigation and witch hunt that would inevitably be undertaken once they knew TV-12 were looking into the Beta issue but crucially take legal action to try and stop the programme being aired.

If the programme was going out on Thursday then twenty four hours notice to the drug company ought to be sufficient she thought but she'd be guided by Toby's view.

Of course the shorter the time the more pressure on her and the television company as well as they'd have less time to deal with and respond to whatever reaction came from Furrina.

Once settled into Toby's office she opened the discussion. 'Right in my view we need to give them no more than twenty four hours before we go on air. That should be more than sufficient for a mighty corporation like Furrina to get themselves organised with a response'.

'Plenty of time for them to get an injunction too! Have you spoken to our legal eagles upstairs?'

'Not yet. I wondered if you'd like to do that?'

'Okay let's go brief the lawyer man' and picking up the phone he punched in some numbers, waited a short while then said 'Tanya this is Toby. I need to talk to Levi right now please'. He waited until he was connected and then said brightly 'Levi we may have an injunction whistling our way shortly preventing us from broadcasting Thursday's edition of Highlight'. There was a pause then he said 'Okay thanks. Kim Harding and I are on our way up. See you in a moment'.

Putting the phone down he grinned at Kim and said 'Right let's go brief the lawyer man'.

They travelled up two floors, walked along a thickly carpeted corridor until they came to a small open space area where two secretaries were sitting at desks. As they approached one stood, smiled at them and walked to a glass panelled door, knocked, opened it and putting her head around the door said 'Kim and Toby are here', and hearing the man beyond telling her to send them in she opened the door wide, stood aside and beckoned Toby and Kim forward, waited until they'd gone in then closed the door behind them.

Levi Edelman was a tall, well built, good looking lawyer in his mid forties, smartly dressed in a black pin striped suit, white shirt, pale yellow tie and highly polished black leather shoes. Known as a toughie in the legal profession he had frequently prevented TV-12 from getting into trouble, as well as on many occasions got them out of difficulties that they'd got themselves into.

Easing himself out of his chair from behind his large wooden desk and indicating some easy chairs, settee and coffee table to the side of his large office as all three made their way to where he'd suggested he asked with a smile 'So who have you been stirring up then?'

'Well no-one yet but we're about to light a bombshell under most of the senior management of Furrina Pharmaceuticals' replied Toby.

'Why?' and as he asked the question his pale grey eyes fixed onto Toby's face.

'We have evidence that they are falsifying results of drug trial tests'.

'To what end?'

'So that they can shortcut the process of getting licence approval to launch this new drug'.

'And what does your evidence tell you then about this drug?'

'That it is causing side effects in some ……. several, of the human guinea pigs involved in the drug trial'.

'Tell me more'.

'I'd like to ask Kim to do that. This is her story. She was approached by a whistleblower, met him, decided that it was worth following up, did so and now has a programme almost ready to go on air'.

'So tell me' said Levi switching his intense gaze to look at Kim 'everything. Leave nothing out. Not even one microscopic point. Don't filter your information and what you know. I'll be the judge of what is relevant and what is not. I want to know *everything* that you know' and putting his fingers together in a pyramid shape he stared at her.

'Right' and she spent the next fifteen minutes detailing all that she had learnt and now knew about Furrina's Beta drug trial.

Levi listened carefully, asked an occasional question, made some notes on a lined pad as she was talking, nodded from time to time and when she came to the end of her explanation looked at her and asked 'Anything else?'

'No I think I've told you everything'.

'Good. That is important because if there is anything, however small, that you've missed it could weaken our case to fight this injunction if and when it lands on our collective desks.

Now then. If you receive anything from Furrina or their lawyers do not, repeat *not* respond or answer it in any way. Do not even acknowledge it. Bring it to me immediately. Clear?'

'Yes quite clear'.

'Good. Now from what you've told me this sounds pretty serious and so I am certain that they *will* try and stop us broadcasting'. Standing up he walked to the door, opened it, peered out and said 'Tanya. Can you kindly get me Golda Lowenthal on the phone please and when you have put her through to me'. Walking back he sat down in one of the armchairs and said 'Golda's good. Expensive but in fighting injunctions she's the best I've come across. So this Brian chap just rang you out of the blue did he Kim?'

'Yes. One day here at the office around lunchtime'.

'What's he like? Do you trust what he's told you?'

'Yes I do'.

'And what you found in India seems to entirely back up his claims and statements?'

'Indeed it did'.

'Good. So it would seem you could have a very strong programme provided our wonderful legal system allows you to put it out to the great

British public'. He paused as his phone rang. 'Ah now that'll be Golda hopefully'. Striding across his office he reached for the phone and said 'Yes?' listened and then continued 'fine so ask her to be good enough to come here for four o'clock then please'.

Looking over to where Toby and Kim were still sitting he smiled 'Right as you heard she'll be here at four. Please make yourselves available to join us then. Anything else at the moment?'

'No' said Toby getting up quickly followed by Kim. 'We'll come back then'.

'Yes do' and moving to again sit behind his desk he nodded and picked up a file of papers.

Toby and Kim left his office, smiled at Tanya and walked towards the lifts where Toby said 'Come on we'll walk down. The exercise will do me good'.

At four o'clock they were with Levi again and also Golda whom they were meeting for the first time. She was quite the opposite of Levi being of medium height, slim, grey haired, around fifty years of age, wearing an elegant trouser suit that fitted perfectly and was of such a dark blue shade it could almost have been black.

'So who's going to try and screw you over then?' she asked Levi.

If Kim was surprised at Golda's language she didn't show it and unsure whether it should be her that answered, she was about to mention Furrina when Levi did so and in a few minutes he'd outlined in an extremely concise way a summary of what it was that TV-12 had discovered through the help of Brian.

'Interesting. This sounds as though it is one of those issues that goes to the very heart of journalistic freedom and *that* is what we have to protect at all costs for the integrity of broadcast journalism in general, TV-12 in particular, and especially the poor souls apparently damaged by this drug.

Your programme hopefully can help them and so we will fight any injunction that this Furrina outfit might whack onto you. And if they do we'll take it and shove it so far up their fat pharmaceutical backsides that it'll be lost forever'. Then she gave a grin and added 'Well that's the theory anyway. It'll all depend on the judge I guess. Right err Kim isn't it?' she asked switching her gaze.

Mike Upton

'Yes'.

'Well now Kim talk me through all that you've found, all that you've learnt and all that you've filmed. How was India by the way? Any problems out there?'

'Err……… no. No problems at all. All quite straightforward. Concerning and worrying as to what Furrina are doing but clear-cut' and once again Kim hid from a third party the terror of being nearly raped.

'Good only it can be difficult for women out there. Now talk me through it all' and she fixed Kim with a steely glance and listened without interruption as the whole story was outlined in detail'.

'Thank you. Now I have four questions' and she fired them at Kim who answered each in detail. Golda sat quite still after Kim finished speaking looking intently at her. 'If we go to court as I think we undoubtedly will, I need to know with *absolute* certainty that you have told me *everything* and kept *nothing* back. Not even a tiny thing. Cases such as we will be fighting have been lost or won, on the tiniest detail and I do not intend to lose this case if we have to fight it. Do you understand?'

'Yes' nodded Kim definitely overawed by this powerful lawyer 'I've told you everything'.

'That is vital. And as the Germans say 'Alles ist klar?' she paused then seeing Kim nodding questioned 'understand?'

'Yes. You asked all is clear?'

'Sehr gut (Very good). Now when are you going to give them the first kick in their collective goolies?'

'Umm'.

'When are you going to tell them what you've got and what you intend to do with it?'

'I thought I'd give them twenty four hours notice'.

'Hmm. My advice would be to make it a little longer. Forty eight. Shows we're reasonable not bouncing them with a possible programme the next day. So if you're going on air on Thursday evening I'd contact them tomorrow morning. Tuesday'.

'Fine. Will do'.

'Then we'll wait and see if these slimy drug rats try and stop us. Any injunction will almost certainly arrive later that day. Possibly Wednesday morning but most likely tomorrow. The process then will be that we'll appeal against the injunction. Assuming we succeed then no doubt they'll appeal against that and if they win then we'll in turn then re-appeal' She smiled 'It's all about appeal and counter appeal'. We should get it all resolved in time for you to go on air Thursday evening'.

'What do you think our chances of defeating any injunction?' Toby wanted to know.

'Well' mused Golda 'the law can be tricky. That's why there are so many highly paid lawyers like me in it' and she gave a quick grin. 'However with the evidence you have collected and provided it's true then I see no way they can stop us going to air. They'll scream confidentiality, commercial secrets, integrity and a whole lot of other bullshit to try and stop the programme being seen, but I would put our chances at better than eighty percent'.

'Yes I agree' nodded Levi.

'Right so we wait to see what happens after you've fired the first missile into their balls' grinned Golda.

'The boss of Furrina is a woman' grinned Kim.

'Hmm. More fool her' grunted Golda. 'Call me when the injunction arrives' she said looking at Levi. He agreed he would and as the meeting was ended he led her out of his office to the lifts, waited until one came, shook hands and once the lift had taken her down returned to his office.

'She has an interesting turn of phrase doesn't she' grinned Toby.

'Indeed. Today she was quite mild! Wait till she gets upset! Then she can become really very ……. err shall we say ……… colourful? Okay well I think we're finished here for now but keep me instantly in touch. Tanya will give you my mobile number Toby. Call me anytime tonight if something kicks off and I've left the office'.

Back on their floor of the building Toby smiled at Kim and said 'Good luck. Keep me posted'.

'Will do'.

First thing Tuesday morning Kim having composed her thoughts picked up the phone, dialled and leant back listening to it ring.

'Furrina Pharmaceuticals. Michelle speaking. Can I help you?'

'Hello. This is Kim Harding from TV-12 television. May I speak with Marylyn Goodrich please' Kim said in a firm but non threatening voice

Mike Upton

to the Furrina switchboard operator. She was asked to hold on and shortly a female voice came on the line.

'Can I help you? I am Miss Goodrich's PA?'

'Hello there' Kim responded in a soft voice. 'I am Kim Harding chief investigator and primary presenter at TV-12 for our current affairs programme Highlight. We are making a episode about some drug trials that your company is running and I have a number of questions which I'd like to put to Miss Goodrich'.

'One moment please' and there was silence for a couple of minutes before the PA came back on the line. 'I am sorry but Miss Goodrich doesn't give telephone interviews about such matters and she suggests that if you have any questions you contact our Public Relations company who she is sure will be able to help you. I'll give you their name and phone number shall I?'

'Thank you but it is Miss Goodrich I really need to speak to'.

'And I have explained that won't be possible'.

'What about Louis Farmer and John Andrews? Can I talk to them please?'

'One moment' and once again the line went dead until this unknown PA came back on the line and advised that it simply wouldn't be possible for Kim to speak to either of the two men.

Realising that the PA was only carrying out her instructions Kim knew that there was no point in getting cross with her and in fact getting upset, angry or difficult would only hinder her potential ability to speak with the Chief Executive or The Head of Drug Development.

'Maybe I could send an e-mail to Miss Goodrich or Mister Farmer?'

'Send it to me and I'll ensure that they see it' was the only slightly positive response.

E-mail details were exchanged with the PA who Kim now knew was called Jules and she said she'd send an e-mail and that was the end of the telephone conversation.

Thinking carefully about exactly what to say she needed to warn Furrina what TV-12 were about to do but to ensure a balance to the programme had to give them some time to respond but not too much. They had the right to reply but the television team were anxious that the time pressure landed on Furrina straight away as they scrambled around to assemble a credible reply to the television company's probe.

After much thought she typed, spell checked, paused to double check it then satisfied pressed the "send" button. Sitting back she looked at what she'd sent.

From: kim.harding-TV-12@btinternet.co.uk
To: jules.oates@furrinapharma.com
Subject: Betanapotraproxiflevien-g3 Drug Trials, India

I am anxious to speak with Miss Marylyn Goodrich and Louis Farmer regarding the trials which Furrina Pharmaceuticals are running in Mumbai on the above new drug.

We have been made aware that significant adverse effects have developed in many of the human subjects taking part in these trials which we have investigated.

We propose to go to air with the results of our investigation in a programme this Thursday evening but before doing so we would appreciate the opportunity to question the above two senior executives of Furrina Pharmaceuticals to enable the company to put its point of view forward and rebuff any suggestions of wrong doing, as well as ensuring a fair and balanced programme.

I look forward to hearing when it will be convenient for me to interview Miss Goodrich and Mr Farmer which can either be here at our London studios, at a Furrina Pharmaceutical office, factory, laboratory - or any other location of the company's choosing.

Kim Harding
Chief Investigator – Highlight – TV12.

'So' she mused aloud 'I wonder how long it'll take for the shit to hit the fan at Furrina?'

The answer was not long!

In less than a quarter of an hour Kim got a phone call from Jules who asked at what time it would be convenient for Marylyn to call her to discuss the outrageous comments Kim had made in her e-mail?

Again recognising that Jules was only doing her job she said she was available at any time. There was a short pause and then Jules said nine thirty then?'

'Fine. I'll await the call'.

At exactly that time Jules rang, checked that she was speaking with Kim and said she'd put her through to Marylyn.

'Is that Kim Harding?' snapped a strident female voice.

'Speaking' she replied motioning for Samita to pick up an extension earpiece.

'Right. Now Miss Harding I don't know what you think you're playing at with these ridiculous accusations of problems with one of our drug trials but I must warn you that making allegations of that sort is a very serious matter and we will not hesitate to go to law not only to prevent you from broadcasting such spurious statements, but we'll also sue you through every court in the land or on the planet if you do. Do I make myself clear?'

'As crystal but before you continue I must tell you that from now on every word of this conversation is being recorded and may be used in our programme' and she pressed the phone record button.

'Record what the hell you like. You won't be using it as you won't be broadcasting anything. Our lawyers will see to that!'

'Miss Goodrich. Are you denying that your company Furrina Pharmaceuticals is involved with trialling a new drug called Betanapotraproxiflevien-g3?'

'I neither deny nor confirm any such thing. What we do is nothing to do with you' she retorted.

'We have evidence that you are doing just that'.

'How? How do you have evidence?'

'We have copies of the documents that you made people in India sign when they agreed to take part in such trials which clearly show the name of that drug, the names of the various human guinea pigs who signed although most did not understand what they were signing as most of them can't read or write English. We also have copies of the statements you made those people who were damaged in the trials sign together with details of the derisory amounts of money you paid the off with'.

'I find it extremely surprising you saying that you have copies of any such documents'.

'Oh but we do. You see we have had a team of people in Mumbai tracking down, finding, meeting, talking to and filming those poor people who have been so badly damaged by your new drug'.

'You've been to India?' and there was a sound of incredulity in Marylyn's voice.

'We have. We've got people who took part in your trial *on film*, have sworn statements from them, have seen and spoken to them for ourselves. You are seriously damaging people's health with the trials of this new drug. You are not just playing with people's lives, you are *ruining* them. Indeed you may be *taking* people's lives if some of the test subjects die as a result of your drug trial'.

There was no response so she asked if Marylyn was still there and received a tetchy 'Yes wait a minute!'

Kim was sure she could hear whispering at the other end of the line and guessed that Marylyn had people with her. Lawyers probably as well as perhaps Louis Farmer their Head of Drug Development.

'Look it may be that we have some trials going on in India' replied Marylyn in a different and more conciliatory tone of voice 'but for reasons of commercial confidentiality I cannot confirm or deny that, nor can I say what any such trials were about, or on which product, or for how long they have been continuing. Neither can I comment on any effects that any such trials might have created in any human subjects who may have of their own free will, with their eyes wide open and fully cognisant of any risks that they might have been running *volunteered* to take part in any such trials'.

'Ah so Furrina *were* running risks were they?'

'I didn't say that. I said .... look why don't we meet for a properly structured discussion'.

'I'd be happy to do that. Indeed Miss Goodrich that is what I suggested in my e-mail to you'.

'I know. Yes alright. Today at one o'clock here at our head office in Milton Keynes? I can free up a slot in my diary at that time and we'll deal with these ridiculous allegations once and for all. Now is that time suitable for you?'

'Perfectly thank you. I will have a colleague with me and probably a cameraman. I trust that is acceptable to you?'

'We'll see. You may bring them with you but I don't guarantee to allow them to be part of the meeting as well as yourself. However there will undoubtedly be others from this company present at the meeting'.

'As you wish'.

'Goodbye'.

'Goodbye Miss Harding'.

Kim replaced the phone then looked at Samita who said 'Gosh what a nasty lady!'

'Sounds like it doesn't she' then picking up the phone again she rang Toby. 'Hi. I've got an interview with the big bad wolf lady this afternoon. I'll take Rick to do the filming but I can't decide whether to take Samita or Fergal with me. Who would you suggest?'

'Definitely Fergal'.

'Why?'

'Because I think you might be better to have a man with you as back up'.

'Hey she may be a thoroughly unpleasant bitch and a real tartar in Furrina but she isn't going to hurt me is she?'

'Not physically, and I'm sorry if this sounds sexist, but you are a slim attractive woman and Samita is a *very* petite young lady. However Fergal looks exactly what he is. A second row forward rugby player and therefore a big guy. Physically impressive and so I feel that psychologically it would be good to have him with you in the devil's lair'.

'Yes okay you are probably right. Big Fergal it is then'.

CHAPTER 18

The three people from TV-12 arrived at Furrina's head office at just before one, parked in a visitor's space and got out of the car. While Fergal stretched his legs and Kim smoothed down her skirt Rick switched on the camera, hefted it onto his shoulder and filmed the front of the building.

'I'll film you from behind as you walk in to reception' he announced after a minute or so. 'Show the intrepid TV reported going into battle'.

'Fine'.

'Also as you've got a really cute bum seeing that will keep our male audience interested. So give a bit of a wiggle as you walk' he laughed.

Kim twisted and stuck her tongue out at him then conscious that Rick was not only filming the company's offices but also her bottom she began walking towards the impressive glass and stainless steel entrance with Fergal to one side and Rick following. Arriving at the swing doors, Rick continued to film as they walked through but stopped immediately they were inside and lowered the TV camera to hold it dangling from his right hand as Kim and Fergal approached the reception desk where she introduced herself and said she had an appointment with Marylyn Goodrich.

'Oh yes Miss Harding. You are expected. I'll let Marylyn's pa know you're here' and picking up a small neat white phone she punched in four numbers, waited and then said that the TV-12 team were in reception, listened, nodded, said 'Three visitors' listened again then said 'of course' and put the phone down.

'Jules will be down directly to collect you' she said. 'In the meantime please wear these visitor's badges if you would.

It wasn't long before one of the three lift doors opened and a smartly dressed woman in her forties stepped out and walked towards the TV-12 team, smiled and said warmly 'Hello there I'm Jules. We spoke on the phone earlier Miss Harding. Please come this way' and gesturing towards the lifts she started back across the large foyer.

'Thanks but do call me Kim' she replied as she, Fergal and Rick followed Jules to the lift, small talked as it rapidly rose to the seventh floor and then trailed behind the fast walking PA along a wood panelled corridor until she stopped outside a room marked CONFERENCE ROOM 1.

Inside was a large highly polished wooden table with upright leather chairs ranged around it. In front of four of the chairs on one side were leather writing pads, note pads, pencils and ballpoint pens. To the side of the room was a long sideboard and at one end the wall held a screen and a range of controls clearly there to operate various kinds of audio visual electrical equipment.

'If you like to take a seat' said Jules indicating the side of the table opposite those laid with the pads and pens 'Marylyn and her colleagues will be with you shortly'.

'Thank you'.

'May I get you some coffee, tea, water?'

'Water would be lovely thanks' Kim said as Rick asked for black coffee with two sugars and Fergal asked for white coffee with no sugar.

'Coming right up' smiled Jules as she left the room, returning shortly with the requested drinks.

Kim, Fergal and Rick sat and waited and shortly the door opened and several people walked into the large conference room. Leading the group was a tall powerfully built woman, smartly if somewhat severely dressed with dark brown horn rimmed glasses, light brunette hair pulled tightly into a bun. Behind her came another woman and two men.

The lead lady approached the TV-12 team and said in a firm voice 'I'm Marylyn Goodrich, Chief Executive of Furrina Pharmaceuticals'.

'Pleased to meet you' replied Kim offering her hand to be shaken.

Taking it and giving a brief but firm shake Marylyn continued as she indicated the other people who'd come in with her. 'This is Louis Farmer the Head of our Drug Development programmes; John Andrews our In Market Drug Test Controller; Suzanne Field our in house Head of Legal Services. Welcome to Furrina. Please sit down' and with that she led the way to the side of the table with the pads and sat in the middle with Louis and Suzanne directly next to her and John beside the lawyer.

The TV-12 team resumed their places on the opposite side of the table.

Pointing at a small device located in the centre of the table Suzanne said 'That is a recording device. We will be recording this meeting'.

'As you wish' smiled Kim and taking out a small digital recorder added 'so will I then we'll both have our own record of the discussions won't we?'

'Fine' nodded Suzanne pressing a switch on her machine then turned to Marylyn obviously handing the meeting over to her who looked at all three members of the TV-12 group before focussing her gaze firmly onto Kim.

'On the phone you made some ridiculous allegations. We utterly refute those and what is more I have to warn you that if you consider going ahead and broadcasting them we will sue. Furthermore if in spite of that warning you confirm that you are intending to broadcast we will immediately go to the High Court and secure an injunction to prevent broadcast. Is that clear?'

'Oh yes quite clear but you see the problem for you is that the points I put to you by phone are not allegations but statements of *fact*. You *have* been conducting trials on human guinea pigs; many of those subjects *are* damaged or are *being* damaged by the drug; there *were* significant flaws to the animal testing regime you undertook in which many if not all normal protocols were *ignored* before proceeding to human trials; *and* you are hiding the results of the problems by buying off the test subjects with an insultingly small amount of money. Finally you have tried to prevent those poor people from seeking any proper redress by having made them sign a document which most didn't understand and thought they were simply signing a receipt for the money they accepted as .... well as what? Compensation for having their health ruined?

What you are doing is unethical, immoral, disreputable, wholly unprincipled and not only plainly wrong but probably criminal'.

'Those are serious allegations which are wholly without foundation' snapped Suzanne leaning forward menacingly.

'On the contrary they are entirely *with* foundation'.

'Bollocks' exclaimed Louis. 'You have got the wrong end of the stick young lady. All trials have problems from time to time ....'

'Not that we are saying there have been problems' interjected Suzanne.

'Err no of course not' muttered Louis 'but all drug companies run trials and tests for new drugs. There is an established industry and legal framework within which they are conducted. Furrina entirely follows those'.

'And as for your suggestion that there was something wrong with the animal testing programme which we ignored before going to human trials that is completely false' snapped Marylyn.

'Are you prepared to repeat that statement and your earlier one refuting our questions on camera?' Kim asked quietly.

'Of course' retorted Marylyn.

'Provided the exact questions are provided and cleared in advance' said Suzanne.

'I've just asked them. I can repeat them and Rick can film your response'.

'One minute please' said Suzanne and she huddled her head close to Marylyn's and then she whispered in Louis's ear before scribbling a note and pushing it over to John Andrews who looked at it and nodded back to her. She then spoke again briefly into Marylyn's ear who listened then eased away and looked at Kim.

'I will answer those questions that you put to me. The rest of the team will be here but not on camera' announced Marylyn.

'Fine. Thank you'.

There was a little shuffling around as Suzanne, Louis and John moved away leaving Marylyn in the centre of the table. Kim nodded at Rick who handed a small microphone to Marylyn. She clipped it to the top of her dress as he put his camera on his shoulder, focussed it on the Furrina Chief Executive and said to Kim 'Ready whenever you want to go'.

'Wait' instructed Marylyn and looking at Jules, who had been sitting quietly on a chair to the side of the room ignored by everyone, said 'mirror?'

'Sure' and rummaging in her bag Jules produced a surprisingly large hand mirror and walked over to hand it to her boss.

Marylyn peered into it, pulled a face, reached into her own bag and extracted a brush which she used to tidy one side of her hair, then taking out a lipstick she freshened the colour on her lips, smiled and putting her own things away and handing the mirror back to her PA and said to Kim 'Right let's do this'.

Rick stood and moved to the end of the table from where he could swing the camera to focus on either Kim or Marylyn and waited.

Kim looked at him and said 'Okay interview with Miss Marylyn Goodrich, Chief Executive of Furrina Pharmaceuticals' paused and raised an eyebrow to Rick who gave a thumbs up then put the camera eye piece back to his left eye.

'Miss Goodrich thank you for allowing TV-12's Highlight programme to ask you some questions about the drug trials you are conducting in India'.

'We are always happy to talk to the media'.

'Good. So can you confirm that you are conducting trials on a new drug which internally you refer to as Beta, rather than its full and correct name of Betanapotraproxiflevien-g3.

'Yes I can'.

'And are you aware that those trials have caused serious problems in several of the human subjects taking part in them?'

'No I am not aware of that'.

'So you have no knowledge of any problems emerging in the human phase of this drug trial?'

'I have just said so'.

'Miss Goodrich we have been to India to interview and film many of the people involved in your drug trials who are now suffering from a wide range of side effects as a result of taking your drug'.

'I don't know who you've seen or spoken to or what health problems they may have told you that they might have, but I totally refute your accusations that any trial of a new drug that we *may*, I repeat *may*, be involved with has caused any health problems for any trial subject. If it had then we would have stopped the trial to ascertain why any such problems might have occurred'.

'You would have stopped the trial?' Is that what you are saying?'

'Of course'.

'But you haven't stopped the trial. You are continuing it and have simply paid off those people that were damaged and recruited new subjects'.

'Rubbish!'

'It isn't rubbish. We have been there, seen the people, been in their houses or in most cases hovels as you recruited uneducated, largely illiterate people who didn't know what they were signing let alone letting themselves in for. Then when it went wrong you paid them off with a paltry amount of money and moved on to the next batch of recruits'.

'I say again that is complete rubbish'.

'Alright what about the animal test results here in your labs in the UK?'

'What about them?'

'Is it not a fact that when the drug trial went wrong on mice you ignored that and switched to testing on rats and when that went wrong you went to dog testing and when that also went wrong you switched to testing on monkeys which seemed to go alright and on the basis of *that* you prepared the necessary documentation for the licensing authorities, doctored the problem results by just using the monkey test data and hence got a licence to test on humans?'

'No absolutely not'.

'Miss Goodrich I must put it to you that you are simply not telling the truth'.

'Prove it!'

'Well that's just the point. You see we *can* prove it. We have signed statements from one of your employees who has passed data and results to us proving that what I am saying to you is correct and therefore your denials are nothing but a complete pack of lies'.

If she wanted to create an impact Kim succeeded splendidly. It was as though she'd dropped a bombshell on the Furrina senior management.

'What did you say?' Marylyn said in a very quiet voice dripping with menace.

'Oh I think you heard me well enough. We have computer printouts, test results, internal memos and e-mails, transcripts of meetings and trial information. These will form a central part of our programme which will go out this Thursday by the way'.

'If you have been looking at confidential company information and data then you've probably broken the law'.

'On the contrary we have simply studied information that has been voluntarily given to us by a Furrina employee who is disgusted with what you have been doing on the Beta project by manipulating the results and ignoring the damage that the drug is causing to many of the people on whom it is being trialled. That employee wants it stopped and so do we. And so will the general public when they discover what you've been doing'.

'Who is this employee?'

'I cannot disclose that'.

'Cannot or will not?'

'Does it make a difference?'

'Yes. You *could* disclose it but *won't*. So I'll ask you again. Who is this misguided ill informed employee?'

'And I've told you that I'm not prepared to give you that information'.

Marylyn glared at Kim with an expression of hatred and anger on her face which was neatly caught by Rick's camera. 'I think we have said all that we can at this stage. This interview is over' and sitting back she removed the small microphone from the top of her dress. Rick continued running the camera as it stayed pointing at Marylyn. 'I said this interview is over. Stop that camera NOW!' she thundered glaring at Rick.

'Kim?' he asked.

'Yes okay stop filming' she confirmed.

As soon as he had Suzanne leaned right forward. 'There is no way you will be able to use any of that. We will move immediately to secure an injunction against you preventing the use of that interview as well as any filming you have done in India or anywhere else for that matter. The injunction will also stop you making your allegations and will wholly thwart you from putting any part of it on air. We will also issue you with a separate injunction to force you to disclose this employee's name'.

For a few moments there was complete silence in the room before a tight lipped Louis said 'Show our visitors out Jules please'.

As Fergal, Rick and Kim stood she stared at the Furrina team one by one then said 'You can try what you like but the programme *will* go out on Thursday night, attempted injunction or not. Good day' and with that she followed Jules out of the room, along the corridor, stood in silence in the lift and walked across the foyer to the swing doors where she turned and smiled at Marylyn's PA.

'Goodbye and thank you for your help'.

Jules said nothing just inclined her head slightly then watched the three TV company employees leave the building.

'Whoa. Kim you've just made that Furrina boss lady mighty pissed off' chuckled Fergal when they were back in the car.

'I'll sort the stuff I filmed to get the best bits and then you and Penny can play around with it in the edit suite. Do you think they'll be able to stop us?' asked Rick. 'I hope not. What we've uncovered needs to be brought to the public's attention'.

'I don't know. We've got the *evidence* from both India and Brian's stuff which should be enough for any judge if they do go to court for an injunction?' Kim replied.

'Great. Mind you what a bitch she is though isn't she?'

'I bet she eats iron bars for breakfast' commented Fergal with a grimace.

'Or men?' grinned Kim.

'Yeah probably balls first! No wedding ring I noticed. Mind you it would be a brave man that took her on and lived!'

'God above. Can you imagine? What a way to die' mused Rick quietly.

'Yes she's a one hundred percent bitch and complete she devil all rolled into one nasty package' replied Kim.

'Back to the office?' asked Fergal.

'Yes back to the office' agreed Kim with a grim smile. 'I need to quickly brief Toby, Peter and Lawrence.

'So how did it go?' queried Toby when Kim walked into his office.

'They're not happy people and have threatened to bring all sorts of hellfire and brimstone down upon us including injunctions, suing us and anything else I guess they can think up to stop us broadcasting'.

'Not surprised. So now we wait and see what happens. Well done and keep me posted so I can in turn keep Levi on side'.

She agreed she would but then returned to her own work area and cleared several outstanding things finally finishing for the day about six. She rang James to see what time he was planning to be home as she thought they might go out to supper somewhere to celebrate the potential success that this programme was going to be but he regretfully declined her offer as he was committed to an evening with clients.

Not wanting to be alone she rang through to Penny and asked if she would like to go out to dinner to celebrate?

'I'd love to but Susan and I are holding a dinner party for some friends. She's a brilliant cook so I'm really sorry but I can't'.

'No problem. Enjoy your party'.

Next she rang Anna who said 'Oh Kim I'm sorry but I've promised to go out with a new guy I met last week'.

'What about Imran and .... err I forget whoever your other man is?'

'Gordon. Oh he and Imran are still around' she said airily 'but it's nice to have a change from time to time and Harry seems like fun. Good in bed too' she laughed.

'You met him last week and have already slept with him?'

'Yes. I don't usually rut on a first date but it just seemed to happen this time'.

'You wicked girl!'

'Nice though. I think it's fun occasionally to be wicked especially like that'.

'So before bed are you going anywhere special?'

'He knows of a new restaurant that's opened off Sloane Street and invited me to go there with him. He's good company and afterwards we'll undoubtedly go back to his apartment which isn't so far away from there so it won't take too long to get from drinking coffee after the meal to some good robust rutting!'

'Right. Enjoy the meal and especially the rutting!' she chuckled.

'I don't know about enjoying the meal we'll have to see what that's like but rutting afterwards? Now that's for certain. Bye!'

She rang three other friends. One the call went straight to voicemail. The other two answered but said they were sorry but already had arrangements for this evening.

Putting down the phone Kim sat and reflected back on her conversation with Anna and just for a moment she envied her carefree love life which bore considerable similarity to how her own had been before she met James, since when she'd been wholly faithful to him.

'Hey cheer up!' said Rick as he walked past her desk on his way home for the evening.

'Yes sorry'.

'You're going to win. The legal guys will stop us being prevented from going on air. You ought to be elated?'

'I am. It's still sinking in and to help that I'd have loved to go out and celebrate but my fiancé is busy with clients; my best friend Anna is going out to dinner and then hoping to get seduced by her new man; Penny's giving a dinner party with her partner Susan; my other friends that I've rung are no goes therefore I'm on my own. So I guess I'll get myself home, go for a run, have a bath, wash my hair, watch some television or listen to some music and wait for James to come back when I can throw myself into his arms and be the loving fiancé'.

'Or you could come out with me and Serena if you like? I'm on my way to meet her now and then we were going to hit a couple of bars, grab something to eat, perhaps do a club before retiring gracefully to bed'.

'Oh you don't want me along'.

'No really you'd be very welcome. Honestly. You'll like Serena. She's fun intelligent and sexy! Do come'.

'You sure? I mean *really* sure?'

'Yep really sure. So come on. Cheer up. Put your "I'm gonna have a good time" face on and let's go'.

She looked at him for a moment then smiled and said 'Okay thanks. I'd love to'.

Serena, who Kim had seen briefly at Heathrow meeting Rick when the TV-12 team got back from India, was tall, black with a wonderful figure, long legs that seemed to go on forever and the shortest skirt that Kim thought she'd even seen an adult female wear. She was also interesting to talk with, had an engaging smile, a quick sense of humour. The evening began well and continued in that vein.

As Rick had said they met at a bar in Soho where he and Serena kissed then held hands as the three of them fought their way through the crowds to order from one of the overworked and heavily sweating bar men or bar girls.

The found a corner where the noise was a bit less and the three of them could sip their drinks and talk. After a while they made their way to another bar further into Soho and again drank and talked against the noisy background of a busy and successful London bar. Around nine Rick said he was hungry and suggested they went to a Chinese restaurant that he'd been to before in Chinatown so the three of them walked the short distance and were soon tucking into an excellent selection of well cooked and nicely served Chinese foods.

Finished Kim took out her credit card but Rick insisted on paying for her meal and would not accept any argument from her about it, so with a shrug and a smile she accepted. When that was done the three of them walked to the door and onto the street.

'Thanks for a nice evening but I must be getting home now' Kim said.

The Beta File

'Hey don't rush off. We were going on to a club only five minutes from here' pleaded Serena.

'Five minutes?' exclaimed Rick.

'Well ten minutes-ish maybe? In a taxi' she grinned. 'Come on Kim. You said you'd like to celebrate so let's go there and do that'.

'Yeah. Don't get all stuffy' chided Rick. 'Join us for some fun'.

'As I said it's really kind of you but no thanks. I'll leave you two guys alone without a gooseberry cramping your style' she laughed.

'Oh nothing cramps Rick's style does it honey?' grinned Serena as leant forward and popped a kiss on his lips at the same time running her fingers around his waist band.

'Nope nothing does' he replied taking her hand and leading her further onto the street.

They waited for a few minutes then a cab appeared so Rick suggested Kim took that one and he and Serena would wait for another so with a smile she accepted his offer, got in and asked the driver to take her to Victoria where she'd get the Northern line underground to Balham.

'Goodnight Kim' called Rick. 'See you in the office tomorrow'.

Traffic was heavy and it took ages to get to Victoria but in the tube station she waited for a while until the train for Balham pulled into the platform where she got on and sat down to read the evening paper as the tube rattled and clattered along until it pulled into her station.

She was soon indoors but skipping her run as after a meal and some drinks she didn't feel like running, so she showered, undressed, sprayed her cleavage and pubic hair with some perfume then got into bed stark naked, switched on the TV and waited for James to come back.

Which he did after about half an hour and the expression of delight on his face as he walked into the bedroom and saw a waiting Kim smiling sexily at him.

'Hi have you had a good evening?' he queried softly.

'Yes. But I think it might be about to get even better' she grinned throwing the duvet aside.

And it did!!

CHAPTER 19

As soon as Kim and her two colleagues had left Furrina's offices all hell broke loose. Marylyn summoned Fay Roper the Head of Human Resources for the Furrina Group and as soon as she arrived in her office the Chief Executive let fly.

'I've just had three people from TV-12 here who claim that they have evidence about the problems that we've been having with the Beta trials in India'.

'Christ how the hell did they get that?'

'Because some miserable little bastard from this company has apparently approached them and given them evidence about it as well as information about how we …… err shall we say ……. took a flexible view of the animal trials for the drug?'

'Flexible view? What do you mean?'

Marylyn paused and looked at both Louis Farmer and John Andrews then slowly returned her gaze to Fay. 'There were some issues with the animal testing which we eventually found a way to resolve'.

'Issues?'

''Yes issues' snapped Marylyn displaying extreme irritation.

'What sort of issues?'

There was a pause before Louis said 'Some of the early animal testing programme indicated that some side effects might be generated by the application of Betanapotraproxiflevien-g3 so we decided to change species and continue with the animal testing programme ……….'

'You decided' corrected Marylyn. '*You* decided Louis. Not *we* decided'.

'Yes alright. *I* decided that it might be a species issue and so we switched to a different species and continued the testing'.

'Two more times' added Marylyn 'before we found that monkey tests seemed alright and as they are our closest relative you felt it okay to proceed to apply to the authorities to move to human testing'.

'Correct' he replied.

'So does this mean that TV-12 have actually got something that they can hit us with?' Fay wanted to know.

'Whether they have or not is irrelevant! We're not going to let them make any sort of fuss or announcements or especially any programme about what they might have discovered!'

'Right. Understood. So what's the next step?'

'We absolutely *must* do several things. First we need to find this bloody traitor and get him out of this business immediately. Second we need to find out how he got the data together. Thirdly we must close any loopholes in our data security that have been exposed by this incident. Lastly I want an injunction on that TV station to stop them broadcasting anything. Repeat anything!'

Fay nodded then Marylyn snarled at her 'So find this little shit, fire him without any notice period or compensation, no redundancy and freeze or cancel his pension. I want him to pay for what he's done for the rest of his life. He'll regret breaking his contract of confidentiality with Furrina. Oh yes he will really regret what he's done. I may even think of something else to do to him? Perhaps get him jailed!'

Her eyes were flashing, her cheeks were red and there were red blotches on her neck as she continued to work herself up into even more of a rage.

'And when you've done so I want it publicised throughout the company as to what's happened to him so it serves as a warning to the rest of our employees. So it tells them not to do what this guy has done and what will happen to them if they do'.

'It might be a woman?' ventured Fay.

'A woman?' Marylyn paused her brow furrowing. 'No I doubt it. Whistleblowers are almost invariably men not women'. Another pause before she continued 'No this treacherous bastard is some stupid weak minded male creep. Find him. Expose him. Fire him. *NOW!*'

Seeing that the Chief Executive was in no mood for a discussion Fay concluded that her best course of action was to get out of Marylyn's office as soon as possible and start to hunt for the mole although exactly how she was going to find him she had no idea so she muttered 'Sure thing' and left to return to her own office.

'Now get me Steve Jackson' demanded Marylyn as Jules came into the room.

He arrived in a very short time having been summoned by Marylyn's PA who'd warned him that her boss was in one hell of a rage and he'd better drop everything to get to her office straight away, so knowing Marylyn's tempers he did just that!

'Steve we've had a leak of extremely sensitive information and data relating to Project Beta' and she quickly ran through what she'd said to Fay. 'I need you to find out exactly what has been taken by this whistleblower'.

'Can you give me any idea where to look?'

'Can *I* give you any idea? No of course I bloody well can't. *You're* the Head of Information Technology in this business. *You* find out what's been taken and quickly. And I mean really quickly'.

'Beta?'

'It's a new drug programme. Go off with Louis and he'll brief you on it but Steve you are to drop everything else to find out what's been taken and by whom? *Nothing* else that you may have on is of greater importance than this. Find out and fast. Got it?'

'Got it. You coming Louis?'

'Yes come on'.

'I'll join you' said John Andrews glad of a reason to get away from Marylyn while she was in this sort of mood and as the three of them left the Chief Executive turned to Suzanne and snapped 'Right. An injunction. How do we get that in place to stop those TV people broadcasting?'

'We need to brief a barrister to obtain a High Court injunction. I'll get on it right way' and without waiting for a response she got up and left the room leaving Marylyn still furious and fuming alone but after a couple of minutes she summoned Jules and dictated a notice which she instructed to be put on all company notice boards throughout the business immediately.

Back in her own office Fay asked her secretary to call Asif Hajjar who was her most trusted subordinate to join her straight away.

'If he's busy or tied up?'

'Tell him to get unbusy, untied up and come here right now please'.

She was soon joined by Asif her deputy who smiled as he entered her office. 'Good morning. I gather you needed me urgently?' he said in his soft voice.

'Yes. We've had a major leak of highly sensitive information which has got to a TV station who are proposing to go on air and blow the whistle on us' announced Fay. 'The detail is highly sensitive and you need to work only with me and Steve Jackson on this. Steve is going to try and track it from an IT perspective to find out who it is and what's been taken while you and I will work at it from a Personnel standpoint.

We have got to discover who this whistleblower is, find out what he or she knows, what has been taken, what has been divulged and what has been stolen? It is *vitally* important'.

The two of them talked for a while before there was nothing further to say at that stage so saying 'Okay I'm on it' Asif walked swiftly out of the room.

When employees of Furrina arrived for work on Wednesday morning the talk was soon buzzing about the notice that had appeared on all the company notice boards.

IMPORTANT NOTICE

All employees of Furrina Pharmaceuticals are reminded that it is a condition of working for this company that any knowledge or information that you may learn, know, acquire or become aware of, is entirely the property of the company and remains so without time limitation. It is not and never becomes the property of any individual and must never be disclosed to anyone outside the company,

This fact is enshrined in your contract of employment.

Any breach of this absolute rule by an employee irrespective of seniority, position or length of service will result in instant dismissal without notice or compensation. Furthermore the company not only reserves the right to seek damages, reimbursement or recompense against any such employee, but may also instigate legal proceedings for breach of contract and possible theft of data

There are **NO EXCEPTIONS** to this rule.

Marylyn Goodrich
Group Chief Executive.

Brian's usual practice on arrival at work around eight o'clock was to set his small document case down on his desk and then before actually starting work he would walk to the area at the end of his floor where there were two drink vending machines. He'd press the appropriate buttons and then while the cup was being slowly filled by the machine idly glance at any notices on the small notice board on the wall between the two machines. Generally there was nothing of much interest but as he saw this morning's notice his chest suddenly felt tight, beads of sweat appeared on his forehead and he felt physically sick as the first waves of panic enveloped him.

Moving away he began returning to his desk when a voice called 'Brian?'

Looking round he saw Emma one of the lab technicians looking at him somewhat strangely. 'You've forgotten your drink'.

'Oh yes. Sorry' he muttered as he quickly returned to the machine and took the now filled cup of coffee from it. 'Forget my head one day' he muttered.

'Hey crikey! Have you seen this?' she queried nodding at the notice.

'Err yes. I just read it'.

'Something must have happened to have Madam Iron Knickers put up a notice like that'.

'Do you think so?'

'Of course. Otherwise why would she be plastering the notice boards with these dire announcements?'

'Err well perhaps she's just reminding us of our contractual obligations. After all, as she says, it is in our contracts of employment'.

'Yes I know but why make such a fuss about it now? What do you think Angie?' she asked turning to another young woman who'd joined them.

'What do I think about what?'

'This' said Emma pointing at the notice board.

'Oh that. It's on all our computer screens when we log on today'.

'Oh really. I haven't logged on this morning. Have you Brian?'

'No but I must be going and do just that' and with that he walked quickly away from the notice board, the vending machines and the discussion.

Back at his desk he logged on, entered his password and taking a sip of his coffee read the same notice that was on the notice boards then clicked to move away from that and onto what he was intending to work on today. But as he peered at his screen he couldn't concentrate. His mind kept returning to what the notice had said and he became even more concerned a little after nine o'clock when his terminal pinged to announce an incoming message. Opening it, his heart really sank as he read what was on the screen.

IMPORTANT ANNOUNCEMENT TO ALL EMPLOYEES

Further to my earlier notice about the need for confidentiality and the fact that it is absolutely forbidden to disclose ANY information about the company, its products, its processes or its developments, we have become aware that a Furrina Pharmaceuticals employee has in fact divulged information to an outside third party about a drug trial which we are conducting.

A senior management team is currently urgently working to establish who this misguided individual(s) is and when they have been identified as they surely will be, they will be dealt with in an appropriate manner and in line with company procedures and policy, as was explained and emphasised in my earlier notice about such matters.

In the meantime if you have any knowledge of who this misguided person or persons might be, please advise Fay Roper our Head of HR immediately.

Any such information will be treated in the strictest confidence.

Marylyn Goodrich
Chief Executive

If Brian had been nervous before, now he was absolutely terrified. A senior team were hunting for *him*. Peering at the screen he re-read the words, pausing on "when" they have been identified noting that it said *when*, not *if* they have been identified. So as far as Furrina was concerned it was only a matter of time before they found him.

Quickly he ran through in his mind the computer searches he'd undertaken when collecting information to pass to TV-12 and although he knew he'd been careful to cover his tracks if there was a really intense search and from the sound of it there certainly was going to be, then it would include electronic tracking and tracing everything to do with Project Beta which would undoubtedly uncover the inevitable electronic traces he'd have left. He knew that everything that anyone did on a computer always left a trail which could be found and in this case traced back to him. As sure as day follows night they'd find the trail leading to him.

'Oh my God' he muttered holding his head in his hands. 'Whatever have I done? What an earth will happen to me?' then after a few moments he added quietly 'what the hell am I going to do if they sue me for damages?'

He looked around his work area and everyone was busy. No-one was taking any notice of him as he continued to speculate on his future.

For the next hour or so he sat at his desk doing nothing just staring ahead and thinking. Indeed he was so inactive that a couple of people stopped and asked if he was alright and the first time he said he was trying to think through a problem and to the second person he said he had a bit of a headache.

By mid morning he couldn't stay at his desk any longer and so went to see Frank Lloyd his boss a fellow scientific researcher who was talking with someone else that he'd seen around the business from time to time but didn't know who he was.

'Ah hello Brian' smiled Frank. 'Bob and I were just talking about these notices that Marylyn has issued this morning'.

'Obviously a bit of a flap on' grinned Bob.

'More than a bit of a flap. Sounds like a right royal who-ha if you ask me. What do you think Brian?'

'Err yes I guess so. Look I'm feeling really grotty. Didn't feel too good when I got up this morning and I've got worse since then. Don't know whether I'm coming down with something but I'm going back home to have a lie down and see if I can shake it off'.

'Sorry to hear that. Yes of course. Hope you feel better soon'.

'Thank you. Cheerio Bob'.

'Bye Brian. You might have picked up this flu type bug that's doing the rounds. Any rate get well soon'.

'Will do. Thanks. Bye' and he walked out of the office, back to his desk, closed down his computer and was soon out of the building and in his car on the way home.

As soon as he came to a convenient point to stop he pulled the car into the side of the road, dialled Kim's number and sat impatiently tapping his fingers on the steering wheel as he listened to it ringing.

'Hi Brian this is Kim' she said brightly. 'How are you today?'

'Oh Kim. I feel awful. There's a big hunt on at work because they say they know someone's leaked information about a drug trial to an outsider. That must be Beta mustn't it? And they're hunting for whoever that is and to do so they've got a senior management team specially convened to find whoever it is. I mean it's me they're looking for and they'll find me and they've said that they'll chuck the person out without notice pay or compensation and they might seek damages, in the courts presumably, and it can only be a matter of time before they find me and I don't know what to do and I wish I'd never come to you or told you about the Beta trials or that you'd been to see them ....'

'Whoa hey calm down a moment'.

'Calm down? How can I calm down? It's *me* they're looking for and they'll be bound to find me. Whatever am I going to do? Kim I just don't know. I'm so frightened'.

'I can understand how worried you must be ....'

'Worried I'm bloody petrified. They are *bound* to find out it was me. *Bound* to'.

'Look you don't *know* that they'll find out that it was you'.

'They will. They will' he wailed.

'Well they won't find out from us I can assure you of that'.

'No I know but they'll trace me internally'.

'Didn't you say that you'd covered your tracks when you got the information out of the computer at work?'

'Yes as best I could. I used a different password not my own ....'

'Well there you are then ....'

'No I'm *not*! If they start to examine downloads from the Beta database they'll discover that someone .... me ...... downloaded a whole lot of data and copied it. They are simply *certain* to be able to trace it back to me'.

'But didn't you tell me that when you went in to Furrina on that Sunday morning to get the information you logged on to a different computer which wasn't yours, to find and download and then copy the data?'

Brian paused for a moment then said 'Yes. Yes I did'.

'Well won't that protect you then? Isn't that exactly why you did it?'

'Yes of course. I don't know. Maybe. But if they find that download and when, then cross check who was in that morning when it was done it won't take them long to work out that it was me. I need to think through everything that I did that morning'.

'You do that and I'm sure you'll find some reassurance for yourself'.

'I hope so' he muttered. 'Bye' and ending the call he sat for a while in his car still concerned and very worried that he would be found out and what would happen to him if it was.

Shortly after that Ronnie the attractive red haired receptionist at TV-12 rang Kim and said that there was a man at reception with an important document which he needed to give to Kim personally.

'Okay I'll come down' and when she reached reception a short man was standing to one side watching one of the many TV screens that were showing current or past shows that the television company had running.

Kim looked at Ronnie who although on the phone smiled at her, waggled the fingers of one hand at her in a little greeting then used the forefinger to point towards the man.

'Hello I believe you have something for me?' she said as she approached the man.

'Are you Miss Kim Harding employed by TV-12?'

'Yes I am'.

'Here you are then Miss' and with that he handed an official looking document to her. 'These are injunctions against you and TV-12. I suggest you immediately refer them to your legal advisers. Good morning Miss' and with that he turned on his heel and walked towards the doors.

'Thank you' she called to his retreating back but he didn't acknowledge her comment in any way.

'Ooh an injunction' said Ronnie as she finished connecting her caller to someone in the building. 'That's heavy stuff isn't it?'

'I guess it can be'.

'Yeah a couple of years ago a friend of my then boyfriend took one of those things out to prevent some former girlfriend harassing him over some pictures she took of him. Nudie ones I gather! Still seemed to work as she backed off'.

'You're not with that same boyfriend then now?'

'God no. He was several ago. I like to play the field a bit where men are concerned. There's always plenty of them around!' she chuckled. 'I mean my current fella ....'

'Sorry to interrupt but could you get Levi on the phone for me'.

'Sure hang on' and she punched a couple of numbers on her phone then pointed at a phone to the side of the reception desk which started ringing. Kim moved to it and picking it up said 'Levi good morning. It's Kim. The injunctions have arrived'. She listened as he said to come up straight away, agreed she would and put down the phone.

'So as I was saying. My current fella Dave he's ....'

'Ronnie you can tell me later but can you ring Toby and ask him to meet me in Levi's office. Sorry but I really have got to rush now' and she walked to the lifts, pressed the appropriate button and was soon travelling up to the correct floor where she exited and walked along the thickly carpeted corridor, paused when she reached Tanya's desk, said she'd just spoken to Levi and he'd said to come straight up.

'Okay. Go on in. Coffee?'

'Umm please. Toby's coming as well. He will be here shortly'.

Inside Levi's office Kim handed over the package of papers. 'A man asked if I was Kim Harding employed by TV-12 and when I said yes he handed this to me' she said indicating the package.

'Fine. Ah morning Toby' Levi smiled as Kim's boss joined the meeting. 'So the shit's hit the fan has it?' he continued as he opened the envelope, extracted the various documents and as he began to read them said 'Right now this is where we legal chaps earn our simply huge salaries!' and looking up briefly at Kim and then Toby his smile was warm and friendly.

Tanya brought in three cups of coffee, set Levi's down on his desk, handed Toby and Kim theirs and looking at Levi asked 'Do you want me to ring Golda?'

'Uh huh' Levi replied without looking up from the papers he was studying. He continued to read in silence, occasionally raising one or other of his bushy eyebrows until coming to the end when he sat back and looked at the other two.

'Right well all quite straightforward. Standard injunction but utterly preventing us from using, broadcasting, retaining or making use of in any way, any material that we have been given, secured, gained or become aware of relating to err 'and he paused and read the drug's name out slowly and carefully 'Betan ..... apot .... raprox .... iflevien .... g3. God what a name'.

'We and the Furrina people tend to just call it Beta' said Kim.

'Good idea' he smiled.

'And the programme we'll put out will be called The Beta File'.

'Put out provided we get this injunction removed' smiled Levi then picked up his phone which had rung once. 'Ah Golda good morning. How are you? .... how is Eli? .... and the children? .... Good. Well the injunction has been served on Kim this morning and she is sitting here in my office trembling with fear and worry as to what it might do to her and whether she's going to be carted off to Holloway prison' and he winked at her, but as he did so she was reminded of Brian's earlier phone call and his obvious fear and worry at being discovered. 'Toby is also here so I'm going to put you on speaker phone so we can all hear what you say'.

He pressed a button on his phone and then said 'Can you still hear me?'

'Yes quite clearly' replied Golda. 'Good morning Kim and Toby. Well they haven't wasted any time have they? You've obviously got them seriously rattled Kim. So Levi anything unusual or odd about the injunction?'

'No. It's a standard injunction signed by a judge in chambers this morning preventing us doing anything with any material that we have obtained by whatever means. Quite clear. A complete blackout'.

'Which judge?'

'Err' and he flicked to the back of the document 'Judge Peter Stevensfield'.

'Ah good. That old fool will sign anything. I am encouraged as Furrina may not have prepared a good case if he's signed it. Gives me cause to hope we will succeed in our application to have the injunction lifted'.

'Okay but at the moment it is binding and watertight'.

'Yes of course. So we need to find a way to torpedo them below their waterline then don't we?'

'Exactly. I'll courier the document round to you shall I?'

'Yes please. The sooner I get it the sooner we can work out how to stuff it up their pharmaceutical backsides and get your programme out'.

'Right'.

'I'll call you after I've received it and had a think about it. Till later then. Bye'.

When the call finished Levi called Tanya in. 'Photocopy this please. Two copies. One for me and one for Kim and then get the original sent to Golda by someone from here in a taxi'. Looking at Kim and with a twinkle in his eyes he continued 'After all you ought to keep a record of the first injunction you've had served against you!'.

'Right but couldn't you have scanned and e-mailed the document to Golda? Surely that would have been quicker'.

'I could .... well Tanya could because I would have absolutely no idea how to scan a document. But you see we legal people like paper documents. Golda will want to see the actual manuscript to ensure nothing is missed. So there isn't anything for you to do for now. I'll let you both know when something begins to happen'.

'What's your honest opinion of our chances of getting this overturned?' Toby wanted to know. 'This could make a stunning programme you know'.

Leaning forward Levi carefully placed his elbows on his desk, raised his arms vertically, slowly intertwined his fingers together and gently rested his chin on the pyramid he'd created. 'The law is complex though logical, yet sometimes a complete ass. In cases of this sort we will need to show and crucially *demonstrate* to a judge that the injunction preventing the publication of this information is firmly *against* the public interest and that such public interest *overrides* the need for Furrina to be able to maintain their commercial secrecy over this matter.

The whole question of whether we succeed will turn on a number of things. Firstly how the judge that we approach will view the need. Judges are of course impartial but evidence of people being damaged especially the potential risk to children from this Betanapot .... err oh hell, this Beta drug that they're testing will weigh heavily. Memories of thalidomide, Bhopal and Chernobyl are still surprisingly fresh in people's minds. Even high court judges'.

'Hang on. Thalidomide was a drug problem but Bhopal and Chernobyl weren't drug issues. They were industrial disasters' queried Toby.

'Strictly speaking yes but it is the *after* effects that stick in people's minds especially where children are damaged. Like with the after effects of Hiroshima and Nagasaki'.

'I see'.

'History is littered ..... err well that's perhaps too strong a description but there are many *many* cases where animal testing has seemed alright but once translated into human usage then serious, indeed sometimes fatal and obviously unexpected side effects have been caused'.

'Really? So Beta isn't a one off then?'

'No not at all' he paused and picking up a file flicked through, found the pages he wanted and then continued speaking. 'For example Flosint an arthritis medication was tested on rats, dogs and monkeys and all tolerated it well but when tested on humans it proved fatal. Zelmid was tested as an anti-depressant on rats and dogs without incident but in humans it caused severe neurological problems. Nomifensine another anti depressant was linked to kidney, liver, anaemia and even death in humans even though animal testing gave it a clean bill of health. Clioquinol an anti diarrheal medication passed all its tests in rats, cats, dogs, and rabbits but it was removed from sale in 1982 after it was found to cause blindness and paralysis in humans. Opren an arthritis medication killed sixty one and seriously damaged three and a half thousand people although it was tested on monkeys and other animals without problems. Eraldin a medication for heart disease caused twenty three deaths despite the fact that no untoward effects could be shown in animals. And closer to the issue of Beta whatever its full name is, then Mitoxantrone was also a potential cancer treatment but it produced heart failure in humans. It was extensively tested on dogs which did not manifest this effect.

So you see there *are* many precedents for problems occurring during new human drug trials but in all those cases there was, as far as I know, no attempt made to cover up these unfortunate effects.

'How the hell do you know all this?'

'A combination of factors. Firstly I rang your man Brian last night and we had a long talk in which he gave me some examples. Secondly though, he pointed me in the right direction on the internet to find other examples all of which are in the public domain and which I have passed on to Golda.

'So now the issue is whether we can persuade the judge that bringing this into the open knowledge of the general public is more important than commercial confidentiality'.

'And do you think we will succeed in doing that?'

'Golda is an expert in mixing points of law, complex facts and heart jerking emotion together. Her background helps her with that of course'.

'Her background?'

'She is as you will have realised, like me Jewish. We Jews hold in our hearts forever the terrible things that were done to us by the Nazis. Indeed even before those monsters. We are a race that has been persecuted, troubled and despised for centuries. Many people still do.

Golda lost all her forebears in the Nazi concentration camps. Her father, two brothers, grandparents, uncles and aunts. Only her mother who at seven was still a child somehow survived thanks be to God. After the war she was taken in and raised by another German Jewish family who'd also survived the camps.

She came here to England when she was just nineteen and made her own life in this country, met a man, married and had three children one of whom was Golda. Thus she's knows about past suffering and crucially knows about experiments with drugs on humans as some of her relatives were damaged and then killed while being experimented on by Nazi so called medical research. It's why Golda speaks German from time to time. To remind herself of the past'.

Therefore I have no doubt that she will do a quite excellent job fighting this wretched injunction for us. Still we will just have to wait and see!'

'Indeed'.

'Right well I guess it is wait and wait some more time eh?' grinned Toby.

'Yes I'll call you when something happens'.

Toby and Kim left Levi's office and returned to Toby's office.

'That's horrible what happened to Golda's parents and family isn't it? And all the other millions of those poor Jewish people?' Kim said quietly.

'Yes we must never forget that and that's why we mustn't let these Furrina bastards get away with this drug disaster'.

'Of course'.

CHAPTER 20

Kim was thinking about what to do about lunch when Levi rang. 'Golda's on her way to court now. If you'd like to come along we can go together?'

'Yes please' she said excitedly quite forgetting about her empty tummy. 'Shall I give Toby a shout?'

'I've already done that and he's busy at the moment so he's happy for just you to come with me. Meet you downstairs in five' and with that he rang off.

Kim had never been to the law courts in London before and couldn't help being impressed as she and Levi got out of the taxi in front of the imposing building. Walking inside they spotted Golda who was standing in the middle of the large central hall talking to a young woman.

'Ah hello' was Golda's cheery greeting. 'Levi, Kim, this is Sally Foster my junior who is helping me with this case'.

After mutual handshakes and "hello pleased to meet you's" Kim asked 'So what are your thoughts on our chances of succeeding?'

'Well where the law in concerned there is *never* a certain outcome. But I believe we have a good case and I shall fight it with all my powers and ability'.

She then explained the process and procedure that would take place and checking her watch said 'Right almost twelve o'clock which is our time. So here we go. Oh by the way you say nothing unless I specifically turn to you and ask you something'.

'Right' nodded Kim.

An usher approached Golda and with a smile said 'Mr Justice George Willington will see you now' and he led off with Golda, Sally and Kim following.

If Kim expected to be taken to a court room she was disappointed as they were led to a door which opened into a corridor. The usher bustled along until stopping in front of a door he knocked, waited and when the sound of "Enter" was heard opened the door, stood aside and motioned Golda to enter. Inside sitting behind a desk sat a well built kindly looking man. Again Kim was surprised that he was dressed in a normal suit, shirt and tie but with no red robes or wig.

'Golda how are you today?'

'Very well thank you my Lord'.

'So what's it all about then?'

'My Lord. If it please you, Sally is my junior on this case, Levi Edelman and Miss Kim Harding are from the television company TV-12 for whom I am acting'.

'Very well please proceed'.

'My Lord we seek leave to appeal against an injunction which has been served on TV-12 in general and Miss Harding in particular in respect of an investigation which she and the company have carried out relating to a particular drug trial. A drug trial which is being conducted in great secrecy and which has created some very worrying side effects in the human beings on whom the drug is being tested.

The test subjects entered into the trial openly and of their own free will but when side effects began to emerge instead of stopping the trial to investigate why that had occurred, the drug company bought off the damaged people by paying each of them a small amount of money; apparently did nothing to investigate why the adverse reactions had occurred; ignored the human suffering they had caused; carried on with the trial and now that TV-12, my client has discovered what they have been doing and hiding and have prepared a programme to broadcast under their Highlight series, then Furrina Pharmaceuticals have imposed these injunctions.

In our view my Lord this is wrong and wholly against the public interest. We fully accept that Furrina Pharmaceuticals has some rights to confidentiality but *not* at the expense of public knowledge of the harm they are doing and concealing out of sight and away from public view and knowledge'.

The judge who Kim guessed was in his late fifties was obviously listening carefully and making several notes on a sheet of paper and she was impressed as Golda spoke eloquently, fluently and only referred to her notes and files occasionally. She even managed to pronounce the full technical name of the Beta drug although she did say that it was generally known by the shorter nomenclature of just Beta and provided his Lordship didn't object then she intended to refer to it by that shortened name in future during her submission. He agreed and even congratulated her on being able to pronounce its full name.

And so the discussion progressed. The judge asked questions which Golda answered without hesitation. At one point she asked for his permission to refer to Kim for clarification on a point. He agreed and having done so she resumed her dissertation to him.

Finally she came to an end of her submission finishing with the words 'And so my Lord it is our belief that preventing the broadcasting of this programme on Thursday evening of this week in spite of any damage that might be done to Furrina Pharmaceuticals as a result, is right ……. is in the public interest …….. and should not be prevented'.

'Thank you. Now I have several more questions' and he proceeded to ask them which Golda answered. They were varied in nature but Golda by her confident and competent responses showed that she had a complete grasp of the issue. Finally the judge nodded, studied his notes and papers for a couple of minutes then looking at Golda said 'You have made a good and clear case, well put to me. I will consider this matter and revert with a ruling by five o'clock as I imagine timescales are getting short for your client to know whether they can or cannot proceed with broadcasting this programme.

In the meantime the injunction of course remains in full force and legally binding. You need to ensure that your client' and here he looked directly at Kim 'is aware of this and also fully understands that any breech of said injunction would be an extremely serious criminal offence'.

'Indeed so my Lord. Thank you'.

'Very well' and with that comment Golda gathered her documents and papers together, indicated that Sally, Kim and Levi should stand and all four did so while the judge walked to the side of the room and exited through a narrow door.

'So that's it?' queried Kim.

'That's it' and checking her watch Golda smiled and went on 'fifty five minutes. Well we got his attention alright. Now the question is whether in his deliberations he considers the public interest to disclose of greater importance than the need to protect Furrina's confidentiality'.

'Your guess?'

'I don't guess in these circumstances. Judges are too unpredictable but I think we have a fair chance. His whole demeanour although impartial seemed to me to err towards us and against Furrina, but you can never tell. Now we must wait. I will call you as soon as I have some response from his Lordship'.

'Great thanks'.

They made their way back to the entrance of the Law Courts where Golda hailed a taxi and all four of them got in. It was only a short journey before Golda and Sally got out leaving Kim and Levi to journey back to TV-12's studios and offices where as soon as she was at her own desk she rang Toby and updated him on what had occurred.

'And what does this Golda think of our chances or didn't she say?'

'She wouldn't give a definite view but said that she thought we had a fair chance but warned that judges are unpredictable. However she thought that his demeanour appeared to err *towards* us and *against* Furrina. But she said you can never tell and we'd have to wait for his judgement'.

'Right. Thanks'.

For the rest of the afternoon she couldn't properly concentrate on anything and kept checking her watch and the wall clock in her office area. Time moved slowly but eventually at about twenty past five her phone rang.

'Kim I have some news for you' said Levi.

'The injunction? Have we got it removed?'

'We have but before you get too excited the judge gave Furrina leave to appeal although he did so only because it is their right to do so and apparently his whole tone in granting such leave of appeal was strongly indicating that he didn't feel his decision to overturn the injunction should be changed or amended'.

'So what happens now?'

'If the other side go back to court tomorrow and lodge an appeal then Golda will also return to court and fight any attempt by Furrina to overturn our judge's decision'.

'Right thanks. I'll tell Toby and the rest of the team'.

The Beta File

Feeling elated she did some more work until checking her watch she saw it was a quarter to six, so shutting down her computer she closed her desk and was soon on the tube travelling home.

As she got off her mobile pinged and she read a message from James saying he was really sorry but that he'd be late home.

'Damn' she muttered as she'd wanted to talk to him about everything that had happened with the court proceedings but once indoors she changed into her running gear and was soon pounding the pavements.

After she'd completed her evening run and again back in her apartment she showered, dressed in clean panties and bra, calf length blue tight fitting slacks and a pink tee shirt emblazoned on the chest with the exhortation

Being bad is naughty
Being naughty is good!

Pouring herself a glass of sparkling water she peered in the fridge, extracted a pack of smoked salmon and another of crayfish tails, knocked up a salad and shortly was eating while listening to some jazz music which was a favourite of hers.

Later she watched the latest episode of a TV drama on TV-12 and at ten o'clock channel hopped between BBC, ITV, Sky and TV-12 news programmes.

James returned just before it finished, kissed her, said he'd eaten but would love a drink, poured himself a large whisky, a small one for her and plonked down on the settee next to her.

'Ready for some news?'

'Yes sure' she replied kneeling next to him.

'I've been offered that job for which I've been interviewed twice'.

'Hey that's terrific. Well done. Are you going to take it?'

'Not sure. I might just use it as leverage with Longtons to force up my salary and bonus earnings'.

'Umm'.

'What do you mean umm?'

'Well you've been saying for a little while now that you felt a bit restricted there and wanted more freedom to act so why not change companies?'

Mike Upton

'You may be right. I like Longtons but in some ways I do feel it's time for a change but then in others I'm not sure. They're nice people there, it's a pleasant environment and I've done well so in many ways I feel comfortable there'.

'Comfort in work isn't always the best thing'.

'No I guess not. I'll think about it for a day or so and then decide. But what about your day? How is the battle of the injunctions going?'

'It's a battle alright. Firstly Furrina got an injunction to stop us broadcasting, then we've now got it overturned ………'

'Hey well done!' exclaimed James.

'Yes but unfortunately the judge gave Furrina leave to appeal against his decision overturning the injunction. So we still can't go on air with this issue'.

'So hang on a minute. Let me get this straight. Furrina got an injunction, now you've got it overturned, but when it goes back to court it might be re-imposed again?'

'Yep' she grinned 'that's right'.

'Then what? You try it to get it rescinded again?'

'I guess so. I'm not sure what happens in those circumstances?'

'Sounds all very complex and expensive. No wonder lawyers are always wealthy men!'

'Men and *women*. Don't be sexist!' she cautioned.

'Sorry'.

'Hmm …… okay. Our barrister is a remarkable lady' and she proceeded to tell James the history of Golda's family tragic misfortunes.

'No wonder she's tough then with that background'.

'Yes so don't forget that women can be tough as well as men you know'.

'I know but they can also be soft, tender, sexy and really often quite naughty!' and he traced a finger along the inscription on her front before moving to touch her breasts beneath the tee shirt.

'Do you think I'm sexy then?' she asked allowing her voice to become quieter and deeper.

'I do' he replied gently pressing first one and then the other breast.

'And naughty?' she wanted to know.

'Oh yes at times. Definitely! Especially when we take this off. Arms up!' and when she willingly complied he pulled it over her head and off then leaned towards her and kissed each bra covered breast in turn before reaching behind her and having unclipped the garment, slid it down her arms and off. 'That's better' he grinned and his lips encased her left nipple.

'Umm. And so now where do your thoughts lead you then?'

Transferring his lips to her other nipple he slowly sucked it deep into his mouth, flicked his tongue across the end then allowing it to slowly slide free he looked up at her and whispered 'Bed?'

'Oh do they now?'

'Yes they certainly do' and he gave both breasts a kiss but this time a little more forcefully.

'Well if that's what's in your mind we'd better go and satisfy it then hadn't we?' she grinned and plonking a smacker of a kiss on his lips, stood, collected her tee shirt and bra, held out a hand and pulling him to his feet continued 'you go and lockup, turn out the lights and then come and join me in bed and we'll see what we can do about those thoughts'.

Later after they'd calmed down she ran a finger around his lips and whispered 'Thank you darling. I do love you'.

'And I love you too'.

Cuddling into his large powerful body and running a hand up and down his chest every now and then entwining a finger in his chest hair she said softly 'I do hope we get this injunction business sorted out. It will make such a good programme, both from a viewers interest point of view but also from the need to let the public know how a major British corporation is misbehaving'.

'If you don't how will you fill the slot?'

'Oh we've got a couple of past investigations on film in case of need. Neither of them are especially hard hitting or dramatic but they'll do as a stop gap. The bosses won't be happy because they're already moaning that some of the recent programmes haven't been sufficiently viewer challenging. Still we have to fill the slot. But that's why this programme about Beta is so vital'.

'And now it's all in the hands of your lady lawyer?'

'Yes'.

'So nothing to do but wait, cross your fingers and hope'.

'I guess so'.

'Right so sleep time now?'

'Err not quite yet if you don't mind'.

'Hey babe you want sex with me again? Man you're one hell of a horny broad' he chuckled putting on a passable American accent.

She laughed. 'Maybe I am but no I don't want sex again. Well at least not tonight. No I'd like to talk'.

'Hey talking ain't sexy. Now you just lie there little lady and I'll ....'

'No you won't! Listen be serious will you?'

'Okay' he grinned and sitting up and leaning back against the headboard pulled her against himself and said 'I'm listening. You going to tell me how brilliant I am at making love?'

'No ....'

'What a stunningly good looking guy I am?'

'No I ....'

'How you can't get enough of ....'

'Shut up and listen'.

'Right I'm all ears. Fire away'.

So she told him of the concerns at TV-12 about the Highlight programme and how it needed a really challenging subject to present in order to stop the station's bosses taking drastic action to curtail its scheduling. He listened, asked several questions then said 'I can see that's a concern. But lying here worrying about it isn't going to change things is it? What will be will be, with the outcome of the injunction issue. Either you'll get it lifted and go on air or you won't. It doesn't seem to me that there is any middle course'.

'No that's the trouble. There isn't' she sighed.

'So in that case I think it's time you stopped lying there worrying and either we went to sleep or you reverted to being a horny broad! Either one of those courses of action is better than lying here getting into a stew about it'.

'Hmm I guess you're right'.

'I am. So which is to be?'

'You've had your horny broad tonight so now it's time for you to calm down, keep your hands *and* your dick away from me and go to sleep'.

'Killjoy' but with a good humoured chuckle he leaned over her, they peck kissed and were soon entwined in each other's arms.

But Kim woke a couple of times, once after a fearsome dream in which she was in the dock at the Old Bailey demanding an injunction to keep James away from her in bed. He was in the public gallery obviously stark naked although the bench which he was sitting behind hid his waist and genitals so she could only see his face, bare chest, waist and legs. Dozens of lawyers were shouting at her with some saying that she could have the injunction some saying not, but eventually a wizened old judge whose face was somewhat unclear but who kept shouting 'Order in court' and banging a gavel on his desk refused to rule on the case. At which point James stood up, leapt over the desk in front of him and ran towards her with his erect penis wobbling violently, grabbed her and ran with her out of the courtroom and into the sea. As she turned to look at the shore she saw their hotel in Sardinia and standing on the beach with a fishing rod was the judge in a blue swimming costume who yelled 'Case dismissed'.

When she got up next morning to do her daily exercise routine she felt quite jaded although she brightened up under the shower and by the time she got to work she felt almost like her old self.

The call from Levi came sharp at nine. 'As expected they have appealed. The case is listed for eleven o'clock this morning. I do not propose to go as there is nothing that I can usefully add or contribute. This is barrister to judge stuff and not for a lowly solicitor like me'.

'Can I go?'

'Yes of course. You don't need me but Golda will probably be glad that you're there in case she needs to check anything with you'.

In the courtroom Kim sat with a combination of worry, anger, awe, excitement, hope, unease, apprehension and trepidation as the court case evolved. As the arguments ranged back and forth she studied the faces of the three judges and tried to gauge whether they were sympathetic or not to TV-12's case. It was such a clear cut case of misleading the public and the authorities that surely they must come down on her side mustn't they?

Once during a particularly complex debate about an obscure point of law she found her mind drifting away and with an internal smile she remembered again her dream from last night.

Eventually though the senior judge announced that the three of them had heard sufficient argument from both sides and that they would retire to consider their verdict.

Kim made her way out of the court and into the main hallway where near to the entrance she rang Levi and updated him on where the proceedings had got to.

'Good. When judges say they've heard enough it generally means that they've come to a decision. Of course it is for them to know and us to guess what that decision might be'.

'How long do you think they will they take to consider the matter? Time is getting short now before we go to air and I know that Toby has made some trailers already so that the moment we get the okay he'll start blasting them out during every commercial break between now and the time that Highlight goes out'.

'I don't know. If the three judges are all agreed then probably not very long. If one or more is against the decision of the other two then who knows? It will depend on how strongly the dissenting judge feels. It is possible to get a majority decision. In other words two of the judges might overrule the third but that is rare and generally if that's going to happen they may reserve judgement at this stage and consider for a longer period of time'.

'Oh God but that might mean we miss this week's slot to put the programme out?'

'No doubt but let's hope it doesn't come to that. The best thing you can do is wait and hope'.

She returned to the court and sat in the courtroom which was almost empty, except for the two teams of lawyers. Golda and Sally for TV-12 and some others on behalf of Furrina.

Alternatively drumming her finger on her knee; studying her nails noting that she'd chipped one slightly; checking her smartphone for messages as she'd switched it to silent and so hadn't heard if any e-mails or texts had come in and finding that some of both had she answered them slightly worried as to whether she was breaking any courtroom rules by doing so.

She found it odd that Golda and Sally were happily chatting to the barristers acting for Furrina and she considered the ironic situation that here were advocates on opposing side happily chatting and talking together, even sharing the occasional little laugh whereas earlier they had been arguing strongly against each other.

While puzzling over that, every now and then she thought about James and how much she loved him. Her mother had always said that when Mister Right came along she would immediately and instinctively know. Anna had also said something similar although her description was considerably more graphic and sexually explicit! And she did know. Without any shadow of doubt James *was* her Mister Right whether considered against either her own, her Mother's or Anna's criteria.

Lost in a pleasant dream like mood remembering his tender caresses and the way he always looked out for her she was startled when the court usher called 'All rise' and as she and the very few other people in the courtroom did so she checked her digital watch which showed 13.34.

The three judges bowed and took their seats, looked around the court then as the one in the middle held a piece of paper in front of him and began to read she crossed her fingers.

He started by outlining the case, setting out the arguments from both sides and summarising the essence of the injunction and why it had been granted.

Pausing he looked first at the Furrina lawyers and then at Golda and Sally before removing his glasses, polishing them with a handkerchief then replaced them on his nose. Kim held her breath as she guessed this was it. The moment when TV-12 would find if they could go ahead and broadcast or not.

'We have examined the evidence on both sides to determine whether the injunction should remain in force or be lifted' said the judge 'and our unanimous judgement is that although the matter of commercial sensitivity for Furrina Pharmaceuticals by the withholding of this matter from the general public is clearly of very great significance, the overriding and indeed paramount importance of the principle of press, or in this case television freedom to expose issues of public importance cannot be prevented'.

He paused again and Kim quickly exhaled then took another breath which as the judge once more started speaking she held and re-crossed the fingers of both hands.

'Therefore and with full cognisance of the implications of our judgement today we rule the injunction should be lifted and that accordingly the television company known as TV-12 be allowed to broadcast their proposed programme.

Kim's heart jumped and she only just prevented herself from jumping up and shouting 'Yes!'

'We further rule that this be an end of the matter and the plaintiff is not granted leave to appeal our decision to the Supreme Court'.

There was absolute silence in the court as the implications of the judgement sunk in to all parties present then the judges stood, bowed and left the court.

Golda turned to Kim and with a broad grin and accompanied by Sally started to make her way towards the young TV executive.

'That's it?' queried Kim running the few paces to the lawyer.

'Yep that's it. You're free to broadcast'.

'They can't stop it?'

'No the judge was quite specific. No appeal. He didn't rule against an appeal to the European Court in Strasburg but there is no way they'd ever get that to happen before you go to air. So yes Kim you've got your approval to expose Furrina so go on girl. Go get 'em!'

'We will. Make no mistake about that. Thank you *so* much. I don't know how to say it sufficiently strongly but *thank* you'.

'My pleasure. Go on off you go. I've got a few things to sign off here but away you go and tell your lot that the programme can go ahead. I look forward to seeing it'.

Kim nodded then walked quickly out of the courtroom, almost ran down the hallways of the ancient building, trotted down the steps outside to the pavement while dialling first Levi to tell him, then she asked him to switch her to Toby.

'Fucking brilliant!' he exclaimed when she told him the news. 'Right get yourself back here and we'll go over everything ready for tonight. I'll let upstairs know that they're going to see a belter of a programme when it goes to air'.

The Beta File

Actually when she arrived back to the TV studios it was almost an anticlimax as there was nothing for her to do with the programme between now and eight o'clock when it went live on air. It was made; had been legally checked by Levi who'd approved it subject to getting the injunction lifted; the senior management were all briefed; her team were thrilled; the trailer was complete and she gathered that the first showing of that had already aired and it was intended to trail the programme in almost every commercial break from now until the time to show the programme.

Kim wandered around the offices chatting to her team, to Toby, even to Peter Holmes the MD who'd come down to congratulate her but at six fifteen she was complete. Nothing more for her to do on the programme, just wait until eight o'clock when it would go out.

Her nerves which had been jangling from the moment she got up, while doing her exercises, on the tube journeying into work and throughout the time of the court case were still tight and tingling at her. She had a lot riding on this particular Highlight programme.

Everyone at TV-12 noticed that she was like a cat on hot bricks and she knew that too as she found she couldn't settle to anything. It was always like this just before a programme she'd created went out, but somehow the Beta File programme was special.

Before the investigative programmes on which she'd worked had generally tended to relate to more abstract subjects and while some had been not as hard hitting as others in the main they'd all generated considerable interest and excitement among the public. Okay she conceded to herself perhaps badgers, and the high street shopping situations hadn't been the most riveting of subjects but others in the past had been.

People dying on trolleys in hospital A & E departments had caused a real furore. As had a new 'pay-day' loan company charging exorbitant rates of interest and then using physical threats of violence to recover the money they were owed. That had led to a police investigation of the company. The RSPCA and Trading Standards had got involved after TV-12's programme on cruelty to chickens in a large apparently free range egg supplier which had also resulted in two large supermarket chains stopping taking supplies from them.

There were other investigations resulting in programmes which the TV station had put out in the Highlight series but now it needed a real hard hitting programme to re-boost the appeal of television documentaries in general, their channel in particular and Highlight especially.

She was convinced that tonight's programme would do everything that was needed for the programme, the station and she admitted her own career.

Forcing herself to work on other matters she'd begun studying some preliminary work that they'd started following an issue that had been brought to them about a series of unexplained dog deaths in two adjacent villages. Although at first sight this might not appear a hard hitting subject she felt that they could take a very sympathetic approach and build in lots of "aaah" factor with many shots of pet dogs before they died; lots of cute puppy or little dog shots and of course grieving owners and especially children mourning the loss of the family pet.

She got quite involved in working on the project including arranging to take Rick out to the villages involved next week to pre-check what to film for background and atmosphere shots, as well as starting to make some appointments with people who'd been affected by the loss of a pet. This was a project that like so many had been stimulated by a member of the public contacting TV-12 and drawing the issue to their attention. Just like Brian had with the matter of the Beta file.

Finally she packed up, said she'd call Toby later that evening as soon the programme had aired and arrived home having been groped on the tube by a very fat man who deliberately touched her bottom. The first time she put it down to an accident but when it happened again she turned to him and hissed 'Touch my bum again and I'll kick you in the balls so hard they'll never recover'. He left her alone after that!

She rang James who said that it was terrific news and he'd be home in good time to watch the programme with her.

CHAPTER 21

But while the TV-12 team were elated and getting ready for the reaction to their programme when it went out, at Furrina Pharmaceuticals Marylyn Goodrich was beside herself with rage when at a quarter to two she'd received the phone call telling her that they'd lost the injunction appeal.

'What else can we do to stop this fucking programme going out?' she yelled at her senior management team who she'd summoned to her office.

While everyone else remained silent it was Louis Farmer the Head of Drug Development who took a deep breath and responded. 'There's nothing that we can do. We lost in the appeal court and that's it. The judge specifically refused us leave to appeal again to the Supreme Court and although we may be entitled to go to the European Court of Justice in Strasburg there is no way on God's earth that we can do that before the programme goes out'.

'Find a way! Find some way to stop it' she snarled. 'Someone. Anyone. I don't care who just find a way to stop it'.

'Marylyn I understand how you feel ....'

'No you bloody well *don't* know how I feel'. She paused and looked in turn at each of the team in front of her. 'I feel like I'm surrounded by idiots. Incompetent buffoons who don't know how to stop a television programme going out! Is that so difficult? Eh?' There was silence so she again asked 'Well?'

'Look getting all het up about it won't change anything' then seeing she was about to explode Louis pointed a hand towards her and went on 'listen Marylyn. The programme *is* going to go out. Like it or not it *is* going on air. We have tried to stop it but regrettably we failed ....'

'Those fucking lawyers failed and if they think I'm going to pay what will be undoubtedly their enormous bill which they'll be sending us they can go and take a large running jump. They failed. They're getting nothing from me. Zilch! Got it?'

'Yes got it. But their fee wasn't on a no win no fee basis. We retained them in good faith and they did their best ....'

'Their best' she screamed. 'Their best? Well if that was their best I'd hate to see their worst!'

Ignoring her tempestuous outburst he went on 'So we are faced with the situation that this programme is going out eight o'clock. We can't stop it so we need to prepare for the undoubted storm that it will generate. We'll have the media all over us. Questions in Parliament is a distinct possibility. They'll also be pressure from TV, newspapers as well as social media which will undoubtedly go wild and we should expect threats probably to our facilities as well as to some of our employees, including us perhaps.

I'll brief the PR people to get ready. We need a statement from you Marylyn and we need professional advice on what it should say. At the moment I'm inclined to err towards being honest about what's happened'.

'Honest? Are you mad?'

'No. The British public generally like people or companies that hold up their hands and say "Yep we screwed up. Sorry. Lessons will be learned to make sure it won't happen again". What they don't like is people or companies who wriggle, lie or try and make excuses. You will need to be ready to be interviewed on TV, radio and probably by press reporters and you'll need to adopt a humble caring sensitive style and approach'.

'Humble? Caring? Sensitive? I don't do those things'.

'But this time for the good of the company and yourself that is what you *need* to do'.

She stared at him for at least a minute before asking 'Why?'

'To try and limit the damage, protect the company's reputation as far as possible and to protect yourself. Protect us'.

'Protect? What the hell from?'

'Prosecution'.

'Prosecution? What prosecution?'

'You ...... we, could be charged with all sorts of offences and serious ones at that. We could be facing prison if we are tried and found guilty'.

'Prison? Don't be so fucking daft. So we screwed up some test results. A few people got some side effects? So what? They signed up for the tests voluntarily and of their own free will. People get damaged in drug trials all the time.

I mean look at that 2006 trial of a drug by a US company at London's Northwick Park Hospital's research unit where six previously healthy volunteers developed serious side effects some even finding their heads swelled up. The worst affected lost fingers and toes and all were told they were likely to contract cancer or other auto-immune diseases in future.

Then there was the trial conducted in Rennes in France of a drug manufactured by a Portuguese drug company in January in which one man died and some others suffered neurological problems. These things happen. There are many other instances of where people have been damaged in drug trials'.

'But not by us. Look you know we didn't follow standard protocol firstly with the animal testing ....'

'YOU didn't follow standard protocol' she snapped.

'*We* didn't. You knew perfectly well that we were cutting corners, switching animal species and that we were taking risks by doing so'.

There was silence for a moment.

'Okay line up your PR people. Are we using Brundells for this?'

'No. They're good for our normal PR requirements, but although I'll brief them this is specialised stuff. We need a PR company that is an expert in crisis management. I've been doing some checking and the one that constantly seems to come up is CML which stands for Crisis Managed Limited. They have lots of experience and have handled many company disaster scenarios. I think they'll be perfect'.

'You'd better get in touch with them then'.

'I have already had a long conversation with Steve Malloy their Managing Director. Without going into any real detail I have told him we have a potential major issue with a TV programme that is going to expose some wrong doing that we have mistakenly allowed to happen. He said that is exactly the sort of thing in which they specialise and they'd be pleased to help if we want to retain them'.

'Right. So you'd better set up a meeting with them'.

'Already done that. He'll watch the programme tonight then be here tomorrow morning at eight o'clock with a couple of others both to plan our counter offensive and our defensive activities'.

'What did he think of our chances of at least getting out of this safely?'

'He couldn't say because I haven't given him any details and he hasn't seen the programme. But I did strongly form the view that he would be a real asset to us in this emergency. He sounded reassuring and confident'.

'Glad someone is. Right now where are we getting to with finding the little bastard who has started this all off by blowing the whistle on us and the Betanapotraproxiflevien-g3 tests?' and with that question she glared at Fay Roper the Head of Human Resources.

'We've been trying to identify anyone who might have a grudge against us, as well as looking at all people who've left in the past two months. We don't think that any of the leavers could be the culprit ....'

'Why?' interrupted Marylyn.

'Because there is no-one with a specific reason to do us harm. We divided the leavers into two groupings. The first were those who left entirely of their own volition and the second are those we asked to leave. In neither of those categories was there anyone, man or woman, who had access to the Beta data or who worked on Beta.

So then we started to look at everyone in the business now that *has* worked on, or *is* currently working on Beta. It's a surprisingly large list but having spoken to every single one of them there is no evidence that any one of them would wish to do us harm'.

'How can you be sure?'

'I can't of course but Asif and I are extremely experienced in interview techniques and our considered judgement is that they're all good'.

'Did you put them through a lie detector test?'

'Err no'.

'Why not?'

'Because .... well firstly because to be honest I didn't think of doing that and secondly now that it's been mentioned I'm not sure it is appropriate'.

'Of *course* it's appropriate! I want everyone on your Beta list lie detected. Got it?'

'Yes I hear that but I'm not sure we *can* do that. I don't know whether we have any legal right to force people to take a lie detector test. In fact thinking about it right now I doubt whether we have. I'll check with Levi but I'm sure it would have to be voluntary'.

'Voluntary! Well if that's the case then if anyone refuses they're obviously guilty. Get on with it. Find someone who can administer those tests. Today. I........ want ...... this .... whistleblower .... found .... and .... quickly'.

'Ok-ay I'll see what we can do'.

'No don't *see* what you can do. Just bloody well DO IT' yelled Marylyn.

There was silence as Fay blushed and felt annoyed and to some extent embarrassed by Marylyn's latest outburst.

'So Steve where are *you* with finding our criminal?' the Chief Executive snarled looking at the Head of IT.

'Making progress. Interestingly we've adopted a similar approach to Fay. We're looking at everyone who's left in the last month as well as people working on Beta. But Loretta who is good at finding solutions to problems ....'

'Loretta? I don't think I've met her'.

'She's been with us about a year but she's very much a backroom person and that's probably why you haven't come across her. She suggested we also look into everyone who has *joined* the company in the last two months in case a sleeper has suddenly infiltrated'.

'Sleeper?'

'Term used by the intelligence services. Someone who joins an organisation, intelligence, armed forces or industry with the intent of doing harm but infiltrates themself and works quietly away without causing problems or challenging anything and is thus seen as an asset, but in reality is plotting against, stealing or maybe in our case leaking information to this TV company. So we're working our way through those people and cross matching them to the Beta list'.

'Okay but I thought those sort of people hid for years before starting to leak information?'

'I think that's probably right in the murky world of military intelligence but maybe not with commercial issues like we've got. Any rate worth checking out her idea'.

'Sure. So when will you have completed the exercise?'

'By tomorrow morning I think'.

'Excellent. At last that's positive' snapped Marylyn again glaring at Fay. 'Right Steve you continue that process, Fay get on with lie detecting and Louis get your PR people in here. Now get out and get on with things. Meeting over!'

CHAPTER 22

At six o'clock in the Furrina Pharmaceuticals board room several people settled themselves down under Marylyn's hostile gaze.

'Right Fay what's happened with the lie detector tests?' she demanded.

'Well first of all we were lucky in finding someone qualified to administer the tests at such short notice'.

'Who was that?'

'Man from a private investigation company. Funnily enough they approached me recently and asked if we wanted any such work doing and they made a point of stressing that they had a qualified lie detector operator on their staff. I remembered that, rang them and managed to get him to come here straight away. They're based in Leicester so not too far away'.

'Yes yes yes' snapped Marylyn. 'So you got someone. Good. What did he find out?'

'We had eleven people who were what the police would call persons of interest' and she gave a little smile but as no-one responded she quickly continued. 'Of those only three agreed to take the test and all were negative'.

'Negative?'

'Were not perceived as having been the whistleblower'.

'But eight refused to take the test?'

'Yes'.

'Well in my view our guilty person is one of those eight! Obviously! Who are they?'

'I guessed you'd want to know that so here's the list' and Fay handed round a sheet of paper to all present with the eight names on it. 'Now you'll see that I've divided it into two sections. The first five I would stake my life on them being *not* the guilty party. The other three .... well I wouldn't say they're guilty but I just don't know. What I mean is that I'm not so certain about them. It doesn't mean that I think they *are* guilty it's just that I can't be as certain that they're *not* as I am of the other five'.

Marylyn stared at her then nodded and turned to Steve. 'So where have IT got?'

'We've got ten names who've all had recent access to or are working on the Beta stuff but four are probably worth a second look to see if they could be the person for whom we are hunting. Interestingly one name crops up on both lists. Fay's and mine'.

'Really?'

'Yes' and getting up he slid the whiteboard at the end of the room into position, picked up a felt pen then glancing at the paper that Fay had handed out he wrote.

HR Suspects: *Angela Harwood*
                 Ray Derbyshire
                 Brian Moffatt

IT Suspects   *Sue Field*
                 Sadiq Kassab
                 Brian Moffatt
                 Penny Castle

Then slowly and deliberately he wrote Brian's name again below the two lists, underlined it and put a tick against it. Turning to the small group of senior people he said quietly 'Brian Moffatt'.

Brian Moffatt √

'Brian Moffatt!' exclaimed Louis. 'Yes. Now he's the guy that objected to the way we switched species in the early testing of this drug. Marylyn you remember. He made a right fuss about it, so you had him in your office, read him the riot act and gave him three options. Accept what we were doing shut up and get on with it; or agree to an alternative position on a different drug development programme. But if he wouldn't accept either of those options then he must leave the company. He chose to stay and we moved him onto the Leukaemia project'.

'Oh yes I do remember vaguely. Unimpressive sort of man. So that's the lousy bastard who has brought all this shit down on us then?'

'In all probability yes but let's discuss that and what we do about him after the television programme has gone out shall we? It's on in a few minutes'.

Hearing that Fay got up, walked to the large television set next to the whiteboard, switched it on, flicked to the TV-12 channel and sat down to watch the programme with the others present.

In Balham Kim's run was uneventful and when she got back James had arrived home. He'd bought some flowers for her, so she gave him an extra kiss to say thank you, wriggled out of his grasp, stripped off her running gear, went and showered, emerged and dressed in fresh panties, no bra and a blue and pink onesie, poured herself a glass of wine, laid the table and sat down to eat the paella that James had prepared for them.

Everything was cleared away by seven forty five so switching on the television and clutching a mug of coffee she sat down on the settee to wait for the programme to start.

When James came and joined her he handed her a glass of whisky. 'Here drink this' he said 'you're all on edge. I've never seen you so hyper about a programme of yours before'.

'No I know but you're right. I am all twitchy about it. I guess it's because of the injunctions and everything that's led up to this point; encouraging Brian to tell us everything; the investigation; going to India and being almost ....' she checked herself as she'd almost mentioned how she was nearly raped.

'Almost what?'

'Oh almost overwhelmed by seeing those poor people who'd been so damaged by Beta; the legal arguments about whether we could go on air or not; the worries that the directors want to reschedule, reduce length and retime Highlight. It's all of those things but if this works tonight then it will all have been worthwhile'.

'I'm sure it will. Now drink your whisky and let's enjoy your programme'. She nodded, took a deep pull of the drink, put down the glass and before snuggling into him popped a quick peck kiss on his cheek as the continuity announcer spoke.

'And now our next programme tonight is the latest edition of our award winning investigative series Highlight which this evening deals with the important issue of drug trials and what happens when they go wrong' he paused and then said 'the Beta File'.

'Good luck' whispered James as he took hold of her hand.

The Beta File

While the usual rather stirring theme music for the programme began shots of various types and colours of pills, capsules, syringes and laboratories paraded across the screen before fading whereupon the camera showed Kim in long shot sitting in a leather swivel chair then panned in to close up on her face.

'Good evening and welcome to this week's edition of Highlight, the programme that fearlessly investigates issues and maters of concern on any subject that is brought to our attention.

Tonight's edition deals with the truly shocking case of a British pharmaceutical company which has been conducting trials on human volunteers of a new drug designed to cure stomach cancer. An important and laudable thing to do as cancer of the stomach is serious, often fatal and always results in serious, debilitating and often life style changing action as the victims have to adapt their lives and personal habits to cope with the effects of the disease and especially the after effects of surgery or other treatments.

But Furrina Pharmaceuticals whose Head Office is based in Milton Keynes has taken dangerous short cuts with its animal testing procedures; ignored warning signs of side effects in those animal tests; undertaken trials on people in blatant disregard of those animal test negatives; and shamelessly paid off those human beings who have been damaged with their new drug with a mere pittance to buy their silence. No proper compensation. No hospital treatment. No after care. Just a tiny payment equivalent to a few pounds to the poor ill educated people in the Indian city of Mumbai who they recruited for the trial via their Indian office and who they threatened with legal action if those people disclosed what had happened to them'.

As she spoke at that point pictures of Indian life, chaotically crowded streets, Mumbai airport terminal, Furrina's Indian Offices and laboratories cascaded slowly across the screen then the camera came back onto her serious looking face.

'It is a story of shame which they have tried to prevent us broadcasting by applying for High Court injunctions to stop us airing this programme. But our lawyers persuaded the three appeal court judges that it was in the public interest to show tonight.

You will be as shocked and horrified as we were about what Furrina Pharmaceuticals have been doing, which would never have been known about unless a brave employee had come to us to expose the company's duplicity.

We have raised what has happened with Furrina's Chief Executive Marylyn Goodrich, Louis Farmer Furrina's Head of Drug development and John Andrews the In Market Test Controller for the company' and as each name was spoken their photograph appeared on the screen until all three were there.

'We have been to India' and the screen again filled with shots of Mumbai's chaotic streets, 'seen and spoken with many of those human guinea pigs, seen for ourselves the physical and mental damage that their taking this drug has caused to them' and quick shots of various of the people interviewed by the team appeared.

'So let's go back to the start of this drug development. To the labs where it was first trialled on mice' and pictures of mice in cages appeared.

The depiction unfolded exposing in enormous detail the results of TV-12's investigation. It was a well constructed programme which Penny as the producer had cleverly crafted together including interspersing extracts from Kim's interview with Marylyn shown against the slum areas of India and the people who explained what had happened to them.

Kim and James were riveted to the screen, Kim especially so when the camera showed the area outside Ashan's house in Mumbai where she was attacked the memory again flooding back but she pushed that to the back of her mind and concentrated on the rest of the programme at the end of which she spoke slowly and seriously directly to the camera.

'This company has refused to come onto the programme tonight but sent us a statement' and a series of words scrolled across the screen as a male voice spoke them aloud.

"Furrina Pharmaceuticals always carefully follows established protocols relating to the health and treatment of animals used in laboratory trials and is scrupulously careful to ensure that any reactions positive or negative are noted and taken fully into account when considering transfer of test programmes from animal to human live trials which are meticulously checked, trialled, monitored and evaluated under extremely strictly controlled procedures and in line with standard pharmaceutical protocols. We therefore utterly refute the suggestions made by TV-12 of any form of wrong doing or misappropriate test programmes on human test subjects".

The camera panned back onto Kim. 'At the moment that statement is the only response that we had have from Furrina, after their failure to prevent us from broadcasting, but we await their fuller and more considered reply in due course when they have seen our programme.

Depending on what that is will determine how *we* in turn respond to any such reaction of Furrina Pharmaceuticals Limited to this programme and the points we have raised and the questions we have asked. Specifically we want to ask them what they intend to do to put right what they have done, what financial compensation they will now pay to those people they have damaged in their drug trial and to give an assurance that never again will they indulge in such shoddy, illegal and dreadful practices'.

She paused and as the theme music began playing quietly in the background looking straight into the camera which was now showing her in real close up finished by saying 'I am Kim Harding. This has been Highlight for TV-12. Thank you for watching. Good night' and the volume of the theme music increased as she faded out and the programme came to an end.

'Well done darling' James said enthusiastically.

'Was it alright. I mean really alright?'

'Yes brilliant'.

'You mean it? You're not just saying that?'

'No I mean it'.

Her mobile rang and she saw it was Brian.

'Hi' she trilled 'have you watched it?'

'Yes'.

'What did you think of it?'

'I thought you came over brilliantly' he said 'really well. 'You are very photogenic aren't you?'

'Ooh I don't know about that but you're happy with the programme?'

'Oh yes'.

'And as you saw no one will recognise you'.

'No. Thank you. So what happens now?'

'Now we sit back and wait to see what they do. Hopefully they'll stop this awful drug trial and make some proper compensation for those people they've damaged'.

'The witch hunt that's been going on at work already will I imagine be nothing to what it's going to be like to tomorrow morning'.

'I guess not'.

'I've been interviewed twice you know. Once by HR and once by IT. They seem to be using those two departments to try to track down and find who leaked the information. HR even wanted me to take a lie detector test'.

'I see'.

'I guess that's logical but it's frightening. I refused and so did one or two other people. Kim I'm really frightened now. If they do discover it was me then I'm finished. Finished with Furrina and finished in the industry. Then what will I do?'

'But your identity was completely protected in the programme'.

'Yes but if through HR and IT they do pin it on me whatever am I going to do?'

'I don't know. I can't answer that question'.

'Yes I know, but even if IT and HR don't get me, what happens if Furrina get a court order to force you to disclose who gave you the information?'

'I don't know but let's cross that bridge when …….. if we come to it shall we?'

He paused for a long time before replying quietly 'Alright. You know I wonder if I did the right thing in blabbing about this?'

'Of course you did. Think of all those poor damaged people we saw in India'.

'Yes I suppose so' but he didn't sound convinced.

Suddenly she said 'Brian I've got to go as I've got another call coming in'.

'Oh right. You will keep in touch won't you?'

'Yes of course. We might even want to do a follow up programme?'.

'Really?'

'Possibly. Depends on the audience reaction to tonight's programme. Bye' and she cut off his call and switched to the new incoming one. 'Oh hello Toby. Came over okay I think don't you?'

The Beta File

'Yes. One of the best we've done. It's funny you can watch it being put together in the studio, see the final programme run through in the studio but somehow watching it on one's own television at home seems to be different'.

'Yes I know exactly what you mean'.

'Any rate. The reaction's started. Have you looked on Facebook and Twitter?'

'No not yet'.

'Well you should. You've not only stirred up a hornet's nest but a nest of vipers as well. Social media is going mad and I'm sure the press and other TV channels will, as well as tomorrow's press'.

'Right I'll look now' then cupping the phone she asked James, 'can you punt around on Twitter and Facebook to find what you can about the programme and reaction to it please darling'.

'Sure thing' and he unwound himself from the settee, walked to a side table and fired up a laptop.

'James is starting to look for me' she said returning to Toby.

'Right. I've had a text from Peter Holmes'.

'Favourable reaction?'

'Yes. Three words. Good programme. Excellent'.

'Praise indeed' she chuckled.

'Indeed. Right see you in the morning.

'Sure. Night and thanks for ringing'.

He'd been right. The reaction on social media was intense and building by the minute and she and James heads close together studied intently what was being posted. She was concentrating on the screen but he began to concentrate on her hair falling forward around her face as she leant forward. Moving his face towards her he whispered 'Will you be staring at that screen for long?' and popped a little kiss on her cheek.

'Umm ages I think'.

'Oh shame'.

'This is important James, really important. To those poor people in Mumbai damaged by the Beta drug; for the employees of Furrina; for Brian having the courage to come forward and tell us about it; for Highlight's future; for our audience; for our advertisers; but especially for me'.

Mike Upton

'I know but you see I'm selfish. I don't like to share you with your television audience'.

'Good' she grinned. 'I like you being selfish like that. Now go and get us some more whisky and let me continue to study this lot' she muttered.

But while the TV-12 people were elated at the programme in Milton Keynes Marylyn's level of anger had shot up several degrees and she was venting it to Fay and Steve in the board room where the three of them had just watched the television exposé.

'It's got to be that bastard Moffatt. Got to be. I know the television company hid his identity but does anyone here think that looked like him?'

'Difficult to tell but at least we know it's a man so we can rule out all the woman on our combined lists' said Fay looking at Steve.

'I agree'.

'So it's one of those three. Sadiq Kassab, Brian Moffatt or Ray Derbyshire then?' announced Marylyn pointing at the white board.

'In all probability yes' agreed Steve.

'What do you mean in all probability? If you and Fay between you have identified those three then it must be one of them. Furthermore as Moffatt was anti what you were doing with the animal trials and he's on both your lists then to my mind the case is clear. It's him!'

'Probably' nodded Steve.

'Look the guy on the screen didn't appear to be Asian or Arabic so that rules out Sadiq. He *is* of Arab origin isn't he?'

'Yes'.

'Right so that's him out. Now the guy on the screen was middle aged and he certainly didn't have long hair which I know Ray Derbyshire does. In fact when he was in a planning meeting a couple of days ago which I sat in on, I thought then what a scruffy sod he is and wondered why doesn't he get his hair cut and tidy himself up. Have a word with him will you Fay?'

'Err yes okay'.

'So it's Moffatt. Clear as daylight' announced Marylyn leaning back in her chair.

'I assume you'll want me to see him in the morning?' Fay wanted to know.

The Beta File

'You bet I do' she snapped sitting bolt upright again. 'And get hold of our lawyers to see if we can bring criminal charges against him. I hope we can as I want him locked up and rotting in jail for years for what he's done'.

'Okay I'll talk to legal and see what they say'.

'Do and tell them not to pussyfoot around with this bastard!'

'Alright I agree that we need to talk to legal but just remember Marylyn that we don't know for sure that he's the one' cautioned Steve.

'*I* know. *I* bloody know. It's Moffatt. *Definitely* him'.

'I'll talk to him first thing in the morning as soon as he arrives at work then I'll call you and let you know what's transpired' stated Fay hoping this meeting would end soon as she was tired at the end of a long day, had a headache and Marylyn's constant angry outbursts didn't help.

'Do. I'll be waiting' she snarled. 'Once he's confessed bring him up to me. I want to tell him what I think of him, what he's done, what we're going to do to him to pay him back and what our revenge will be'.

'Do you think that's wise?' queried Steve. 'Wouldn't it be better to keep you out of it in case it goes to an employment tribunal?'

'Maybe it would but I don't care. I want that creep in front of me and when I crucify him I want to see his eyes, his face, his body, his whole being and I want to watch as he contemplates just what's he done and more importantly what's going to happen to him'.

'I think we're done then for tonight aren't we' queried Fay mentally crossing her fingers.

'Yes. Meet and review in the morning when you've got Moffatt to confess. Goodnight'.

After leaving the Chief Executive's office Fay and Steve walked thoughtfully side by side along the corridor to the stairs. As they began to descend Steve said 'Fancy a quick drink at the Crown?'

'Oh Steve that would have been lovely but I've got a splitting headache and I think I just want to get out of this place, home and relax with a large gin'.

'Oh come on. I'll buy you that gin at the pub. Needn't stay long'.

She looked at him as they continued downstairs then said 'Yes okay. Tom's away tonight so I'll take a couple of paracetamol before I leave here and hope they work quickly'.

Mike Upton

'The gin will speed 'em up' he chuckled. 'See you there in a few minutes?'

'Okay'.

When she arrived Steve was sitting in the corner of the bar with a pint of beer and a gin and tonic on the small table in front of him. Seeing her he jumped up, grinned, bowed his head and said 'Your drink awaits my lady'.

'Thanks' she sighed as she sat down, took the drink, poured in half the tonic and took a large sip. 'Umm. God I needed that. I hate Marylyn you know. I've never really liked her but the more I see of her the more I dislike her and it's got to the extent that dislike is becoming hate!'

'Yes she's a nasty piece of work alright. If it is Moffatt and as it sure looks that way then Heaven help him when she gets hold of him'.

'Indeed. Silly fool. If it is him?' she cautioned.

'Looks pretty clear though doesn't it?'

'Yes unfortunately'.

'Does he have a family. Wife? Kids?' he wanted to know.

'No I looked him up before I left tonight. He's single'.

'Gay?'

'No I don't think so' she laughed. 'Just because a guy's not married doesn't mean he's gay. Plenty of eligible single bachelors'.

'Guess so. Any rate change of subject. You said Tom's away tonight. Does he go away often?'

Always at least once a week sometimes twice. But every now and then he's off for a week or so if he's travelling abroad on business. He's a sales manager for a medium sized distribution company so he spends his time selling to potential new clients and schmoozing existing customers'.

'Do you mind him being away?'

'No. Gives me some *me* time'.

'Doing what?'

'Oh just girl things. Washing my hair mid week, painting my toe nails, stuffing the washing machine with his and my dirty laundry, bits of gardening in the summer, reading slushy novels, listening to classical music as he hates that, going for long solitary walks with the dog. Lots of things'.

'And you don't get lonely?'

'I miss him in the evenings of course and especially at weekends but needs must. He's got a good job and is in line for promotion. His firm have recently merged with a Canadian distribution company and that's why he's over there now. He's hoping that the next UK Managing Director's job that comes up could be his'.

'So I guess him being away right now is more than just a one or two nighter?'

'Indeed. He's in Canada. Flew off at the weekend. He'll be there for five days then he's going to Chicago for two days, flying down to Atlanta for three days then he's off to Brazil for a couple of days, followed by Argentina and finally Chile before coming back home. He'll be way for the best part of three weeks'.

She looked at him. 'The trips are getting longer. I wonder ....'

'You wonder what?'

She sighed 'I wonder if ....'

'If?'

'I wonder if he's having an affair? No actually that's not quite correct. I don't wonder if he is. I'm sure that he is'.

'What makes you say that?'

'Oh several things. Woman's intuition? He's bought himself some new underwear, now wears aftershave which he never did before, his new assistant is an attractive female several years younger than him, and me' she grimaced. 'And she goes off on several of these trips with him. He gets texts late in the evening and always deletes them after reading and sometimes I've discovered him talking on the phone at odd hours. You know weekends, evenings. He always says it's work but that's never happened until recently .... until this Laura joined the firm. She's single, pretty and I'm sure any man would fancy the pants off her'.

'Okay but that doesn't necessarily mean ....'

'He's having an affair with her? No I know it doesn't. But I think he is. There's something else too'.

He didn't ask the obviously question just smiled and waited for her to answer it herself which she did after a short while. 'Things in the bedroom aren't too good between Tom and me now'.

'Not too good?'

'Infrequent. Usually says he's too tired or got to leave early. Any number of excuses to avoid us getting it on together'.

'I'm sorry'.

'Ah well' and she took a deep breath then exhaled quickly 'enough of my problems. Forget it. Let's talk about you. How are you after, err well after ....?'

'It's okay. After Steff walked out?'

'Yes'.

'I'm fine. It wasn't really a surprise. Things had been pretty ropey between us for some time but nevertheless it was a shock when it happened and she upped and went. Still I've got over it and when we actually divorced it was a relief in a way as although I'd have loved her to come back, knowing she wouldn't kind of meant that whatever we had was unfinished, but the divorce stopped that and made it final'.

'I understand. So have you got a new lady?'

'Not really. I've had a few dalliances but no-one special'.

'Dalliances?' and raising an eyebrow she continued 'leading anywhere?'

'Apart from bed you mean?'

'Yes' she laughed.

'No only to bed'.

'Shame for you'.

'Ooh I don't know' he said quietly. 'Bed with a new lady for the first time is fun' and he seemed to stare at her rather intently for a moment or two.

'No doubt' she replied quickly taking another sip of her drink.

'Especially if you know it isn't going to lead anywhere long term and it's just fun for the night or maybe a few nights but not a permanent relationship'.

'Sounds a bit shallow doesn't it?'

'No not shallow. Just fun. Bit like going out for a nice meal at a new restaurant or having a first drink in a wine bar you've not visited before. Savour the anticipation, enjoy the experience then think about whether you'd eat or drink there again'.

'A very interesting analogy!'

'Umm I think so. Another drink?'

'Phew' she said slowly blowing out a long breath. 'I'd love one but I'm driving'.

'I don't think two G and T's will cause you a problem. I say what about something to eat? I don't know about you but I'm hungry. It'll also help soak up the gin or if you prefer skip the second gin and have a glass of wine with the meal?'

'Now that's a better idea. Can you get a menu?'

'Okay. How's the head by the way?'

'Getting better thanks. The food will probably help that too as well as soaking up the booze!'

He collected a menu from which she chose salmon steak and salad with a glass of Chablis and he plumped for a sirloin steak, chips, green beans and broccoli with which he had another pint of bitter.

They left the pub about ten thirty and as they got to her car he took her hand and said quietly 'Thanks for coming here tonight. I've really enjoyed our time together this evening'.

'Yes I've enjoyed it too' and she removed her hand from his gentle grip.

'Good and remember if you get lonely when Tom's away and want a night out with some friendly company just give me a shout'.

'Thanks I will. That would be nice'.

'Yes it would but you know what I'd like to do now?'

'What'.

'Have you come back to my place for the night?'

'Steve!'

'Yes?'

She looked into his eyes, flicked her own eyes around his face then said quietly 'I am very flattered that you've asked me but the answer is no. So now I'm going home'.

'Okay. Can't blame a guy for trying though. Fay I've fancied you for a long time you know and I'd just love to take you to bed. It would be so good'.

'Perhaps it would but .... no. Now goodnight' and she unlocked the door and slid behind the wheel. Closing the door she started the car, pressed the button to lower the window and with a smile said 'Thanks for supper. And for asking. Sorry to disappoint you. Nite Steve' and with that she drove slowly out of the car park.

Steve watching her VW Golf disappear muttered 'Shame' and walked towards his own car.

Fay though as she set off ran Steve's invitation through in her mind and for a second was tempted to turn round and see if he was still in the car park. Because what she hadn't said to him was that relations between her and Tom her partner of five years were at a really dire state with the sex infrequent and disappointing when it happened, constant rows and disagreements and before he'd left for North America they'd had a real humdinger of an argument. As so often happens in these kinds of situations it had started over a minor issue and quickly escalated into a full blown yelling match.

As she drove she began to speculate as to what Steve would be like in bed? After all he was reasonably good looking, tall, slim build, always dressed smartly not scruffily like many computer people, had a nice sense of humour and the more she thought about him the more she found herself regretting that she'd turned him down. After a few minutes she pulled into a small lay-by, got out her smartphone, scrolled through to Steve's mobile number, paused, took a deep breath and pressed the dial button.

It began ringing and she was about to end the call when Steve's voice came down the line. 'Hello Steve Jackson'.

'Steve this is Fay'.

'Hi. Forget something?'

'No'.

'Look if you're upset about what I asked then ....'

'No I'm not upset' she replied 'at least not with you. Just with myself'.

'I don't understand. Why are you upset with yourself?'

For a moment she couldn't bring herself to answer his question.

'Fay?'

'Sorry'.

'Why are you upset with yourself?'

'For saying no to you' she replied quietly.

'You mean you will come and spend the night with me?'

'Yes please .... if .... well I mean yes if the offer's still there?'

'Oh the offer is most certainly still there. Do you know where I live?'

'Not here in the car I don't. At the office I could look it up but not right now'.

'Got a pen?'

'If you go slowly I'll put it straight into the sat-nav'. She paused to switch it on then said 'right go ahead' and carefully tapped in the details he gave her, said 'okay it says it'll take thirty one minutes'.

'Thirty one minutes too long. When you get to the apartment block there's usually space in the visitors parking area but if by chance there's not then park in space nineteen. It belongs to my neighbours and they're away on holiday'.

In was in fact twenty five minutes later when she rang his doorbell and waited, heart bumping, for him to open the door.

'I'll have to be away early in the morning as I've got to go home, change into different clothes and get back to the office in good time especially as Marylyn wants me to interview Brian first thing' she said when the door opened and he stood framed in the space. Then she continued 'Sorry silly thing to have said as soon as I arrive. I guess I'm a bit nervous. You know about' she tailed off 'well about why I've come here. About what we're going to do. You and me' and again she lapsed into silence.

'Come in and don't be nervous. It'll be fine'.

After everyone had left for the night Marylyn sat quietly alone in her office contemplating the debacle that would unfold after the TV-12 expose went out. It would be a disaster for the company but a catastrophe for her.

She was aware that the company's main shareholders were unhappy with the financial results that the company had been producing recently and the Non-Executive Chairman had already warned her that their patience was wearing thin and that if Furrina did not firstly generate better results and secondly find something new in the drug field that would enable them to continue their past corporate growth which had stalled about eighteen months ago, then those shareholders would be looking to replace her as Chief Executive.

Unfortunately she knew that the next set of financial results for the half year's trading were dire, as costs had spiralled upwards, sales had declined yet again and innovative developments were disappointing. They were the things which could have helped offset the City's reaction to the below par sales and increasing costs issues.

That was why she had been pinning her hopes on the g3 variant of Betanapotraproxiflevien. The g1 and g2 variations had proved in the very early stages of testing to be ineffective which was why this g3 development had generated high hopes of a breakthrough for the latest variant of the drug.

Staring into space she put her head in her hands and for a moment felt like crying but as the first tears were about to appear she sniffed, rubbed her eyes with the ball of her hands, muttered 'Pull yourself together you stupid woman' and turned to her computer screen to finish the document she'd been working on earlier.

But progress was slow, the words wouldn't come and after a few minutes she decided to stop for the night, logged off, locked her desk and cupboards, collected her coat walked out for the office, paused to lock her door and strode confidently through the empty outer office where her secretary Jules worked, exited into the corridor, paused again to lock Jules's door and was soon in the lift travelling down to the foyer where she nodded goodnight to Harry the night security man and was soon in her red Mercedes on the M1 heading home to her large house in the small village of Keysoe in Northamptonshire.

Wholly unaware of the sword of Damocles now hanging over him Brian was at home, eating an Indian takeaway that he'd ordered and which had been delivered a few minutes ago. Since going to India and trying different Indian foods he'd come to quite like the spicy and hot food and so sitting at his small dining table with the dishes he'd ordered spread about, he was enjoying his food, as well as the porn DVD film that he was playing through his large television.

Indeed it was mainly to better enjoy porn films that he'd treated himself to the new bigger set.

Eventually he went to bed where he ran through in his mind the film he'd enjoyed and then letting his mind turn to Kim he started to think about her. But as he was about to sink into a happy sexy imagination of her he remembered Furrina and the witch hunt that was going on and seeing himself, albeit in shadow and with a disguised voice, he began to worry whether he could have been recognised by anyone at the company.

This concern took porn films and Kim right away from his brain and he lay in bed tossing and turning in an increasing state of worry and fear until he got up, went to his model soldiers room and switching on a tape recorder filled the room with the sounds of battle as he briefly re-enacted a small part of the D Day landings on Gold beach. His gaming lasted until gone two o'clock when yawning and now tired he went back to bed and soon dropped off into a fitful sleep.

CHAPTER 23

On Friday morning Marylyn woke looking forward to utterly destroying Brian Moffatt.

Louis started the day contemplating the implications of what the whistleblower had done and the repercussions from last night's TV-12 programme..

John Andrews thought about their problem but he also thought about another drug trial that they had running which fortunately wasn't causing problems.

Steve had woken earlier and studied the naked attractive woman next to him for a short while before deciding to shake her gently awake as to his surprise and intense pleasure last night she'd proved to be a good lover and he wanted to put his morning erection to good use with her.

Fay was now in the shower at her home having left Steve's around six fifteen after a quick but surprisingly good lovemaking session and was getting ready to go to Furrina to deal with the Brian Moffatt problem. But as she stepped out of the shower she glanced at her body in the full length bathroom mirror and smiled remembering how Steve had last night slowly and sensuously trailed his tongue from her lips to her pussy and given her a stunningly good oral orgasm before giving her another couple when he made love to her properly.

Kim busily conducting her morning exercise workout was bright and cheerful and looking forward to the day and hearing what more people thought about last night's programme.

James was dressing and pondering how to extract maximum value out of the fact that he had a firm offer from a rival company and did he use that to force better terms, conditions and salary from his current employer or accept the alternative offer?

Toby pensively ate his breakfast cereal and knew that today would be manic at TV-12 from the reaction to last night's Highlight programme.

Peter Holmes reminded himself that the TV station's advertising sales teams ought to have a field day in booking airtime both with new clients and existing ones following the positive audience reaction to that

Highlight programme and with more ad slots to coincide with next week's programme, as he was certain that audience response to last night's programme would have been good and as a result they could expect higher audience levels next week. As MD then audience levels was one of the key measures on which his performance was judged.

But Brian woke still desperately worried about what he'd done and anxious as to what would happen at work this morning and whether anyone would have guessed it was him on last night's programme.

He soon found out because as he walked into the glass fronted building Emily the brunette receptionist called to him as he made his way towards the lifts 'Oh Brian can you ring Fay Roper please? She said it was really urgent and for you to do so as soon as you got in'.

Heart dropping he muttered 'Yes okay'.

Arriving at his desk he saw there was a note propped against his computer.

Brian
Call me as soon as you arrive.
Thanks.
Fay Roper

Heart now banging furiously he checked in the company directory found her number and dialled. It was answered straight away.

'Oh Fay this is Brian Moffatt ....'

Without waiting for him to finish speaking she interrupted. 'Brian will you come up to my office straight away please. There's something we need to talk about'.

'Yes right' and putting the phone down he *knew* they'd discovered it was him. His feet felt like lead as he walked to the lifts and took one to the fifth floor. Slowly he padded along the corridor to Fay's office where he knocked and waited. The door opened and Asif Hajjar looking grim stood aside and motioned for him to enter.

Fay who was sitting behind her desk stood up and with a stern expression walked round to stand in front of it. Asif moved to stand close to her. As he waited for her to speak Brian couldn't help thinking that she looked very attractive this morning wearing a pale cream short skirted suit where the jacket was unbuttoned revealing a buttercup yellow blouse and as she stared at him there seemed to be a radiant glow on her face. However any thoughts about her appearance that he was having disappeared as soon as she spoke.

'Last night TV-12 showed a documentary about a drug trial which we are running in India. The drug is one that is undergoing human trials with which you are familiar. Betanapotraproxiflevien-g3. Did you see the programme?'

'Err no'.

Her face showed a clear expression of doubt as raising an eyebrow she continued 'It was *extremely* damaging to Furrina Pharmaceuticals. Part of the programme contained statements from a whistleblower whose identity was disguised and an actor spoke his words. However we believe that whistleblower was *you*'.

'No it wasn't. I wouldn't do something like that'.

'I'm afraid I don't believe you. Having had prior notification from the television company that they were going to show the programme and that it contained statements from a company employee who was going to make allegations against Furrina we investigated who that might be. Indeed you know that you and several others have already been interviewed about this matter as part of our investigations.

'We investigated not only from an HR perspective but also as you know Steve Jackson and one of his team looked into it from an IT angle. I have to tell you that the results of both Steve's and my enquiries led each of us to a short list of possible suspects. Your name was the only one on both lists. Furthermore looking carefully at the disguised person on last night's programme the profile of the head appeared to be very similar to yours. Also it is a matter of record that you disagreed with some of the animal trials we were conducting on this particular drug development and as a result you were moved off it and transferred to a leukaemia project.

'Therefore I am asking you again. Were you that whistleblower? I suggest you think very carefully about your answer and tell me the truth'.

Brian stared at the floor and shuffled his feet.

'I'm waiting for an answer Brian. Were you that whistleblower?'

He looked at her, then at Asif, around the room and then back to Fay whose dark brown eyes stared straight at him. His face was flushed and his breathing was faster than normal but unable to continue holding her gaze he stared at the floor.

'Well?' she asked very quietly. 'Did you go to TV-12?'

For a few moments he couldn't bring himself to reply then Asif snapped 'Fay has asked you a simple question Brian for which there is a simple answer. Please answer her. Did you disclose confidential information to TV-12? Yes or no?'

There was another pause then Brian said quietly 'Yes. I did. It was me'.

'You are confirming to me and Asif that it *was* you who went to TV-12 and gave them verbal information, computer printouts, and other materials about the human and animal test phases of Betanapotraproxiflevien-g3? Is that what you are saying?' demanded Fay.

'Yes but let me explain. You see ....'

'I am not interested in explanations. Come with me please. Marylyn wants to see you before you leave the building. Asif ring her and tell her we're on our way up to her office now please'.

Fay and Brian left the office and walked in silence along the corridor to the stairwell at the end, climbed one flight and were soon entering Jules's outer office. She nodded and said 'Go right in. Marylyn is waiting'.

Feeling exceptionally nervous Brian followed Fay into the large office which he'd only been in once before when Marylyn threatened to fire him if he didn't accept the transfer offered to the leukaemia project. As they walked in this time she was standing in the middle of the room, legs slightly apart, her arms folded across her chest, leaning slightly forward.

'Brian has confessed that it was him who gave TV-12 the information and appeared on the programme last night' stated Fay then she moved back a little leaving Brian about a yard way from the Chief Executive.

'You interfering, pathetic, no good, little shit' Marylyn said surprisingly quietly. 'I have no idea why you did what you did ....'

'Because of ....'

'Be *quiet* and listen to me. What you have done will undoubtedly have caused serious and possibly long term damage to the reputation of this company which will unquestionably affect its standing in the industry, with the public at large, with regulatory authorities and the Government,

The Beta File

not to mention its employees some of whom will certainly lose their jobs as we will have to restructure and probably shut down some research work while we deal with the damage fallout and mess to the company that you have caused'.

Her voice started to rise in pitch and volume as she continued. 'I don't know whether you thought you were being clever, had an axe to grind or whatever reason you had for this shameful and wilful act of vandalism and sabotage.

But company reputations take time and are hard to build. However they can be lost in a instant especially through the result of a sensationalist television programme misrepresenting the facts such as TV-12 broadcast last night.

You are worse than a maggot. A miserable useless little man that has no place on this earth never mind in this company. You are dismissed with *immediate* effect. You will receive no notice or severance payment. If ever any other employer is daft enough to consider employing you and asks us for a reference we will ensure that they are made aware of what you've done here. We will publicise why we fired you and thus be certain that you are blacklisted throughout the industry. You'll never work again in the pharmaceutical industry and we'll do our best to ensure that you never work for any sort of major company again in *any* industry. You will be seen as a pariah. A person who cannot be trusted. Someone for whom confidentiality just doesn't exist'.

Her voice now rose to full shouting volume as she threatened 'When we're finished with you you'll become an utter nobody. Useless, worthless, a person of no consequence, irrelevant, immaterial and someone not even worth mentioning. We will also be giving serious consideration to instigating legal action against you and if we can get you convicted and locked up in prison where you can rot for several years then I for one will be absolutely delighted'.

Although he could feel tears pricking the back of his eyes he wanted to speak but yelling 'Now *GET OUT AND NEVER COME BACK!*' she turned away from him and headed back to her desk.

'Look I need to explain ………' he stammered.

'*OUT. GET OUT!*'

Mike Upton

'Come on Brian we're done here' said Fay and taking his elbow she gently but firmly turned him round and led him out of Marylyn office and back to her own office.

As soon as they got there she said 'Technically you'll be dismissed for gross misconduct, misappropriating company property.........'

'I haven't misappropriated anything' he protested.

'Computer sheets; data that you downloaded presumably onto a memory stick; company records. Shall I go on?'

'No' he replied miserably.

'Contravening the terms of your contract of employment and breach of confidence. We will set that out in writing and it will be sent to your home address by recorded delivery. From this moment on you are not allowed onto any company premises anywhere, and are forbidden to talk to any company employees.

Asif will accompany you to your work station and you will be allowed ten minutes to collect any personal belongings or materials and then you will be escorted off the premises never to return. Do you have any questions?'

'What about an appeal against my dismissal? How do I go about that?'

'Are you serious? Brian are you really thinking you can overturn this decision with what you've done and the damage you've caused to Furrina? Well do you? Because if you do then you are living in cloud cuckoo land. Forget it. Leave here and never come back. Go away forever. Far far away. Abroad maybe. But forget Furrina. Remember what you've done. Now leave'.

He stood there and now the tears did start to fall but Fay was unimpressed and simply said 'Asif take him away please to his work station and then see him right off the premises. Goodbye Brian'.

With that she watched as Asif muttered 'Come on this way' and the two men left her office.

Turning to her computer she wrote up the details of the first brief meeting that she'd had that morning with him, the meeting with Marylyn and her final review with Brian Moffatt.

Asif returned to Fay's office about a quarter of an hour later. 'Right he's gone' he announced. 'What a stupid man. Utterly daft to do what he did'.

'You saw him right off the premises?'

'Yep. After he'd cleared his desk and work area I escorted him to his car in the car park and watched as he drove out of the gates. Briefed the security men on duty that he wasn't to come back. I'll also take his photograph out of his file, copy and enlarge it and let security and reception have copies telling them he is under no circumstances to be allowed in. I'll also circulate it to our other plants'.

'Good thanks. Just write up your part in this morning's proceedings will you and let me have it as soon as possible'.

He said he would and left her office where Fay rang Marylyn and briefing her was glad that the Chief Executive seemed to have calmed down a little and listened to what Fay said in silence and muttered 'Right good' when she finished her explanation.

Putting down the phone she decided that she needed a coffee so walking out and along the corridor she dropped in the appropriate coins and waited while the machine whirred and buzzed before beginning to dispense the drink. As the cup slowly filled she re-read the two notices that had appeared on the notice boards about the incident and decided to leave them in place for a little longer. Taking her coffee she began to walk back to her office when another door opened and Steve appeared.

'Good morning Fay' he grinned looking her up and down. 'You look rather lovely this morning I must say'.

'Thank you'.

'But ....' he paused.

'But?'

'But not as lovely as you were last night or earlier this morning at six o'clock both times when you were naked in my bed' he grinned.

'Hmm'.

'You free tonight?'

'As a matter of fact I am yes'.

'Meet up for dinner?'

'Come to my place and I'll cook. Oh and bring your toothbrush, razor, a fresh shirt and clean pair of pants for tomorrow' she smiled. 'Then you won't have to rush away will you?'

'Thank you. By the way I don't eat shellfish. It has a nasty effect on me'.

'Okay no shellfish but I hope I'll have a nice effect on you'.

'You will'.

'I'll e-mail you my address but now I must rush. Bye. Till tonight'.

'Sure. About seven?'

'Make it seven thirty'.

'Done. See you later'.

Back in her office she smiled to herself as she contemplated the evening and night to come. She'd enjoyed making love with him and knew that tonight would be even more pleasurable as they got to know each other better. With that happy thought at the front of her mind she settled down to some work.

Brian though had driven less than half a mile when he broke down and started crying and howling from distress, worry, fear and just the sheer shock of what had happened to him and so quickly. He rang for Kim but it clicked to answer phone so he left a message saying he'd been identified and fired.

He sat for ages wondering what to do then started the car and drove home where as soon as he was indoors he went upstairs and lay down on his bed and the tears started again.

Alan Fordhurst was Furrina's lawyer. Medium height, smart, late forties, well dressed and highly paid had been busy since first thing this morning dealing with the aftermath of the TV-12 programme but at around eleven he wandered into Marylyn's office.

'How are things developing?' she asked.

'Brewing nicely' he grinned. That was one of the things that people in the company liked about Alan. He never panicked, never flapped and took all manner of hassle and legal problems in his stride.

'Right. Well if you need any help or there's anything I can do let me know'.

'I will. There'll undoubtedly be a need for you to be interviewed by the press and other TV stations. When I judge the time is right we'll set up one session so you can get it all out of the way in one go'.

'Good. Is there any way we can blame Brian Moffatt for the actual incident?'

'No I doubt it. Best leave him out of it altogether'.

'What about taking him to court and getting the little bastard locked up for years?'

'We-ll we probably could' he mused 'but it would be in a few week's time and would undoubtedly open up the case again, allow the press and TV to crawl all over us once more and for what purpose? Revenge? I assume you've fired him?'

'You bet we have. No notice or compensation. Can we sequester his pension fund?'

'No you can't. It isn't the company's to do so. It belongs to the pension fund not the company so you have to leave that alone. He's legally entitled to that'.

'Shame'.

'Look forget him. He's gone. Now we all need to focus on damage limitation, then damage correction and finally rebuilding reputation'.

'Alright ……… if that's your advice'.

'It is. Forget him. He's history. Just think about Furrina and the future'.

Kim checked her mobile and saw that there were several messages one of which told her she had a voicemail. Moments later she was listening with sudden sadness as she heard Bran's tearful message. She immediately rang his number.

'Hello?'

'Brian it's Kim. I've got your message'.

'They've fired me. They knew it was me'.

'That's awful and I'm really really sorry but they can't have identified you from the Highlight programme?'

'No they trapped me via HR and IT. I'm not quite sure how HR thought it was me but IT tracked my downloading all the data on Beta. They cross matched that to the HR analysis and then with me having been identified they studied your film last night and matched the profile to it being me. Oh Kim whatever am I going to do? I'm out of a job; they'll black list me in the industry; I've not got a lot of money saved: I'm finished. And all because I told you people about Beta. I wish I'd never come to you in the first place. I should have kept quiet'.

'No Brian what you did was right. Think of all those poor people in Mumbai? You did the right thing'.

He paused and considered what she'd said. 'Maybe. But I'm still out of a job!'

'I'll see if there's anything we can do. I really am most awfully sorry about what's happened to you'.

'Thanks but it doesn't solve the issue does it? You being sorry for me I mean?'

'No it doesn't I'm afraid' she replied quietly.

He slumped back onto his bed and stared at the ceiling contemplating a very bleak future. He knew that Furrina would definitely black list him throughout the industry. There was no question of that and it would be effective as the pharmaceutical industry although enormous was in some ways quite a tight knit community and whilst Furrina would be careful about how they did it they would certainly ensure that he never managed to find work again in that industry.

His thoughts then ranged onwards and he asked himself over and over again what he was going to do with his life in the future. The only thing he knew was working as a scientist and not an especially innovative or clever one at that. He knew he wasn't good at administration or paperwork so a job as a clerk wouldn't suit him, even if he could get one. He didn't speak any foreign languages so there was no point in trying to find work abroad. In summary he was condemned to low grade, lowly paid work. That was provided he could find some employer, *any* employer, who would take him on with his background baggage comprising a lack of other skills and the problems caused by his being a whistleblower.

CHAPTER 24

> *He that can't endure the bad*
> *will not live to see the good.*
> *Yiddish proverb*

1 YEAR LATER

Things had really changed for Kim since the night that the programme had aired.

She'd been really pleased with the furore that the Highlight programme had created with questions raised in Parliament followed by a Parliamentary Sub Committee being formed which summoned Marylyn Goodrich, Louis Farmer and John Andrews to give evidence before it; most television stations running the story as a major item for a few days but TV-12 especially constantly re-running extracts of the programme and continuing to feature the exposé for the next three weeks; Buckinghamshire Police announcing that they were beginning an investigation to determine whether any criminal acts had been committed; several newspapers on the hue and cry for justice against what Furrina had done; the UK Medicines and Healthcare products Regulatory Agency, who are the regulatory body responsible for medicinal products, announced that they were to investigate all aspects of Furrina's work and development process for Betanapotraproxiflevien-g3 but in the meantime their temporary licence to test the drug on humans was revoked. Yes the programme had indeed done what it was intended to do by exposing Furrina's wrongdoing.

It had also brought her to the attention of others and a couple of months later she'd received a phone call one afternoon at work from a man calling himself Sebastian Lynchwood, a name she'd vaguely heard but couldn't quite place who he was, but that became clear as he started to talk.

'Kim I've been watching you and your work from afar for some time and have to say I've been mightily impressed with the standard of work that you have produced. Several of your Highlight programme have really caught my eye but the Furrina expose was outstanding. And the one TV-12 aired this week on under age sexploitation in the fashion industry was another belter of a programme'.

'Thank you I was pleased with both of them but I have to say I feel that the Furrina one was the highlight of my career so far. Sorry about the pun'.

'Pun?'

'Highlight of my career. Highlight programme?'

'Oh yes very good' and he gave a short quiet laugh. 'Look I'd like to talk with you about other opportunities. I am senior Programme Planner for Challenge TV. You've heard of us of course?'

'Indeed I have. Who hasn't?'

'Good. Now we are looking for a new head of our Investigations Unit; so much more than just Head Reporter and investigator. I need you to bring your skill, expertise and especially flair to a whole new range of programmes which will go head to head with your existing Highlight show, as well as taking on BBC1, ITV and any other station's similar investigative programmes or shows.

You'll have a free hand …… well within reason' he chuckled 'a team of about a dozen and you can pick your own staff. Interested?'

'You bet'.

'Alright let's meet for lunch'.

They arranged a date and location for tomorrow but for the rest of that day she was like a cat on hot bricks.

'This could be my big moment' she said to James that night after supper when she'd told him all about it.

He was full of enthusiasm and clearly as excited for her opportunity as she was and their whole evening kind of floated past in a sense of euphoria which was enhanced around ten thirty when after they'd got into bed he said quietly 'So you'll be investigating and exposing all sorts of things presumably in this new role?'

'Yes I guess so'.

'And your interview is tomorrow?'

'Yes over lunch which is rather nice. Kind of civilised'.

'Umm. So if you're going to be exposing things I wonder if you might like to get in a little practice tonight so you're fully ready for your meeting tomorrow?' he said rolling onto his back.

'Practice? What sort of practice?' she queried a frown appearing on her forehead as she slid on top of him.

'Well a good investigative head of department needs to be ready to expose anything that's interesting at any time doesn't she?' he grinned.

'Oh I see. That sort of exposure? The sort that requires me to do this' and throwing off the lightweight summer duvet she wriggled down the bed kissing his chin, chest, tummy and belly as she did so 'and this' as she slipped her hands into the elastic top of his boxers 'ensuring I have a good look at all relevant matters' she slipped both hands inside the waist band of his boxers and eased them away then over his rapidly erecting prick before slowly sliding them down to his ankles. 'Hmm this looks as though it could be *most* interesting but perhaps I need to get a little closer to the main area of investigation?'

'I'm sure you do' he said quietly.

'Yes indeed' and as her tongue licked along the length of him he completed his erection process. 'Of course' she continued giving him first a kiss then another long slow lick 'I guess I need to marshal all my resources' and her hands gently cupped his balls before beginning to tenderly squeeze and massage them 'don't I? Now I wonder how this investigation is going? What do you think?'

'Quite good so far'.

'Oh dear! Only *quite* good. I'd better try a little harder hadn't I? Mind you speaking of harder this seems pretty hard to me but I believe there's a choice of two ways to find out for sure'.

'Is there?'

'Definitely and this is the first' and as she spoke she leaned forward and using one hand to play with his balls and the other to direct his now throbingly hard prick between her lips. She paused, clamped her lips tightly onto him then pushed her face forward so he slid deep into the warm wet embrace of her mouth.

Looking up at him she saw he'd closed his eyes as he allowed himself to be taken on a trip to ecstasy by her lips, tongue and mouth. She took time until she felt she'd brought him a long way along the path to a climax.

'It sounds and looks as though you're benefitting from my investigation' she whispered letting him slip out from her lips.

'Indeed' he muttered slightly with his eyes still closed.

'So I now think I need to broaden the basis of the investigation' and slithering on top of him she wriggled up his body, kissed his lips tenderly before allowing her tongue to flick around his face.

'Kim I was almost there' he wailed quietly.

'I know but I've finished *that* part of my investigation. However I do believe that it needs to be taken to a more advanced stage' and teasing him she rolled her belly from side to side gently squashing his extremely hard prick between the two of them. 'So I suggest you relax and enjoy what might happen next' she chuckled softly as she eased herself up, felt for and found his prick and holding it in position lowered herself onto him and began to move slowly at first and then more quickly.

'Oh God Kim that is just so-oo wonderful' he sighed as he started to move with her.

'Good' and leaning forward she clamped her lips firmly to his, pushed her tongue into his willingly open mouth and using all her skill and expertise slowly but inexorably brought him to a stupendous climax.

Next day the interview went well. In fact it was more like a discussion than a formal interview and she found Sebastian not only easy to talk to but very willing to listen to ideas and thoughts that she had. As the conversation progressed she became more and more enthusiastic especially when he said that they needed a really experienced producer to take charge of their production unit and she immediately thought of Penny. The salary and other elements of the financial package were extremely generous and would mean that her earnings would shoot up by about forty percent.

The conversation finished with her formally accepting the role at Challenge TV while Sebastian said he'd put it all in writing to her.

Back at the office she went to see Penny and in confidence told her about the offer she'd accepted as well as the opportunity to take charge of Challenge TV's production unit.

'Go and meet Sebastian and see if you think it would suit you' suggested Kim. Penny agreed to do just that and one week later she'd had the meeting, accepted the role and like Kim resigned from TV-12.

Toby reeling from Kim's resignation was rocked when he learnt that Penny was also resigning but he was a pragmatist and wished them well and settled down to recruiting new people for both jobs. He promoted

The Beta File

Jamie Wilson to be chief investigator in Kim's place, recruited a new investigator from the BBC to replace Jamie and soon found another senior producer to take over from Penny.

Both Kim and Penny made great successes of their new jobs as did James who had decided to stay with his present firm although he used the offer which he had of an opportunity at another company to negotiate an increase in salary where he was currently working.

But while life was good for Penny and especially Kim it was the reverse for Brian. Time and again over the past twelve months he'd asked himself why had he done what he did? If only he'd never made that phone call? But he *had* made it; he *had* blown the whistle; he *had* exposed what Furrina were doing; he *had* risked his career and life; he had *destroyed* himself.

He'd constantly tell himself okay at least his actions had helped those poor people in India and undoubtedly prevented more human beings from being used in such a dreadful manner by Furrina and maybe other drug companies. But at huge cost to him personally.

He now had nothing. No job. No money. No home. He'd done a little work for cash in hand. Labouring, grass cutting, washing cars but he'd been unable to find what he deemed a proper job. Without an appropriate reference just simply a short statement from Furrina confirming the date he'd joined and the date he'd finished working for them, no other employer would take him on. It was well known in business that although an employer is not allowed to put anything detrimental in writing about an employee in a reference for another employer, the plain fact that the reference was so short, deficient of any detail, glaringly shouted that here was an employee who'd been fired for serious misconduct.

The Job Centre was utterly unhelpful; both in helping him apply for benefits as well as assisting him getting another job. Eventually he did begin to receive some small amount of money from The State but it was wholly insufficient to maintain his existing lifestyle which although by no mean extravagant was at least reasonably comfortable.

He applied for lots of jobs, some that he saw on the Job Centre notice boards and others in local newspapers but in most cases he didn't even get a reply to his application. Occasionally he did but it was usually a

"Thanks but no thanks" response. A couple of times he actually got an interview but his explanations of why he was without a job rang hollow to the interviewer who usually realised straight away that he'd been fired. In one instance he was honest at the start of the interview and explained that he'd been dismissed for blowing the whistle on nefarious practices at his employer, but after making polite comments about that the interviewer cut the interview short obviously worried that Brian might go public and blow the whistle on any issues he discovered within their company.

All in all Brian was astonished at how quickly his life unravelled into disaster and despair.

Having fallen behind on his mortgage payments after a very short time his building society gave him an ultimatum to pay all the arrears within fourteen days or they'd begin eviction proceedings. He pleaded but to no avail and therefore after those two weeks had elapsed they gave him twenty eight days notice to leave his home. On day twenty nine they repossessed the property.

He moved into a cheap somewhat less than clean one room in a boarding house which he hated but at least he had a roof over his head.

The finance company repossessed his car.

All his furniture and other belongings including his beloved model soldiers and battle scene boards he put into storage but after six months he could no longer even afford to continue to pay the storage fees and so following several telephone warnings from them to his mobile phone, until that was cut off by Vodafone for unpaid charges, they said that unless the storage amount outstandings were paid in full plus interest, all his possessions would be sold.

As he *didn't* pay because he *couldn't* everything that he'd owned was sent to auction. The storage company kept seventy five percent of what they realised from the auction and the balance was paid to Brian's bank account.

But even that little amount didn't help and was soon gone along with all his meagre savings. He was completely broke. He was jobless. And as he could no longer pay his rent he was asked to leave the boarding house. He became homeless.

With no close friends on whom he could rely to give him shelter and with no money he started to live on the streets, begging for cash but he

The Beta File

wasn't even very good at that. Twice he got robbed by a fellow street dweller of what he'd collected from his day's begging.

So over the months he just drifted and lived on the streets. He got moved on several times by the police in Milton Keyes and as the nearest big town to where he'd lived was Northampton he walked there. He wasn't sure why he did. It just seemed to be something he ought to do.

It was about twenty miles and took him two days because on the first day not long after he'd set off it started to absolutely teem with rain so he spent a miserable late morning and all afternoon huddled in a barn which he'd found unlocked in a field and going inside waited for it to stop. But it didn't and continued pouring with rain so he stayed in the straw for the rest of the day and then all that night. He heard rustlings and guessed it was rats or mice but he was too grateful for being out of the wet to care.

Eventually he got to Northampton late the next day and over the following days found some locations where kindly souls gave out hot soup or a sandwich, often stale but at least edible, to down and outs like him. He found a night shelter where he could sleep but the beds were filthy and he thought lice or flee ridden; the other occupants were often off their heads on booze or drugs and always viciously unpleasant to him.

By nature Brian was a gentle man and this dreadful life on the streets where only the toughest survived was wholly unsuitable to him. Frequently his thoughts turned to killing himself but he didn't probably because he lacked the determination as well as the means the wherewithal but especially the courage to do so.

So his life continued unravelling and becoming more and more desperate, increasingly hideous and progressively more horrendous. He lost a lot of weight and developed sores on his neck, arms and legs as well as a hacking cough from constantly getting wet and having nowhere warm and dry to sleep at night. With winter approaching he was never properly warm but always cold. Often very cold indeed.

Many times he cried as he thought about his former life and the happiness that he had then even if at the time he hadn't fully realised how lucky contented and happy he'd been. A small house which with the help of a just about manageable building society loan he been buying and only had sixteen years to go before it was his; a car; spending money in his pocket; his hobby of model soldiers and of course his regular sex visits to prostitutes.

All those were gone as he roamed the streets by day looking in waste bins for any discarded food. By night he slept where he could. Most often in shop doorways but also occasionally in derelict houses, sheds, bus shelters, anywhere he could get out of the weather and be reasonably safe.

His walk once firm and upright was now more of a shuffle and he avoided eye contact with other passersby. Indeed they physically avoided him, stepping well aside to avoid getting too close to him. To start with this irritated him but now he accepted it as the rule for the way a normal happy, employed person with money in their pocket would treat him - a dirty, unwashed, unshaven, street tramp.

Not only had his self esteem completely disappeared he continually struggled although increasingly ineffectually to try and survive in the harsh street environment in which he now found himself.

But even in that simple objective Brian failed.

THE END

**Death does not wait to see if things are done or not.
Kularnava.**

References:-

- *Information relating to various drug trials that have gone wrong taken from internet article "50 deadly consequences of Lab Animal Experiments" from US Doctors Group Americans for Medical Advancement available on the Vivisection Information Network.*
- *Other references to drug trial problems taken from published articles on the internet.*

To learn more about the author
visit his website:-

www.mikeuptonauthor.com

A list of other titles by this author is
shown below and there is a précis
of them on the following pages:-

Ambitions End
Winners Never Lose
Arrow of Truth
The Boss

A Twist In The Tale
The End Is Always Final

Footprints in The Snow
Vortex Rising
Open To Persuasion
The Last Change

A Surrogate Dilemma
The Track in a Forest

AMBITIONS END©

Ambitions End was Mike Upton's first novel and is a story of ambition and one man's quest to avenge his father.

As a teenager Mark Watson sees the devastating effect on his parents when his father's business is bankrupted and he vows to get even with the industrialist who caused this event.

The book follows Mark's early years, schooling, his entry into the business world and his single minded climb up the corporate ranks until he becomes Chief Executive of a multi-national conglomerate.

His marriage, affairs and tangled love life are interwoven throughout the fast moving story which alternates between Britain, America and Europe as Mark manages his increasingly complex business empire whilst never losing sight of his long term goal.

He ruthlessly exploits and discards people, manoeuvres, manipulates and plots using all means at his disposal. Industrial espionage, blackmail all find a place in his pitiless progress as he seeks to achieve his overriding ambition to gain revenge for his father.

As the story reaches a climax one question is on the readers mind and that question is – will Mark Watson reach the end of his Ambition?

Ambitions End draws on Mike's own business experience honed over many years to create a story with authenticity, interest and excitement.

WINNERS NEVER LOSE©

Winners Never Lose, Mike's second novel is a direct sequel to Ambitions End.

This time it starts in the Oil Industry as primary character Mark Watson once again generates his own unique, tough and demanding approach to this complex industry before he is head hunted into the Pharmaceutical Industry where he hones and develops his skills to turn an ailing business around to regain its former good financial results.

He has to find out who is leaking vital information to competitors and stop it, whilst at the same time re-energising the company's complex but moribund new product development programmes; manage and defeat cut throat competition; sell off unprofitable companies within the Group and acquire competitors. His wheeling and dealing is much to the fore as he tackles the challenges in these two important industries.

As well as seeing and understanding Mark's tough minded approach to the business problems, difficulties and opportunities that emerge during the story we also see how he copes with the tragedy of the loss of a child and follow his continued betrayal of his wife with a string of affairs.

The juxtaposition of Mark's ruthless attitude to business and people interwoven into his complex personal life creates a fast moving, interesting and absorbing story where the action moves from Britain to America, India and Europe before finally finishing in Australia.

Winners Never Lose like his first novel Ambitions End, draws on Mike's extensive knowledge and experience of large multi-national corporations. His first hand familiarity with the way that big business operates is fully utilised in this exciting and fast paced novel.

ARROW OF TRUTH©

Arrow of Truth is Mike's third novel and his first "who-dun-it".

The story tells how William Hardy the third generation owner and Chairman of a family manufacturing business, struggles to keep his business going in the face of increased demands from his customers and ruthless competition from his competitors as well as suffering arson attacks, bomb threats and blackmail letters from an unknown assailant. But he is finding business life more and more difficult and doesn't have the natural business flair of his forebears.

Meanwhile the company's bank believing that the business is on the verge of bankruptcy installs a team of specialist turnaround experts to work with him to try and save the business from collapse and then rebuild it towards its former glories and fortunes. Tensions rise and challenges appear as the turnaround team take over from William leaving him feeling frustrated and sidelined.

But while William is battling with these complex and demanding business issues, he is totally unaware that his wife, obsessed with a secret lover is betraying and cheating on him. However in a twist of delightful irony it is also she who is betrayed by her lover but not in the way that might be expected.

Set in Norfolk in the East of England, the story is a fast moving thriller set within a business background where the many characters and events interact with each other, as they unfold towards the surprising ending.

Arrow of Truth (like his previous novels - Ambitions End and Winners Never Lose) draws on Mike's considerable experience and knowledge of business in general and turnaround teams in particular and how they operate to try and save businesses that are in difficulty.

THE BOSS©

The Boss is Mike's fourth novel and is a challenging story set in the world of business and tells how Helen Buckley, an accountant by training and profession, attempts to fight her way to the top in a highly competitive and difficult corporate world controlled and dominated by men.

It follows her early life, her many love affairs, her marriage and the reasons for its failure, as well as charting her progress as she struggles to prove that she is as good as a man in solving company problems and confronting business difficulties.

Innovative in finding solutions to business problems, she gains a reputation as an expert wheeler dealer which leads her to decide to branch out on her own by setting up her own business consultancy which soon becomes highly successful.

However the stress of her business life leads her on an increasingly steep downward path towards alcoholism which threatens to destroy her business, her personal relationships and ultimately, her life.

Her battle against the ravages and effects of alcoholism are well and accurately documented as are her attempts to overcome the effects of this awful illness.

The Boss is a moving and sensitive story, with an interesting twist in that there is choice of two different endings.

A TWIST IN THE TALE©

A Twist in the Tale – Mike's fifth book is a collection of four different stories of varying lengths and subjects, but all of them have a surprise at the end. An unexpected twist - hence the title.

Two of them were originally conceived as plots to be turned into full length books but as he had always wanted to write a book of short stories then the decision was taken to use these ideas and thoughts as they stood and turn each into a short story in its own right. The topics are widely varied but hopefully that adds to the interest of the book.

Sea Deep Advertising man Pete loses his high flying job in London and so after struggling to find something similar or better, to the dismay of his wife he decides to pursue a dream and embark on a wholly new way of life?

Illusion During the Second World War a chance meeting between an 11 year old boy exploring the moors above his village and an Italian prisoner of war in a newly constructed prison camp leads the lad in later life to pursue a dream. But dreams don't always have happy endings.

Choice Dave is Head of Marketing for a company making a range of cleaning products. While trying to decide on which of three potential advertising agencies to choose he also has to make a choice about his personal and private life but having made that decision fate intervenes in an unexpected and threatening way.

Gone One Sunday afternoon in winter, a happily married and successful middle aged businessman walks out of his house to find out why his dogs seem restless, but he doesn't come back. He simply disappears. Why? Where has he gone and who is the mysterious Bulgarian lady? A tense thriller unfolds as the police quickly uncover information about his secret double life.

FOOTPRINTS IN THE SNOW©

Footprints In The Snow is the sixth book Mike has written and significantly departs from the previous themes, scenarios and styles of his earlier novels which were generally set within a business or corporate environment as in this book, each of the four stories deals with a happening that might be described as supernatural, or ghostly.

The first three stories in this book are purely based upon Mike's imagination. But within the fourth - The College - there is an element of a strange happening which he himself experienced.

So do ghosts really exist? If so can you talk to them? Can they talk to you? Well read Footprints and then make up your mind about ghosts and whether they exist or not?

Footprints Jeff is out walking his dog in the snow when he comes across something peculiar in the woods. What has he seen? Was it imagined, real or just an apparition?

Alice Was That Really You? Russell takes a six month career break from his job to write a book. But he meets Alice and after a brief passionate affair their final meeting is very bizarre.

Tom's Oak Matt and Sarah have renovated an old cottage to create their dream home and all is well until one day out riding he meets a strange man by an old oak tree.

The College Greg Thorbone enrols at a Business Management College to attend a four week career development programme but he soon finds that all is not as it seems in the old house.

VORTEX RISING©

Vortex Rising is Mike's seventh book was intended to be the third and final part of a trilogy about businessman Mark Watson who featured in AMBITIONS END and WINNERS NEVER LOSE. However as time has passed a fourth book is now in the process of being written, which will turn the trilogy into a quadrilogy! After that there is also the possibility of a fifth book in the series turning the sequence into a quintology!

However this latest novel again has Mark as the central character but much older than in the first two books as he is now in his fifties and has been knighted for services to Industry.

Chairman of several companies as well as a Non-Executive Director of two charities, he continues to wheel and deal in the cut throat world of big business something at which he excels.

But he also gets involved in politics at the highest level where his acumen, tough approach to life and avid desire to succeed enables him to make a real impact in the top secret project in which he becomes enmeshed.

Vortex Rising, as well as weaving its way through the environment of big business, also encompasses many aspects of recent past as well as current political life, as the worlds, desires and challenges of business, Government and Monarchy intermingle, until finally it inexorably builds towards a dramatic ending.

OPEN TO PERSUASION©

Open To Persuasion explores attitudes to greed and illicit gain and how individuals might be prepared to go beyond their usually established norms of what is right and wrong, when there is a major prize on offer.

Following Steven Marsh's surprise announcement that he will be relinquishing his role as Managing Director of a major food company in order to spend more time caring for his wife who is suffering from a life threatening illness, this is a story of two ambitious executives as they each fight to secure the one big job that has unexpectedly become available, with both of them determined that it should be they who is the one that succeeds in gaining the promotion.

Caroline the very attractive Marketing Director deploys all her feminine wiles and seductive charms to persuade various members of the interview panel that they should give the job to her.

But her rival for the job is Rob, the Sales Director who in his anxiousness to be the one that succeeds starts to utilise illegal incentives and methods with his customers to gain large amounts of new business and thus put himself into pole position for the promotion.

The intriguing question though is whether either Caroline or Rob will succeed through their unusual approach to achieving business success?

Open To Persuasion is an absorbing and compelling story about business, but it is also an interesting study in just how far people will go in disregarding their normal scruples and beliefs to persuade others to their point of view.

THE LAST CHANGE©

The Last Change once again features Sir Mark Watson, businessman and womaniser is the primary character of Mike's ninth novel and the 4th in the series featuring Watson and his complex business and private life as he embarks on yet another major change of career direction.

Fed up with the constant demands from The City, Financial Institutions, Pension Fund and Insurance company bosses and many others, he decides to give up the responsibilities of being Chairman of several publically quoted businesses and to take on the challenge of buying a number of businesses which he will personally own.

It is a significant and major change in his career life pattern and one that he undertakes after considerable soul searching and worry, but eventually he makes the decision to go ahead.

Wheeling and dealing to make the acquisitions, in spite of many pitfalls and difficulties he gradually begins to acquire a diverse range of companies while at the same time managing his convoluted love life, with affairs aplenty as well as facing up to a personal health issue.

But following his divorce and having passed the aged of 60, he is becoming disenchanted with his complex single life style and years for the comfort and satisfaction of married life again.

A fast moving story of business, love and life.

A SURROGATE DILEMMA©

A Surrogate Dilemma is the story of Andrew Noble, heir to the Noble Speciality Foods business. After leaving university he spends a year travelling the world then returns to the UK and takes up a position in Marketing in an electronics firm where over the next few years he builds his career eventually becoming Marketing Manager. But after that period of time there, he believes that he is now ready to enter his family business in a position of some importance.

However his father who heads the family firm disagrees and insists that he runs another business before joining Noble Speciality Foods and to this end arranges for Andrew to go to Africa to run a business there, learning the ins and outs of being head of a company before allowing him to join the family business with an eventual view to succeeding him as Managing Director.

Although reluctant but realising that he has no option, Andrew agrees and soon discovers the trials and tribulations of being head of a business, especially one located in Zambia. However he quickly settles into the life there becoming a member of golf, tennis and ex-pats clubs and enjoys his rather privileged life, while also discovering that attractive female company is not too difficult to find.

Returning to England almost three years later, wiser, more experienced and now ready to enter the family company, he rapidly settles into his destined role in the firm. He also meets and marries Becky and they have a charmed and delightful life together – until they decide to start a family.

The book weaves together Andrew's business activities with the challenge and intimate experience of surrogacy that he and Becky undertake with their friend Linda. However none of the three people involved anticipate the outcome that follows from their fateful decision.

THE END IS ALWAYS FINAL©

The End Is Always Final begins in the middle of the year 2016 and is the fifth and last in the series about Sir Mark Watson - businessman and serial philanderer. It again follows Mark's activities in his various companies as he tries to pull off his most complicated piece of wheeler dealing so far in which he attempts to buy a multipart but bankrupt conglomerate for the sole purpose of breaking it up, in order to sell the various component parts to make a lot of money which he could then use to buy further companies.

The action is mainly set in the UK but does include a crucial business trip to the USA in his search for funds to make the acquisition.

He has a tight timescale as he wants to get everything completed before his impending marriage to his former wife Abi who having accepted his assurance that his dalliances with other women are over, has forgiven him his past affairs and accepted his proposal of re-marriage. But she is completely unaware that his protestations of current and future faithfulness are wholly insincere as he doggedly continues to seduce and bed other women.

Mark is an extremely complex man showing flashes of great kindness and sympathy; a genuine interest in the charity of which he is non-executive Chief Executive and a real desire to help the unfortunate young people that the charity assists; but quite ruthless in his business activities; genuinely in love with Abi; although completely unable to stop himself constantly wanting to sleep with other women.

With a dramatic finale it is a fitting end to the Mark Watson series of novels.

THE TRACK IN A FOREST©

The Track In A Forest is Mike Upton's 12th novel and his 2nd book of ghost stories. Five separate erotic tales of ghosts and unusual occurrences all set in his home county of Norfolk. He again poses the same questions about ghosts as he did in his 1st ghost book. Are ghosts real? Do they exist? If so can you see them? Can you talk to them?

Billy: An old ghostly fisherman long dead appears to recently divorced Theo in the small sailing harbour where he keeps his own boat. But can he convince either Hannah with whom he is having a torrid affair and then Patsy of what he's seen?

The Roman: A family move into an old cottage but soon strange happenings occur in one of the bedrooms as they uncover a past story of the missing Roman Legion.

The Track in A Forest: A young couple walking in a forest stumble on a past event which inexplicably seems to be re-enacted to them in the present day. But are they themselves all they seem?

The White Lady: Who is the mysterious beautiful lady reputed to haunt the old Barnton Manor house and will Peter be lucky enough to meet with her?

Millie: After discovering love and then betrayal, she finds solace with the ghost of her beloved horse Jupiter.

mikeuptonauthor.com

Printed in Great Britain
by Amazon